SEASON

OF

WAITING

SEASON

OF

WAITING

Book One of the
Utopian Testament

Jim Christopher

Published by Jim Christopher.

ISBN-13: 978-1-7355362-0-0 (ebook)
ISBN-13: 978-1-7355362-1-7 (paperback)

Cover design by Nicole Lecht

First edition
Published 17 November 2020

Hey Mom, watch what I can do!

Are you watching?

Mom?

We are our choices.

— J. P. Sartre

Chapter 1

EMERSON

"I wouldn't do this if I didn't have to, Em," Mom said. "You know that."

Emerson turned to face the passenger door of the car. This was their neighbor's car. It was full of old-people smells, and Emerson didn't like it. He didn't want it to be today. The only thing he wanted was to keep his dog. He loved his dog. And he didn't want to say good-bye to her.

The car slowed to a stop at a red light as the sign for Tarpley, Texas, rolled into view. Emerson counted three bullet holes in it. From behind him, Barfly poked her wet snout into the tight space between the window and the seat, trying to get closer to Emerson's face. He nuzzled up to the dog's snout, letting her tongue lap out against his salty cheeks and her kibble breath stink up his nose.

"It's not fair," he said into the dog's loose and dusty curls. He pulled away, turning to face his mother. "Barfly didn't do anything wrong."

Mom sighed, releasing another wave of cigarette smoke against the car's windshield before it drifted out of the cracked window. "I know, Em. None of this is fair." She placed the cigarette back between her thin lips and tucked a lock of her bright red hair behind her ear. "Barfly is a good dog, but we can't take care of her anymore."

The traffic light changed. As the car eased forward, Emerson turned back toward his window and Barfly's searching tongue. Emerson knew that Mom didn't want to do this. He could see it on her face. He could see it in the way her halo wavered from its normal Scarlet, flickered to Desert Sand and back again.

"Hey," Mom said, her hand stroking his head, "there's Mac & Ernie's, we ain't been there in a stretch. Maybe on the way home, we can stop there for lunch. You can get the 'Mac-n-Ernie and cheese.'"

The restaurant's sign scrolled by against the pale, empty sky. He thought about how delicious not-from-the-box mac and cheese would be, and then his colors became dark. He didn't want to eat macaroni and cheese. He wanted to keep his dog. He sat up straight in the seat, the bargain reaching his tongue before his mind could stop it. "If we skip lunch, can we keep Barfly for another day?"

He knew he had upset her, even before her eyes glanced away from the road to find his. Her voice was stone as she said, "I'm not gonna coat it in honey for you." Emerson swallowed his hope, wishing he could swallow his words with it. Mom pressed him, "I know you understand. So you tell me, why do we have to sell Barfly?"

His heart quickened. Emerson didn't want to talk about this again. Every time his father came up, Mom would get madder. And madder. Until she lashed out. But Emerson knew better than to stay quiet. That would send her into a rage. "Because we don't have money to buy her food," he whimpered.

"And why is that?" Mom asked.

An ugly, sickening feeling bloomed in Emerson's tummy. "Because Daddy took it all when he left. And you don't make enough at the Silverleaf." He pushed the rising feelings back down his gullet. "And I'm not old enough to work yet." Mom had pulled those words out of him so many times. Each time, Emerson wanted to feel like they were just words, instead of the tingling panic and shame they wrung from him.

Mom sucked on her cigarette. She released the smoke with a tight nod, adding, "And a dog like Barfly is very expensive to take care of. Your daddy bought her back when we were a family. And well, that's over now." Flares of Maroon in Mom's halo marked the last few words as she pelted the cigarette out of the car window.

Emerson sat silent and still, watching the rage build in his mother. The pulses from Mom's light were patternless. All willy-nilly and outside the lines, like the drawings the younger kids made at school. Emerson could hear the creaking tension as she tightened her grip on the steering wheel. Her lips lost their color. The car sped up. She would lash her tongue soon. Yell at him. About Dad's new family. Their delightful house. Our borrowed trailer. Their new car. Our empty wallets. Their full bellies. Our stomachs rumbling around a few scraps and leftovers from the diner. Dad's lover and her tight body. The ruins Emerson had left behind as his mother carried him to term.

Emerson unbuckled himself. He reached across the bench seat with his hand, placing it on her stomach, in the center of her erratic halo. He laid his head on her shoulder. "It's okay, Mommy," he whispered, smoothing the light back into a silky shade of deep Red. After a few quiet moments, it was where it needed to be. Emerson could hear his mom's breathing getting calm again. Her heartbeat became regular. She slowed the car to a reasonable speed.

She lifted her arm and hugged Emerson to her chest. "You always know how to calm me down," she said, kissing his head and sucking in a deep sniff of his hair. Not to be left out, Barfly craned her head over the bench seat. She nosed her way between them, slapping sloppy kisses on each of their faces.

Mom laughed. Emerson loved that sound. He loved the way the Yellow exploded out of her with each joyful gasp. He loved it, and it was so rare since Dad disappeared. He felt a smile break across his face, and Barfly licked his exposed teeth.

"All right, girl, get back down there," Mom said as she gave the dog a firm shove into the backseat with her elbow. "And you buckle yourself back up, kiddo." Emerson slid back to his seat, pulled the seat belt over his shoulder, and clicked it into the buckle. Then he went to work cleaning the dog slobber from his lips with his T-shirt.

The sound of the turn signal shifted Emerson's joy to panic. Mom confirmed his fears as she sang, "Here we are at Uncle Terry's." Cracks and pops replaced the hum of the tires on the road as the car moved onto a gravel drive. They passed a wide field dotted with large rolls of straw, recently baled.

Tears welled in his eyes. His chest tightened. Maybe he could jump out of the car with Barfly. They could run into the field and disappear into one of those bales. Mom wouldn't find them. Then they could live together for the rest of their lives.

He lost his chance as the car passed through a line of trees. Uncle Terry's kennels rimmed the edges of the property, filled with the dark, shifting forms of dogs. At the first bark, Barfly rose to attention—ears up, tail slapping, and eyes searching. Emerson sat up straight, watching the enclosures. Some dogs barreled against the chicken wire, yelping at the intruders. Others stood tense, shaking in whatever shadow they could find from the roasting sun.

Past the kennels, a single thick black dog watched their arrival with a lazy interest. It lay in a bald patch in the middle of the scrub yard, chained to a flagpole that carried a limp and faded Texas flag.

Barfly's excitement grew with the volume of the barking canines, the backseat barely containing her as she hopped from window to window. Emerson knew she did not understand they would leave her here. Forever.

Mom pulled up to the trailer on the other side of the property. Barfly's anticipation burst out of her in leaps, twirls, and *ruff*s. Mom slammed the car into park as she asked, "Can you hand me her leash, Em?"

This was it. It would happen. Emerson's vision blurred as the tears came. He found the leash on the floor by his feet. As he turned to hand the leash to his mother, he found Mom looking at him. Her halo faded to Copper as she reached for his face, gently brushing away the tears. "I know you love her, Em. And I am sorry we have to do this. I really am. If there was another road, I would take it in a heartbeat."

Emerson felt the leash leave his hands. The dog's excitement shook Emerson in his seat. Wiping away tears with one hand, his other found the door handle and pulled.

"Oh sweetie," Mom pressed, her voice tense, "wait until I get her on the leash!"

The click of the opening door was all the permission Barfly needed. She squeezed over the bench seat and across his lap, and she was out the car door before Emerson knew it was happening.

For a moment, he hoped that Barfly would keep running. She would run away and then come find him again when they had money to take care of her. But as Emerson left the car, he saw Barfly had no such plan. She lopped across the yard in uncoordinated bounds toward the first dog she saw. As Barfly got near, the large rottie stood up. Its chain rattled against the flagpole, then snapped tight as the dog pulled forward. Her back and neck bristled with raised fur and Violet light.

Barfly landed in front of the rottie with a flop. Her Cerulean halo was welcoming and bright, and her tush raised above her head and swaying with each crooked wag of her tail. It was a pose that Mom called her "play-now bow." But the rottie wasn't play-now bowing back. The enormous dog pulled its chain as far as it could, light spewing out in splotches of Purple and Fern.

"No!" Mom screamed. The breeze swiped Emerson's face as she ran past him, shouting "Barfly! Come to Mama! Barfly!"

The bang of the trailer door whipped Emerson's head around. Shirtless Uncle Terry bolted from the trailer, screaming something about "not letting her near Lucy." Emerson's gaze followed Terry as he ran past, his naked belly jiggling. Emerson's eyes stretched from Terry to Mom. From Mom to his dog.

Just in time to see the rottie clamp its jaws around Barfly's throat.

Chapter 2

BLAIR

Blair's scream tore at her chest and ears. Yet she could still hear the yelps of the goddamned dog as it thrashed on the ground.

That dumb dog was her last chance to pull some money together. Her husband had paid thousands of dollars for Barfly. The dog even had papers for Christ's sake. It was the one valuable thing her whore of a husband left for them when he walked out. And now Barfly's life—and her hope of a livelihood—was disappearing in ragged spurts into the parched ground.

The weight of it was too much. Blair's legs wobbled, and she fell to her knees in the dirt. Selling Barfly would have gotten them out of the hole. Given her a month or two to figure things out. What the hell was she going to do now?

Lucy's bloodied maw broke into a wide grin as Terry ran up to her. Her gaze fell to her violent handiwork, then back to her human. Pride brightened her eyes until Terry slapped her snout. The dog's stare remained lowered, her nub of a tail pointed at the ground as Terry dragged her away by the chain.

Barfly stopped moving, except for her frantic panting. Someone was talking to Blair. She looked over. It was her son. She sucked in a breath, filling the void left behind by her scream.

"I'm sorry, Mama," Emerson whispered.

Blair turned back to the dog. She'd never seen so much blood. How could there be that much blood in a dog?

"I'm sorry, Mama," her son echoed. Blair's eyes found his face. His skin glittered with tears and sweat. A lick of his dark hair stuck to his forehead, the same way his father's would after he'd been working outside. "I didn't know it would happen."

A spark of anger shoved Blair into the moment, and she felt her fingernails dig into her palms. That phrase—"I didn't know it would happen." The same fucking thing Emerson's father would say. Whenever she caught him wrapped up in some young pussy. That was his excuse. He didn't plan it. He didn't know it would happen. And yet, it kept happening. Again and again. For years, in their home. In their bed.

Her fingernails pierced the flesh of her fisted hands. Her jaw joint twinged as her teeth ground together. She looked into the eyes of her son. In the deep brown, she saw the eyes of his father. Pleading. Lying. Flames of hate licked out from her tongue. "Get the fuck away from me, you shit!"

Emerson broke. His form shrank from her, like Lucy had cowered from Terry's hand. His head pulled into his shoulders, eyes wide and mouth gaped in shame. The sight of her crushed son broke Blair too. She screamed again, the terror of the moment giving way to regret. She fell back on her haunches, raised her fists over her head, and slammed them into the ground at her knees.

The sting of her knuckles splitting gave her something to focus on. Her eyes opened on the ground beneath her. Her breath rippled across the dusty earth. She stayed prone for a minute, letting her breath come back to her. Finding her calm. Blair strained to ignore the yapping dogs as she collected her thoughts and boxed her feelings.

Sitting up, she examined her busted knuckles. The cuts were deep. They needed stitches. She could wait long enough to apologize to Em. To hold him for a moment. Smell his honeysuckle hair. They would reset, move forward from this moment fresh, like they always did.

Blair glanced up to find Emerson kneeling over his dog, his back to her. His head bowed over the animal. The dog had gone silent during her outburst. Its tail lay still in the dirt, the rest of its body hidden behind Emerson's sulking form.

"Emerson," Blair warbled.

His head pivoted. Her voice had reached him, but he wouldn't acknowledge her. She had hurt him this time. Her words had been excessively harsh. She needed patience to bring him back around.

Emerson leaned closer to Barfly's carcass. Blair's brow furrowed as she tried to make sense of what she was seeing. Was Emerson hugging the dog?

"Emerson, don't do that, honey."

He leaned farther over Barfly, his hands moving in front of him in ways Blair couldn't make out. What the hell was he doing?

"Emerson?" Blair shifted to sitting on her hip, the pain of her cuts increasing with each throb of her pulse. "Emerson, please, just come here, sweetness."

He didn't move. A bead of sweat fell into Blair's eyebrow. She went to wipe it away, but her bleeding hands stopped her. The air was stale and still, and the sun burned close. But she would wait here until Emerson finished saying good-bye to his dog.

The goddamned dog. Barfly's tail rose and hit the ground with a dull thud. Blair's brow scrunched. Then a second, more deliberate wag sent up a puff of dust. Blair was still processing this as Emerson sat back on his shoes and held his hands up by his head. They were wet with blood.

Shock clamped on Blair's throat. "Emerson!" she screeched. "What the hell are you doing?"

From behind her boy, Barfly rose to all four feet. Mud from the Texas dirt and her own blood mottled her fur. The dog tried to shake it off in a clumsy rattle across her body. She walked around the boy, sniffing his face and hands. After she gave Emerson's fingers a few licks, Barfly's eyes found Blair.

The dog's mouth fell open in a smile. Her eyes brightened as she pounced over to Blair and licked her stunned face, bringing a wave of metallic and dusty odors.

"Wh-what?"

"I'm sorry, Mama. I didn't know Barfly would get hurt." Emerson's voice shrank. Her boy was scared.

"What the hell just happened?" she mumbled. The dog wandered over toward the ground stained with its blood and sniffed. Barfly scratched the spot with a gentle paw, then squatted and pissed on Lucy's napping spot under the flagpole.

Emerson sat down in front of Blair, pulling her gaze away from the dog. He looked down at the ground. Em asked, "Are you mad?"

Blair had no response. She lifted her son's chin with her fingertips until their eyes met. "What did you just do?" The words barely made it out of her mouth as Blair's breath caught in her chest.

Emerson pursed his lips in thought. "To Barfly, you mean?"

Blair nodded.

Emerson heaved his shoulders and replied, "I fixed her light. It was all bent, but I made it pretty again." His voice was tentative, like it was when he was afraid of telling Blair the truth.

Blair kept nodding, even though she didn't understand what Emerson meant. "What do you mean, Em? What light?"

Her son looked down at her knuckles. Steady flows of blood merged between her fingers. Raising an uncertain glance at his mother, Emerson said, "Hold still, Mama."

He leaned close and held his blood-caked hand close to her abdomen. Blair shut her eyes as a wave of calm reached out from her belly, then moved up her torso. It fell through her legs and arms and finally tickled across her face and scalp. The sense of serenity pushed away the worries about money and the anger toward her husband. When the rush ebbed, a chill rattled her body. Her skin tightened to gooseflesh despite the warm Texas afternoon. She opened her eyes to find Emerson looking at her. Blair blinked away her haze. She pulled in a lazy breath that, regardless of the barren paddock around them, carried a deep floral scent.

Emerson smiled at her. She grinned back on instinct, disoriented as if she had just sneezed. She followed his face as it fell to her hands. They remained dirty and bloody. Emerson's thin fingers wiped away the crust on her skin, and Blair's mind cleared.

She found no sign of her lacerations.

"How?" she asked.

Emerson squeezed her hand tight. "I fixed your light too, Mama."

Blair swallowed. Her throat felt cool, hydrated. Her jaw muscles were slack. She opened and closed her hands a few times, checking for injury. Even her palms were fresh and pink, without a mark from her fingernails.

Blair's attention shot over to the kennels, captured by Terry's voice. "Jesus Christ, Blair!" he hollered across the yard. He had found a stained white T-shirt to cover his beer belly. "I'm sorry, but also-too-is, you should've known better than to let that dog run up to Lucifer like—"

Terry's mouth and feet stopped moving when he saw the dog. Barfly pranced up to him and sniffed his crotch. He pulled her head up, going over her face and neck. Not finding a wound, he checked over the rest of the dog's body. Terry stood erect, mouth hung open in dismay, and he pulled his clinging shirt away from his sweaty gut. He murmured, "Where the hell did all this blood come from, then?"

He looked up at Blair and Emerson. "You two all right? You ain't hurt?"

Blair shook her head—they were fine. She felt fine. In fact, she felt wonderful. Hell, when was the last time she'd been hurt? Or sick? She couldn't remember so much as a runny nose since the time Emerson could walk. She shifted onto her knees in front of her son, lowering her face to his.

"Emerson? You ever ... um ... fix Mama's light before?" she asked.

He blushed, but didn't look away. He nodded once, his lip curling around a worry. "Sometimes, when you're asleep. Are you mad?" he asked.

Blair shook her head, holding his gaze as her lips tightened into a thin smile. "Of course not, sweetness."

Blair nuzzled him into her bosom, squeezing him close. She rocked him for a moment before gently asking, "Can you do that ... to anybody you want?"

Her heart leaped as she felt Emerson nod against her breast. She pivoted back onto her hip and clutched him tighter. They held each other for a few seconds in the merciless sun. Barfly trotted over to them. Blair turned her face away to avoid the dog's disgusting fur as Barfly tried to pry the mother and son apart with her nose. Blair nudged the dog away with her elbow.

"Mama?"

"What is it, Em?"

Emerson said nothing for a few moments. Blair felt his breath expand and release in her arms. She relaxed and looked at his face. He finally whispered, "Can we please keep Barfly?"

The goddamned dog. The perky, bloody beast parked herself a dozen feet away. Barfly lifted a hind leg, and started licking herself in a slow, sloppy cadence as she tipped over onto her side.

Blair laughed and kissed the top of her son's head, inhaling the bouquet that radiated from him. "Yeah, honey," she whispered, "I think I can work with this."

TRUTH OR CONSEQUENCES

Chapter 3

CALEB

The box in Caleb Allard's hand would kill him. At least, that was Caleb's hope. It wasn't heavy. The metal felt thin. Almost cheap. Caleb had enough experience with medical devices to know that despite its feel, a set of rigorous standards had governed its construction. Whoever built it designed it to do one thing. It would do that one thing.

Dr. Pavle Miloje used his fingers to trace the pair of wires leaving the box, finding the plastic plug at the end. In his pointed Eastern European accent, he explained, "This we connect to the controller module." The doctor mimed attaching the cable as he gestured to an oblong device gripping the IV stand. "That unit governs the flow of tranquilizers and narcotics."

The sterile chrome of the stand was out of place in the doctor's comfortable office. The bourbon leather armchair in which Caleb sat was twisted and stretched in the reflection on the pole, the mild sea-green walls framing his elongated face as it stared back at him. Caleb followed the metal pole with his eyes, up to two circular hooks that were empty. Eventually the drug cocktail would hang there, and even then the contraption would weigh less than ten pounds.

"When everything is connected and enabled, the button there will glow. You'll be ready to go," the doctor added, gesturing toward the box.

Caleb swallowed and returned his gaze to the black box in his hand. The surface was slick and flat, with a single transparent plastic cover protecting a square red button.

"So, once he activates it, how long?" asked Irene. Caleb was thankful his daughter was here to ask the questions he wasn't thinking about. He had assumed it would be over in an instant. Irene was adept at rooting out assumptions.

"Configurable," the doctor offered. "At a minimum, Mr. Allard will experience about four seconds of consciousness. We can dial it out longer," Dr. Pav explained. "Although I must admit that none of my patients have opted for that."

Irene took her father's hand. Her flesh was warm against his, her color vibrant and smooth against his petechiae. She continued, "And after that, how long until ..."

"Seconds." The doctor looked from Irene to Caleb and explained, "You push the button, you feel good, you go to sleep, and you die. All of it happens in less than ten seconds."

Ten seconds. Not instantaneous. Caleb hadn't considered there might be a period where he would be aware he had committed suicide. Could he keep his composure? Would those ten seconds be an endless train of regret? Would those last moments of awareness be serene, or terrifying?

Irene squeezed his hand. "You still want to do this, Dad?" She must have sensed his ambivalence.

"Want?" Caleb croaked. The idea was obscene—that anyone would want this. "I want to see you finish school. Watch you build your life and career." Her fingers tightened around his. "I want to see your brother sober and happy." The rest remained unsaid: Caleb would see none of those things.

Pancreatic cancer. The same disease that had killed Irene's mother, Ivy. They caught Caleb's cancer earlier, at stage three. That had given him some hope. His fight would be easier, his outcome different.

But even as the first few rounds of chemotherapy worked, Caleb received a stage four diagnosis in a matter of weeks. His lungs, his brain, and the deathblow: the cancer made roots in his liver.

At first, the oncologist talked about Caleb's life in terms of probabilities. Fifteen percent chance of survival. Then three percent. Then it changed to time. Months. Then weeks. After the last consult, they inverted the scale. With the size of the tumors in his brain and liver, Caleb was lucky to be walking around at all. The conversations were hard. The emotions were turbulent. And all of it was too familiar. The only things left in his control were his own pain and how tidy his end would be for his family.

"I know, Dad," Irene offered. Her eyes rose, glistening. "And you know if you want to try to beat this, I'll support you. Either way."

Caleb returned his daughter's squeeze. "I guess 'want' is the wrong word," he said, unable to keep the sadness out of his voice. After a few moments, he continued, "But we've seen this opera. We lived it with your mother. Once is enough for any family, Starlight." Irene let go of his hand to wipe a tear from her cheek.

A dull thud in his right ear brought a grimace to Caleb's face. He dropped the metal box into his lap and pulled down on his earlobe, the percussive whomps turning into an itch. He apologized as he crammed his index finger into the ear and wiggled it around.

"Everything okay?" Dr. Pav asked.

Caleb nodded. "Yeah, my ear's been itchy. I think a muscle is spasming in there or something." Given his body's condition, a tickle in his ear was nothing.

"I can look?" the doctor offered.

"Nah, Doc, thanks. That ear's never worked, anyway."

Dr. Pav looked confused until Irene clarified, "He's deaf in that ear. Since birth." She looked at her dad with a wistful grin. "It's why he makes me drive everywhere, so he can hear the conversation."

Caleb smiled. She was right. He preferred the passenger seat when there was someone else in the car, for that very reason. Irene had never mentioned she had picked up on that.

Resting on the edge of his heavy wood desk, Dr. Pav returned to the matter at hand with a small nod. "Okay then, hospice will be by your home tomorrow to deliver the system.

Call them to tie the IVs into your existing chemo port when you're ready. They'll make you a priority, but if you can, give them about two hours' notice. Do either of you have questions for me?"

A rush of anxiety filled him as Caleb realized the doctor was wrapping up their visit. Their final appointment before his death. He would never see Dr. Pav again. The words he shared with the doctor would be the last. It was unexpected. Not quite regret, something closer to dread. He hoped these good-byes wouldn't all carry this angst.

"Oh wait," the doctor added with a snap of his fingers. "There is one thing you need to do." Caleb's chest unknotted at the delay. The doctor reached behind him and retrieved a small coil of wire. He gestured to Caleb's lap as he hooked up the wires to the terminals on the device. Caleb traced the wires back to the doctor's desk, where they ended at a tiny speaker. "I know this may be uncomfortable, Mr. Allard, but I would ask that you give the button a push while you're here. I want patients to appreciate the slight pressure it takes to activate."

Caleb looked down at the metal box and swallowed. The flat red button emitted a steady glow now that it had a power source. Holding the box in one hand, he lifted open the clear plastic cover.

With his thumb, he traced a flange along the edge of the button as it rose a few millimeters above the surface of the metal box. A tactile mark, he realized. Something a person could find using only a finger. As the pad of Caleb's thumb glided over the center of the red plastic, the speaker on Dr. Pav's desk buzzed.

Caleb's eyes widened. "That's all it takes?"

Dr. Pav nodded as he disconnected the leads. "It is very sensitive. When the time comes, you may not have a lot of strength. So the trigger responds to minimal pressure. Legally, the patient has to instigate their own Final Release. If anyone else pushes that button while you're wired into it, the state can charge them with manslaughter." The doctor leaned in closer and captured Caleb's gaze. "To work in the legal boundaries of the Final Release, the choice and effort to push the button must be yours, Mr. Allard. Your will must activate the machine. No one else can do it for you. Do you understand?"

Caleb nodded. He knew this already, but he didn't mind hearing it again. End-of-life situations were never easy, but they could always become more complicated. After a few moments of silence, Dr. Pav turned to Irene. "Keep the button covered until the device is in your father's possession, and he's ready to use it."

Caleb released the breath he hadn't realized he was holding in.

Chapter 4

IRENE

"Thank you again, Starlight," Dad said. Irene smiled. He hadn't called her that since she had left for college. It surprised her she still found it endearing. The name "Starlight" stuck after her presentation at the seventh-grade science fair. She'd discussed how the stars are a forge for all atoms in the universe, even those that make up our bodies and brains. When stars go nova, the violent explosion spreads those atoms across the cosmos.

They walked down the hallway, away from Dr. Pav's office, until they reached the elevators. Dad poked the down button as he spoke. "And I know I keep saying this, but I'm sorry to pull you from school mid-semester. I don't think I could do this without you."

"It's not like there's ever a perfect time for this stuff to happen. Grad school will be there." Irene knew there was no way he could do this on his own. He'd tried, though, pulling plans together after his terminal diagnosis. But the legal and medical requirements for a Final Release were complex. The time he needed for the forms, appointments, and hearings? His pain consumed it, along with its treatment and the aftereffects. So Irene stepped up, like she always did. She took a leave of absence from the university and came back to New Mexico. Dad signed power of attorney over to her. Designated her his medical point of decision. Irene used these bureaucratic superpowers to bring his Final Release across the finish line made of red tape.

She stroked her hand on his back as they waited for the elevator. His spine rippled against her fingers. The fragility of his slight frame still shocked her. Dad wore a flannel shirt she'd given him for his birthday a few years ago. At the time it had been unflattering, accenting the various lumps and bulges that come with age and a sedentary life. Now the shirt swallowed him. Every day, there was less of her father.

Dad shook his head, replying, "I know, I know. But it feels unfair, you jetting back here to help when Wes lives here."

Irene sighed, "Yeah, but my brother isn't here, is he?"

Dad turned to face her. "No, he's not. He's where he needs to be, though. He's sick too, Irene. His addiction isn't his fault any more than the cancer is mine." She clenched her jaw against a flurry of sharp words. Wes had made choices to get where he ended up. Dad didn't. Wes had every opportunity to turn himself around. Dad couldn't help but enable his destructive behavior. Irene wanted nothing more than her father to stop giving Wes a lifeline. Maybe then, her brother might realize how simple life is when you don't make it hard.

Dad reached up to pull on his earlobe again, his face pulling into a half grimace. "Is your ear still bothering you?" she asked, thankful for the change in subject.

He nodded, using a knuckle to massage the soft tissue behind his earlobe. "Oh, so that reminds me. There's another finance thing," he said. "I got an email from Del Rio."

Irene released an exasperated breath. "Del Rio" was short for "the Del Rio Rehabilitation and Assisted Living Center," the vacation resort where Wes was being treated for his opioid addiction. This would be his third attempt through the program. Irene had little faith that this time would be any different, but Dad hoped otherwise. And he paid through the nose to make it happen. "And?" she replied, expecting the worst.

He swallowed. "Well, it looks like we'll need to use more of the liquidity from my estate to cover the cost of rehab. There was supposed to be enough left to cover some of your school expenses. But then, your brother ..." Dad trailed off, pulling on his earlobe again.

"It's okay, Dad," Irene replied. "I'll figure it out. Just forward me the email, okay?" She turned back to the elevators as the doors opened. She helped him shuffle inside and then pushed the button for the lobby.

Rehab was expensive. Without health insurance, Wes once again turned to their father for financial help. And once again, Irene had to bend. Figure out how to make it work. This time it was putting a pause on her bioinformatics degree so she could help Dad through the end of his life. Meanwhile, Wes did whatever the hell he wanted.

Dad's chest rattled as he spoke. "I wanted to do so much more, Starlight. I just ... never got around to it. When your mom died, I fell down. And I never managed to get my feet back under me, you know?" He pulled a tissue from his front pocket and wiped his nose. "I had all that time. Christ, if I could have it back, I would ..." His voice broke as he trailed off. "I wish I was leaving a legacy besides some well-organized books for my clients, I guess."

Irene leaned into him, hugging his frail waist from the side. "What would you want that to be?" she asked. "Your legacy?"

Dad snorted. "I don't know," he said with lethargy. "I'm not sure I'm up for thinking about it today." After a few moments, he added, "This sucks."

This sucked, he was right. Irene refused to let it be any worse than it needed to. Memories of her mother's ordeal asserted themselves. People Irene loved, waiting for the mercy of her mother's death, then coping with the guilt of going back to living their lives. She'd experienced it once, and it would be anguish for everyone all over again.

Her father's ever-present fanny pack pressed into her side. The firm bulge of a tumor brushed against her hand as her arms reached around his torso. Her head found his bony shoulder and she gave him a gentle squeeze.

Dad flinched in pain.

Irene let go of him. "Oh shit! I'm sorry, did I hurt you?"

He shook his head, holding his breath.

"Breakthrough?" Irene asked. She took his arm, helping him stay balanced.

He nodded.

Irene asked, "Where is it on the scale?"

"Seven," he replied through clenched teeth. Irene knew more about pain classification and management than she'd ever wanted to know. Whenever there was pain, she would ask Dad where it was on a ten-point scale. In the last two weeks, he hadn't responded with anything below a six. Irene had tracked his responses, using a simple data-collection app on her phone. She had eighteen data points—nineteen once she recorded this one—but the trends were already obvious. The numbers were getting higher, and the time between them shorter.

She checked the time on her cell phone. "Shit. We missed an ATC dose." ATC was one acronym she'd picked up recently. It was short for "around the clock," and referred to medication taken at regular intervals to deal with persistent pain. That was in contrast to PRN medication, which was something in Latin that Irene guessed meant "right fucking now."

"Do you have your PRN on you?" she asked.

He shook his head, his breath coming out of him in semi-controlled rasps.

"Dammit, Dad. We talked about this," she scolded. He had put up a fight about taking the liquid morphine. Dad didn't like the inconsistency of a dosage that came with using an eyedropper to place the drug under his tongue. That was her father, the consummate accountant, wanting to make sure the numbers added up.

The wince eased off his face, leaving him pale. His breathing steadied, a sign that his wave of pain was ebbing. "I'll take the ATC, but I'll need to eat something first." Dad had been throwing up after his ATC medication for the last two days. Ingesting small bits of food with tea or water before taking the pills seemed to help. "I'm not hungry, though," he said as the elevator doors opened to the lobby of the medical office building.

"I'm not hungry either," Irene replied. "So let's go find something to eat."

They moved into the atrium, where tall windows created a greenhouse in which a lush slurry of vines grew around an artificial indoor stream. The air was thick with moisture, and it was a welcome respite from the skin-splitting dryness of the New Mexico desert outside.

"Are you going to wait for Wes to finish rehab before scheduling the Final Release?" Irene asked. Her brother still had two weeks left in his program. Not a long time under normal circumstances. Fourteen days of increasing and unmanageable pain was not something she wanted her father to experience.

Dad nodded. "I'd like to," he said. "I'd like to try to explain it to him." After a few paces toward the door, he continued, "I definitely want him there. You too."

Irene cringed. She had tried to come to terms with the fact that she would see Wes again as the Final Release came together. This was the first time she had to acknowledge that it would happen.

Dad heard her thoughts. "I know, Starlight. He might not agree with everything we've put together."

Irene sighed. "I doubt he'll take to it, Dad. You know he could derail the entire plan if he wanted to, right?" After they crossed the walkway over the stream, she continued, "Maybe you should explain to him how you're setting him up financially. That might make him more amenable to it."

Dad stopped moving and faced Irene, his eyes wide with hurt.

A fire burned in her cheeks. "What?" she demanded. "Do you think he's more concerned about ending your suffering? Or losing his financial support network?"

"Irene!" Her father's voice tightened. "He hasn't had it easy. And this will scare the shit out of him."

She watched his eyes in silence, having nothing to add.

"Wes isn't motivated the way you are, Starlight. And that isn't all his fault. I'm sure I have some blame there."

Irene scoffed, folding an arm across her chest. Her hand went to her jaw. It wasn't true. Wes was a damned wrecking ball off its chain, creating rubble from everything he touched. Dad kept sweeping up behind him, making it okay for him to shirk any responsibility for his choices. She wanted to argue, to show her father how wrong he was, but by the time the words came together, he wasn't looking at her anymore.

Instead, he stared past her, through the wide glass windows into the baking parking lot outside. His eyes glazed over in thought, and in a near whisper, he said, "Wes."

Irene blew out her breath. The conversation was consuming her patience. "What about him?"

Dad shook his head, his brow knotted in confusion. He pointed over her shoulder and said, louder this time, "No, I mean, there's Wes!"

Irene turned around. Outside the revolving door, stubbing a cigarette against one of the potted succulents, was her asshole brother. Through her teeth, Irene hissed, "What the hell is that fatass doing out of rehab?"

Chapter 5

WES

"Once you told me Irene was in town, I started talking to the doctors about letting me out. To check on you, Pop," Wes explained. He downed the rest of his coffee and looked behind him for the waiter to signal for more. He'd picked this spot because it was close and the plates were huge, but he had forgotten about the shit service. Failing to catch anyone's attention, Wes turned back to his sister and father. "I figured something bad happened if Irene left school to come back here."

Dad nodded. He looked wrung out. Irene sat still, her eyes on a hole in the plastic checkered tablecloth between them. She folded her arms across her chest as she said, "I left school because you were in rehab. I came here so you would finish the damned program this time."

Wes leaned his elbows on the table. "No, see, I will finish the program, Sis. This is just a ... what's the word they used? 'Furlough'?"

Irene smirked. Her hand dropped to the table, and she picked at the small hole in the tablecloth with her fingernail.

"Look, I can return to the program as long as I test clean when I go back. They wouldn't have let me out if I wasn't kicking ass in there, all right?"

Irene snarked, "They probably want to give your bed to someone with health insurance. Or maybe to someone who wants to be a better person."

"Oh fuck off, Irene," Wes blurted out.

Irene jabbered over him, "Do you have any idea how expensive that place is? How much money each of your little vacations costs?" Her voice exploded in volume and pitch. "The least you could do, the literal least amount of effort you could have exerted, would have been to just stay there, Wes!"

Dad raised a gentle hand, trying to quiet her. Wes felt customers and staff behind him staring their way. Irene heeded her father, her eyes falling back to the tablecloth.

She glowered at Wes. "What the hell do you offer here, anyway?"

"Please, that's enough," Pop said. "We have things to discuss."

Irene shifted her gaze to their father. Her expression immediately softened into ... what was that? Concern? Panic filled Wes's chest when Irene reached out and took their dad's hand.

"Oh shit," Wes sighed. He sat back in his seat, hands on the table for support. "It's real bad, isn't it?"

Dad nodded. "Irene and I ... we've been preparing. We've known my illness is terminal for a while now, and there are a lot of things I wanted to make happen."

Wes swallowed the lump in his throat as Pop continued. "I'm taking care of you both as best I can. My accounting business, the house, the car, the boat, all of it will be sold off. My retirement will be cashed out. After taxes, the money will go toward your rehabilitation, and provide a small nest egg for both of you to start your own lives."

Dad stopped to take a sip of water. His hand was unsteady on the glass, and he ended up moving his head down to the straw. Sitting back up, Dad shook his head and added, "I wish there was more."

Wes waved him off. "It's more than enough, Pop." His panic thickened into guilt.

Irene snorted, but held her tongue. Dad released her hand and sighed. He placed both hands flat on the table, propping himself up. His eyes rose to Wes's. They were wet. There was something else. Something worse. What could be worse than him dying? Wes looked from Irene to his father and back, unsure of what to ask.

It was Dad who broke the silence. "Son, I've decided not to fight this disease. I don't want to put you two through that, when the diagnosis is so ..." His voice faded as he shook his head. His lips tightened into a line. "Fighting it would be pointless."

Wes tried to process what that meant.

After a moment, Pop took in a rattling breath and continued, "I'm ending my life, Wes."

The guilt melted back into panic. Sitting up in his chair, Wes shook his head. "You're ... what?"

"I will not throw our lives into chaos when we all know how this ends up. I don't want to rot away in hospice while you and your sister watch. I want to avoid becoming any more of a burden than I already am."

"This can't be legal?" Wes heard himself ask.

Irene replied, "It is legal. At least in New Mexico. Has been for about two years now."

"So you're ... what? ... gonna blow your brains out? How can this be legal?" The spreading alarm in his chest warmed up as he looked from one of their calm faces to the other.

"No, son, of course not," Dad appeased. His tone was the one he used when he talked about ways Wes could be a better person. "It's a medical device. The end is quick and painless."

Wes grabbed the sides of his head with his hands and tried to shake off the confusion. This wasn't making sense. "How ... You're just giving up?"

Dad kept talking. "There's no road from here that doesn't lead to my death, son. I have ..." He leaned on the table as he gestured to the three of them. "None of us have any illusions here. Fighting this would be painful. For all of us. And it would be pointless. And expensive."

Wes's mouth hung open, words failing him. How could this be happening? What perverted logic had Irene used to get Pop to this decision?

His father's face fell. "I want to save what little I have for you and your sister. Not waste it on false hopes."

The heat in his chest exploded. Wes's fist hit the table, rattling the dirty plates and silverware. Dad and Irene flinched away from him. Their startled reaction egged Wes forward. "'False' hope?" he yelled, staring down his father. "There is no such thing as 'false' hope, Pop! It's just hope!" Wes's throat burned from the words. He took a breath to calm himself. "That's literally the first skill they drill into you at Del Rio! Life trips you up, but you can't do anything lying down. So you stand up, dust yourself off, and take another step. Even when that means starting over!"

Dad swallowed hard. He had one hand raised, palm toward his son, in a placating gesture while the other massaged his ear. When he spoke, his voice was soft and calm. "I'm not giving up, Wes. I'm making the best of a terrible situation. My body is already dead." He shrugged his shoulders in a slow surrender. "We're just waiting on the biological paperwork."

Wes's face hardened. Slamming his hands flat on the table, he darted his stare between his father and sister and said, "There's no way I'm letting you do this. No. Fucking. Way."

"Do you even remember Mom?" Irene's voice was gentle, but direct. She was picking at the hole in the tablecloth again. "I'll bet you don't. You were young. Hell, I barely remember her," she said, raising her eyes to Wes's and folding her arms back over her chest.

Wes went to shake his head, but Irene continued.

"I remember. Parts of her, at least," she sighed. As her tears welled, her eyes and fingers fell to the hole she picked wider in the tablecloth. "I try to remember cheerful things, but I mostly remember her dying. Wes, it took so long. So many days. I don't know how many." Irene stared into the red underlayer visible through the tear. "There was my birthday, then yours. The end of school. Summer, then starting the next grade. Halloween. Thanksgiving. And a Christmas. I think she made it to Valentine's Day? I can't remember that part anymore."

Wes swallowed, the fiery rush running out of his face. Irene exhaled a slow breath before speaking, "She fought. Hard. Tooth and nail for every moment she could get. That's what she wanted, because we were ..." She stopped to wipe a tear that found its way down her cheek. "Hell, Wes, we were just babies. She used to say something, what was it? 'Babies need a mother'? Something like that. I guess I don't remember that anymore either."

Her eyes snapped back to Wes, her face hard. "She smelled, Wes. She smelled awful, all the time. Like metal and chemicals and mold. That's how I remember her." Another tear fell, and Irene let it fall. "I remember Mom wanting a hug, and I didn't want to hug her because I thought she smelled like a monster."

Irene wiped both sides of her face with her hands, leaving a thin streak of wetness across her cheeks. "That's how I remember Mom."

Pop took his hand. "That's not what I want, for any of us. What money I have I want for you and your sister, not dumped into pointless efforts to prolong the pain. What time I have I want to spend in peace. And I want to leave this life knowing you'll not have to cope with memories like ..." Instead of finishing the thought, Pop reached out and took Irene's hand too.

The three of them sat for a pregnant minute, letting the clinks and tings and murmurs of the other customers fill the space. It was their father who broke the stillness when he let go of their hands to scratch his ear. He turned to his fanny pack and rummaged for something. Wes blanched as Pop placed a thick orange prescription bottle on the table.

Wes felt it. A chilling tickle. Eating a hollow in him he wanted to fill. He recognized it. Acknowledged the anxious craving. He'd known this would happen. The therapists warned him. Made him come up with a plan. Simple options.

Before the craving became an ugly thirst, Wes stood and kicked in his seat. "I'm going outside to smoke," he croaked. He turned, walked through the maze of tables and customers to the door outside. The restaurant sat in a strip of small shops, flanked by an out-of-business appliance place and an antique store. He crossed the sidewalk toward the line of cars parked along the street. In the falling sun of the New Mexico afternoon, he lit a cigarette. The first drag smothered the longing tickle like a heavy blanket on a fire. As he exhaled the smoke, the diner door popped open.

Irene arrived in a wind of hair and fury, yelling at him before the door closed behind her.

"Just who the fuck do you think you are?" she demanded. Her fist jabbed his chest, the recoil knocking the cigarette from his lips. "You! You shouldn't even be here! You should be in the goddamned rehab Dad is paying so much money for!"

She shoved him, hard enough that he stumbled against one of the parked cars. "How dare you, how dare you say those things to him! You selfish prick!"

Wes straightened and grabbed her flailing hand before she struck him again. "Selfish?" he barked. "What's selfish about wanting him to live? To at least try?"

Irene wrested her hands away from him. "You? Try? When the fuck have you ever tried, Wes? When have you ever made any effort? Who the fuck are you to make that demand of him!"

The whack of the diner door bursting open halted his sister's rant. Wes looked past Irene. Dad leaned out of the restaurant, his hands clutching the door. He cupped his right ear, his eyes boring into them, his face twisted in ... in what? Was he in pain? Or did he eat a lemon?

"Be quiet!" Pop shouted. His head nodded forward, pulling his body away from the door. His feet followed in a clumsy dance. "Just be quiet!"

He teetered through the line of parked cars. Toward the road. Before Wes could move, Pop disappeared under a passing car with a sickening thunk.

Chapter 6

CALEB

Caleb found the ATC in his fanny pack and set it on the table. It rattled in thick clunks, containing more pills than he would ever need at this point.

Wes shot up from his seat, his movements abrupt and decisive. "I'm gonna go smoke."

Caleb nodded as his son left, then unscrewed the bottle and fished out one of the stout capsules. He placed it in his mouth, said a small prayer that it wouldn't get stuck in his throat, and reached for his water. It took three swallows, but the pill made it down.

As he took another drink, the fluttering itch in his ear grew into a series of languid pops. Caleb pulled hard on his earlobe, trying to calm the sensation. Instead, it wormed deeper into his head. Christ, what if a damned bug had crawled into his ear on top of everything else?

He looked up to find Irene stomping toward the glass door, beyond which his son lit a cigarette. He recognized her posture. The tensed shoulders. The stiff gait. A fight brewed in her. The popping in his ear canal grew into thumps inside of his head.

Irene blasted open the door. Her momentum moved her forward as she punched at Wes's sternum. His daughter's yelling carried back to the rear of the diner as she shoved Wes against a car parked on the street.

A percussive snap shook the room. Caleb felt the sound before he heard it. On reflex, he bent toward the table and clenched his eyes shut.

The sound passed, replaced by a heavy and steady reverberation. It came through the floor, up his legs, through his body, and into his jaw. He peeled open his eyes. Other patrons sat laughing and talking as the intense vibration pressed around them.

The hum grew as it moved into his head. The single tone split into a chord that rose in pitch and volume until his teeth rattled. Raising his hands over his ears, he searched for the source and saw nothing obvious.

"What the hell is that?" Caleb screamed over the noise. His voice was stuffy and muddled. Patrons stared at him now. A rotund man at the next table was asking him something. The man's lips vibrated, his eyes searching, but Caleb heard nothing except the infernal hum.

The pitch rose past his ability to sense it, but the rattle moved through his body. His head. His ear. The sound searched for a place to land.

Caleb?

Someone was bellowing at him. He turned to the right, toward the monstrous sound, and saw only the diner wall.

Caleb, can you hear me?

The volume of the voice rocked Caleb up as he tightened his hands on his ears. His leg knocked the table, toppling glassware and plates to the floor. Those things—the glasses breaking, the plates scattering, the silverware dancing on the tiles—they should have made noise. Caleb heard nothing.

"What the hell is this?" he screamed. He needed Irene. He looked up. She was outside, with Wes. Everyone had stopped eating and stared at him now.

Hey.

A young waitress stood close by, reaching for his left arm. Her face wrinkled with concern, and her mouth moved. There was no sound. Her grip tightened on his arm as he stumbled into another patron, unable to find his balance.

Hey! Can you hear me?

The voice wasn't from the waitress. It didn't sound like she would sound. She was on his left, supporting his arm, and the voice was …

The voice was in his right ear.

His deaf ear.

You can finally hear me, can't you?

Caleb took a step toward the door. Toward Irene. The restaurant lurched under his feet. The right side of his body seized as the voice pushed against his skull.

I need to know that you can hear me.

The pressure abated. Caleb was on the floor now. He didn't remember falling. He rose up to one knee, whispering, "Please, please be quiet." He needed Irene. He looked up. She was outside. Arguing with Wes.

People were standing now. He could see their legs and feel their hands as they helped him to his feet. A rising pressure built behind his eyes. It was coming again. Caleb held his breath as the gale of noise crested against his skull.

Are you speaking to me? I can't tell.

The voice racked the right side of Caleb's body. He leaned into the strangers, trying to maintain a focus on his children outside. Wes was holding Irene's wrists. But he wasn't. No, there were two of Wes now. Two Irenes. One Wes held both hands tight around Irene's wrists; the other Wes raised a hand to strike her. One Irene struggled to free her hands; the other shrank away from the impending blow. The view unfolded in front of him, and a third Irene appeared in the fray. She was kicking another Wes in the groin.

The world split around him. A kaleidoscope of scenes and people bent into an impossible space. Caleb squeezed his eyes shut, unable to process what he was seeing.

Wait, am I doing that? Or is that you?

Caleb spit through his clenched teeth, "You be quiet!" He moved forward, eyes clamped against the visual cacophony around him. He left the supporting hands behind and lunged for the door—for where the door should be in the darkness.

The solid edges of the tables guided him, until they passed, and Caleb braved opening his eyes.

The door. Irene was outside. All the Irenes. So many. A wave of nausea grew in his gut as the door gave way. The ground bent away from him in every direction. An angry roar built in his ear. The voice. It was coming again.

He grabbed at his right ear. He had to stem it. To pull the voice from his head. His other hand gripped the frame of the door. Caleb sucked in a thick, dusty breath. His children. They were staring at him now. Every Irene and Wes. The crackle ignited in his ear. The sun dimmed in the sky as the voice approached.

Caleb hollered, "Be quiet!" He had to get to Irene before the voice hit him. This next one might kill him.

Is this too much?

The world grayed at the loudness of the words. His right leg buckled as the voice slammed through his bones. Caleb drifted from the door, away from Irene.

"Just. Be. Quiet!" he screamed. It should have been loud. The scream tore at the inside of his chest. It grated at the nerves in his throat. But he heard nothing.

Yeah, okay, this is too much. Let me dial it back a bit, hang on.

Caleb's feet flopped, trying to find the ground that flowed beneath him. Above him. Around him. His foot fell off the curb. His body followed. He spun around, arms reaching out, bending in impossible directions. His mind registered a car moments before he stumbled into it.

Pain. Everywhere. And relief. The voice was quiet. His eyes opened. There was color again. There was Irene. One Irene. Her face was close. She was speaking. He could hear her.

"Dad? Don't move!" She was looking him over. "Jesus Christ, don't move." Her face tight. Shocked. Concerned.

The ground was beneath him. Where it should be. It was warm, solid, and supportive. Irene's eyes found his. She felt his head with her hands, gently probing for injury. He reached up to touch her face, and a surge of pain radiated through his body. He moaned. And then he smiled, because he could hear himself again too.

"I said don't move, Dad!" Irene spoke in apneic gasps. "Christ, they could have killed you." Wes appeared behind her, gawking.

Pressure. Against his skull. It pushed tears out of his eyes. No. No, no, it was coming again. The voice. Turning back to him. A growling throb grew with each pound of his heart. It scraped against his skull until it reached his right ear. Caleb tensed as it took ahold of him.

I guess she's not ready for you to die after all.

Chapter 7

WES

Wes ran back to his father. Irene squatted over Dad as he lay on the road. Onlookers had gathered from the diner and surrounding businesses.

"The driver fucking took off!" Wes cried. "Is he okay?" Without waiting for her answer, Wes leaned over his sister to examine his father. Sucking in a breath, he asked, "What the hell is happening with his face?"

The right side of Dad's face twitched on and off. In one moment, he scrunched up, as if he was experiencing intense pain. In the next, the eye relaxed, and his cheek and mouth released their tension, leaving his face slack with palsy. While this happened, the other side of his face stayed locked in a mask of constant terror.

Irene turned to face Wes. "He needs to get to a hospital. This is some kind of seizure."

"I'll call an ambulance," Wes offered.

Irene waved him off as her phone went to her ear. "You stay with him, I'll call." She leaped to her feet and stepped back toward the diner. More people stood there, at a respectful distance, gawking at their dad on the ground.

Wes knelt next to him. "Hey, Pop, you're gonna be okay. Irene's calling an ambulance and ..."

Dad reached out and took Wes's hand. He heaved out a thick breath, squeezing Wes's fingers until his knuckles cracked.

Wes winced at the pressure. "Jesus, take it easy!" He would never have guessed Pop had that strength in him.

No response. Wes felt the grip relax in his hand. His father's body rag-dolled against the pavement, his face now slack, eyes unfocused.

"Pop?" Anxiety bloomed in Wes as he waited for his father to breathe. To blink. Nothing. "Shit! *Dad?*" Seconds passed. Too many. Wes turned to his sister and shouted, "Something's wrong!"

Irene turned around, her phone to her ear. She was holding her breath too. A violent rasp exploded out of Pop, snapping Wes around. Dad was back. Sputtering. His face tightened around his cheeks, eyes pleading.

"Stop," he coughed.

"Stop what?" Wes asked.

Dad collapsed back to the pavement. His face lost all tension as his stare drifted to Wes's forehead. Wes put a hand to his dad's chest, shaking him. *"Pop?"*

The murmurs of the crowd filled the surrounding air. "What the hell's wrong with him?" "I don't know CPR, but I think my cousin does, should I call him?" "Hey, is he dead? He looks dead." "Shit, I've never seen a live dead guy before, this is messed up!" Through it all, Wes watched his father's chest. It didn't move.

Panic squeezed Wes's throat. Before he could call to his sister, Pop's hand shot up, grabbing Wes's shirt. His mouth gaped as he sucked in a deep breath, releasing it with a ragged cough as he writhed on the street. "Oh, thank God!" Wes said, relief exploding through him.

"Don't," Dad spit between coughs, "don't let me go, please!"

"What? I'm not doing anything!" Wes's hands trembled helpless in the air over his father. Dad's breathing became labored and deliberate.

Irene leaned over them, speaking into her phone. Her words clipped, her tone calm. Fifty-nine years old. Hit-and-run. No visible injury. Something about an existing condition.

Their father's face tensed, as if he was concentrating. His cheeks reddened, his teeth pressed together, cracking lips stretched in a tight grimace. Pop's eyes lifted. His right pupil opened. Wider. Too wide, as if it wanted to suck the sun from the sky.

Hissing through clenched teeth, he spurted, "Two ... seven ... one eight ... two eight ... one ... eight three."

Wes turned to his sister. Her face locked on Dad, her calm veneer cracking around her eyes. "Irene, what the hell is he saying? What is this?"

Season of Waiting

"Two seven one eight ... two eight one ... eight three," Pop repeated. Wes felt Dad's grip relax on his shirt as the tension left his face.

Irene's throat swelled as she swallowed. In her matter-of-fact tone, she spoke into her phone. "I think he's having a stroke. Please hurry."

Chapter 8

CALEB

I realize this is hard on you, and I'm sorry.

The impact of the voice had blunted.

Give me a few seconds to dial this in.

Caleb watched his body from above. It lay prone on the pavement, Wes kneeling over it—over him—and Irene standing close, on her phone. Caleb tried to speak, tried to ask, "Jesus Christ, am I dead?" No words came.

No, you're not dead. Hang on a second.

Caleb felt his awareness of the scene expand. Details became clear. The texture of the pavement. The particulates in the air, suspended as if the moment had hardened in amber. The tension in the tiny muscles around the eyes of the looky-loos in the small crowd gathered on the sidewalk. The swirl of smoke from Wes's abandoned cigarette, sketching the current in the air with a wispy tendril.

Okay, this looks good. You can see everything, right?

Caleb nodded. Or tried to. There was nothing for him to nod.

Good, good. Are you able to move?

Caleb felt no part of his body. No, he couldn't move. He no longer knew how.

Huh. Okay, give me another second.

The stillness of the moment rattled, the details still there, but wiggling.

How about now?

The idea didn't seem possible. Caleb had nothing to move. No way to move. He had nowhere to go. He was already everywhere.

Shit. Um ... okay, I'll need a minute. I've never done this before.

Caleb waited in the pulsing moment. Cycles became apparent around him. Small and benign details, but Caleb was immediately aware of every one of them. Irene's body rotated toward his; then the movement was undone. The smoke and particulates in the air flowed on currents he could not feel. Then they moved back, as if the moment gasped them in.

Nothing?

No, nothing. The voice filled the space, pushed on him with immense pressure. It was tolerable now. Or here. Whatever this was.

Dammit. This should work, I don't see why ...

The cycling details tore themselves apart. Caleb was moving. Or the surrounding scene was moving. He felt nothing—no air on his skin, no tingle in his gut. Yet space bent into something new. Something familiar.

The boat. Caleb was on the boat now. He could see himself standing at the bow, in front of the small gate, heaving the anchor into Elephant Butte Lake. Behind him, around him, were his children. When his children were kids. Sitting at the boat's small table, facing each other. The moment was static. Irene separated a peanut butter and jelly sandwich for her brother to share. Wes hunched over a soda held between two tiny hands sticking out of an oversized life jacket. His lips pursed as they reached for the can. Caleb knew this day. This was the day Wes first went in the water.

Whoa, okay, that worked. Did you do that? Or did I?

Caleb didn't know.

I guess it was me, then. Let me check something.

The scene flailed back to the road. Caleb felt the intimate and still details fade as his perspective moved into his body lying on the pavement. The warm asphalt supported his body. The air moved on his skin. Pain coursed through him. The moment was living again. Caleb heaved in a breath, the effort immense. His chest seized in an involuntary spasm.

"Stop," he hissed between hacking coughs. He found his son's face. It gaped with concern.

"Stop what?" Wes asked. Caleb didn't get to answer before he snapped out of himself once more. He hovered over the moment, the air gone, his body not part of himself anymore.

Sorry, let me try that again.

Details thickened. The movements of the crowd magnified. Tics on their faces, wrinkling of their lips, shifts in their stances, the subtle changes smeared into a blur.

This isn't working like it should.

Everything sped up. The smears of slight differences grew to broad strokes, overlapping and pressing together. At first, Caleb could make out individuals. Irene, Wes. But their forms smudged as they moved, a kaleidoscope capturing several seconds.

Hang on. This might be rough.

The scene became visual noise. People lost their edges. Caleb stopped trying to process any of it.

No, I need your help with this. Try to focus on something.

Like what? There was nothing around him except swirls of color.

Anything. Just one thing. Pull something out of all of this.

He couldn't. There wasn't anything solid.

Fine! One second, I'll be right back.

The colors brightened, blending together into a single view of the sky. Caleb was on the road again. Wes sat over him still, and Caleb reached out, fisting a hand into his son's shirt. An anchor, to hold him here.

Caleb coughed, the air in his lungs stale and wanting to escape. "Don't!" he cried. He tightened his grip on his son. "Don't let go, please!"

Okay, I think I've got it this time.

Caleb tried to protest. He didn't get the chance. The moment trembled; the sky opened behind his son. Caleb's vision filled with new details. Edges. Shapes. Light.

Focus. Identify one thing.

A room. Pricks of light. Three dark edges meeting in a corner. A television.

Good, come on, hone it in. We've almost got it!

Caleb pushed his perception. The facets of the scene were innumerable. The screen dissolved into millions of points, individual lights. Caleb could see each one.

Relax a bit.

The dots of color merged into shapes.

Good! What do you see?

The shapes were familiar. Caleb knew what they were. They were numbers.

Yes, can you read them?

He could. The first was a two.

Yes, okay. Keep going, this is helping!

More numbers congealed from the details. Seven ... one, eight ... two eight ... one ... eight three.

Yes, yes, I think we got it!

A jolt through his body. He was prone. Strapped to a stretcher. Being rolled into an ambulance. The voice was gone. He could think again. But he didn't want to. He was so tired. He didn't know anyone could be this tired. He wanted to go home. Sleep. Maybe forever.

Season of Waiting

A man climbed in, his blue uniform crisp. He closed the ambulance doors, the frame to the street shrinking around Irene and Wes. She was biting the skin by her thumbnail and shifting her weight from one foot to the other. Wes stood behind her, his hands clenching his shaggy head.

Caleb felt a gentle rocking as the vehicle moved. He tried to relax as the paramedic poked and prodded him.

"BT is 97.3. BP is ..." The man leaned over Caleb, staring intensely at something connected to his right arm, and whistled. "Jesus, 170 over 110. Pulse is 122 BPM, and respiration ..." He paused for a stretch, gazing at Caleb's chest and mouth. "Huh ... 12." Caleb flinched as a brilliant light filled one eye, then the other.

Caleb blinked away the fading colors. He took in the back of the ambulance. The space was tight with secured supplies and filled with the sharp smells of chemical cleansers. The only sign of their movement was the swaying of the medic's torso above him.

"Who were you speaking to?" Caleb asked him. "There's no one else here."

The medic smiled down at him, his eyes kind as his hands gently probed Caleb's left arm. "It's just how we do, sir."

Chapter 9

IRENE

Irene paced the waiting area at Sierra Vista Hospital. The muted television mounted in the corner above their heads played the montage introduction for a popular show that reviewed video clips and home movies. The local news program she was ignoring must have ended. That would make it ninety minutes since they arrived.

They had hurried to the hospital, just to wait in this stale room to find out if their father was okay. The waiting room was almost empty. The only sounds were the jiggling taps of Wes's frenetic foot bouncing on the tile floor, and the adolescent girl crying in her mother's arms on the other side of the room. As she paced, Irene couldn't help but notice the pattern between Wes's tapping and the girl's staccato gasps. Five taps, one sob. Five taps, one sob. Seeing the pattern irritated her, more so when she noticed her strides were falling into the rhythm.

The television mounted in the corner showed a video. It was amateur, based on the camerawork. A doe stumbled away from a young Hispanic boy. The animal was wild, framed by asphalt on one side, small sun-bleached buildings on the other. It wasn't where it should have been. Like her, in New Mexico. Like Dad back in the emergency room. Like Wes out of rehab.

"So?" Wes asked.

Her eyes moved from the television to her brother. He sat in one of the hard plastic chairs in front of the window, his right leg bouncing like it was trying to get away from him. She had sat with him for a while after they first arrived. The uncomfortable silence between them, the hardness of the chair on her bad back, and the vibrations of his wild leg got her moving around the room.

She crossed her arms over her belly. "I wish there was a way to hurry through the waiting."

Wes nodded. "I know, Sis. I'm sorry this happened."

Irene shrugged and shifted her weight. They had driven to the emergency room together in Dad's car. Her panic had worn off. Now the discomfort of being around her brother—of being alone with him—had fully bloomed.

She scowled. "Yeah, me too." She turned at the sound of the hospital doors opening. A man in green scrubs entered the waiting room and looked their way for a moment. Irene's breath caught, but the man turned toward the only other people in the waiting room and called them through the door.

Irene sat in a chair and leaned into the hard plastic. She pushed her feet into the floor and arched her back until she felt a series of cavitations in her backbone. She relaxed forward, savoring the release of tension. Wes slid across the seats between them, closing the distance she would have preferred.

He moved to a whispering distance from her. "So what do you think that was?" Stale cigarettes and pastrami stained his quiet voice.

Irene shrugged and leaned away from his rancid breath. "What?"

Wes waved toward the doors with his hand. "That thing with Pop? What the hell was all that?"

Irene glanced out the window. The sun would breach the edge of the mini-blind in a few moments. "I don't know for sure, Wes. If I had to guess, I'd say he's had a stroke. On top of everything else."

Wes nodded. "Because of that face stuff he was doing? How one side of it would, like, scrunch up and then ... melt back?"

Irene folded her arms across her chest. "Yeah. That and the way he was speaking. I don't think he was saying what he wanted to say."

Wes sat up, rubbing his palms on his jeans. "God, I thought he was dead when I heard the car hit him."

Irene sighed. Part of her hated the minor comfort from Wes. "So did I. I just ... I froze. I couldn't move. It was all I could do to watch him stumble into the road like it was a ..." She waved up at the television above their heads. "... a show."

She hugged herself tight and continued, "I should have acted. I should have grabbed him, but I didn't process what was happening." The ebb of her adrenaline rush had left a wake of emotional turbulence, and the tears swelled in her eyes again.

Wes patted her shoulder. "He'll be okay, Sis. He didn't seem badly injured, did he? Could have been way worse. I guess he's got an angel watching out for him."

She shrugged off his hand and stood back up, shaking her head. "His injuries might be on the inside. If he's paralyzed from a stroke, if he loses the ability to use his hands, I'm not sure he can still do his Final Release. He'll suffer until he wastes away."

Wes released an elongated sigh. He had something to add, Irene was sure of it.

The approach of another physician captured their attention. The woman was short and round, with dark features and a practiced smile. She tugged on her green scrubs, straightening them as she spoke. "Are you Caleb Allard's family?" Her voice sing-songed and was way too chipper for Irene's dour mood.

Irene nodded. "I'm his daughter."

The doctor held out her hand. "Dr. Marybeth Cass." Motioning toward the chairs in the room's corner, she added, "Let's sit. I can update you on your father."

Irene sat on the hard seat again, her back screaming in protest. She oriented herself to keep the falling sun from blinding her. Dr. Cass sat across from her, shielding her eyes as she spoke. "Caleb didn't sustain any serious injuries from the accident. He has a fractured wrist, but beyond that, we don't see any physical issues."

Irene released her breath. Dad was okay. Physically at least.

"Now, I am concerned," the doctor continued, her voice taking on an edge. "His behavior indicates some kind of brain trauma. But with the tumors in his head, our data is difficult to interpret. We're waiting to hear from his oncologist, get a recent scan, and compare them."

Irene shook her head. "He's terminal, Doctor. Is that necessary?"

The doctor nodded with enthusiasm. "Of course! I wouldn't be doing my job otherwise." A shadow now reached her face, and she lowered her hand to her lap. The sun must have fallen behind the foothills.

"No, that's just it. My father's registered for the Final Release. He's terminal. We had the last appointment with hospice this morning. The equipment is being delivered tomorrow."

Dr. Cass's expression chilled, her eyes losing their kindness, her lips moving from a smile to a curt pucker. "I see," Dr. Cass said, her emotion leveling off. The vibration of Wes's bouncing leg came through Irene's chair.

Irene raised her eyebrows at the change in the doctor's demeanor. The Final Release program didn't fit with everyone's moral code. She pressed, her voice lacking confidence, "So you'll release him—he's okay to leave here?"

Season of Waiting

The doctor stood, tugging her clinging scrubs away from her round belly. "I'm sorry, but we need to watch your father overnight." Her tone had cooled, dropping the concern it contained before.

Irene shot out the chair. "You're admitting him for a broken wrist?" This wasn't what she needed now, not what Dad needed. A sideline martyr wanting to make sure her father's suffering contributed to her moral code.

Dr. Cass swallowed as she shook her head. "No. Not for that injury. We had to sedate your father. So we need to monitor him until he comes out of it."

Irene clenched her teeth. "I'm sorry, you sedated a terminally ill man? For a fucking broken wrist?" she asked, slapping her thigh in aggravation.

"No, well ... yes, a mild sedative." The doctor's eyes fell to her wringing hands. "I was getting to that. We had to sedate your father, and ... I'm afraid ... restrain him too. To keep him from injuring himself."

Irene stared at the doctor in dismay, waiting for some plausible explanation. Dr. Cass fisted her hands together. "Sometime between me and the nurses doting on him, he ..." The doctor shrugged her shoulders and sighed, "He apparently tried to tear off his own ear."

Chapter 10

CALEB

A voice approached him. Not the crippling voice. Someone he knew and loved. The sound of it tickled the edge of his consciousness.

"Hey ..."

Was that Ivy? Was she here now?

"You coming around?"

Caleb cracked his eyes, but the scream of lights forced them shut again. Odors assaulted him. Astringent. The violent smells of medicine. Ivy. She's sick again. Goddammit. We were done with all that.

"C'mon, Dad, open them peepers," Ivy sang.

Not Ivy. Ivy couldn't be here. But she was squeezing his hand. Caleb pried his eyes open a slit. Shadows and light. He blinked once, twice, opening his eyes wider. The shadows became a person. The light became a room.

Not Ivy. Irene. She leaned over him and touched his cheek. "Hey there, sleepy. You've had quite the night."

Caleb tried to swallow the paste that stuck his tongue to his palate. He tried speaking through it, but there was no moisture in him.

Irene lifted a tumbler to his lips. "Take a pull."

Caleb sucked on the straw. The water cleaned his mouth and cooled his throat. When it hit his stomach, his body checked in. His arms ached. The tumor in his belly was angry. His ear—his deaf ear—it itched, but on the outside now. Caleb tried to reach up and scratch it, but his arms wouldn't move. Looking down, he saw that his left arm disappeared into a thick roll of gauze. A Velcro cuff secured his right arm to a rail.

Caleb was in a hospital.

"Am I okay?" he croaked.

Irene smiled at him. She was on his right side, and Caleb turned his head to better hear her.

"Yeah, you're lucky," Irene said. "Do you remember what happened?"

The monstrous words. The crippling effect their sound had on him. The world breaking to pieces when the voice spoke. Caleb's gut churned.

"No," he lied. His voice broke again.

"That's okay." She brought the straw to his lips, and the few sips Caleb took lapped away the fog in his mind.

He glanced around the room. Wes sat in a chair, leaning his head against the wall. He looked from Caleb to the television mounted in the corner.

"Dad, can you squeeze my hand?" Irene asked.

His grip pressed on her fingers, and a modicum of tension melted off Irene. "Thank you," she whispered through a calm smile.

Her brother shot Irene a scolding glare. "Subtle," he mumbled, before turning his attention back to the television.

The itch on Caleb's right ear became aggravating. He tried again to rub it, but neither arm moved that far. "It itches," he said, pointing a thumb toward his ear. "Can you help?"

Relief came as Irene tenderly massaged the skin behind his right temple. "Yeah, so, what happened there?"

Caleb shrugged. "What do you mean?"

Irene paused. "Do you remember what you did to your ear?"

Fireworks of panic burst in Caleb's head. His ear. The voice. Did he do that to himself? He shook his head.

Irene turned and reached to the floor, pulling up her backpack. Rummaging through the front pocket, she fished out a compact mirror and let the pack fall back to the floor. She spun the mirror toward Caleb. "Can you see your ear?"

Caleb shifted his head, following his face in the mirror. He gasped when his ear came into view. At the top, a ragged wound ran under several clean stitches and a thin line of tape. The skin was bruised and angry.

"What happened, Dad?"

He looked away from the mirror. Caleb held his breath for a moment, unsure what to say to his daughter. Her eyes waited on his words. He sighed, "I'm ... Look, I don't really understand what happened."

Irene's warm hands wrapped over his. "It's okay, Dad. Start at the beginning."

The beginning. When was that? The restaurant?

Irene cleared her throat. "Wes and I were having a ... passionate debate over things, and you, sort of, fell out of the restaurant. Do you remember that?"

Lunch. When everything split apart. Caleb nodded.

"You were shouting at us, to be quiet. Do you remember that too?"

He didn't remember. Yet he nodded.

Irene smiled. "Okay, good. So our fighting upset you?"

Caleb thought back. To the feelings. Not anger. Just fear. Helpless under the compressing immensity of the voice. He shook his head. "No. No, I wasn't ... It's not ..." Caleb racked his brain to find a plausible explanation. A story that made sense. Something that Irene wouldn't find insane.

Irene rubbed his hand, encouraging him to continue. When he couldn't, she offered, "Okay, so if we didn't agitate you, then what did?" She sat for a moment, waiting for him to speak. "Did anything happen in the diner? After me and Wes left?"

Caleb swallowed and nodded.

Irene's face brightened. "Okay, good. Let's start there, Dad. What happened inside the restaurant?"

Caleb's eyes darted around the room as he debated his answer.

"Did someone say something to upset you?" she offered.

Caleb coughed out a few huffs of uncomfortable laughter. He met her pleading eyes. She wanted to understand, but there was no way she would. Caleb had only memories of feelings. Irene required facts.

The snapping of Wes's fingers pulled Caleb's attention from his daughter. "Pop, what were those numbers? The ones you were yelling at the accident?" Wes was standing now, gawking at the television.

Irene let go of Caleb's hand and turned to her brother. She snipped, "Why? What the hell does it matter?"

Wes's finger-snapping had shifted into an excited hand-flapping. "Two seven, one, eight two ... eight, one eight ... three, right?" His face turned from the television, eyes white with excitement and his mouth open in joy. His flailing hand formed into a pointed finger jabbing at the screen. "That's right, isn't it!" He danced, tapping his finger on the television screen.

The screen, made up of millions of pixels, each luminating a single spot of color, when viewed together displayed the day's winning numbers for the Four Corners lottery: 27, 1, 82, 8, 18, and 3.

Chapter 11

WES

Wes's fingernail tap-tap-tapped against the glass of the television screen.

"That's right, isn't it!"

The crease in Pop's brow deepened; his mouth drew to a frown as he looked from Wes to the television and back. Irene stood next to Dad, glowering.

"Irene!" Wes called. "You're a numbers girl, right? You remember the numbers, don't you?" He turned back to the television, where a dog-food commercial had replaced the lottery numbers.

"What numbers?" Pop asked. "I didn't see any numbers, son."

Wes felt the excitement peak, beginning the hard fall into frustration. "The ... the jackpot numbers? They were just on the TV! They were the numbers you were repeating when you ..." Wes waved a hand at his father. "When you ... were on the ground. They're the same!"

Irene heaved out a breath, her irritation on her face. "I don't remember the numbers, Wes. What the hell does it matter?"

He turned to his father, flapping his hand for some show of support. Dad faded to a lighter shade as he swallowed and looked away. "Come on," Wes pleaded. "I know one of you remembers!"

Irene released Pop's hand and crossed her arms. A defensive gesture. She was prepping for a fight. "The numbers. Are you sure you remember them right?" she asked.

The question surprised him. Wes had been expecting an insult. He straightened, the tingle of embarrassment in his cheeks. "Yes, I'm sure," he said.

"How?" she pressed, tightening her arms.

Shame blossomed in him, but he swallowed it down. "Well, Irene," Wes said, running a hand through his hair, "Dad repeated them, and there was this kind of rhythm to it, and ..." He licked his lips and swallowed. "Well, I made up a little tune around 'em."

Irene's face was stone. Pop's concern broke into a patronizing smirk as he looked down at his bandaged hand.

Wes groaned. "Dammit, you're going to make me sing it, aren't you?"

Irene's eyebrows rose with expectation, while Pop's face lit with amusement.

Wes sighed, weighing his need to be right with the humiliation of proving it. He swallowed his pride and cleared his throat. His voice came out in a jitter. He half sang, half spoke the Numbers Song he'd composed in front of the diner. "Two seven one, eight two eight, one eight three, that's all there be." He caught himself bouncing from foot to foot with each line of the tune.

Irene's eyebrows crawled farther toward her hairline. Dismissing Wes with a shake of her head, she uncrossed her arms and turned back to their dad. She paused for a moment before turning back to Wes. Her face pursed in confusion, she asked, "Wait, can you sing ... say those numbers again for us?"

Wes repeated the Numbers Song, this time without the bouncy jig. "They were the same order as the lottery numbers!" He thumbed toward the television. Turning to his father, he asked, "Why did you say those numbers, Pop?"

Irene waved Wes off. "That's Euler's number, isn't it?" She turned to Pop, and he shrugged.

Wes didn't know what Oiler's number was, but he wasn't about to admit that to his sister. She stared up at the ceiling, a tell that she was scouring her brain for something. Blinking her eyes, she said, "Yeah, two point seven one eight two eight, blah, blah, blah. Euler's number."

Her eyes fell down to Pop, and she looked back at Wes. His face must have betrayed his ignorance. "So, it's a well-known constant, like pi, but another value. It's denoted by a lowercase *e*. The base of the natural logarithm?"

Wes tucked his hands into his jean pockets and shrugged.

Irene elaborated, "It comes up in interest calculations and statistics. That's probably why Dad was using it."

Pop chimed in. "Using it? For what, honey?" His voice was dusty and dry.

Irene lifted the water sipper from the tray to Pop's lips, saying, "Well, you were in a lot of pain, right? It's a common tactic, to repeat some mantra to distract from the pain. That's what you were doing, right?"

She was taking the conversation to the wrong place. The muscles in Wes's neck tensed from shaking his head in a tight arc as he spoke. "No, Irene. That's not the point. That doesn't explain the lottery numbers!"

His sister waved him off. "There's nothing to explain. It's a coincidence." Irene moved to the sink to refill the tumbler. "And besides," she continued, "I'm not sure what numbers were on the television. I missed it."

Wes pulled his phone from his pocket, incensed. "Well, Irene, that's why God invented the Internet." He opened his web browser and thumbed in a query for the Four Corners Lotto. The first result linked to the website for the local news station they were just watching. In bold, stylized numbers, it showed that Wes was right.

The rush at proving his sister wrong spread to a grin as he pushed the phone to her face. Turning back toward him, Irene glanced at the phone and shrugged. "Christ, Wes, it doesn't matter."

"How can you think that!" he pleaded. This was important—he would not let her overthink this one. As she put the water on Pop's bed tray, Wes pushed his phone back in his pocket with a huff. "The universe is trying to tell us something!"

Irene turned to their father. Her shoulders dropped; her head lilted. Wes recognized the movements. He knew what a dismissal from Irene looked like, from any angle. She had rolled her eyes, made a grimace.

Before Wes could call her out, his sister chided, "It's telling us you're an idiot who can't see what's important." Her voice dripped with condescension. "What matters is getting Dad back home."

Heat rose in his throat. "Fuck off, Irene!" Wes shoved a hand into his sister's back. She spun around, hands up to her face in a defensive stance. In the haze of anger, Wes raised his voice. "Do you hear yourself right now? Look where we are, Sis! We're in a hospital, and you wanna get Dad out of here ... get him home ... just to kill him!"

In a flash, Wes faced the floor. Irene gripped his wrist. She twisted his arm around. Pressure built on his elbow and shoulder, teetering on injury as Irene pressed her other hand into his back. The shock of his sister's physical reaction, along with the excruciating pain in his arm, froze Wes to silence.

"Keep your fucking voice down," Irene said, her movements at odds with her calm. "Trouble from the hospital staff is the last thing we need. And if you keep making a ruckus, trouble is what we'll get." His shoulder and elbow protested as she continued, "I'm here to help Dad get what he needs, Wes. I will not let your dumb ass get in our way."

"I saw those numbers." Pop's voice was distant, quiet.

Irene rose from Wes's face. He felt the blood rush from his pounding head into his arm as she released him with a shove. He stood, rolling his tender shoulder as he took a few steps away from his sister.

"What do you mean? Like, you've seen Euler's number before?" she asked as she turned toward their father. Wes moved to the foot of the bed so he could see Pop's face.

Clearing his throat with a messy grumble, Pop shook his head. "No, I mean yeah, I've heard of it, but that's not what I mean. What I mean is, I saw them. Well, I guess … they were shown to me?" His gaze fell to the sheet on his bed, his face tight. The cuff tethering his right arm to the bed rattled as he tried to point at his ear. Looking up at Wes and Irene, Pop licked his lips and nodded to the right. "I heard a voice. In my ear. My deaf ear. It showed me those numbers."

After searching Wes's face, and then his sister's, Pop continued, "It … it hurt when it spoke. It filled my head. I felt it through my body. There's a lot of … pressure, it's paralyzing. Made it hard to walk." Tears worked their way down his sunken cheeks as he spoke, landing on the blanket in his lap. "I wanted it to stop, and it just kept … insisting."

"Holy shit," Wes whispered.

Irene spoke over him, through the hands on her mouth as she shook her head. "Oh my God."

Wes gulped down the rising tingle in his chest. He was right. For once, he was right. The universe was correcting itself, giving Pop a gift to pay him back for his suffering. Wes looked to his sister with the fire of vindication and pride, but she didn't see him. She stared at Pop, the terror on her face dampening his itch to gloat over her.

Their father's tears rolled into breathy sobs, and the three of them waited in a heavy silence. The corner of Pop's mouth tightened. Wes placed a hand on his blanketed leg. "Go on, it's okay, Pop."

"No, this is bad," Irene warned, moving her hands to the sides of her face.

Wes ignored her. This was fucking amazing. He squeezed his father's calf, offering him support. Dad had an ally here. More than one, it would seem. Between sobs, Pop's mouth ticked up into a slight smile, and Wes mirrored it. The moment was warm, a rare connection with his father.

It faded as Dad's smile grew into an exaggerated smirk. The right side of his face stretched. His lips tightened. The corner of his mouth pursed and relaxed in a spastic rhythm. Pop's eyes grew wide. Pleading. Wanting. Needing something.

"Hey, Pop?" Wes sputtered, giving his leg a firm shake.

His father didn't respond.

Chapter 12

CALEB

Caleb's vision blurred with each heartbeat. He could make out his children's faces against the distorting ceiling tiles. This time, there was only one Wes, one Irene, and one room as the voice gripped him.

This should be easier on you.

Caleb could still breathe through the tension and pressure in his body. His face formed a fist around his right ear as the voice spoke. The seizure was painful, and Caleb had to focus on the rasps of his breathing to avoid choking on his own spit. His face came back under control, the voice letting go of him.

Irene's face stretched with panic, eyes wide and focused. Wes bubbled with excitement.

Wes whispered, "Are you ... are you hearing it right now?"

Caleb nodded, still focusing on the breath entering and leaving his body.

"Holy shit, that's amazing!" Wes whispered. His eyes darted around the room. "We need paper. And a pen." He turned and opened a drawer, heaving wads of gauze and tape onto the floor.

The tickle worked its way deeper into Caleb's ear.

I'm sorry about before. This is ... tricky.

"Irene, don't you have a notebook in your damned bag? A pencil or something?" Wes was getting frantic. Irene's attention remained locked on her father. At her lack of action, Wes snapped, "C'mon, Sis, we need to write this down!"

I need to show you a few things, Caleb. I'm not sure I can. You must believe that this isn't some figment of your imagination or sickness.

Caleb forced out a breath as the voice released him. He sucked in another.

This might feel strange.

Irene's hands moved into the bed, searching. "We need a doctor," she cried. "Where's the damned bed remote? With the call button?"

That's a superb idea, let's start with the remote.

Caleb felt a sharp pop inside his head. The room shrank until he could see all of it. Sound evaporated. Irene and Wes were still. Her hands had lifted a corner of the hospital blanket, and his were in the middle of shoving a cabinet door closed. And Caleb saw himself, swallowed up by the gaping bed. There was no motion to see. No odors, no sounds. The moment only existed in front of him.

Can you see the remote?

He became aware of the device. It dangled in the air under the side of the hospital bed. A thick cable tethered it to the rail close to his cuffed arm. He could see it from all sides, in an odd panoramic focus. The grid of buttons. The cable's stretch to the serpentine knot around the bed rail. The gummy underside that needed cleaning. The scratched-up beveled edge. All visible at once.

Yes, that's right. There it is. Now, can you tell how it ended up there?

Caleb's mind knotted. How the hell was he supposed to know how it got there? And yet, he knew. There was a ... line. A thread. Leading away from here. He couldn't hold it, but it was there. Caleb followed as it led behind them, dropping into another moment. Here, in this same hospital room, Irene heaved her backpack off the bed. As she did, the remote nudged through the gap in the bed railing. This must have happened when Irene retrieved her mirror to show Caleb the stitches in his ear. This scene was like the first—quiet and stale. Yet it looked different—there was less color here, everything a similar shade of tepid gray.

Good! That's good!

The thread went on. Caleb sensed he could follow it as long as he wished, but he resisted the urge to go further. He expected some fear, confusion. There were no feelings in this lukewarm space.

Now, are you able to see what else could have happened?

Caleb focused on the line connecting this moment to the next. He could sense a fray in the thread—a barb. Caleb focused on it, finding it to be another line, attached to the first. He knew he could follow that line forward. He could see where it would go. Irene would leave the backpack on the bed instead of throwing it over the railing to the floor.

Very nice, Caleb. You seem to be a natural at this.

He saw both moments now. In the first—the one he'd lived—Irene scoured the bed looking for the remote, while her brother opened a cabinet door. This scene was full of color, as if it might pop to life and change at a whim. The second moment was colorless and static, like unfinished plaster. There, Irene lifted the backpack with one hand. With the other, she grabbed the remote. Wes still rummaged through the cabinet. Caleb's accountant mind isolated the difference between the scenes: the backpack.

Sort of. Not the backpack itself, but Irene's choice of what to do with it. Irene chose to move her backpack. The consequence was the remote dropping from the bed. If she chose to leave it, the remote would still be on the bed. Two moments, stemming from a single choice.

Caleb moved into the colored scene. He was in his bed again, staring up at Irene. He gasped and watched as Irene found the cable to the remote under the blanket. She followed the cable to the knot on the railing and pulled up the remote. Caleb released his breath as the moment slowed to a pause, and he left his body.

No, don't stop. This is fun, and helpful. Let's see what else we can do. Should we follow Irene back a ways?

Caleb didn't want to. Yet he moved back along her thread from this moment. It flowed through the accident, through the visit to the hospice offices that morning, and back through the entire week with Irene. Then the previous week. And the one before. Moments stacked together, books filling an endless shelf that told the story of their recent time together. He watched her record his pain numbers several times a day. The thread wound backward, racing through scenes until it was a month ago. Irene was arriving at his house. Caleb followed the thread to Irene getting her luggage at the Las Cruces Airport. Then further back to her leaving school. Scenes came faster. Patterns of activity. Driving. Class. Friends. Work. Sleep. Class. Friends. Work. Sleep. On and on. Then the beach. A boardwalk.

The flow calmed. Caleb found himself in a tattoo parlor. Somewhere near Boston. He'd never seen the place, yet knew the name of it was Stinky's Ink. Irene lay facedown on a padded table. A woolly man—Stinky himself—held her exposed buttock in one hand. The other worked a motionless tattoo gun against her skin. Irene's face turned away from him, soured in mild discomfort. A fist on her forehead, her lips parting as if speaking to the woman standing in the corner. Her friend, stuck in the middle of a laugh, face round, wrinkles of joy carved into the alabaster of her face. Caleb could see the details of the lipstick image imbued on his daughter's ass by the needle. He felt the lecherous smile beneath the artist's burly face hair. Caleb absorbed the regret carried in Irene's fixed shoulders, her clenched hands, the bead of sweat on her forehead.

Whoops. Um ... maybe this wasn't such a good idea.

Caleb snapped back to the hospital room. There was color again. He could breathe. The remote clattered against the bed as Irene pulled at its cable. Wes slammed the cabinet door with a thud.

"Stop!" Caleb said. Irene paused, remote in hand, thumb over the nurse call button, and locked eyes with him.

"Dad," she said, her eyes still wide with panic, "are you okay?"

"Just hold on a second." Caleb stopped to take a breath. The scene still vivid in his mind, feelings of shame bloomed in him at his intrusion into her privacy. Still, he couldn't reconcile what he saw with the Irene he knew. "You got a tattoo?"

Irene dropped the remote, her eyes widening. They collapsed to a squint as she asked, "How do you know about that?"

Wes stopped scouring the other cabinet. His face turned toward them, eyebrows raised with interest. "Irene got a tattoo?" he parroted.

Irene waved her hands, silencing her brother. "How the hell do you know about that? It was months ago."

Caleb shook his head. "Just ... seriously? Irene!"

"Wow, what did you get?" Wes cajoled. "A tramp stamp of a spreadsheet or something?"

Irene put a hand on the railing of the bed, squeezing. "What the hell! How ... Did I tell you about it?"

"I saw it. I saw you getting it," Caleb replied.

Wes rushed over to the bed. "Oh shit! The voice! It showed you, didn't it?"

Caleb nodded, appalled at his daughter's choices. "It's ... it's a tattoo of a lipstick kiss."

"Aww, that's sweet," Wes said. "Where'd she get it?"

Irene's hand shot from the bed to her left buttock. As if covering it would prevent further discussion. Wes drew the implication and cackled.

Irene blanched, covering her gaping mouth with her other hand and turning away from the bed.

"This is amazing," Wes sputtered. "This is just all-around perfect." He looked up to the ceiling, his hands splayed in offering. "Thank you, Lord, for these gifts we are receiving!" he clucked in a dramatic Southern accent.

"Stuff it!" Irene spit, as she turned back to Caleb. "I told you about it, I must have. I just don't remember." Her voice was tentative, lacking her natural confidence.

Wes chuckled, shoving his hands into the front pockets of his jeans. "Pretty sure one of you would have remembered that conversation, Sis. This has to be something else."

Caleb shook his head. He was fading. This ... whatever it was ... it drained him. Between that and the growing pain in his gut, Caleb wanted his meds and then he wanted to sleep.

His pain management. Anxiety lapped across his broken body as he looked around the room. What happened to his ATC prescription? Christ, if he lost it ...

I can help with that, hang on a sec.

He was outside himself again. Color dissolved as he followed the thread back to the accident outside the diner. The street and the cars were a sickening taupe color, a muted canvas stretched over a frame. Caleb saw the statue form of himself in the street. His left arm cradled on his chest, his right hand pulled on his ear, his body captured mid-writhe. His face was chiseled in a mask of terror—eyes bulging, mouth stretched wide. Irene stood over him, hands quiet in the air as she either approached him or moved away, Caleb couldn't tell. He followed the invisible thread into the diner. It spiraled through the tables and frozen patrons, most of whom were standing to look at the scene in the street. The thread led to the back table of the diner where Caleb had first heard the voice.

There was Wes. His lumpy plaster form knelt by the table, his head cocked toward the diner entrance. His fingers delicately lifted Caleb's bottle of ATC medication off the diner floor.

Chapter 13

WES

"Pretty sure one of you would have remembered that conversation, Sis. This has to be something else," he chuckled.

"Oh, fuck off," she retorted. "It's the only logical explanation."

Wes lapped up her discomfort. He eased into her personal space. "What the hell about any of this seems logical to you, Irene?"

She kept her face turned to Pop. Her brow tightened. "Dad?" She touched his arm.

Wes looked at Pop. "He's passed out again. It must take a lot out of him."

"What?" she asked, her tone shitty. "The cancer? Or being hit by a car?"

Wes huffed. "This—" He waved his hand toward their father. "Whatever is happening to him. You can't shrug it off or explain it away."

Irene turned to face him. She crossed her arms, waited a moment to respond. "There's nothing extraordinary here, Wes. This is just his illness. Or his meds. Or both."

"Or something else," Wes interrupted. "Something we can't understand."

Irene sighed, "I prefer not to make up stories where a sensible set of facts will suffice. Occam's razor, you know?"

Wes didn't know. Irene knew he didn't. She was baiting him. Trying to get him to say something stupid so she could jump on it. "Is there any room in your head for things like hope?" he redirected. "Or wonder? Don't you ever just ditch the facts and imagine how things could be?"

"You keep your hope. I'll stick with probability theory. We'll see who lands on their feet," she sniped.

"What the fuck does that mean?"

Irene smirked, and her eyes fell. A look of pity.

"What?" he demanded. "If you don't have hope, what's the point of doing anything?"

"Like rehab?" she chided. "What did you say earlier? Something like, 'There is no false hope'?"

Wes rolled his shoulder into a shrug. It was still sore from Irene's death-hold ninja grip.

She licked her lips and continued, "Because statistically, you will relapse. You know that, right?"

He tried to swallow his unease.

"I mean, in all probability, you will end up killing yourself. Maybe directly, via an overdose. Or indirectly, given the company you keep. Can you name a single person in your life who would stick around if you cleaned the fuck up?"

Wes tightened his lips to cover their tremble. Irene cut deeper into him. "So, hope all you want, little brother. Because the numbers don't lie. I'll bet hard money against you. Every damned time."

Silence wedged between them. Wes wanted to speak. To tell Irene to piss off. To get bent. That all he could do was prove it. To himself. To Pop. To her. Every day from this point on. He knew if he said any of it, tears would come. And Irene would lash out harder. A cycle, highlighted by his therapist, which ended with Wes self-destructing. They'd put a plan together for this. Ways to disengage with her. Irene didn't owe him the benefit of a doubt, and Wes owed her zero promises. He gulped down the lump in his throat and broke eye contact. "Well, Sis," he said, "you're a numbers person and all. I guess it must be a solid bet."

Her eyes crawled on him. Judging. Her mind working out ways to make him feel dumb. He ignored her. He could not control her words or actions. Only his own. Wes focused on the bed. On Pop's relaxed form lumped up under the blanket. His face wore a dour expression of slumber. After a few moments of uneasy silence, Pop's eyes blinked. Wes realized he wasn't sleeping at all.

"Pop?" Wes cracked an uncomfortable smile. "Sorry you had to hear that. We thought you were asleep."

His father glared at him, his frown deepening. "Where is it, son?" he croaked.

"Where's what?" Wes asked.

"Don't," he scolded. "Don't do that. Give it back to me, please."

Wes knotted his brow, confused. "Pop, I'm not sure ..." Wes turned to Irene, who offered a shrug of her shoulder.

"Stop it!" Pop spit. Wes jumped at the anger in his voice. Where was this coming from? "I'm giving you a chance here! A chance to come clean and explain yourself!"

The tingle of anxiety rose in Wes's gut. "What the hell are you on about? I haven't done anything."

"Stop lying!" Pop yelled, rattling the arm cuff on the bed rail. "I saw you! I saw you back at the restaurant. While I was lying in the street!"

Oh shit. Wes knew exactly what this was about.

"Look, it isn't what—" he started.

His father snapped over him, "No! Just stop! I don't want to hear it! What did you do with my medication, Wes? Where is it?"

Wes bit his lip. Irene unfolded her arms, her face turning rotten. She balled up her fists, and he raised his hands in surrender. "Okay, look, it's right here, okay?" He stepped over to the armchair where his denim jacket lay. He unzipped the pocket in the lining. His hand wrapped around the thick prescription bottle, and Wes pulled it out, rattling it in front of his dad and sister. "See? It's safe! I picked it up after your accident. I just forgot about it, is all."

"You piece of absolute shit," Irene hissed. "Two hours out of rehab, and you're seeking? From your dying father's pain management?"

"No!" Wes flushed. "Really," he pleaded, "I went back to check, saw them on the floor, and grabbed them." He placed the medication on the bed tray. "I just ... I didn't want some kid to find them and ... you know." Christ, even he didn't believe what he was saying.

"Get out," Irene huffed. "Just fucking leave."

"Wait, what?" Wes stuttered. "No, I wouldn't keep them!" He turned to his father. "Pop, look, you know how hard I've been working at this. You've seen the progress, right?"

His dad looked into the wall, his eyes glinting. Wes turned to his sister. "Irene, no. Don't throw me out. I swear to fucking God or whoever. I took the meds to keep them safe. There just hasn't been a chance to bring it up with you guys, okay?"

Something clicked in Wes's mind. He was right. They hadn't discussed the meds yet. So how did Pop know? His stomach flipped. His brow unfurled. "Holy shit, Pop! Did it show you? Did the voice show me taking it? Like Irene's ass tat?"

Pop remained silent and still.

"No, no, come on! This is huge!" Wes bellowed. He turned to Irene. "Even you see that—"

Season of Waiting

Irene interrupted him with a fist to his mouth.

Chapter 14

Irene

Her ears closed. Wes's mouth moved. She couldn't hear what he said. Wes's fat face turned to her, eyes begging. Her fists balled. His gums flapped, excuses dripping from his tongue. She couldn't do this. Have Wes go off the rails while she needed to focus on her father. Her knuckles landed square on his mouth. His head snapped back, and his body followed it to the floor.

"Get the hell out of here!" Irene screamed. Wes scrambled backward until he reached the armchair. "Get out!"

He raised a defensive palm. "Goddammit, Irene, stop! Let me explain!"

"Oh, fuck no!" she spit. She stepped toward him, and he cowered toward the floor.

"I know how this looks, but—" he started.

"But nothing!" she hollered. "It is always exactly how it looks with you!"

Wes backpedaled up the armchair, finding his jacket. Irene sidestepped him, grabbing handfuls of his collar and waist. She heaved his bulk forward, moving his fat ass toward the door.

Wes didn't resist, but pleaded, "Irene, I swear, I was just trying to help!"

She shoved him into the closed door. The smack of his face against the heavy metal frame indulged something ugly inside of her. She did it again, harder. Her rage tempered with a sickening pleasure.

"All right!" Wes cried. His hand flapped against the door's handle, pulling it open as Irene yanked him back. She shoved him through the threshold, releasing her grip to let him tumble to the hallway floor. He turned over and gaped at her.

"Go!" Irene roared. She stomped toward him, raising a hand. His awkward feet found the floor, and Wes stood. His face was wide, his eyes wet. He stumbled a few steps, avoiding staff and equipment in the hallway. Irene felt a wave of righteousness radiate from her belly. It exploded out of her mouth. "Get the hell out of here!"

Wes ran down the hall. His sneakers squealed as they bounced off the tile floor. He wiped a hand across his eyes as he disappeared around the corner. "And don't come back!" Irene bellowed after him.

Every eye in the hallway bored into her. Doctors, nurses, staff, and patients took her in with confused faces. Irene felt a flush of shame at the shitty dynamics of her family bleeding into a public space. She shook it off as fast as it came. As long as Wes stayed away from Dad, the embarrassment was worth it.

She turned back to Dad's room. In her periphery, she could see someone approaching her at a wobbling jog. She stopped in the doorway as the round form of Dr. Cass closed in.

"I'm sorry," the doctor began in a clipped tone, "but, Ms. Allard, this is unacceptable. This is a hospital, not a wrestling ring."

Irene gathered her calm before responding. "I'm sorry, Doctor. That was my brother I chased out of here. He's a train wreck."

"Regardless, I'm going to have to call somebody."

Irene smiled. "Please do. Let's get security down here. They can make sure that asshole doesn't come back—"

"No," Dr. Cass insisted, "that's not what I mean. Ms. Allard, what I've seen over the last twenty-four hours has me very concerned."

Irene's dander went up. "How so?"

The doctor cleared her throat. "Your father. He is showing signs of psychological distress."

"Sure," Irene laughed. "A fucking car ran into him, and he's already dying."

Cass shook her head. "He hasn't been able to explain how he ended up in the street. His explanation was 'I fell down,' which I find suspect."

Irene's brow curled. "What are you saying, exactly?"

"You and your brother obviously have different opinions," the doctor continued, speaking over her. "He doesn't think the Final Release is right for your father, does he?"

A hole opened in Irene's chest. "No, now you wait—"

"I'm not convinced your father isn't trying to isolate himself from you. To protect himself. I have to ask if that's why he walked into traffic, yet sustained such trivial injuries. And then why he hurt himself, requiring sedation. I have to consider the possibility that he doesn't want to go home with you. So I've called social services, Ms. Allard." Cass's face hardened, her lips a tight line as she raised her chin to Irene in defiance. "I feel that there is a genuine risk that your father is being pushed into a medically enabled suicide. And I cannot, in any good conscience, allow that to happen."

"Oh, fuck." Irene had intended to keep the thought to herself.

Dr. Cass raised an eyebrow at the colorful language. "Indeed," the doctor sneered. Her round face expanded in a chilly smile as she turned back toward the nurses' station. Irene's gaze stuck on her squat form as her mind raced through this fresh problem.

Her research into the Final Release had been extensive. There were three requirements to avoid criminal prosecution. First, Dad had to have a terminal diagnosis from a qualified medical professional. That was covered; no one could make an argument that Dad wasn't dying.

The second requirement—he had to activate the Final Release by his own volition. No one could do it for him. It had to result from his own will, rather than stemming from a seizure or other involuntary movement. Physically, Dad's right hand could push the button. After the seizures she saw today, could Dr. Cass build a case that he might not have the capacity to execute voluntary activation of the device?

Irene knew why this part of the law existed. There was a heavy backlash around the first iteration of the Final Release program. Stories of people murdering invalid parents for inheritance. Spouses looking to ditch their sick partners. Most of the stories proved unfounded. Enough of them made headlines for the public to push policy in a more conservative direction. The state mandated a witness—someone outside the family who could monitor the event and ensure the patient acted on his or her own behalf. Their hospice nurse would sign as that witness. Since Dad wasn't wealthy or famous, nobody should have given a shit.

But Dr. Cass had inserted herself, changing the dynamics. What should be a quiet moment of sorrow and relief for her and her father had become everyone's fucking business. Irene backed through the threshold into Dad's room, turning around as the door closed behind her. Dad slept, no doubt drained by the emotional ordeals of the day.

She remembered more stories as she watched him sleep. The comatose or elderly wasting away in front of their families for years. One device rested in their still hands, waiting to end their suffering. Another pumped nutrients into their body to keep them alive. Righteous volunteers from local churches rotated in and out of the room around the clock. They wanted to ensure that the family didn't perform one last act of mercy for someone they loved.

Government policy and social acceptance orbited each other for years. They collided in a place that was not perfect, easy, or caring. Hell, it was barely workable. At least now there was a safe, if obtuse, path through the program.

Irene wanted none of these troubles for her father. Getting through this was hard enough without these new indignities. She watched him, and her breathing synchronized with the tide of Dad's rhythmic rattle and sigh. The shackle fixed Dad's arm to the bed. She imagined the Final Release device just out of his reach—him unable to use it, her having to let him suffer or go to prison herself. If Dad's disease had to run its course, how long would that take? How many mile markers of the living would Dad pass rotting in bed before he could rest? Would Irene remember the better things when it was over? Or would the scars left by the sharp teeth of these awful moments be the thing she carried away?

None of it mattered, because of the third legal mandate— mental fitness. Dad must be capable of describing the results of his choices and actions. Dr. Cass could cause trouble, depending on what she had seen today. Irene's eyes traced Dad's arm to his bruised ear and the barbed stitches there. The bleeding was dry and brown now, flaking off in plates onto his pillow as he snored.

For a moment, she considered suffocating Dad with the pillow. Give him that mercy, to hell with the consequences for her. The pillow was there, next to Dad's head. Just pick it up. Lean over him. Let him sleep until he's gone. Irene had no idea how long it would take. She would need to research it first. She didn't know how awful the experience would be for him. What if he woke up? How much physical strength would she need? The idea dissolved into unknowns.

Irene needed help. She unpeeled her feet from the floor, eased open the door, and padded into the hallway. Time of day meant little in the walls of a hospital, but even after the fight with Wes, there was a calm indicative of night. Irene passed the nurses' station, ignoring the side glance from the night nurse at the desk. She found a quiet corner away from the patient rooms and scrolled through her contacts until she found the one she needed.

"*Molim* ... um, hello?" Dr. Pav's voice was groggy as he answered his phone. It was later than Irene had thought.

"Dr. Pav, this is Irene Allard. I'm sorry to call you so late. I don't even know what time it is."

He cleared his throat. "Do not worry about the time. I'm happy to hear from you, Irene. Is everything all right?"

She sighed, "Can you come to the hospital tomorrow?"

Chapter 15

CALEB

C aleb stirred at the sound of the door clicking into its latch. His hands clenched around the blanket in his lap. He worked his body to a seated position. A stab ripped from his gut as he felt his tumor grind against one of his ribs. He adjusted the pillows to allow his body to lean to the side, relieving the pressure.

The constant hum of silence pressed on him, broken by the beep of a monitor. It reminded Caleb to breathe.

He swallowed, the wet clicking sound filling his head. "Why is this happening to me?"

Caleb's face contorted as the voice arrived.

Because I need your help.

It didn't hurt like before. Instead of a pressure, Caleb felt a mild vibration in his skull. The effect didn't spread to his other senses. He could breathe through it without issue.

"That was a rhetorical question," Caleb murmured. He shifted his weight off his side. "Who ... what even are you?" he asked.

I've been trying to reach you for a while now. We haven't really had a chance to talk. Like I said, I need your help, Caleb.

"What could I possibly do to help you? What would you need from a terminally ill accountant?"

It will take some explaining, but I promise that you have a rather grand purpose, Caleb. Our time is running out, for obvious reasons.

Caleb snorted. "What does that even mean?"

It means that despite spending your life counting beans and cross validating columns, you can still have a significant impact. Even this close to your death, you can still affect the fate of everything and everyone.

Caleb stared into the wall. The lack of another face in this conversation was uncomfortable. "How?"

Are you willing to help me?

He sighed at the coy responses and demands. "I don't know. What the hell do you need me to do?"

That's fair. I'll show you the problem. Then you can decide.

The sensation was familiar. The pop in his head. The unfolding of the room. Caleb filling in the space. The growing awareness of every nuance in the moment as he left his body in the bed. Threads wove through him, passing into the walls and floor. They joined with others, lines connecting everything by choice. Even his daughter, down the corridor from his room and on the phone with ... Caleb followed the thread ... with Dr. Pav.

What was he doing back in this strange space?

This is the only way I can show you. This moment you're in, this is now.

He understood. He didn't see any problem, though.

We'll get to the problem soon. You've already figured out how to follow choices into new moments. You did it before, with the television remote, remember?

Caleb remembered.

Good. I need you to do it again. Forward from here. See the possibilities.

The space was a tapestry, fibers leading off in directions without names. Which one should he follow?

It doesn't matter. Just pick one.

Caleb latched on to a thread weaving from the plump doctor in the hallway. It was the woman who'd worked on him when he first came to the emergency room. He didn't remember her name, but in this space he knew it was Marybeth. Dr. Marybeth Cass. He traced the fiber out, feeling it branch and split into thousands of directions. Which one was he supposed to trace?

Can you do all of them?

He couldn't.

I can help you. You okay with that?

He was. He wanted to understand. A shimmer formed at the edge of this moment. More dimensions folded into it, and Caleb's perception changed to make sense of it. The room, the hospital, earth, and everything beyond it collapsed into a point of light. Countless other brilliant sparks appeared with it. An infinite field of stars bathing itself in a bottomless glow.

This is ... well, I guess this is also "now." Each light is a "now" that could have happened. Can you still see the threads? Leading away to the next moments?

No, all the light made it difficult to see anything. Caleb felt he was looking into the night sky with no dark. No air. No ground. Only stars.

Focus a bit. Like the numbers on the television.

Caleb's mind centered on one glowing spot. He tightened his attention around it. The ambient light of the surrounding field tapered away. With some struggle, Caleb found it, buried deep in the fluorescence. A single translucent cable.

There, yes! Follow it. Follow it forward to one of the next possible moments.

Caleb had no trouble moving along the cable. Threads split away and branched off into the light around him, weaving into another point of light. Another moment, a universe of detail condensed into a gleaming barb.

Don't stop. Carry forward.

For how long? Caleb wondered.

You'll know it when you see it.

Caleb traced the thread ahead, through a moment, another star of light. And then another. They came faster, Caleb skipping from one point to the next without thinking now. It was easy. The field of stars smeared together, a burning mosaic as his mind flew through this alien space. He passed seconds, minutes, days. Then years scrolled by, and he reached forward with greater ease, through greater distance. Decades past him. Centuries. Epochs.

And then Caleb stopped. Not because he wanted to. The thread spiraled into nothing. Where there was light before, Caleb floated in boundless space. His mind scoured the black for something on which to focus. Anything. He found no gradations, no edges, no detail at all.

This is why I need your help.

Caleb realized the thread was missing too. He flailed in the void. The lack of depth and difference left him adrift. Falling. What happened to the stars?

They're gone. There are no possibilities here, Caleb. No choices. No more moments to come.

How could that be? What could extinguish so much light?

This rift in the cosmic tapestry? This nothingness? This is where all threads are heading.

But, why? Why would this happen?

Will you help me?

The voice pressed, the endlessness around him stifling. Caleb couldn't understand. What did this emptiness mean? What was the voice asking him to do?

Caleb, this is the end. This is the end of everyone and everything. I'm begging you to stop it from happening.

Caleb felt the darkness fold around him. A flash, and he was back in his body. Warmth. He was in the hospital bed, clutching the blanket in his lap. He took a moment as his vertigo waned. He tried to hold on to the experience, but something about being in that strange space was impossible to process. And yet, it was real. It left Caleb with authentic emotions. Exhilaration. Liberation. And abject terror.

So? What do you say? Will you help me?

Caleb's hands relaxed their grip on the blanket. The familiar pain of his illness returned. His breath was steady, marked with a phlegmy rasp. "What do I need to do?" he asked.

Well, first, tell me what time it is.

Caleb shrugged and pointed at the clock on the wall. Incredulous, he said, "It's six thirty-eight?" As he sat up straighter, Caleb's brow tightened at the discomfort in his gut. "How can you not ..."

Okay, that's good. Any chance you get the History Channel in here?

Caleb's hands went up in irritation. "I ... I don't know. I feel like these are things you should know already!"

Sometimes a list of channels is taped to the remote. Or the bed tray.

Caleb pulled the tray closer, finding a list taped neatly on its surface. "Okay, yeah, it's channel fifty-four."

Okay, turn it on. Hopefully, we haven't missed it.

Caleb's secured hand reached the remote's cable tied to the bed rail, and pulled it until he could reach. He thumbed the power button.

Yeah, fifty-four, if you please.

Caleb sighed, his frustration coming out as he jabbed his sore fingers against the remote. The television changed to a show he recognized. One of Wes's favorites. A host offered colorful commentary on videos from the Internet. At the moment, the overgroomed twenty-something was interviewing a disheveled loon, spouting some nonsense about the Mayans and alien visitors.

No, ignore this guy, sorry. Just hang tight a minute.

As the interview wrapped up, the host returned to the green-screen studio. His voice was emotive but vapid, as if he didn't believe his own words. "Next, the miracle from Texas. If you haven't seen this one yet, I need to warn you—this video is graphic. If you are squeamish, I urge you ... look away ... now!"

Yep, this is it. But don't worry, it's not that bad. And you need to see this.

The television showed a fawn and its mother walking along a road. The doe stopped, staring back to the camera. It flicked its tail in a white warning, stamping a front leg onto the road. As the fawn stumbled forward in the frame toward its mother, a warbling sound filled the scene. Unable to discern what it was, Caleb increased the volume.

Murmurs and coos filled the hospital room. Children off-camera, excited to see something from the wild misplaced in the middle of their sleepy town. Behind the deer, new stores occupied former workshops and warehouses. The shoulder of the road was asphalt crumbling back into nature. This was a place a lot like Truth or Consequences, New Mexico. The ground was dust, but the sun landed less harsh on everything. The sky was deeper, more blue. The foliage was softer, more abundant, and more green.

The fawn nuzzled its mother, evoking more sounds of wonder and pleasure from the children. It was a lovely scene, and Caleb smiled. His smile faded as the video halted, and the grinning head of the host appeared in the screen's corner. Around bleached teeth, he explained, "A group of kids are walking to school, and they find this mama deer and her baby wandering through the quaint streets of Utopia, about ninety miles west of San Antonio in the Texas Hill Country."

The talking head's expression darkened, his voice tainted with suspense and hesitation. "But all that ... is about to change."

Caleb jumped at an indecipherable shout of warning, the volume of the television too loud. A sudden jolt of the camera. The screeching of tires. The blur of children shoved into and out of frame. The tail end of a car swerved across the screen. The camera followed as it broadsided the fawn. The young deer's hindquarters twisted against the rear of the car as the animal flopped in an uncontrolled tumble. The car heaved over the fawn with a dull whomp and the tiny animal disappeared.

The fawn rolled out. Its momentum carried it across the road for several turns. Waves of pavement flowed as the person holding the camera broke into a run. The video stabilized on the broken animal. Its hind legs and hips bent at the wrong angles. Blood gushed from wounds across the animal's hindquarters. A sound rose above the squealing children. A frantic bleat, staccato pain and panic. The camera panned up the road, catching the mother doe as she disappeared around a stone building. The sounds of children crying brought the camera back to the fawn. It lay prone in the dirt, panting as it bled.

The video paused, the talking head reappearing in a corner of the picture. His face full of concern that didn't carry to his voice, the host said, "... but this tragedy is only the beginning." His eyes widened with incredulity. "You won't believe what happens next!"

The program resumed, and the sound of the children's cries faded. The view tightened on the mauled animal as it hollered in pain. Clambering at the ground with its front legs, the baby deer tried to convince its broken rear half to move. To get away from the throes of a painful death. Above the sobs and whines of the children, a woman off-camera hissed in a scolding tone, "What are you doing!"

The camera zoomed out, revealing a dark-haired boy approaching the dying fawn. His pixelated face turned to look out of frame, his hands held in ambivalent fists at his side, shoulders pulled close to his neck. He turned back toward the deer on the ground, which had stopped moving save for its rapid breathing. Other voices floated in from off-camera. Grown men chattering in confusion. Someone asking if everyone was okay.

"Bleep!" the woman yelled. The boy's name. They censored it. The video centered on the boy as he stood over the fawn. The voice of the woman offscreen became insistent. "Get back here right now or sure as sin, I'll break out the hickory!"

He stooped over the deer with his hands open, placating the wounded animal. The fawn's breath became frantic at his approach, its eyes wide with fear. Children hushed as the boy bent over the fawn. His body blocked everything from the camera except the animal's head, which eased to the pavement in resignation. Another kid's voice arrived from off-camera, his voice derisive, "What's the weirdo doing?" A man's voice, disgusted, screeched, "Naw, kid, don't touch that!" The animal's head heaved once, releasing its last breath in a sputtering cough.

The video stopped again as the host's voice interrupted. "What on earth is this kid thinking, approaching a wounded animal like that?" The talking head appeared, full of attractive concern. "Doesn't he know how dangerous this is? That might be a baby deer, but it could kill him with one kick to the head! But hang on a second, because you'll never expect what the boy does next!"

Caleb sighed in frustration, "For fuck's sake, get on with it."

I know, I know, just hang in there, here it comes.

The voices in the video muted in disgust at the sight of the boy lying over the deer. The woman's voice broke the silence with a stern warning, "Bleep! Stop!" Hands appeared in frame, grabbing at the boy like a bird of prey. As she snagged his T-shirt, a murmur rose from the children. The fawn moved on the ground as hands pulled the boy out of the camera's view.

The broken animal raised its head. It stretched its legs—all its legs—and heaved itself into a seated position. Its back legs folded beneath it. It panted, regarding the moment.

Then the fawn stood, to a chorus of adult gasps. People clapped and cheered. Censor tones covered expletives. The bloodied animal stumbled a few tentative steps up the road. With each step, the fawn moved with more confidence. As it approached the stone building, its mother poked around the corner, stamping the ground with her front leg. The fawn quickened into a wobbly gallop, and the video blurred as the operator zoomed in on the reunion. Above the excited and dismayed murmurs of the children, a man's voice said, "Praise Jesus!" Another asked, "Holy bleep, do you smell that?"

So? What do you think?

Caleb muted the television as the host's perfect jawline began flapping again. He shrugged, unimpressed. "A fake video?"

I get why you would say that. But what if it's real? What would you do if I told you it was real?

Caleb scoffed, grunting as he turned off the television.

I'm serious, Caleb. That kid is the real deal. What do you think that means for everyone?

"I don't see how that could be," he replied. "People fake this stuff all the time. I could find a dozen of these on the web right now."

You saw the deer, right? Did it look fake?

Caleb swallowed. That was the thing—the video didn't strike him as contrived. Watching it felt like observing something natural. Something he shouldn't be witnessing. The pain was visceral, the details too mundane. The deer's mottled blood was rusty, not thick and red like it was in the movies.

This couldn't be happening. "Are you ... are you serious?"

Yes.

Caleb flushed, his breathing quickening. "There's no way."

What if there is?

Caleb stiffened, fending off the flirtations of hope. "No. I mean ... Could he ..."

You asked me what I want from you. You asked me what you need to do. It's simple. Get to that boy, Caleb.

He blinked away tears. How could this be happening? Where the hell was this coming from?

Live long enough to get to that boy. Find him. Then your life can have the purpose you want it to have.

Incredulous. There was no way this could be real. Why Caleb? Why now?

You, because there is no one else. Now, because you have no time.

Caleb's hand covered his mouth. This feeling—this seed of hope germinating. It shocked him. That it would find purchase in him after everything he'd been through. Ivy's epic death, his own pain, the indignities of treatment and hospice, and arranging his own end. "I can ... I can survive this?"

Get to the boy. That's the tricky part. You're sick, and you can't do it by yourself. You need help. And, Caleb ...

The click of the door grabbed Caleb's attention. Irene skulked into the room, her expression tired and broken.

Move on this as soon as you can. You've got maybe four days left in you.

Chapter 16

IRENE

Irene was eager to get back to the hospital.

She'd stayed with Dad overnight. Between her brother's bullshit and the anxiety of Dr. Cass's attention on her father, Irene was physically and emotionally wrung out. Despite that, the hospital rabble wouldn't let her sleep. In the morning, Dr. Pav arrived to pull together Dad's discharge. Irene used that time to run back to Dad's house and take delivery of the Final Release equipment. The hospice nurse ran through setups and protocols, which took a few hours. After that, Irene ate some leftover posole and passed the hell out on the couch. She needed the food and sleep, but napped longer than she wanted. When she woke, several texts from Dr. Pav waited for her. Dad was ready to come home.

She negotiated Dad's BMW into a parking space. The sun was approaching the horizon, and she wanted to get him home before they gave up the day. Those feelings intensified as she walked toward the hospital entrance. The important building was diminutive. Shanty. Sun-worn, ramshackle, clinging to the edge of town. Scrub and desert threatened to swallow it up, reclaim the lot. Hell, the parking lot contained fifty spaces. Grocery stores back in the suburbs of Boston were bigger than this.

Walking through the automatic doors, Irene heaved her backpack onto her shoulders. This would be the last time she would need to come here. Dad would come home, and they would settle in for his Final Release. She wasn't sure if that made her happy or sad. Without giving it more consideration, Irene was grateful. She appreciated the help from Dr. Pav, his willingness to placate Dr. Cass and social services. As she passed through the entrance, Irene smiled. He might still be with Dad right now.

The smile waned at the prickling stimuli of the hospital. The revolting chemical cleanliness. The squeaks of her shoes against the floor tiles grated her ears. She hated this place. She always had. Irene had good health, but she'd been here enough times to develop an aversion. Once was her fault, a severe bout of food poisoning after ordering seafood at a restaurant in the desert. Every other time was because of Wes. Either he needed medical treatment or someone else did because of him. The last time she was here, he'd fractured her jaw during an intervention. Irene opened her mouth, feeling the joint pop.

Her feet carried her around the turn to the wing that housed Dad's room. In the last twenty-four hours, this walk had become another mind-numbing pattern to her. She queued up the sequence in her mind, a hypothesis to test against her memory. First would come the elderly woman. Once she caught sight of Irene, the woman would call out to her. Irene passed the door, and screams rattled from the room, "Help me! Please help me! They're gonna kill me!" Hypothesis confirmed.

Four more steps to the happy giggly couple. Irene listened as she passed the doorway. He was reading to her, from a magazine.

Six more steps to the silence of the stoic room. One or two corn-fed boys. Bowl-cut hair. Eyes locked on the bed as they tried to figure out how to fix their problem with their muscles.

And then, the last four steps to Dad's room. The door was halfway open, and Irene stopped at the threshold. A voice was coming from the room. Not her father's. Someone whose lips sputtered from uncontained emotions. "I'm so sorry, I didn't mean for this to happen. ..."

Wes. What gumption. How dare he come back after the shit he tried to pull! She had warned him: *Stay away. Do not impede Dad's plans.* He couldn't help but put his own wants first. A fire lit in Irene's gut, and she pounded the door open with the side of her fist. Teeth bared, she entered the room tensed to fight. She hissed, "I fucking told you ..."

A stranger, about her age. Brunette instead of Wes's dirty blond. His face shot up to her, his eyes round and wet with grief. Who the hell was this?

Irene looked to the bed. A child prone on the sheets. Bandages swallowed most of the tiny body and head.

"Ma'am?" The baritone voice boomed from the hall, and Irene turned. A police officer gestured her out of the room. "You can't be in here."

"Sorry, wrong room, I guess." Her pattern-seeking brain was still recovering from the trauma of the last few days. Not surprising, considering she'd had one actual meal and three hours of sleep.

Skirting past the officer, Irene checked the room number. A quick stab of panic and doubt hit her. Her father should be here, in this room. "I'm sorry, sir?" Irene captured the officer's attention as he placed himself in the doorframe. "Can you tell me where they moved the previous patient?"

He shook his jowled face, frowning. "Check with the nurses' station," he said, pointing down the hall with his chin.

Irene moved that direction, peeking into the rooms she passed. Her father wasn't in any of them. At the counter, a woman was hanging up the phone. Her pale eyes met Irene's and widened. She rose from her chair and leaned toward the counter. With a thin smile, she asked, "How can I help, dear?"

"My dad's been moved to another room. I need you to tell me where he is."

The nurse nodded. "Sure, honey, what's the name?"

"Caleb Allard."

She sat back down, typing on her computer. The woman's eyes probed the screen as her fingers poked at the keyboard like it might bite them off. Irene considered rounding the counter and running the search herself.

"And you are?" the nurse asked, her eyebrows accenting the question.

"Irene Allard. His daughter." After a moment of silence from the nurse, Irene added, "And his medical power of attorney."

The nurse nodded, raising her face to Irene. Her smile was warm and calm as she said, "Sweetie, this says we discharged him. About ninety minutes ago."

"Discharged?" Irene couldn't hide her confusion. "On his own?" She shook her head, scanning the hallway for her father. "What the hell is wrong with this place?"

The nurse's lips tightened as she looked back at her computer. "No, of course not," she said. Her warmth had dissipated. "According to Dr. Cass's notes"—she tapped the screen with a finger—"she released Caleb Allard into the care of his son. Wes Allard."

HIGHWAY

Chapter 17

WES

The El Camino topped out at sixty-five miles per hour. Any faster and the vehicle shuddered and threatened to come apart under them. Wes took that into account when he penciled out the trip from Truth or Consequences to Utopia. South on I-25 to I-10, then east into Texas for a wide stretch. A few country roads later and they'd be there. The numbers comforted Wes. About 650 miles from here to there, and they were looking at ten hours in the car. Easy math. A nice round, clean number. It was a sign that this was the right thing to do.

The call from Pop had surprised Wes. He answered the phone blubbering and apologizing. Then he pulled out the letter he'd written in rehab, in which he took responsibility for his choices. His behavior. Where he'd written his promise to never drag his family into his personal struggles again. Before he could read it, his father had interrupted him with those three magic words.

"I need help."

And Pop hadn't asked Irene. He came to Wes.

Once Pop explained what was happening—the voice, the video, this miracle healer boy—Wes realized why he hadn't called his sister. Irene would have scrutinized everything. Analyzed every detail. "How could the video be real? How do you know it wasn't staged? What evidence suggests they shot it in Utopia?" Once she had worn those paths to dirt, she would attack Pop's intellect. Belittle him until he was too tired to argue anymore. "How could you believe this tripe? Why would you be so special? How can you think this is a solid plan? What do you do when you get there and there is no boy? You're just sick, let's go home and die—that would be easier on me." Irene's head had no room for wonder. She thought about things too much. Dad was out of time, and thinking about things wasn't doing the things. Wes would do the things. Wes would make this happen for Pop.

As they pulled away from the hospital, Pop insisted they call Irene and let her know where they were going. Wes disagreed. She would freak the hell out over this, demand they come home. Hell, he'd already turned off their phones because she was lighting them up with calls and texts. As a compromise, Wes agreed they would call her after they were on the freeway for an hour or two. Dad didn't want Irene to worry, and Wes didn't want that either. A nervous Irene was a mean Irene. Although, if he was honest, the thought of his sister freaking out for a little while gave him some wicked pleasure. Besides, he wanted to get some miles in. Some distance from her. As soon as the car hit the freeway, Pop passed out. That had been an hour ago.

Wes sighed. Las Cruces was approaching. He might as well eat this shit sandwich while it was still fresh. He rummaged through the small plastic basket zip-tied under the dashboard. He found his flip phone by feel, flicked it open with his thumb, powered it on, and ran down his contacts to find Irene's number. Wes took a deep breath and made the call.

He looked over at his father in the passenger seat. Dad remained asleep. The click and thump of Wes's tires vibrated the thin bags hanging from his father's cheekbones. The call connected after one ring.

"Where the fuck are you? Where is Dad!" she yelled. Wes yanked his head away from the phone, from her yells. He should have expected this.

"We're okay, Sis." Wes spoke with a calm voice, returning his ear to the phone. He didn't want to wake his dad. "Pop's fine, okay? He's asked me to take him somewhere."

"Bullshit!" she screamed. The speaker in Wes's phone rasped, unable to re-create his sister's loudness.

"No. He called me from the hospital," Wes explained. He focused on keeping his tone cool. "He needs to get ..." How much should he say? Irene was smart—she could fuck this up for them. "He needs to get someplace, to see someone. So we're taking a quick trip."

Irene hissed a sigh. "Let me talk to him."

"He's asleep."

"Well, wake his ass up, dipshit! I need to hear this from him!" she spit.

"No, he's exhausted, and he needs to rest. Maybe he'll call you later, okay?"

"Fuck no, this isn't okay!" Irene returned to screaming. "Wes, I swear to Christ, I will call the fucking cops!"

Wes chuckled. "Go ahead, Sis. We've done nothing wrong."

Irene was silent for a long moment, the sound of the road filling the space. "Just tell me where you're going." She had regained some composure.

Wes knew he wouldn't do that. "I don't think that'll help, Sis. We'll only be a day or two, okay? Trust me."

On the other end of the line, Irene exploded in a profanity-laden wall of noise. Wes pushed away the guilt. He couldn't control his sister's feelings. He could control only himself. His own choices. His own obligations. He'd promised Pop he would let Irene know they were okay. He'd done that, and Wes didn't want to put up with this shit. Enunciating into the phone, not so loud that it would wake Dad, Wes said, "Hey, Irene, can you tell me something?" The line went silent. He hoped Irene was listening. "Does this sound like a phone hanging up on you?" Wes disconnected the call. He turned off his phone and tossed it back into the plastic tray with a thin clatter.

That had gone as expected. Irene's head was hard. Her ego refused to bend. There was no way Dad could have gone to her with his current problem. If he was being honest, Wes didn't think that the video was legitimate at first. He never would have, except Pop insisted that it was real, that the voice told him so. After Wes found the Utopia video online, his dad explained the voice's instructions—get to this healer kid, find your purpose. Wes couldn't even pretend to understand. But that didn't matter. Pop needed this, and he needed his son to make it happen. So Wes didn't think about it; he gathered what he had and stepped up to help. Ten hours away—that's how close they were to ending his suffering and saving his life. The approaching sign for Las Cruces reminded him to adjust his math. Wes smiled. Make that nine hours.

Beyond his father, the sun blazed below the horizon. It hit a sky iced with clouds that turned the threat of rain into glowing purples and reds. Color rose tall into the sky and carried away to the north. It would be the first monsoon of the season, a promise of much-needed rain back home.

Pop stirred a bit, coughing. His clothes swallowed him, like he was three pounds of dirt in a ten-pound sack. The fanny pack secured tight around his waist cinched his oxford shirt into messy folds. He could tell the zipper lay open without looking down. The cap of the script bottle peeked out from behind the smirking metal mouth of the pack. Wes acknowledged the itch, the toothache all over his body. He wanted to push on it. To create some pain only for the pleasure of releasing it. He ignored the thought, turning his head back to the road.

A random thought made Wes chuckle. How much product was his dad holding? This might be the largest haul Wes had made south on I-25. Usually he was heading the other direction, hauling loads of "Mexication" up from the border to Albuquerque. Most of his customers turned out to be around Pop's age. They needed anything from Oxy to antibiotics to boner pills. They could convince a doctor to fill a bogus script, but most couldn't afford the price of the legal drugs. It was low risk for decent money, and Wes enjoyed helping people. And now he was helping Pop, by hauling his ass and his drugs in the opposite direction. The experience was familiar, and Wes couldn't help but feel he had been preparing for this trip for a long time.

Wes jumped as a splotch of rain smacked the windshield. Then he smiled. It was another sign of impending relief, telling him they were on the correct path. It would rain. The ground would swallow it down. The stubble that grew here needed the water, just like the world needed his father. Like Wes needed his father.

He flipped on the wipers, which puttered across the windshield with a squeal. The windshield was too dry. Wes realized his mistake, turning them off before they woke up his dad.

But it was too late. From the passenger seat, Wes heard a painful groan pierce his father's sleep.

Chapter 18

CALEB

Caleb was moving. No, he was being moved. Forward. The sigh of road noise replaced the shudder that had stirred him awake. He was in a car. Driving his BMW. He could see the road ahead of him. The lines were in the wrong place. And the steering wheel was missing. Why did it smell like a wet ashtray?

Caleb wasn't driving. He was being driven. His mind cleared, and he could see the cracked vinyl of the dashboard. His son's El Camino. They were on a trip. Were they leaving? Or coming back?

A flicker of lightning pulled his attention out the passenger window. The sun was setting. Or was it rising into the storm? He massaged his eyelids, trying to force the fever dreams out of the way so he could remember.

His body ached all over. A crankiness that came from inactivity. On top of it, a sharp pain punctured his stomach. A brace wrapped his wrist. He had been in a hospital, but now he was in a car. Traveling to the boy.

Or had that happened already? He might not remember. The doctors said that would happen sometimes. "You might feel better some days, but the sickness is in your brain, and it changes how you see things." His hand went to his stomach. The hard knot was still there. Cancer still riddled his body, squeezed his liver like a vise. He remembered the deer, broken, then whole. Would there be holes where the cancer was, after he was healed? A hole in his liver, his pancreas, his brain? Or would Caleb be whole again?

The pain crested. He groaned. The noise displaced his fugue. He lifted his head from the window, stretching his cramped neck and shoulder. He turned to find Wes driving.

"I need food. To take my medication."

His son's mouth moved. Caleb concentrated, focusing hard on the thin lips as they ebbed and flowed into shapes. Restaurant. They have food. Caleb nodded and closed his eyes.

He smelled toast. Wasn't that a sign of a stroke? He opened his eyes. He could see toast too. He must be okay. He had wanted toast, but he didn't remember ordering it. There were other people here. He didn't know them. He could see his hand, holding a glass of water. The glass moved close to his mouth, and the straw found his lips. He pulled in the water and swallowed.

The cold worked its way down his throat. It hit his stomach and anchored him. He was in a restaurant. Wes was holding the glass, asking him a question. Caleb pulled another gulp from the straw and nodded. He was unsure if the response was appropriate as the water washed away the last of his haze.

Wes sat across from him, ignoring an omelet and hash browns as he fiddled with Caleb's glass. Wes's hands moved to the condiment tray on the table, pulling out the single-serving jellies into a pile. His son was looking for a grape packet, unaware that since chemotherapy, Caleb could no longer tolerate the cloying sweetness. He chewed a bite from the corner of the dry toast.

Seeing his father didn't need the jelly, Wes grabbed the ketchup and sprayed it over everything on the plate. As he put the bottle back into its cubby, he asked, "So, what's it sound like?" His voice was discernible over the room noise.

Caleb paused his chewing. "What?"

"The voice! What else would I be asking about?" he chuckled as he forked a wad of egg into his mouth. "What's it sound like?"

Caleb considered the question as he resumed chewing and swallowed. "I'm ... I'm not sure."

Wes raised a brow. "How can you not be sure when you're the only one who can hear it?"

Caleb put down his food. He shook his head, considering how to convey the experience. "I don't know how to describe it to you."

"Well," Wes said between lip smacks, "is it a guy's voice? Or is God a woman?"

The question furrowed Caleb's brow. He hadn't noticed or considered it before his son had asked. "You know what? I can't tell. The voice ... it doesn't speak as much as ..." He puffed a sigh, trying to find the right word. "The words just sort of arrive."

Wes stopped chewing, motioning for his dad to elaborate. Caleb shrugged, unsure of what else to offer. "It's kind of like understanding something. Like recognizing someone's face. Or identifying an odor. It just ... happens."

"Okay," Wes said, "so you and I, we're chatting here. You're listening to me, and I'm speaking. Then you speak and I listen to you."

Caleb nodded.

Wes stabbed some potatoes as he asked, "So is it like that? A conversation?"

Caleb's nod became more animated. "Oh, yes, it's absolutely a conversation."

Wes filled his mouth before continuing, "But you don't listen to the voice. You ... what?"

Caleb leaned against the back of the chair to relieve some pressure growing in his abdomen. "I hadn't thought about it, but now that you ask, it feels strange. I definitely hear words, like I hear yours. But I can tell that you said your words. I can tell it's coming from you. But this voice ... I hear it only in my right ear. I can't tell you where it comes from. It comes from everywhere. I can't describe what the words sound like, but ..." He thought some more, his son's eager face encouraging him.

"There is inflection around the words. Like they're coming from someone with ... I don't know, feelings? Sometimes I sense anger behind the words, sometimes they're playful. But I can only describe the voice they travel on as ..." Caleb swallowed, remembering the emotions. The compulsion to move, the undeniable urge to appease. Almost like dealing with a bully. "It's crippling. Overwhelming."

Wes had stopped chewing, hostage to his father's story. He finally swallowed and asked, "Like, loud, you mean?"

Caleb shook his head, "Naw, not loud. Not really. More like, authoritative. Impossible to ignore."

Wes nodded, staring down at his food. Caleb hadn't captured the experience, but he wasn't sure it was possible. They ate a few minutes, the sounds of his own soft chewing unable to compete against Wes's lip-smacking fervor.

Taking a breath between shovels, Wes waved his fork in a probing circle. He said, "So this kid in Texas, if he is the real deal, like the voice says"—he swallowed some coffee—"I wonder why we haven't heard about him before." Wes gazed up and to his right. A sign that his son wasn't speaking to him, but was thinking out loud. "I mean, maybe he developed the ability just recently, you know?" He piled more egg into his mouth, adding, "Sort of how you started hearing that voice, or those words. Or however you put it."

Caleb shrugged, unsure what to contribute to his son's meandering thoughts. Wes wanted something from him. Validation? A flush of foolishness grabbed him by the chest.

Their logic was thinner than the paper napkin in his lap. His son continued to eat as Caleb asked, "How are we going to find him? The boy? I mean, how do we know he lives where the video was taken?"

The clatter of Wes's utensils on the plate snapped Caleb's attention up. His son beamed, his face relaxed with satiation. Wes's eyes widened, sharp with confidence. "Oh, he lives there," he said. "Remember the video?"

Caleb nodded, hopeful.

"It was morning. Kids heading to school. The adult knew the boy's name. Could be his mom. Or a teacher."

The clues fit. Caleb smiled, surprised at the details Wes had pulled out of only two viewings.

Wes reached across the table, yanking his dad's smartphone from his shirt pocket. He continued, "And I don't think finding him will be difficult either. I checked out the town online—it's built around a single street." He powered on the phone, poked and swiped for a few moments, then turned it so Caleb could see the screen.

Wes had the video open, stopped on an image somewhere near the end of the clip. He pointed with his stubby finger at the cream building in the background. Brick-red trim and roofing were just visible at the corner of the frame. Next to it, highlighted against a pale sky, was a rusted-out sign that read: SILVERLEAF.

"This place," Wes said, "is the only restaurant in town. The town's school is just up the road." He powered off the phone, handing it back. "He'll pass it every morning and afternoon on the way to school and back. If that fails, we can scope the school and try not to look like two pedos."

His son was proving to be quite the sleuth. Caleb smiled, feeling more confident in their journey and purpose. Then, a wave of pain crashed against his gut. His reminder to take his ATC medication. He reached down, unzipped the fanny pack at his waist. The massive bottle took up most of the pack. He unscrewed the cap as Wes excused himself to go smoke.

Caleb fished out a pill before packing the bottle back into its pouch. He swallowed the medication, then picked the check off the table and waded through his discomfort to the cashier station near the door.

The teen woman operating the register asked if everything was good, and Caleb said that it was fine, thank you. He handed her his credit card and turned to look for Wes out the restaurant windows. And things were fine. Caleb felt confident. He'd eaten a little food. The meds would kick in soon. And his son was solving problems instead of creating them. Trepidations and doubts lifted, and it wasn't until then that Caleb realized he had been carrying them. As odd as this all was, it felt right.

"Sir." The woman tapped Caleb on the shoulder. He turned back to the cashier. Her face had lost its cordiality. "They declined your card," she explained.

Caleb's positive feelings poured into a rift of confusion. "What?" he asked. There was no way he was over his credit limit. "Can you try it again, please?"

"I've tried it three times, sir. Do you have another form of payment?"

Chapter 19

IRENE

Irene passed the door from the kitchen to the dining room of her father's house. She stepped around the bench of the heavy oak dining table and into the living room. Massaging her temples, she skirted the perimeter of the room. At the edge of the crisp ivory sofa, she turned again, moving into the home's foyer. From there, she headed back into the kitchen.

The house was still unfamiliar. Dad moved into it after she had left for school. She'd been here a few times, for holidays. She expected the house from her childhood, but this wasn't that place. This bungalow was small, but Dad described it as "just enough for me." Irene imagined that many of the rooms went unused, especially in these last few weeks as Dad moved from his bed to the sofa and back again. He would occasionally disappear into his office for a bit. Irene assumed to organize things for after his Final Release.

While the topology of Dad's home was novel, the odors were not. Irene could have walked into the place blindfolded and known this was his house by the mix of his musky deodorant and the wood cleaner he used on his office desk. And tonight, the air carried the smell of petrichor through the open windows. An earthy anticipation of relief, the desert's sigh before a rain. She stopped to enjoy the vivid memories of that smell luring children outside. Teasing them to play in the cooling air. She opened her eyes, and the loamy vapor again compelled her to leave, to act, to do something. But what was there to do? Where would she go? So she resumed walking, chewing on the skin around her thumbnail. Back in the kitchen, she repeated the loop one more time.

Right after Wes had hung up on her, she called the police. The authorities were helpful, taking the details from her: Dad's name, address, cell phone, description. They immediately issued a Silver Alert for Caleb Allard, age fifty-nine, height five feet ten inches, weight somewhere way under his precancer 180 pounds, mixed gray and blond hair, brown eyes. Wearing khakis, a button-down oxford, sneakers, a wrist brace on his left arm, a small bandage over his right ear, and a goddamned fanny pack cinched at his waist, filled with opiates. Traveling with Wes Allard, an intellectually stunted overweight man-child with dirty blond hair and pale blue eyes with a history of addiction and thinking of no one but himself. At least authorities would look for them. When they found Dad, they would take him into protective custody until she could get him home. Safe from Wes.

Irene pressed the authorities to cut access to Dad's bank and credit accounts. This would flag the authorities if anyone attempted to use his credit or debit cards. Dad had made it easy. He'd collected his account numbers as part of his end-of-life packet. Irene had expected some pushback from the cops. She was ready to get a lawyer involved, but the police were more than happy to oblige. Evidence to her that this situation was more common than she'd thought.

As she passed through the kitchen, Irene wished she had information about Wes's accounts. Wes's pockets were nowhere near as deep as their father's. He wouldn't get far on his own. At some point Wes would fuck up and need to rely on Dad. On Dad's money.

She slogged through another circle of the house. Reaching the kitchen, she stopped to check her phone. Still nothing. An hour since Wes hung up on her, and since then, her calls to him went unanswered. Thirty minutes since she wrapped up the Silver Alert with the authorities. But it had felt like hours. Irene was in a spiral, in her head and through this house. She broke her path, walked to the cabinets on the other side of the kitchen. Fetching a tall glass, she filled it with water from the tap and downed it all, ignoring the sulfurous tang of the aquifer water. She refilled the glass, turning away from the dining room and heading down the hallway that led to Dad's bedroom and his office.

She stopped at the open office door. The room was immaculate and still. Heavy built-in shelving and file drawers consumed one wall. Dad's oak desk anchored the room, facing the one window. Beyond, the sky was dreary, the ink of night in the desert hiding the storm she could smell.

She moved farther down the hall to her father's bedroom. Since she'd shifted furniture to make room for the hospice equipment, the room was in a chaotic state. Thick drops of rain thumped against the windows on either side of Dad's bed. Irene rounded to the side not crowded by medical equipment. The unsteady staccato of the rain grew into a consistent static as the storm arrived.

She sat on the edge of Dad's bed, watching the rain pelt the other side of the window. The water ran down the pane in thick streams, pooling at the rail before falling out of view. On the nightstand under the window sat a framed photo of the three of them—herself, her dad, and her brother. The boys were in front, Irene behind them with her arms around their shoulders. She couldn't remember who'd taken the photo, or when. They were outdoors somewhere, the sky behind them. Maybe on the pontoon boat.

The hiss of rain crescendoed into a low roar. The kids would run inside now. The rain wasn't fun when it didn't feel safe.

The jangle of her ringing phone surprised her, and water spilled from her glass onto her jeans. She set her water on the nightstand, checking the caller ID on the phone's display. Her heart quickened. It was her father.

"Dad! Are you all right?" she asked.

"Yes, honey, I'm fine." Dad cleared his throat into the phone. "I'm with Wes. We're taking a small road trip."

Irene stood and walked across the bedroom. "What the hell? Dad, why wouldn't you tell me about this?"

"It's okay, Starlight. It's only a day or two. Which"—he chuckled—"I guess 'only' is a relative term now, isn't it?"

Irene massaged her temples. "Dad, are you okay? Is Wes forcing you to do something?"

"What? Naw, not at all. I asked him to take me." Dad sounded tired, but not distressed. Still, Wes was manipulative. Dad might not realize Wes was grooming him, preparing to take advantage of him.

"You asked him? To take you where? Where are you going?" The questions came too fast to wait for answers. "Has he taken any of your meds? Have you counted them?"

Dad was silent. Irene could feel him running the numbers on the other end of the line. Whatever they were up to, Dad knew she wouldn't go along with it. She interrupted his thoughts, "Never mind, just tell Wes to bring you home. You're sick, and I don't think you're thinking right."

The line was quiet. "Dad, are you there?" Irene's hand fell to her hip, her eyes welling with tears as she paced back toward the window. "Please, Dad, just come back. We can talk through it."

The sound of Dad swallowing was thick and sharp over the phone. "It's gonna be all right, Starlight. I will be okay. I promise." He sounded convinced, sure of himself. "I just need your trust for a few days. We'll come back and I'll explain everything then."

Irene felt a flush of heat through her face, her tongue loosening in her mouth. "Dad, I can't trust you. Not after the last few days. And I won't trust Wes. I think that together you two are dangerous to one another." She sat on the bed, staring at the photo of her family for a breath.

"Honey," Dad started, but Irene interrupted.

"Why don't I come with you? Wherever you're going, I want to go with you," she offered. The idea came out pleading and desperate. She tried to recover, making her tone light, "We could make it a family trip."

She concentrated to hear the muffled conversation on the other end of the phone. Irene recognized the sound of her brother's murmurs.

Dad came back to the phone, asking, "Listen, honey, my credit card was just declined. Do you know anything about that?"

Irene sighed, "Yeah, Dad. I didn't know what happened to you. I assumed Wes was ..." Irene wanted to say that Wes was kidnapping her father, but she knew Dad didn't see it that way. Not yet, anyway. She took a breath, choosing her words. "I didn't know if you two were okay. So I called the police. They asked for your card numbers as part of the Silver Alert."

Dad stuttered for a moment before saying, "Wait, a Silver Alert? That's like, one of those old farts who wanders out of the nursing homes?"

There was agitated conversation away from the phone. Irene heard her brother's muted voice exclaim, "Fuck!"

"Yes," Irene replied, loud enough to capture her father's attention from her brother. "I asked them to issue a Silver Alert. The police are looking for you both."

"Why would you do that, Irene?" He sounded the way he did when Wes fucked up. She closed her eyes, the afterimage of the family photo fading into purples and greens behind her eyelids.

"After the last couple of days, I don't think you're in a place to take on choices like this. And I know Wes isn't either. To be blunt, I think he's taking advantage of you. For your medication."

The sizzle of rain filled the silence. "Dad?" Irene prodded.

She heard him sigh with resignation. This was it—he had decided. He was coming home, or going with Wes. Dad's voice was calm as he said, "We love you, Starlight, and we'll see you in a few days."

The call disconnected. Tears ran down her cheeks as Irene lowered the phone to the bed. Bleary-eyed, she reached for the box of tissues on the nightstand. As she pulled one, she knocked the photo off the edge and onto the floor with a tink of cracking glass.

She wiped her eyes and lowered a hand to the floor to collect the photo. The glass had split diagonally from one corner to the other, creating a chasm separating Dad from Irene and her brother.

She dropped the photo again when her phone rang. She pounced, lifting it to her ear.

"Dad, I'm sorry," she sobbed.

A low, gravelly voice interrupted her, "Miss Allard? This is Officer Blakely from the Las Cruces Sheriff's Office."

Irene took a moment to swallow her embarrassment, pinching the bridge of her nose to stop the tears as she spoke. "Yes, sorry, that's me. What do you need?"

"There's a Silver Alert out for your father, Caleb Allard?" the officer asked. Without waiting for her to confirm, he continued. "He used his credit card at a diner outside of Las Cruces a few minutes ago. We have officers on the way."

Chapter 20

WES

"Pop, just pay with cash!" Wes prodded, his hand on his dad's back. They were burning precious seconds. "Quick, we need to go!"

Dad opened his wallet, thumbing through the few bills it contained. Wes reached in and threw thirty dollars at the cashier, muttering, "Keep it, okay? Keep it."

Pop resisted. "Hey!"

Wes moved him to the door. "Keep moving, Pop!"

His dad let out a grunt of protest, but Wes pressed toward the car. He scanned the parking lot. No cops yet. The frontage road carried no telltale red and blue lights.

"Just wait a damned minute, son!" Dad moved Wes's arm away from his back.

They were feet from the El Camino. Wes had his keys out and continued toward the car, unlocking the passenger door. "We don't have a minute! Let's talk in the car, okay?" He waved his father over.

Dad eyeballed him, but didn't move. "Did you do something?"

Wes shook his head, but kept waving his hand, as if it would reel in his father and put him in the El Camino. "No, but Irene thinks I did." The wail of a siren rose above the traffic noise.

Pop took a step toward the car, asking, "What do you mean?"

Wes's heart raced. "In the car, okay? Then I'll explain."

Pop shrugged with his hands and moved between Wes and the car. Wes eased his father's diminutive frame into the passenger seat and helped him with the seat belt. As he rounded the driver's side, he glanced back at the highway. Strobes of blue pierced through the white globes of headlights.

He cursed Irene under his breath. This simple overnighter was a goddamned race now. He opened his door and fell into the seat. He rammed home the key and turned. The car started with a throaty whomp that lowered into the whirl of the idling engine.

As they approached the road, the blue lights entered the off-ramp on the other side of the highway, heading to the overpass. Wes breathed slow, moving onto the access road. His eyes shot between the road and his rearview mirror. Another set of blue strobes appeared behind them. Wes resisted the urge to floor the gas pedal.

"What the hell did you mean back there?" Pop asked. "Why would Irene think you've done something wrong?"

Highway patrol was approaching fast, emergency lights bouncing off Wes's grimy windshield. He tightened his grip on the steering wheel, tensed the muscles in his calf. "One second, Pop," he mumbled. Wes felt his foot press against the gas, his car speeding up the on-ramp to I-25 South. The blue light around them disappeared, the cruisers turning into the restaurant parking lot. He blinked at the spots left in his eyes.

"Son?" his dad prodded, sounding frustrated.

Wes took a breath as he merged onto the highway before responding. "Irene's issued a Silver Alert," he explained.

"Yeah? But it's a mistake." Pop's tone was dismissive, like this was a misunderstanding. "She doesn't know what we were doing. We can explain—"

"No, that's not gonna work," Wes interrupted, rubbing the remaining spots from his eyes. "Irene knows I'm with you."

His father said nothing. How the fuck could he not understand?

"Dad, you know a Silver Alert is like an Amber Alert, right? But for ... old people?"

"Sure. There are several a year around here. Lots of old folks who—"

Wes snapped, his patience stretched. "Irene knows you're with me, I talked to her earlier. She issued the Silver Alert after that." He turned to his father.

Pop shook his head again. "Right, so, let's fix the mistake—"

"No, that's just it, it's not a mistake," Wes sighed, emphasizing his words by hammering the steering wheel with his palm. "She's issued the alert ... *because* you're with me."

Pop's face relaxed into a dour frown. Finally, he got it. His eyes wandered to the windshield. "She said something about you taking advantage of me."

Wes nodded. "According to her, I'm doing this to you. Not with you."

"To steal my pills." Dad sounded tentative.

The relish of his father's understanding was at odds with the embarrassment it provoked. "Yes, that. And she assumes I'm trying to prevent you from ... you know, from ending it all."

At that, Pop snorted and broke into laughter. The reaction brought Wes close to swerving off the road. "Why in hell are you laughing?" He didn't mean to sound so angry. He looked over at his father, who covered his smile with a delicate hand.

Dad wiped his hand down his mouth. "What can she be thinking? That you want to steal me away? From death? That your plan is to outrun the Grim Reaper? In an El Camino?"

The humor brought a smile to Wes's face. Dad was right, this was all absurd. The miraculous situation, this road trip, Irene's logic. "That'll be tough," Wes added in a teasing tone, "unless death moves slower than sixty-five miles per hour. Any faster and this car might shatter, and death won't have to catch us at all."

"At least we'd die in style," Pop replied, patting the dashboard.

They drove in the light silence, carried by the rhythm of the tires on the road. Scrub passed at the outer edge of their headlights. After a time, Wes asked, "How the hell are we going to explain any of this to her?"

Pop grunted. "No idea. I won't know until I see her again."

Wes didn't know either. Hell, he would never see Irene again after all of this. She wasn't one to forgive. And Wes, well, he couldn't adult his way out of a bag according to his sister, and she never let him forget it. It was a cycle of distrust and hate between them. Wes would make an honest mistake. Irene would pounce on him and make him feel like shit. His self-esteem nose-dived, and he'd fuck up again. Lather, rinse, repeat, until Wes didn't even want to try anymore. And here, Wes stepped up where she wouldn't. Wes was saving Pop, not Irene. Regardless of the outcome, she would never forgive or forget this trespass. It would kill her to admit that Wes had done something right. Something good.

The stakes were higher than Irene knew, but Wes understood. It was a battle now, between his will and his sister's brains. The road ahead rolled toward them. Wes tightened his grip on the wheel. Nine hours. They could do this.

"I promise I'll get you there," Wes said. "Whatever it takes. I won't let Irene stop us from reaching Utopia."

"I don't think it'll come to that," Pop replied. "I hope not, anyway."

Wes shrugged. "I don't know. I wasn't expecting the Silver Alert. Or losing access to your cards. Irene's made this road trip into something a lot more complicated. I don't have a lot in my checking account. I sort of thought you would pay for gas and food."

"I still have my ATM card," he offered. "Cash still works, doesn't it?"

Wes chuckled at Pop's lack of common sense. "If she stopped your credit cards, your ATM cards are no good either."

Wes wouldn't outbrain his sister. His street smarts didn't compare well with his sister's book smarts on paper. Irene could plan. Expect their moves. But Wes could act and react way better than his sister. The trick with Irene was to play the right game. She wanted to win, and she would if he played her game. But Wes didn't need to beat Irene; he needed time. He had to give her something else to think about. Occupy her long enough for them to reach Utopia. An idea formed. A simple one, but it might buy them the few hours they needed.

The turn signal clacked as Wes moved the El Camino into the exit lane. Dad stirred in his seat and asked, "What's up? We need gas already?"

Wes shook his head. "Not yet." He crossed the overpass and drove into the busy truck stop on the other side of the highway. He parked the car and scanned the parking lot.

He locked on to his father's curious eyes. "Pop, do you trust me?"

His father curled up his brow, nodding. "Why?"

Wes sighed. "I need to know how much cash you have on you."

Dad scooted down in the seat, twisting his torso to fish his wallet from the pocket of his khakis. "Sure, one second."

"And I need your credit and ATM cards," Wes added. "All of them."

Chapter 21

IRENE

"This doesn't make any damned sense!" Irene cursed to no one. She stood at her father's desk, in the middle of scouring the once pristine office. Piles of papers covered the floor. Dad's shelves were empty now, Irene having scavenged them for a clue to her father's behavior. "Dad won't take a shit without a plan."

Irene pulled open the wide center drawer of the desk. She dumped the contents onto the desktop, shoving the pens and office supplies onto the floor. She wanted a note, a receipt, anything. She found nothing helpful.

She turned her attention to the three drawers on the right side of the desk. The bottom drawer was business files. It contained no surprises. Dad had walked her through its contents after giving her power of attorney. Each thick file contained smaller manila folders. Dad had labeled each folder: "Accounts," "Fixed Assets," "Current Year Taxes." Boring, necessary stuff. He'd even gone as far as creating a vertical file named "Final Release." It contained various legal and medical forms, and the do-not-resuscitate orders needed for the procedure. The thickest vertical file carried the label "Wes Rehab Expenses." It held three other folders, each named by the month and year. One for every time her brother had gone into treatment.

"So where's your file on this shit show, Dad?" Irene slammed the drawer with a loud clap. She jerked open the middle drawer, rummaged through the pile of legal pads there. Finding them blank, she tossed them to the floor, revealing a single black writer's notebook. The kind jobless hipster writers scribbled in at coffee shops back in Boston.

Irene had found several of these scattered through the house. Each had a specific purpose noted on the flyleaf. One notebook from the office shelves contained something like an engineering day log, but for an accountant. It listed daily activities, notes on his work throughout the day. He kept impeccable records.

Another she had found in the kitchen, buried among the cooking magazines in the small rack on the floor. Dad had used it as a food diary, tracking his reactions to different foods after he started chemo. Irene had thumbed through it. Tidy columns showed meals, times, food eaten, and quantities. Dad's accounting was pristine. He would have made an excellent data wrangler. After a few months, the entries in the log became sporadic, skipping meals, then days, then weeks at a time. The last entry was a note that said, "I'm dying of cancer. I'll eat what I want."

Irene sat in Dad's chair. She slapped the notebook open to the middle. This one appeared to be a diary. She flipped back to the blank flyleaf, finding Dad's chunky letters on the page. Irene's heart broke. This was a cancer journal. He documented his illness.

She noted the date of the first entry and blanched. Almost a year before he told her about the diagnosis. Why would he wait so long to talk to her? The simplest answer was that he hadn't wanted to put her through it again. She shook her head at his selfishness.

Irene shucked forward a few pages, skimming. Words stood out to her: "positive," "enthusiastic," "assured." These were hope-laden chronicles of trips to the doctors. They discussed options available to Dad at the beginning. The pages that followed turned more methodical, Dad falling back to his habits. Lists of where the cancer appeared. Tables of body parts shifting columns from healthy to sick, asset to liability, black to red. Why the hell would he go through this alone, without telling her?

Irene snapped out of her self-pity. If Dad had kept up with this journal, maybe the more recent entries would offer a clue to his current thinking. She thumbed through the book, looking for empty pages. A sudden visual break caused her to stop.

The page started with an entry. A terse note about how Dad was increasing his use of ATC. "The more of these damned pills I take, the less pain I have, but it comes at the cost of time. I sleep so much more now, and I can't imagine it—"

The sentence stopped in the middle of the phrase. A thick, dark line jutted from the last letter. It sliced straight across both pages of the fold, breaking Dad's consistent crisp margins.

Irene swallowed her shock. "God, he must have been in so much pain here," she whispered. She ran a finger over it, the chasm in the paper evidence of the force he had applied. Irene bounced her eyes to the top of the page. Three months ago.

The next spread returned to Dad's standard clean and squat letters. She flipped forward a few more pages, finding more journal entries. Dad had been consistent, at least. Irene turned the page, and she gasped.

The date on the page was six weeks ago, right before she arrived here to help. The date was the only readable thing on the spread. Messy lines and swirls covered the paper. Sloppy shapes, drawn with purpose. She realized Dad may have been trying to write, may have even thought he was writing. Jesus Christ. Irene felt a sharp pang of guilt at having this intimate view into her father's failing mind. This journal was personal. Under other circumstances Irene could never bring herself to read it. But these weren't other circumstances. She needed data to develop insight into what her father was thinking. She turned the page.

The top of the entry contained the date, written in her father's compact block letters. Three weeks ago. The rest of the page looked as if someone else had written it. It was full of writing, but it looked nothing like her father's signature boxy print. Instead this writing was loopy, light. Elegant. Wide curves, elongated letters, the spacing consistent but not contained within the lines.

It was not her father's writing.

Each line started with a wide oval, giving the page a visual pattern Irene noticed right away. It took her a moment to realize that each line of script repeated the same words.

"Caleb, can you hear me?" Across the fold, another phrase repeated down the page. "I need to know if you can hear me."

What the hell was this? Irene turned the page, finding the same refined script, the same lines repeated over and over. "Caleb, can you hear me? I need to know if you can hear me." She checked the top of the page. The date jotted in Dad's normal hand.

She thumbed another page, finding the same script, the same words, another dated entry. Who the hell could have written this? Irene had been living here, in his house, when these entries were written. She had been with her father the whole time. No one else had been in Dad's office. She flipped the page, finding the same terrifying clean swirls scribed on the paper. Her heartbeat mirrored the rhythm of the pages as they snapped by. Her pattern brain noted the same words over and over, "Caleb can you hear me? I need to know if you can hear me." Elegant. Stately. Repeating. Page after page after page.

Irene froze. The pattern broke. She had reached a blank spread. No graceful writing. No stumpy date. Swallowing her dread, Irene slid back the left page of the fold. Three lines composed her father's last entry in the journal.

The first line contained the date. Two days ago.

The second line was in her father's stodgy hand, beginning the journal entry: "I am afraid. I am so afraid to die."

A line wormed away from the end of those words, the pen having been held steady on the paper. The writing transitioned into the lacy, graceful cursive of the third and final line:

Don't be afraid. You're mine now.

Chapter 22

WES

Wes glanced at the gas gauge. His chest tightened every time he noticed the needle dip lower. They had two-thirds of a tank, but it wasn't enough to get them all the way to Utopia. They would need to fill the car, but first they had to fix their cash situation. Their options weren't great. This stretch of I-10 was unfamiliar to him, but Wes knew an opportunity would present itself. They were on a mission, and the voice would help them.

The headlights pierced a few yards into the night. A large green sign crept into view. They were approaching Van Horn. Wes brought up the paper map in his mind. He tried to recall the markers he'd identified along their route. El Paso had been the first, marking their entry into Texas. They had passed through El Paso about ninety minutes ago. He recognized Van Horn as the next milestone. What was the one after that? Fort Something? He had made up a song with the names of the towns, but it hadn't stuck. Hell, it didn't matter. He needed to go east on I-10. The rest would work itself out. Besides, this wasn't some ordinary road trip. They had a mandate. Wes had faith.

A line of traffic cones forced him to merge into the right lane. Ahead, portable lights split the darkness with a haze of white. A construction site. Traffic slowed as everyone tried to get into the single lane. Wes applied the brake, and the car shuddered.

Fort Stockton! That was the next marker! Wes smiled at himself as the tune came back to him: El Paso we'll pass through, across the Van Horn; east to Fort Stockton, and east we go on; Ozona, we'll own ya, but Junction's the cap; that's where we stop to look at the map. The rhymes weren't great, which explained why it hadn't come to him right away.

Traffic crawled, and Wes sighed. This would waste their precious gas, force the money issue sooner. Why the hell were so many damned people on the road at this hour? The sodium lights were blinding, and Wes lowered his sun visor to block them. The eighteen-wheeler riding his ass wasn't helping either. Wes tapped the level on the rearview mirror to get the high beams out of his eyes. The dashboard and visor limited his view of the road to a few inches. It was enough to follow the bumper of the car ahead of him. The orange traffic cones appeared and disappeared as they inched down the freeway, never stopping but always slowing down.

The car rolled over a rumble strip, stirring Pop. He exhaled with a rattle, clearing his throat in phlegmy grunts. Wes looked over as his dad massaged his eyes and coughed out the sleep from his throat.

"Sorry, Pop, didn't mean to wake you," Wes murmured.

Dad sucked in a breath, shielding his eyes from the brilliant white light ahead. "Are we there already?"

"No, Pop, not even close. We're hitting some construction, I think."

Dad swallowed, the sound thick and crackling. "Is that why we're leaving the highway, then?"

Wes shook his head, replying, "No, we're just in traffic. It'll clear once we're past."

Dad turned his head away from the light, toward Wes. "We're on an exit ramp, aren't we?"

Wes shrugged as the car came to a stop. He lifted the visor enough to take in the scene ahead. Dad was right—the line of cars was off the highway. They were driving straight into the middle of the blinding light. That was weird. Why would they divert traffic into a construction site instead of around it?

The car ahead slugged forward half a length. Wes lifted his foot from the brake, letting the El Camino pour into the space. He winced as the high beams of the truck crawled up his side-view mirror and reached his eyes. Blinded with blue and red strobing afterimages, Wes hunched down in the driver's seat. Staring off into the scrub on the side of the road, he waited for the visual splotches to dissolve. His stomach dropped. The colors didn't fade. They were becoming sharper.

Dad cleared his throat again and said, "I don't see any construction. This looks like a DUI checkpoint, maybe."

Wes bolted upright. Police. He whipped his head around, taking in their situation. Pop flinched at the quick movement.

Wes looked for a way out. They were in the middle of a line of vehicles, in a single-lane exit ramp. There was no shoulder. With the truck behind them, there was no backing out onto the highway. How could he be so dumb? How could he not have seen this?

"Wes, what's wrong?" Pop gaped at him, eyes wide.

Wes looked in the mirrors again, gauging how close the truck was to their bumper. "We gotta get out of this line!"

Pop's voice was pleasant, almost teasing. "Why, son?" After a pregnant moment, his braced hand landed on Wes's shoulder. "Oh my God, Wes, do you have drugs in the car?" His tone had fallen, and it dripped with disappointment.

He turned to face his dad, scowling at him. "The only damned drugs in this car are yours!"

Pop let go of him, holding up his hands. "Okay, then what's the matter?"

How could somebody so smart have such little common sense? Wes pointed to the line of traffic ahead of them. Shadows moved in the blue and red strobes. "The checkpoint, Dad! Who do you think they're looking for?"

Wes watched realization and despair take turns on his father's face. Pop's head pivoted back to the windshield, the lights giving his skin a pallid and yellow hue. Wes explained,

"Irene has everyone searching for a sick old man being kidnapped by his son. That looks a lot like us right now."

Pop fidgeted in his seat. He turned to Wes and asked, "What can we do?"

Wes needed some way to hide his dad. The bed wasn't an option. Too exposed. The car had no backseat, but there was a small area behind the bench seat. If he could work his way under the soda cans and fast-food wrappers, it might hide him long enough to get waved through.

The slap of the semi's horn pulled Wes's head up. The line of traffic had moved forward again. Three cars separated them from the checkpoint. They were running out of time. Wes lifted a hand to shield his eyes from the sodium lights. One of the shadowy blobs ahead congealed as an officer approached the car ahead. Another officer appeared at the passenger side. The first stooped to the window and, after a moment, waved the car through.

"Oh shit, they're not searching cars. They're checking passengers. They're looking for us." Wes's heart sank.

"So what do we do?" Pop repeated in a strained voice. The next car filled the hole at the head of the line, leaving a space for Wes to move forward.

Two cars left. Wes shook his head. He was out of ideas. The next car moved through the checkpoint and headed back onto the highway. As the car in front of them approached the officers, Wes kept his foot on the brake. The officer leaned to the car ahead, shone a light through the interior of the car, and waved them on.

Wes's foot bounced off his brake when the semi behind him belched out a hydraulic squeal. He scanned left and right again, frantic. There was nowhere to go. "I've got nothing here, Pop." The El Camino rolled forward, carrying the two men into the checkpoint.

"If they are looking for us, I'll just explain, okay?" His dad's voice broke, betraying his lack of confidence. Wes's hope shattered. He would fail. And Pop knew it.

The blue and red strobes from the cruisers bounced around the inside of the car. Patterns of moving colors left Wes disoriented as the cops and cruisers appeared in two places at once.

He rolled to a stop next to the immense shadow of an officer. Wes scanned for a way to bolt through the checkpoint and make a run for Utopia. More officers stood ahead. More patrol cars. A half dozen or so. He saw the long shadows of shotguns. The shifting and impatient shapes of dogs.

They were absolutely fucked.

A light shone through the passenger window. Dad shielded his eyes with his unbraced hand. The black nose of a dog smeared across the bottom of the window as it sniffed the air coming from the car. The dog would smell their fear, Wes's terror. His failure.

Two heavy thunks pulled Wes's attention to his window. Outside the car, a wide and thick officer held a Maglite in his left hand, knocking it on the glass. The officer motioned with his other hand. A swirling motion, indicating he wanted the window rolled down.

Wes's hands trembled as he reached for the knob on the window handle. He whispered to his father, "It'll be okay." He lowered the window in starts and spurts. The officer raised his light into Wes's face. He flinched and squinted at the bright light. The officer leaned close, eyes on Wes. Cataloging. Measuring. Wes felt hunted, as if this shadow knew his weakness and would use it to consume him whole.

He could floor the gas. Run, hope for the best. It would take the cops a few moments to organize, get in their cars. They might evade the cops, take the back roads across Texas, find another way to Utopia.

The light moved from Wes's face, and on to Dad's. Wes worked to control his breathing and hide his panic as the officer took in Pop.

Wes swallowed his dread as he did the math. How far would they get, running from the cops in a shitmobile that wouldn't top seventy miles per hour? A tremble rattled through his dad's hand. Pop whimpered, and Wes realized he was clutching his wrist brace. He released it, trying to convey some sense of calm. To himself. To his father. To the officer leaning into his car.

The cop's face emerged from the shadow. His voice was rough, alert. "Well now, good evening, gentlemen."

Chapter 23

IRENE

Irene maneuvered her dad's BMW into the parking area outside Wes's apartment. The units were single story. Each shared walls with the apartments beside it. From the front, they were the same repeating pattern of cheap screen doors separated by windows.

Irene approached Wes's place—second from the end. She found the door locked, but her hard shoulder and desire to break things made quick work of the flimsy frame.

The acrid odor of fresh pot poked her nose. Her hand found the light switch. The place was a shithole. Irene imagined the entire row of apartments had the same simple layout. An open studio with a small kitchenette. There was an identifiable living space, but no separate bedroom.

She scanned the room. There was a futon sofa and a table for a television, but there was no television. On the couch was a stack of mail secured with a rubber band with an attached hold notice. Overflowing ashtrays were everywhere. Empty soda and beer cans. Fast-food containers, months old, judging from the crust on them. Dirty clothing. More mail. A glass bong sat on the floor by the sofa. The water was clean, a delicate ash in the bowl. Wes had used it today. He must have returned home to get high before kidnapping Dad.

Irene shuddered. Wes stoned with their mentally fragile father and a bottle of opiates wouldn't lead to a positive outcome. Whatever his intent, wherever they were going, things would get tough. Wes would fuck it all up to get those pills, and Dad would find himself on his own.

Wes was self-serving and lazy. Everything he did was to make things easy on himself. She rescanned the room in this mental context. A hypothesis formed in her mind—these piles were chronological. Older piles would be farther from the sofa, newer items higher in the stacks. If there was any clue about where Wes was taking Dad, it would be close to the futon, on the top of the piles.

Irene toed through a pile of clothes by the couch. There was at least a week's worth of shirts. On top was the shirt Wes had worn to the diner where Dad lost it and had his accident. Hypothesis confirmed: Wes had been here.

She moved on to a leaning stack of papers on the TV tray next to the futon. On the top of the pile was a crisp envelope with the name "Del Rio Rehabilitation and Assisted Living Center" printed in a soft, comforting font. Irene opened it, yanking out a typed letter. She skimmed its contents, scanning down to the last paragraph.

"We do not feel Wes Allard is ready to be released on his own recognizance and recommend he completes the program before leaving." Irene felt a rush of warm vindication in her chest, another hypothesis confirmed. But the rush evaporated to worry. The letter proved Wes was a liar, but that wasn't helpful now.

She dug through the rest of the stack, scouring for any hint of where Wes was heading. It was piece after piece of junk mail, credit card offers and power-washing coupons. She checked a postmark—the mail was eight months old. Useless. She let the pile spill onto the floor, along with her expectation of learning something from this disgusting place.

Her hands found her hair. They clenched into tight fists, pulling her scalp away from her skull. She looked around the apartment, taking in the context. There was no planning here. No strategy. Her brother lived from opportunity to opportunity. He let them pile up, one on top of the last, until his life exploded into the space and people around him.

A vibration in her pocket broke her thoughts. Her phone rang. She retreated out of the apartment, answering the call. "Yes?" she said, hoping the call was bringing some news.

"Irene Allard?" The male voice coming from the phone was slow, pedantic.

"Yes?" she repeated, her voice rising in pitch.

"Oh good, good. Ma'am, this is Sheriff Smelly, from the Las Cruces Sheriff's Office."

She waited for the voice to continue. After a few seconds of silence, she spit into the phone, "How can I help you, Sheriff?"

"Oh, well ... there's a Silver Alert on your father?"

"Yes, Caleb Allard." She held her breath. "Do you have any information?"

"Oh ... yes, ma'am," the man drawled. "See, they took him into custody. And I wanted to call you and let you know."

Irene's heart threatened to break from her chest. "He's safe?" She was yelling. She didn't mean to yell. She opened the car door and dropped into the driver's seat.

"Well ... yes. He's on his way here, Miss Allard, yes. Should be here in an hour. Um, so ... how soon would you be able to come down here? Because, see, he ain't talkin' to us, and we're hoping you can help figure all this out."

Chapter 24

WES

Wes's eyes ached as he squinted against the brilliance of the officer's LED flashlight. As the light moved off his face, the world swam in his vision. Panic welled up his throat. The scene was tense, but familiar. Wes had been here; he knew what to do. Play nice, smile, but not too much. He and Pop needed to get through this checkpoint. They had done nothing wrong. If the cops thought that too, they'd be back on the road. God willing.

Wes looked sideways at his dad, his face now the target of the cop's light. Dad lifted his braced arm to shield his eyes from the portable sun.

"Sir, can you please lower your arm?" the officer asked. His thick voice carried a level of kindness absent before. "Please look at me, sir."

The canine officer by Pop's window choked up the leash. The shepherd reared up on its hind legs, sniffing the air. As the dog glared at Wes, its gleaming nose twitched. Wes huffed a sigh of relief. This wasn't a people search, he realized. This was a drug search.

The dog's snout left a line of snot on the window, and his calm vanished. Wes had hit a bowl earlier. It was before Pop called—how long ago was that? Wes had changed his shirt, but the dog could still pick up the scent.

Dad lowered his arm, raising his face into the light like he was sunning himself. The dog disappeared beneath the window. They were fucked if the dog signaled. The cops would hold them and learn who they were, and that would be the end of Pop.

"You all right, sir?" the officer questioned.

Before he could stop himself, Wes replied, "He's fine, Officer, we're just ..."

A hard stare from the patrolman sucked the breath from Wes.

"Sure, I'm okay, Officer." Pop's thin voice carried the officer's attention off Wes.

The patrolman leaned forward, moving the light over Pop's fragile frame, pausing for a moment on his brace. "Are you sure about that?" he asked.

Pop nodded, swallowing.

The officer continued, "Because you look ill. Are you ill? Do you need a hospital?"

A smile broke across Pop's face. Wes worked to stuff his dread back into his belly. Please, Pop, just be cool.

The officer's voice chilled as he asked, "Did I say something funny?" Wes wiped his hands down his jeans.

Dad raised his face, meeting the officer's gaze, and shook his head around his wide smile. "No, it's just ... I mean yes, I'm fine. Except, you know, for the terminal cancer. But we're managing it, as best we can, Officer."

Wes heard the officer swallow. He turned to see the cop nodding as he pulled away from the window. The patrolman waved. Wes followed his gaze to the officer controlling the detection dog. He could see the dog's face again through the window, staring at him with accusation and purpose. The dog's controller nodded as another grim figure emerged from the light carrying a long stick.

Not a stick, a shotgun.

The dog had signaled.

Wes could throw the car into drive, stomp the gas, push the El Camino as hard as he could until it collapsed. What were their odds on getting to Utopia that way? He didn't know. He had to try. Get past this, to the next thing, and go from there.

"Y'all comin' from New Mexico?" The officer's voice broke Wes's frantic thoughts, his plan collapsing to dust in his mind. Did the officer know who they were?

Dad replied from across the car, "Yes, sir."

Christ, Pop had no idea what he was doing. Sweat beaded over Wes's lip.

The officer straightened, looking over the hood of the car. He addressed the others with two curt waves of his hand. "It's medical," Wes heard the man say to the other officers. "They're from New Mexico." Through the windshield, Wes watched the shadows step away from the car. What the hell was happening?

The officer leaned in, closer this time. His voice lost its rough edge as he cautioned, "Y'all are gonna want to keep his marijuana use a secret while you're in Texas." Wes blinked, the officer holding his gaze for a long moment. "The medical stuff might be legal in New Mexico, but here in Texas it's still felony possession. Don't use it in public, don't flaunt that you're holding. Can you do that, please?"

Wes slowly nodded. He waited for the cop to yank him from the car, tell him to pull aside, tear his El Camino apart, beat the shit out of him, something.

"Have a safe trip, gentlemen. And Godspeed." The patrolman rose up from the window. He waved them on and turned his attention to the impatient semi on their bumper.

Chapter 25

IRENE

Irene lifted her foot off the gas. She maneuvered the BMW around the plodding Oldsmobuick. The car responded, gripping the road as she whipped around the land yacht. She slammed the pedal to the floor. The engine rejoiced with a growl as it chewed up the miles.

As the mile markers zipped past her, Irene shoved off any notion of relief. She wouldn't have peace until she was with Dad, until she was talking to him, hearing his voice, touching his hands. A pair of assholes took up both lanes ahead. Irene took the car onto the shoulder, passing the cars at a rapid clip. A stalled semi forced a last-second swerve back into the lane. The close call incited the other driver to slam on his brakes. That earned her a few honks and a rude gesture. She deserved it. After a few minutes, the adrenaline rush from the near accident faded. Her leg shook against the gas pedal and her stomach turned. She was doing her best to drive calm, but the desire to get to Dad was forcing terrible choices out of her.

The headlights reflected off a large green sign: Las Cruces was only twenty miles away. She was almost there. Almost to her father.

Ahead, brake lights slogged in the left lane, and she was approaching them fast. She was in the passing lane, so they should move over. But as she closed the distance, the lights remained in her lane.

She flashed her brights and slammed the horn. "Fucking move over," she hissed. The car squatted in the left lane. She repeated her high beams, and in response the sedan's brake lights pulsed. "Goddammit!" Her hands tightened on the steering wheel. Her body full of anger and impatience, she shot into the open lane. Speeding past the car, Irene growled along with the engine as it perked up at the acceleration.

The blur of red and blue lights danced across her dashboard and reflected off her mirrors. She blew out a frustrated sigh. The air filled with the voice of the officer behind her: "Pull over, now."

She slapped the leather steering wheel. The car slowed as she eased onto the shoulder. She didn't need this delay. Dad was only a few miles away. Once she rolled to a stop, Irene killed the engine.

She opened her door and stepped out of the car, looking back at the cruiser behind her. Amid the emergency strobes, she spied the form of the officer exiting his car. The shadowy blob stopped, and a light blazed into Irene's eyes.

"Ma'am, I need you to get back in your car!" As she adjusted to the lights, she could see his hand tensed on the butt of the revolver at his hip.

Her hands floated up. "Okay, okay," she placated. She considered spooling up tears. Getting emotional with the cops might speed things along. Then she realized she didn't need to; she was already crying. "I'm trying to get to the sheriff's office in Las Cruces. They have my dad." The desperation in her voice frustrated her. "I need to get to him, okay?"

The officer responded, "Ma'am, you were flying like a bat out of hell back there. You got no business driving in the state you're in right now." His light pointed at the ground by her feet. The pelts of rain had created hundreds of small craters that cast long shadows across the earth. His features congealed out of the dark. Irene expected a scolding face, but found concern.

"Can you get me to the Las Cruces Sheriff's Office? Please?" Her voice cracked. "I'll take any ticket you want to write with a fucking smile and pay it on the spot. But right now I need to get to my dad and make sure he's okay!"

The officer moved to the front of his vehicle, motioning for Irene to lean against the trunk of Dad's car. A woman's voice asked from the dark, "Your father is at the Las Cruces sheriff's station?"

Irene nodded, searching the flashing lights for the female officer. "They asked me to come get him." It was a lie of omission; she'd been told to come get some answers out of him.

The male officer pulled out his radio, spouting out a series of call signs and numbers and commands. He glanced up at her. "What's your name, ma'am?"

"Irene Allard."

He repeated her name into the radio, listening to the squawks that came back as if they had meaning. He nodded, satisfied with whatever he heard. He asked her for her license, glanced at it, and handed it back.

"Okay, here's what's gonna happen. You'll ride with Officer McHay in the cruiser, and I'm gonna drive your car to the sheriff's station. Once we're there, we'll give your keys to the sheriff. He can decide when you're in a state to drive again." The male officer opened his hand, waiting for her to deposit her keys.

Not seeing an alternative, Irene nodded and relinquished the fob. The officers moved. Irene followed McHay. She opened the rear door of the cruiser, and Irene folded into the backseat. Metal bars covering the windows and the thick Plexiglas shield separating her from the front of the car consumed Irene's personal space.

As McHay slid behind the wheel, Irene noted the discolored smears across the barrier. A shoe print stamped on the shield between her and the officer. Irene felt a sinking shame. She'd never ridden in a cruiser before, much less in the back where they keep the criminals. The space was strange, foreign enough that she would never learn the customs.

The BMW merged onto the highway, and McHay followed. As they sped up, Irene leaned back. If she wasn't driving, she may as well try to rest during the quick sprint to Las Cruces. A sharp prong dug into her lumbar, and Irene reached behind her to examine the protrusion. Her fingers found a solid metal bar, secured to the frame of the seat. At first she figured it was a LATCH point, designed to secure baby seats. Irene had only ever used them to tie down storage containers when she moved. But this bar was too thick, and it stuck out farther.

Her other hand found her first, and both ran a tactile analysis of the thing. It was her posture that snapped the solution together. With both hands behind her back, the purpose of the bar was clear. The officers would use this bar to secure someone's wrists to the frame of the seat.

Her fingers closed around the metal. She swayed side to side, the pressure of her limited movement tightening her shoulders and neck. The tension of incarceration, of isolation. Losing choices. How many times had Wes experienced this discomfort? Hell, had Wes been in this cruiser? Maybe attached to this specific lump of pointy metal she was holding? Was she breathing in atoms of his skin, right now?

Her jaw joint ached. It was psychological. A reminder of Wes exploding when Dad had him committed years ago. Her brother put up a struggle when they confronted him. Irene stepped in to help, but Wes knocked her down and stomped on the side of her face. She had to hold her jaw in manual traction for forty minutes until an ambulance arrived for her. By that point, Wes was sitting in this backseat, or one like it. On his way to a cushy room at rehab, where he drank sodas and complained about his shitty family.

Wes meant to hurt her that day. He made a choice to do so. Dad never thought that was true, calling it an "unfortunate accident." He never would see Wes for the broken person he was.

Irene brought her hands to her lap as the cruiser pulled into a parking slot next to the Beamer. She looked out the window at the large municipal building. It dwarfed any structure in Truth or Consequences, both in girth and quality. The landscaping was well-maintained grass and shrubs, a small oasis in the desert, likely requiring a conspicuous use of water.

McHay opened the cruiser door, gesturing toward the other officer, waiting outside the lobby doors. Irene followed them into the building. They entered a wide area of cubicles where several other officers milled about in the quiet.

They stopped at a desk supporting the elbows of a round man, his bulk stressing the buttons of his olive uniform. Vapid eyes searched the air ahead of him, and his white hair clung to the sweat on his brow. Irene glanced at the melamine nameplate on the desk. This was Sheriff Smelly, the man who had called her earlier.

Season of Waiting

The male officer stepped ahead of McHay. "Hey, Sheriff, this here is Irene Allard. She's here to help with her father."

The sheriff's vacuous gaze stayed on her face for a long moment. "You're the daughter?"

Irene's patience frayed. Christ, what part of that was so hard to understand? She forced a calm to her voice. "Yes, I am Irene Allard. May I see my father, please?"

The sheriff stretched a sigh. The drawl from the phone call became more prominent as he replied, "Um ... yes, but first I think we should—"

Her impatience asserted itself. Irene commanded the sheriff, "Show me my goddamned father!"

McHay and her colleague both jumped at the change in her tone. Irene regretted losing her cool as Sheriff Smelly's hands shot into the air, as if she were mugging him. Before anyone could speak, Irene recovered. "I'm sorry, it's been a long day, and it would bring me great peace of mind to see that my father is here. Is he here?"

The sheriff kept one hand up as the other shoved his body out of his chair. He wobbled around the desk, waving at her to follow. They passed through the cube farm, Irene feeling the side-eyes from many of the young officers. They entered a short hallway with two doors on either side. Smelly raised a finger. He poked his head into a door on the left, then called Irene over with a wiggle of his stubby finger.

Irene stood in the doorway, staring at the middle-aged Latino cuffed to the massive metal table in the tight space. His scared, wide eyes bounced to each of them, his voice stressed and shaking in fright. *"No hice nada, no ... no hice nada malo. ..."*

Irene took in the room, glancing at the corners. She turned to the sheriff and shrugged. "Who's this? Where's my dad?"

Sheriff Smelly licked his thin lips, turning from Irene to this mystery man. He sighed, resting a hand on his ample gut. "This ... um, isn't your father, then?"

Irene waved him off. "No, my dad, where is he?"

"¡No hice nada!" the man shouted.

The sheriff raised a thick finger at the man attached to the table. "See ... so, this man was ... um, trying to use your father's credit card ... at a, um, gas station. Officers happened to be at the scene already, and that's how, um ... we got him into custody."

Irene looked at the Latino, his chestnut skin and black hair in sharp contrast to the "Allard pallor" of her family. "But that's not him!"

The sheriff sighed again, opening and closing his mouth to untie his tongue. "Well, see ... there was a younger man too that, um ... ran off, so we thought ..." The sheriff pulled a bandanna from his back pocket and rubbed his damp forehead. "And see ... he ain't, um, talking to us, ain't said nothing except 'No heece nahdah,' over and over. We hoped that, um ... getting you here would help ... you know, get him talking."

Irene heard the sheriff's words, but their meaning wasn't snapping together. "Wait, you assumed that's my father?" she asked, stabbing a finger at the agitated man in the chair. "Given the description I gave the police?"

The sheriff nodded, regret forming a frown that looked to drip off his thick chin. "We had hoped, I guess, um ... yes."

Irene turned back to the cuffed man. His features blurred together as her tears returned.

Chapter 26

WES

Wes groaned, exasperated. "All I'm saying is that it felt like we had some guardian-angel shit happening back there."

His heart danced in his chest, but not from panic. Wes's mood had improved a lot. Back at the checkpoint, he was sure they were done, that he'd failed Dad one last time. Instead, the angst had turned into elation. And here they were, disappearing into the ink of night in West Texas.

"I mean, don't you think someone was looking out for us?" he asked.

Pop sighed, stammering, "I dunno about that, son. I think we got lucky."

Wes snorted with derision. "Fuck your luck, Pop."

"I don't get it," he replied. "We got an understanding highway patrolman who reasoned about what he perceived. A terminal cancer patient, marijuana odors. He assumed that I was using medical marijuana as part of my treatment."

"Okay, for starters," Wes said, "there are no sensible or reasonable cops. And second," he added, turning to his father, "just call it 'weed,' okay?"

Pop shrugged with his unbraced hand, his shoulders tense. The conversation must have made him uncomfortable. Wes turned back to the road and continued, "So let me reverse the question back to you. Why couldn't it have been divine intervention?"

"I don't see what that matters," Dad replied. "And besides, how would we know if it was or wasn't God's hand back there? How would we even test that?"

Wes lifted his gaze to the car's roof and groaned. Beneath the playful noise, his irritation grew. "Ugh, Pop, you sound like Irene! Admit that something amazing happened there! Okay? Just do that and I'll drop it!"

Dad turned in his seat a bit. "And why is that important to you?"

"Well, because!" Wes's eyebrows wrinkled. Why was it such a thing with him? He wanted to be right. To prove Irene wrong and show her way of thinking was inadequate. This miracle was happening around their dad—the voice, the boy, this trip. But this wasn't about Dad. Wes had a stake in this too. This was his chance to do something right, for once. "Because it means we're doing the right thing."

"I'm not sure what you mean."

"Well, take the voice," Wes started, doing his best impression of the professors he'd seen on PBS. "It offers you knowledge, right? But only you, Pop."

His dad nodded, noncommittal.

Wes continued, "It's leading us to the healer, to get your cancer taken away. Right? Is that not a miracle?"

Dad's face turned thoughtful. Wes smiled, knowing he was getting through. "You can't deny those things. You experienced them firsthand, I didn't. And back there, the voice or ... whatever it is ... got us through the checkpoint, somehow. God, or fate, or the universe, or Brahma, whatever you want to call it? It's looking out for us."

Pop turned to the windshield, his hand finding his stubbled face. Wes recognized the behavior—Dad was thinking through what he heard.

Wes went on, "Something bigger than us. Bigger than all of us. It wants you healed, and it's pushing the obstacles out of our way."

After a few moments, Pop sighed and shook his head. "I can't believe that, Wes. I mean, that was terrifying back there, wasn't it?"

"Hell yeah, it was a real pants-ruiner!" Wes laughed.

"So if the universe wanted to intervene, why not remove the entire roadblock?"

Wes snorted, raising a hand. "What, like with a meteor? I mean—"

"No, I'm serious," Pop interrupted. "If this voice I'm hearing is God or some omnipotent thing, then why didn't it even tell us about the checkpoint? Give us a chance to drive around it?"

Wes's head shook with more fervor. Dad wasn't getting it. "Nah, it didn't need to, see? We managed our way through it. The voice could see that we would be okay! It would have helped us if it needed to. Or it did help us, and we just don't know."

"But that's the thing, you've got this circle of logic that's self-fulfilling and—"

"Stop, okay?" Wes snapped. His patience stretched to near breaking, and he raised a hand to block Pop's words. "Just stop with the Irene-speak and hear me out. There's this story a friend of mine was telling, about a man who ended up trapped in his house during a massive flood. In like, Louisiana, I think. Katrina, maybe."

Wes glanced over at his father's face. He was listening, his eyes focused with curiosity. Wes continued, "So yeah, the flood comes, and the army, or whatever? They issue an evacuation, but this guy, he stays. He refuses to get on the truck, saying that God will take care of him, see? So the water keeps coming, and now he's trapped in his house. He prays for God to help him. When someone in a boat comes by and offers him a ride, the guy says, 'No, I'm good. God will take care of me.' More floods come, and they get so high he's got to go up onto his roof. He's got nowhere else to go, he's gonna die if the water keeps rising, and he prays more, see?"

Pop nodded.

"Then a helicopter flies in. The pilot lowers a ladder and shouts at the guy through his megaphone thing to get aboard. But the guy is still, 'Oh naw, God will take care of me.' So, long story short, the waters keep coming, and they reach the roof."

Wes paused for effect, trying to stretch the reveal. "So he drowns! And he dies and goes up to heaven, and he's all pissed, so when he sees God, he lays into him real good. Like, 'What the hell, man, I prayed for your help!' And that's where God tells him, 'Hey, dude, I sent you a truck, a boat, and a helicopter to get you out of there, what else was I supposed to do?'"

A smile broke across Pop's face. A smirk. Shit! Wes wasn't shooting for funny with his story. When the therapist had told Wes the tale, the spiritual impact was profound.

"The point is," Wes stammered, recovering the momentum of his story, "you won't always see where God's stepping in. Especially if you're spending all your effort looking for it."

"Okay," Pop said, "but how can you cherry-pick which actions to classify as God's hand?"

Wes looked over at his father, trying to work out the question.

Dad elaborated, "I mean, wouldn't the floods in your story be God's doing as well?"

Wes turned back to the road. He hadn't considered that. He tried to reimagine the story, figure out how God making the flood supported the moral. A coherent plot failed to form. He stalled, "I mean, sure, there would have to have been a bigger picture, right? Like, the flood would have been for a reason—"

Pop interrupted his thoughts. "So you're saying that every incident, every action anyone takes on this planet, is according to some plan from God?"

Wes nodded, unsure. "Something like that, I guess."

"But why would anyone worry about their decisions, then? If God guides us to every consequence? People would do whatever they pleased, chucking it all up to God's will."

Wes's face soured with confusion.

"Take murder," Pop offered. "Or rape. Or genocide. By your logic, it's all justified after it happens. That it happens at all means it was God's plan. The act of doing something implies God wanted it to happen."

Wes raised a hand. "Well, no, you can't justify that stuff on its own. Consider the ... situation. Or the aftereffects."

"Such as?" Pop asked. He folded his arms across his chest, wincing as his elbow knocked his wrist brace.

Wes could feel his face reddening. He turned back to the road, speaking around his waving hand. "I dunno. Maybe the person murdered was going to do something awful." What the hell was Pop's problem? Wes's tone was becoming sharp with his growing impatience.

Pop let out a tiny laugh. "How could the murderer know that, though?"

The rush through his face became a pounding in his head. "Fuck, Dad, how the hell should I know!" Wes was angry now, punctuating his questions with a slap against the steering wheel. "How the hell did you know the lottery numbers? How the hell did you know about this healer in Texas? *Huh?*"

Dad went quiet for a moment. "And your addictions? God's plan?"

Wes's fist found the steering wheel and tightened around it. His teeth ground together. He could feel his dad staring at him, waiting for him to say something dumb, but Wes kept his eyes on the road.

"Breaking your sister's jaw, when we were trying to help you? God's master plan? Where do we take personal responsibility? Where are the consequences of our actions, son?"

The frayed thread holding back Wes's tongue snapped. He turned to his father, veering the El Camino off the highway as he screamed, "I don't know!"

Dad flinched into his seat, his eyes wide with shock and terror.

"I don't know! I have no fucking clue!" Wes's voice grew louder, tighter. "And fuck you for throwing that shit in my face!"

Wes sucked in a breath, pulling the car back into the lane. The two men rode in silence for several minutes, Wes's breath heaving as he calmed down. His dad's fear left a cold vapor between them, his posture frozen in defense. He wouldn't look at his son. That was fine. Wes didn't want to see Pop right now either.

Wes swallowed, clearing his throat and relaxing his grip on the steering wheel. His voice came out raspy, deeper than normal. "Look, man, most everyone I know is focused on getting through the day, all right? Everyone. Junkies. Doctors. Criminals. Judges. Everyone is waiting for the day to end, so they can hurry up and do it again tomorrow." He swallowed again, gaining back more control and composure. "All I'm saying is that this is different. For us. This," he said, motioning toward the road ahead, "feels different. What we're doing here. We have a ... I dunno ... a purpose. You're getting a second life, and that must mean something to you. I'm helping make it happen, and that sure as shit means something to me, Pop."

Dad relaxed a bit, staying close to the passenger door, and turned to his window.

Wes continued after a moment, his voice breaking, "And yeah, all of that negative shit we ..." He sighed. Shame and regret over his tantrum pushed tears out of his eyes. "All the shit that I put us through, I need to believe that was to get us here. To this moment. To fulfill our purpose." Wes rubbed his nose on the back of his hand. "I have to believe that, Pop."

His father didn't speak, didn't turn from the window. Wes figured he was crying.

"I've apologized so many times, I know it's meaningless to do it again, so I won't. But this thing we're doing?" Wes stopped to wipe his own tears. "You need to understand, this is redemption for me. A chance to make up for all that shit I put you through. I'm so sick of getting by, getting through today. Waiting for the next today to come so I can be sick of that too. I want to do something more, something good. For once in my fucking life, Pop."

Dad remained quiet and still.

"Are you awake?" Wes asked after several seconds.

Pop nodded, turning forward and wiping his eyes.

They rode without speaking for a long while, the cadence of the road noise filling the space between them. Wes felt the time was right. He needed to share his letter, the one he'd put together in rehab. A contract. A promise. He hadn't finished yet, but he remembered enough to fill in the gaps. When he had his thoughts formed, he broke the silent tension.

"Okay, so here's the deal," he began, looking over at Pop. "There's nothing I can do about what's happened. I take full responsibility for all the damage I've caused over my life. And I can't promise I won't fuck up again, okay?"

Wes sighed, slowing the car as they approached the ass end of a Greyhound bus. He swallowed, girding himself for his next words. "But if I fuck up again, I promise not to pull you or Irene into it. I'll deal with it myself."

His father turned in his seat, stiff and grimacing. "And what does that mean exactly, son?"

Wes shrugged. "I don't know. I won't know until it happens. If it happens, I mean." He followed the bus as it lilted right onto an exit ramp and left the highway. "I guess I'm saying that if I slip again, I'll do it away from you guys. I'll ... up and disappear. Do my best to work it out on my own, without pulling you or Irene into it with me." Wes pulled the car into the restaurant parking lot, careful not to park too close to the bus.

Pop exhaled. "Wes, I don't want you to ..." He stopped, looking out the window, confused. "What are we doing here? My God, son, are you hungry again?"

Wes threw the El Camino in park and killed the engine. "No, Pop." He pointed at the bus. A stream of passengers were unloading, stretching their legs and arms, and wandering into the restaurant. "I think it's time we deal with our cash shortage."

Chapter 27

VICTORIA

"I swear to God, you bring this burger back to me again with mayonnaise on it and I'm gonna get you fired!" The old man punctuated his demands with a gnarled finger aimed at Victoria's face.

"Of course, I'm so sorry," Victoria soothed. She lifted the plate from the table and turned toward the service bar. The old man's hand shot to the hem of her apron and held her in place.

"This is the second time I've had to send it back!" The man's wrinkled face was sour with contempt. "How hard is it to leave off mayonnaise? It's less work than adding it, for Pete's sake!"

"I know, and I'm sure it's very frustrating, sir. I'll get this fixed right away," she replied, keeping her tone civil. The mistake was an honest one. Customers had packed the diner at this late hour, a bus full of seniors making an unexpected stop so the driver could load up on coffee. Victoria worked the floor by herself tonight. She had jumped at the extra shift. It made for a long day on her feet, but the extra cash was too enticing to pass up.

"Oh, stop badgering the poor girl. She's all alone here and doing her best!" His wife slapped the man's hand away from Vic's apron. Victoria smiled as she walked from the table. The wife continued to dig into her husband. "You're still put out about the busted air-conditioning on the bus. Don't take it out on our waitress, you grouchy old fart."

Victoria set the plate on the service bar and called Samson over from the grill. She explained the issue to him, emphasizing the "no" part of "no mayonnaise." Samson rolled his eyes, but took the burger. Vic smirked at him. The buses were great for business, but the later ones made for a long shift for them both.

Patting down her apron, Victoria found her ticket pad. She turned toward the counter seats. After the bus had unloaded, two men wandered in and had been waiting for her to take their order. Pulling her pencil from behind her ear, she sucked in a deep breath, and approached them with a fresh smile.

"So sorry for the wait, y'all—it's just me tonight. What can I getcha?"

"Um, coffee," the younger man ordered. Before she could ask, he added, "Lots of cream, lots of sugar, please."

As she pulled out a mug from beneath the counter, Victoria turned to the older gentleman. His stare remained locked on his hands in front of him. "And you, sir? What'll ya have?" He didn't respond, keeping his gaze low.

After a moment, the younger man placed a hand on the man's back and responded, "How about tea, Pop?" Looking at Victoria, he said, "He'll have hot tea. Nothing caffeinated, though."

Victoria nodded and ducked under the counter. She rummaged around for the box of herbal samplers, finding it tucked behind the sugar canisters. Before standing, she wiped off the dust, using her apron. Grabbing another mug, Vic rose to the men.

"Well, at least you'll make more tips, right?" The young man's smile was all pink and gums.

Vic set down the mug and tea. "Sorry? I don't follow."

"It's busy, and you're working the place alone, but that means more tips for you, right?" he elaborated.

Vic smiled and nodded with enthusiasm as she replaced the unused pad and pencil back in her apron. "It sure does," she replied. Spying a woman returning from the bathroom to her table, Victoria excused herself. She walked over to take the woman's order. The thought of extra cash lightened her aching feet. With her daughter's birthday later this week, she was running out of time. She needed another hundred bucks to make their trip to the San Antonio Zoo a reality. Her daughter loved elephants, and she'd never seen a real one. Vic hadn't either, and if she was honest, she was at least as excited as her kid. She had saved what she could for a while now, but she wasn't sure if they could afford the trip. After paying for rent, food, gas, laundry, clothing, and everything else, there was never wiggle room in their budget. But tonight, with this crowd, she just might pull enough together to make the trip happen. And that idea made the crabby crowd worth the hassle.

Bathroom Lady ordered the Salisbury steak with mashed potatoes and carrots. She asked to have it prepared medium, and Vic nodded as if it would make any difference with Samson. Vic walked back to the counter, delivering the order onto the spindle and hollering at Samson. He acknowledged her by raising his spatula next to his head without turning from the griddle.

Orders were in, and there was no food up for service. Victoria picked up the pot of stale coffee. She approached the men at the counter, the older man still hunched small, as if he was trying to crawl into himself. The younger man waved her off, covering his mug with his hand. Vic saw some tension between the two of them. Everyone passing through carried a story, and sometimes Vic made up her own. She knew better than to get involved. She was here to smile, serve the food, and take the money.

"Service," Samson mumbled, slapping the call bell with the dirty spatula. The old man's burger was ready. Vic put the coffee back on the scarred heating element and pulled the plate from the bar. She walked over to Mr. Grumpyfarts, forcing a smile as she approached. She eased the food in front of him and sang, "Here you are, sir, and again I apologize for the inconvenience."

The man responded with a grunt, lifting the bun and checking the mayonnaise status. His hands moved to the burger, shaking as they lifted it to his mouth. He took a bite, smacking his thin lips with each sucking chomp.

"How is it?" Victoria asked.

"Finally edible," replied Mr. Grumpyfarts. "Congratulations for doing your damned job." He spoke around a mouthful of processed cow. Vic could see that there was no mayonnaise on it.

The call bell rang again—that would be Bathroom Lady's Salisbury steak. "Let me know if you need anything else," she said, turning back and crossing the floor. As she rounded the counter, she sensed the smiling young man watching her. Not a casual glance, more of an intense fucking-with-his-eyes stare across her body. She hated it when customers leered, but she couldn't afford to lose a tip—or, worse, her job—over calling out the shitty behavior. If the guy got too creepy, Samson was more than capable of protecting her.

She picked up the order and delivered it to Bathroom Lady. All orders out, none in the kitchen, she walked the floor, making sure everyone had what they needed.

Grumpyfarts waved her over. Vic hid her sigh, wondering what the man wanted this time. Vic stole a glance at his plate as she approached the booth. He had stopped eating halfway through his burger. His wife had finished her BLT and was poking at a game on her phone with tentative fingers. "Yes, sir? Is everything okay?"

"Bring me some of that sweet potato pie I see in the case over there," he grunted.

At that, his wife looked up, moving her finger from her phone and shaking it at her husband. "Dammit, your diet, Phil ..."

"You shut your damned hole. I'll eat what I want," Grumpyfarts interrupted. With a pout, he added, "And I want that pie."

Vic smiled at them both, updating their ticket before leaving it on the table. She walked to the counter, again aware of the man's sideways stare. She opened the glass case and found the thickest slice of the sickly yellow pie. A crack ran along the surface, and a discolored blotch had formed after a full day in the dry heat. Grumpyfarts would complain about it. Vic pulled the can of whipped topping from the fridge and used it to spackle over the less inviting parts of the dessert.

Delivering the pie and finishing her checkup of the diners, Vic returned to her spot behind the counter. She took a moment, leaning against the short wall by the register. She lifted each foot from the floor and rotated her ankles, feeling the blood flow into her achy calves as her back tightened. Her shift would be over in an hour. Then, she'd go home and collapse into bed for a few hours before kiddo needed to get to school.

As she stretched out a kink in her neck, the driver announced the bus would leave in ten minutes. Vic took a deep, calming breath. This final bit of chaos would be the last thing she'd have to put up with tonight. One by one, the seniors lined up at the register, their eyes wide in worry that the driver would abandon them here. She worked through the tickets one at a time. Most of the customers paid in cash, thankfully, and were patient and kind with her.

After a few minutes of hustling at the register, Victoria regarded the remaining customers. Grumpyfarts scowled at her from the back of the line. She met his gaze with a smile. In moments, he'd be out of her life forever.

"May I borrow a pen?"

Vic slammed the register drawer. A reflex. The eye-fucker from the end of the counter. He stood next to the line at the register. The odor of cigarettes stained the air. She handed him a pen from the cup behind the register, nodding back at him. Vic returned her attention to the customer waiting to pay. Behind them, patrons returned to the tables to drop their tips before leaving the diner and her life forever.

"Can you move your ass, sweetheart?" mumbled Grumpyfarts. His fleshy arms folded across his sunken chest. Vic opened her hand for the ticket, and he wadded it into a ball as he gave it to her. She forced her smile as she took the paper, opened it flat, and tallied the cost of their meal. "And you need to comp that pie, given the shitty service!" His wife stood a few feet behind him, face lowered with shame at his behavior.

Vic caught herself before she huffed—a comp would come out of her pay for the night. She needed every penny of that money. "I understand, sir, but we're short-staffed tonight.

We're doing the best we can, you know?" she offered with a light laugh. For Christ's sake. This old fart probably had more money in his wallet than she'd seen in three months, and he wanted a slice of pie for nothing.

She rang up the total. The man's chest puffed out as he leaned into her space. "Listen, sugartits, I'm not paying for the pie. I had to send my meal back twice so Guapo back there could get it right!" Vic's eyes widened as she turned to the kitchen, finding Samson's gaze stabbing the old man.

Turning back, Vic forced a smile through her irritation. With a stern voice she said, "I apologize if the service wasn't up to your expectations, but we don't comp food on demand here. You order it, you pay for it." She kept her cool as Grumpyfarts fumed to a shade resembling the roasted beets no one ever ordered.

After a few breaths, the man's lips pursed in a forced exhalation. "Fine!" he mumbled. He dug his thick paw into his pocket, pulling out a wad of cash. He separated the bills, licking a finger and flattening them out one at a time. Once he had his money organized, he pulled out a few bills and threw them behind the register. They spun around Vic's head and tumbled on the air until reaching the floor. Vic groaned as she stooped to pick them up. A few minutes more, that's all she had to endure. As she rose with the collected bills, Vic faced a ten-dollar bill clutched between Mr. Grumpyfart's talons. Once she saw it, the old man whisked it back into his pocket. "Kiss your fucking tip good-bye!" he laughed.

Victoria cleared the couple's ticket and offered the man his change. Mr. Grumpyfarts shoved open the diner door and wandered into the night. Behind him, his wife held up a twenty, waving it to capture Victoria's attention, and set the bill on their table before moving to the door. She stopped long enough to mouth the words, "I'm so sorry." Then, like a fart in the wind, she disappeared from Vic's life.

Vic cleared the Grumpyfarts sale and speared the ticket on the spindle. She was ready to clean up, collect her tips, and go home.

A phlegmy rattle pulled her gaze up to the older man from the counter. He stood in front of the register, holding out a few creased dollars to her. He looked tired, or scared, or both. After tonight, Vic wasn't sure she cared which it was. She made his change for the two drinks, the man's son calling from the door in a brisk tone, "Get a move on, Pops!"

With his thumb, the father motioned back toward the counter where they had been sitting. "I left you a note," he creaked. His tone was meek, apologetic. Vic smiled her professional service smile. Jesus Christ, the leering son and now the father leaving her his number, or a lewd comment on a napkin? Would tonight end, please? She watched the last two patrons exit, and the diner became quiet and still.

Vic took a moment to enjoy it. She waited several deep breaths to collect herself, massaging the plaster smile out of her cheeks. She reached under the counter for the dish tub. Rounding to the tables, she stretched her arms and back. She knew how to pack an entire section in a single trip. Larger plates on the bottom, then the smaller plates, bowls stacked to the side, glassware on top, and silverware collected in the drink glasses.

She approached the farthest table from the kitchen. Mr. and Mrs. Grumpyfarts. Remembering the twenty the wife left, her face cracked into a smile. A genuine one. Vic mocked the old man to herself, "Guess who paid for their pie, sugartits!"

She cleared their plates into the tub. Not finding a tip, she felt a pang of disappointment and scanned the table again. She was sure she'd seen the wife leave a twenty. A quick glance at the surrounding booths yielded nothing either. She checked the floor under the table. Nothing. Maybe it stuck to one of their plates? That happened sometimes. She shuffled the dishes in the tub. No money there either.

Figuring it would turn up, she moved on to the next cluttered table. This time she scanned the tabletop to locate her tip before misplacing it. No tip on this table either. Her disappointment deepened. What the hell? She set the tub on an empty table and walked the diner floor, the ache in her legs growing as she checked each messy table, looking for cash.

There was none, anywhere. It made no sense—she'd seen people leaving money for her!

She stood stunned for a moment, unsure whether to trust her memory or her eyes. She scoured the room, looking for anything green. Her eyes landed on the two mugs at the counter. The stinky eye-fucker and his gross father. She walked over, eyes on the stools where they had sat.

No tip. Instead, Vic found a napkin folded in front of the mug of untouched tea. She lifted the thin paper and opened it. For a moment she hoped money would fall out of it. But none did. She saw writing.

This was the note the strange old man had mentioned. She read the clean, straight print: "I'm very sorry. We'll pay you back in a few days. With interest."

Chapter 28

WES

Scraping tips broke something in Pop. He hadn't been keen on the idea when Wes explained it to him. The way he acted back there at the restaurant in Fort Stockton, it amazed Wes that the waitress didn't call the police on them. "Just act natural," Wes had told him, "and I'll do the heavy lifting." The pun was intended, but Pop missed it.

Holy Christ, could he have been more rigid? He wouldn't even look at the waitress, much less talk to her. Wes hadn't seen Dad touch his tea at all. "Act natural." *Pffft.* Maybe Wes should have just kept the plan from him, let Pop enjoy his tea while Wes did the dirty work. Of course, then he risked his dad asking lots of dumb questions. *Like he does.* It would have drawn unwanted attention. "Where ya goin', Wes? Whatcha doin' at that table, Wes? Why are you picking up that money, Wes? That's not yours, so don't put it in your pocket, Wes! Aren't you going to give it back to the hot waitress, Wes? Why are we running away, Wes?"

And what the hell was that note? Wes had almost bitten off his own lip when Pop asked for a pen. Pop threatened to scream that the cops were looking for them, unless Wes got him a goddamned pen. Wouldn't explain why. So Wes got him a pen, and Pop wrote the waitress a note, promising that he'd pay her back.

His dad might be smart, but it was the same smart as Irene. It was all from books and school, and none of it from knowing people or the way shit got done. Until an hour ago, they had done nothing wrong. Then they committed a petty crime. It might put a bigger spotlight on them, but the waitress would sure as shit remember Pop's odd behavior. That could come back to bite them in the ass. Wes hoped they could get to Utopia before anyone put together the Silver Alert and the description of the two odd diners who'd scraped tips on their way out the door. They could deal with the slap on the wrist later, but at the moment, Pop was running out of time.

After they were back on the road, Pop summed up their petty crime at almost $150. It would be enough to get them to Utopia and back. For Wes, that was the end of it. One less problem to deal with. But Pop couldn't let it rest. He sat there silent, plodding, sketching out a list on a napkin from the diner. The location, date, time, and take from their brief adventure. Then he started working out a payback schedule. "To be fair to the waitress," he kept saying, "to compensate her for the inconvenience." After a while, he became quiet. His face was wet whenever Wes stole a glance at him, and his breathing was sharp. He never started sobbing, but he turned into a melty, whining mess.

"Pop, it'll be fine," Wes consoled. "This is temporary. Fixable. Nothing we can't deal with later."

"It doesn't change the fact that it's wrong," Pop lamented. "I mean, I've never done anything like that before. Never needed to."

Wes sighed, "Yeah, well, these are kind of extraordinary times, aren't they? We wouldn't have had to do it if Irene hadn't freaked the fuck out."

A rising whine escaped Pop's lips, the sound a kid makes at being treated unfairly. "That's the thing, though, Wes! Why is this getting so difficult?" He wiped his nose on his unbraced hand. "I mean, the checkpoint? The voice couldn't tell us about that? Given us a way around it?"

"Yeah but we talked about that and—"

"I know," Dad interrupted, "but now stealing? It's getting worse! Why do we have to resort to crimes if we have some larger power on our side? What about that poor waitress? What if she needed this money?"

"Please, Pop," Wes begged, "just stop! Everything will be fine, okay?" He reached over to take his dad's hand, finding the hard brace instead of skin. "Remember, this is a loan. A temporary fix. We can pay her back. But we need time to do that. Time we won't have unless we get you to that kid in Utopia."

"It's not right, son." Wes saw Pop shake his head in the corner of his vision. "This feels wrong."

Silence marked the next few minutes. Thoughts and excuses bounced inside Wes's skull. None of them felt helpful now. It didn't matter. Wes could tell Pop was pretending to sleep to avoid the conversation. That was fine. His father's mood was temporary too. His cancer was not. Fix Pop, then they'd have time to fix their mistakes.

Another few minutes, and Dad fell asleep, his breathing moving into the deep wet rattle Wes recognized from the hospital. Wes pushed the argument from his head and focused on the road passing beneath them. A steady sixty-five miles per hour, moving them closer and closer to his dad's salvation. The coffee's effects were ebbing, the focus of the caffeine turning into a distraction in his bladder. He would need to stop at some point, but he also wanted Pop to get some proper sleep. When he woke, he should feel better about things.

Wes noted the subtle shift of color in the sky, allowing him to find the horizon in the muddy blackness ahead of his headlights. The sun would rise soon. The marked division between land and sky expanded around him, the land pushing up in black swells to prop up the kindling sky. The El Camino's speed was deceptive, creating lethargic shifts in the inky waves of land.

The sky blushed, as if they'd embarrassed the night with their behavior in the diner. Wes shrugged off the thought, stretching out his shoulders and yawning, taking notice of the dramatic change in the landscape that the coming day was reluctant to reveal. Texas was flat, but it wasn't without curves. The oranges and reds stained the vegetation all around, giving the night's flat canvas sudden texture and shape and motion, rising and falling away in long undulations of land painted with ruby shadows and pink highlights. Everything here seemed covered in something living, not like the real desert back home, where dust was king. The rotating blades of dozens of wind turbines became visible on the hills to the north. They twisted with the air, the lackadaisical patterns of light and shadow, rise and fall, mesmerizing Wes. The land glowed pink and then red and then purple, and finally exploded in greens around them.

Wes turned back to the road as the sun thundered over the horizon. The landscape disappeared again, lost in a brilliant haze. He lowered the visor. It blocked out the center of the ball of fire without covering up the road ahead. The asphalt congealed out of the light, forming a solid just yards in front of his car. Wes stared into this transition, where the sun reflected off particles in the road. The steady stream of flashing glints lulled him into a daze.

The El Camino shuddered against the rumble strip on the shoulder. Wes jumped at the adrenaline spike, steering the car back onto the road. Christ, he was tired. He needed to rest too, at least give the sun a chance to get out of their way.

Out of the morning glow, the sign for the exit to Junction appeared. Wes sang his little tune in his head: "El Paso we'll pass through, across the Van Horn; east to Fort Stockton, and east we go on; Ozona, we'll own ya, but Junction's the cap; that's where we stop to look at the map."

Junction, Texas. Wes smiled. This was where they would leave the interstate for the state roads that would lead them to Utopia. They were so close.

Wes slid the car onto the exit ramp, scanning the frontage road for a place to stop. Next to a large truck stop sat an off-brand motel. Its marquee contained three words, only one of which Wes cared about: CASH OR CREDIT. Perfect.

He pulled into the parking lot, slamming the car into park and rubbing the burn from his eyes. They just needed to get through the next day or two. Then they could fix everything with the waitress, Irene, and the cops. Once Pop was healthy again. Once time wasn't so limited. Whatever he had to do, Wes would get his father to Utopia, and get him healed.

After that, Wes would be grateful to pay whatever bills came due.

Chapter 29

IRENE

Irene woke in the shadow of a frantic dream. The sounds were wrong—keyboards, polite conversations. She wasn't at Dad's house. This wasn't the hospital either. The smells weren't clean enough.

Her eyes peeled open. She blinked through the morning haze, rediscovering the Las Cruces Sheriff's Office. She was here to pick up Dad. But it wasn't Dad. Her arm pricked as nerves decompressed and allowed signals to reach her brain. She shook her hand, trying to speed up the process. Her other hand found her phone. She checked for messages or voicemails from Dad or Wes. Nothing.

She revived her laptop and waited for her analysis to come back up. It ran over eight hundred scenarios overnight. Irene paged to the summary report. Seventy-seven percent of the models favored Wes taking Dad west. Most predicted Wes heading to Phoenix or Tucson. It made sense. Farther from the border, prices for drugs would be higher than in, say, El Paso. A few took Wes east, to San Antonio or Houston.

Irene stared at the map. Was she missing something? This was where an assumption would bite her in the ass. Would Wes have doubled back north? Irene didn't think so. Wes was dumb, but he wasn't an idiot. Reversing toward Truth or Consequences would mean more trouble for him. That assumption felt valid.

Irene scrolled the map up a few inches on her screen. A wide swath of empty white filled her screen. Would Wes have headed south? Into Mexico? None of her models could have considered it, since she didn't have any data for the country. Her focus sharpened in a moment of panic. He wouldn't do that, right? Drugs in Mexico were cheap and available. It made little sense for Wes to run there if he was planning to sell them for cash. He wanted to be where the drugs had value.

She could feel the grain of sand in her mind. If she was honest, Irene didn't know what the Mexican drug trade looked like. She didn't understand much about it in the States either, but at least she had some data points to work from. The sand grew to a stone as she considered the previous evening. Wes started out with some goal, but Irene messed that up for him with the Silver Alert. Maybe Wes's goal had changed, then? Evade instead of arrive? Would he run to Mexico? The political border would offer a buffer against the authorities looking for him. Why run for hundreds of miles when you can relax and hide after a few dozen? Then he could wait for the heat to die off before making his way back.

Her heart fell. What if he wasn't planning on selling the drugs? What if his goal was to use them? If that was the case, why take Dad with him? To milk him for money?

The possibilities were growing out of control. There were too many unknowns, stacking up in a feeble house of cards that had no chance of holding weight. She needed clarity. A place to focus. A single question she could chew up with her mind. A knock on the table pulled her gaze.

It was Officer McHay. Irene smiled at her, but it waned when she didn't smile back.

"Ms. Allard," she said, her tone all business, "I thought you should know that officers in Junction, Texas, have located your brother's car. Shouldn't be long now before they have your father safe in custody." She punctuated this report with another knock on the tabletop.

Junction? Where the hell was that? She bounced to her map, scrolling along I-10 through Texas. She found it. About a hundred miles west of San Antonio. The town looked too small to matter. The closest city in her model was San Antonio, and even then, the estimated probability of Wes heading there was almost zero. She'd have to dig further to find out why. She could guess that the city had a saturated drug market, bringing prices down. Wes wouldn't know that, though. Or would he? Was there a Dow Jones for illicit drugs?

Fuck it. She shook her head to purge the logic tree from her mind. There was no time to understand. She needed to get there. Irene opened her web browser, looking for flights out of

Las Cruces that would get her close to Junction. A little math, and she concluded that the universe was patronizing her. If the town were any closer to San Antonio, she could have flown there and saved time. Any farther west and driving would have been the faster route. Instead, Wes had landed in the sweet spot, with the same travel time by car or by plane. If she didn't know her brother, she might think he planned it that way to make her life more difficult.

Her laptop dropped into her backpack with a thud, and Irene crossed the cube farm to the exit. She jogged to the BMW, threw her pack in the backseat, and fell behind the wheel.

The car chewed up the interstate. El Paso was a blur, Irene ignoring the sprawling city as she forced the vehicle to its limits. While she was thankful for light traffic, the endless construction was slowing her down and pissing her off.

The road ahead of her was undeviating. The empty expanse of red-and-brown desert disappeared in the haze of heat and sunshine. The gas pedal reached the floor. The car cut through the distance cleanly, with no fanfare or complaints. Another mile closer to Dad.

Irene moved to the passing lane and glided around an RV like it was sitting still. She glimpsed the silver-capped man in the cab as she passed. The RV's horn wailed a nasal chord that fell in pitch and volume as she flew down the road. The Doppler effect. The pitch of a sound rising as it sped toward you and falling as it headed away. An insight that wasn't helping her get to her father.

Her mind wandered back to Wes. To the unknowns. Why would he pick a place so far away? Tucson was closer and off I-10. Hell, he could have headed to Albuquerque and disappeared in less time if that's what he wanted. But he'd run south, not north. Then he went east, not west. The facts didn't fit Wes's motivations. The questions piled up in her head, hypotheses getting filed away for later testing.

Hypothesis: Wes knew someone in San Antonio who could help him.

Hypothesis: Wes wasn't selling Dad's drugs; he was planning to use them for himself. He wanted to crash in a place where prices would be low when his supply ran out.

Hypothesis: Her assumptions about Wes's motivations were wrong.

Hypothesis: Wes was an unpredictable idiot.

Chapter 30

WES

On stirring, it took a moment for Wes to remember the cheap motel. A pair of blackout curtains held back the sun. Enough light managed its way around them to show the shabby fixtures and stained walls. The room wasn't much more than two twin beds. The one in which Pop slept prevented the door from fully opening.

What time was it? Wes grabbed his phone from the nightstand, then remembered it was powered off. He reached for the alarm clock, turning the red glow to his face. It was late morning now. He had gotten a few hours of sleep, and that was all he wanted. They needed to get moving. Time and money were going to run out soon.

He planted his socked feet on the carpet and rubbed the sleep from his face with his palms. A pang in his stomach reminded him how empty it was. If Wes was hungry, his dad needed to eat too, at least to keep his pain meds down. He recalled a truck stop next door, large enough that it might offer warm food.

He slipped on his sneakers and looked for a piece of paper so he could leave Pop a note. The room had no amenities. Remembering their adventure at the diner last night, Wes scanned for Pop's fanny pack. He found it on the floor by the bed and eased open the zipper.

Inside he spotted what he needed—paper napkins and a pen. He left the zipper open, not wanting to chance waking his father with more noise. Last night was hard on him. Having been unable to wake him enough to get him walking, Wes carried him from the car to the room. Well, two rooms. The petite *abuela* that ran the place had given them a room that smelled like literal shit. Wes had to ask for a different one. Once they settled in a clean-enough space, Pop was in dreamland. Wes glanced over at him. His body lay in the same position he'd landed in when Wes got him into the bed.

Stooping to the nightstand, Wes jotted a note for his dad on the paper napkin: "I'll be back." He looked at it, wondering if a "Love, Wes" would seem genuine. He sighed, thinking again through the events of the night and early morning. He replayed the uncomfortable conversations. Dad's lack of trust. Lack of belief. Wes licked his lips and finished the note: "Trust me."

Leaving the message propped against the alarm clock was best, he figured. Pop's eyes would open right to it if he woke. Wes grabbed the room key from the floor where he'd dropped it last night. It was chained to an obnoxious hunk of barn wood. He had to cram the key in the small change pocket of his jeans, and let the big wooden plank bounce against his leg as he walked. He unlocked the door, but it refused to open. After a few moments of fiddling with it, Wes gave it a solid yank. It popped open, and he lighted into the breezeway of the motel.

The air felt soothing and warm on his skin, but his eyes expected the dank of the room. He rounded the back side of the motel, where the shadows gave his eyes time to adjust.

Wes walked the tall and weather-worn fence separating the motel from the truck stop. When he reached the access road, he stopped a moment to glance at the El Camino parked out front. It was still there, but of course it was. This trip had angels watching over it.

He crossed into the bustling truck stop. So many people passing through this place, at this particular time. How many possibilities could come from a mere second in this lot? How many interactions could there be? Wes knew he didn't have the brains to figure it out. Irene would know. She could rattle it off the top of her head and still have breath to tell him why he was so dumb. The image made him smile—the innate brilliance in his own sister, his own flesh and blood. He must have gotten a bit of that too.

The smile faded as he thought back over their history, looking for places where his gut stood up to her logic. There weren't many. The scenes that came to mind were more fights than arguments. Not just emotional shit, but physical too. It was no wonder his sister hated him so much. Hell, Wes hated himself. It had been no surprise when Irene left home. And she went as far as she could afford to go. If Wes could, he'd leave himself behind and never come back.

The hard wind of a passing truck snapped him from his self-pity. He walked the edge of the lot to avoid the muddled traffic around the pumps and approached the expansive building. A hand-painted sign in the window heralded Wes's favorite word: TACOS.

Nature's perfect food!

The truck stop was as busy inside as it was outside. The entrance led to a general store, and a small extension provided access to a food counter. The savory odors of sausage and spices pulled Wes in that direction. On the wall hung a chalkboard scrawled with a menu of breakfast tacos.

He got in line, with six people in front of him. The man ahead of Wes danced and shifted, mumbling to himself that having to wait was bullshit. The cooks filled orders at a steady pace. The line shortened until the irritated man reached the order window.

The round cook acknowledged the man with raised eyebrows. To Wes's dismay, the customer had the nerve to ask for a menu. The cook grimaced and stuck a thick stubby arm through the window. He reached over the uncomfortable angle to tap a gloved finger against the chalkboard. The customer stammered, processing his options now that he was aware of them.

A hatred filled Wes, centered on this self-important dickhead. The arrogant ass had wasted that time waiting in line. Doing nothing to help himself. Instead, frothed up, lashing out at someone innocent and undeserving. Someone making the world better. With tacos.

After asking what "chorizo" was and what animal it came from, the man ordered plain egg tacos. As the cook handed the asshole two foil-wrapped packets, he looked to Wes. Wes smiled, his order ready: one egg taco and two egg and chorizo tacos. Receiving the warm foil wads of portable flavor perfection, Wes felt his irritation melt away. He thanked the cook, paid at the register, and carried his food out of the station.

The pumps were full with cars and trucks, and some had vehicles waiting. Wes fished a smoke out of his jacket pocket and lit the cigarette as he skirted the lot. As he approached, he noticed a gap in the fence he had missed earlier. Walking through, Wes faced the brick front of the motel. He turned left, heading around toward the office and stairs. He took two steps around the corner, then froze.

His mouth opened. His cigarette peeled from his lips and fell to the ground.

Parked at an angle behind his El Camino was a police cruiser. The emergency lights were on, and an officer peered through the passenger-side window of his car. As Wes gaped, another cop stood upright on the driver's side. Wes slunk back around the corner, praying they hadn't seen him.

Chapter 31

Caleb

Fire razed his body, burning Caleb conscious. He sat up as fast as he could. The pain localized to his gut and throat, and Caleb recognized the sting. His liver tumors pressed into his belly while he slept. Gastric liquids roiled up into his esophagus. The acid reached his throat, but the burn he was feeling wasn't heartburn. He had aspirated on fluids from his stomach.

Sputtering, Caleb rose to his feet. He coughed, sending a vaporous burn into his sinuses. He pulled himself toward the bathroom. A rancid sweetness filled his palate, threatening to make him retch. He made it to the bathroom before his stomach contracted. His torso locked, the pain intense as he vomited what little he had in him.

As the heaving subsided, Caleb's skin wept a cold sweat. Any energy regained from his sleep had just gone into the toilet. He braced himself on the sink, afraid that the black haze in his vision was a sign he would pass out. He opened the small window, wanting some fresh air to clear out the acrid smell.

The cloying odor of wet trash wafted in. He closed it, needing no more prompts to throw up.

Caleb ran the water. He cupped several handfuls into his mouth, clearing out the acid tang. After he swallowed a few sips, the burn subsided. Caleb grabbed a washcloth from the towel bar. Hoping it was clean, he scraped out the thick paste that had accumulated in his mouth.

The cool water felt good. It calmed him as he rubbed his wet hands on his face, cleaning out the gunk from his eyes and around his mouth. He sucked in a few more breaths, trying to bring his body back under control. The pain was falling, but he would need to dose up soon and stay ahead of it. He raised his head to the mirror over the sink. The surface was disgusting, an amber film staining the reflection of himself. Even his eyes had a yellow tint to them.

Caleb pulled the towel from off its hanger, wetting a corner and wiping down the mirror. This stain wasn't coming off. Caleb stopped wiping the mirror, realizing that the stain was moving across the mirror with him.

It wasn't a stain. It was him.

He had jaundiced overnight. The dark scoops under his eyes. The ochre tint in his sclera. His face wasn't the right shape either. It was gaunt. At first he thought it was the crack running down the height of the mirror. Moving from one side of the crack to the other made the sullen cheeks and sharp bones worse. Caleb had lost considerable weight in the last few days.

His face tightened in a grimace. The shock of seeing such rapid decline in himself transformed into prickling fear. His frown intensified. He would lose what composure he had left. A familiar pressure filled his skull. A knot formed around the right side of his mouth as the voice arrived.

It's not long now. Two days, maybe.

His face unknotted, but his lips continued to tremble. The terror of death being so close. He knew it was coming, and he wanted to meet it standing, with acceptance. But he could see it now, painted on him. As if death had caressed him while he slept. Seeing it draped on his own face made him want to run. Claw away from it, kicking and screaming. To wring out another day, another minute, another moment of living.

Stop. It will be okay, Caleb. There is still plenty of time. And you're so close now, you know that? An hour from the boy. I knew you'd make the right choices.

In a heartbeat, the rattling fear in his chest turned into rage. "Where the hell did you go?"

What do you mean?

"You've been silent! We've had to deal with some intense stuff! Why didn't you come to help us?"

I guess ... I mean I'm confused. You're on the right path. Where you need to be. What should I have done?

"For starters, tell us about that police checkpoint? Or warn us Irene would freeze my accounts so we could have left home with enough money?"

The voice was silent. Caleb stared at himself in the mirror, waiting for the telltale tic on his lips. The face that stared back was angry and tired.

Caleb slapped the edge of the sink, stinging his hand. "Answer me!"

Look, you're doing fine on your own, right? And besides, how was I supposed to know those things would happen?

Caleb's eyes widened. Incredulity spit from his lips, "What the hell does that mean?" He tightened his grip on the sink, feeling it give a little from the wall. He leaned closer to his reflection in the mirror. "How could you not—"

A stern pounding on the door interrupted the thought. He scanned the tiny room. His son was missing.

"Where's Wes?"

The door burst open.

Chapter 32

NESTOR

The little orange light on the dashboard blinked. The car was running on fumes. Nestor lifted his foot from the gas, hoping to keep the car alive long enough to make it to the truck stop ahead.

"Please," he asked the beat-up Nissan, "please make it to the gas station." The subcompact sputtered in protest. He pulled up to the red light. "It's only another fifty feet."

His phone rang. The opening harmony of "Fat Bottomed Girls." It was Caterina again. He answered the call, not waiting for her to speak. "I'm on my way. I just need gas."

"You should've been here ten minutes ago," she jabbed. "Why am I not surprised?"

"I said I'm on my way, Cat! Ten more minutes is all."

"You're making me late for work!" Her voice went shrill. "I'm calling my mother. I should have asked her to watch Armand. She would have been on time!"

Dammit, there it was. "You know you have to ask me first."

"I called you first, asshole!" Caterina hissed. "And you had every chance to say you couldn't make it, Nes!"

"Cut me some slack, Cat!" She loved throwing the separation agreement in his face. Following it to the letter. Cataloging Nestor's mistakes to use against him later. "I'm not dumb, you know? I know what you're doing."

"What? Trying to get to my job? So I can earn a living? Pay for rent and food?"

Nestor laughed, "No, you know better. You keep setting me up to fail. You already got full custody, and now you want to take away my visitation too."

Caterina sighed. "I don't have time for your shit. I'm calling my mother and leaving as soon as she gets here."

"No, wait, Cat!" Nestor pleaded. "I'll be there in a few minutes, okay?" Silence. "Cat?" The line went dead. Nestor huffed and threw his phone on the floor. He'd already been to court several times to keep the visitation he had. He saw Armand one day a week, and every other weekend. It was like not seeing him at all. Every week the boy was bigger, different, using unexpected words. Nestor had a few hours every week to get to know his own son. And yeah, he had missed two or three visits, but paying child support means you need money. Money came from working. Work was where and when you could find it. Nestor had to be flexible, but his ex-wife had no such demand on her in making Armand available to him.

The traffic light changed to green. Nestor whispered a prayer to Saint Christopher and lifted his foot from the brake.

He set his eyes on the truck stop ahead and tapped the accelerator. The car bucked. Nestor switched from silent prayers to verbal cursing, willing the car forward with spite. The car stuttered.

Nestor steered the car into the station as the Nissan belched one last gasp and the dashboard lit up. The breathy noise of the tires on the pavement became prominent, his engine no longer active. The pump crept up alongside as the car coasted into place.

He released the breath he was holding, thanking heaven for small miracles. He heaved himself out of the car, the struts protesting until his feet found the ground. He headed toward the building, reaching into his pocket and pulling out a wad of bills. Sifting through them, Nestor made sure he had at least ten bucks for gas. He smiled as he counted out eighteen dollars. Another miracle.

Nestor signaled the cashier, giving her two fives and pointing to his car. He walked back to the pump, checking his watch. He was cutting it close on time, but he still had a few minutes to pick up tacos from Sammy. Armand would like that. Cat might even appreciate it.

Nestor shook his head as he fitted the nozzle into the open gas tank. No, she wouldn't appreciate it. She would complain about it. "Nestor, the boy's sick and doesn't need tacos!" she'd say. It didn't matter what he brought. Food? "It will make Armand sick." Medicine? "That's the wrong kind." Games? "Too engaging, the boy needs rest." A movie? "Too violent."

Nothing Nestor did was right, and Caterina made sure he knew it.

His anger pumped in time with the gasoline. Why should he have to choose between seeing his son and working to pay child support? That's the position Cat was forcing on him. See Armand, then miss a job and be short on his support payment. Or miss his visitation so he could work and earn the funds. See his son and go to court, or not see his son and work to pay the boy's mother. It was a shit sandwich, and it was the only food Cat knew how to make.

He would set her straight, though. He'd show Cat what a father does. He'd figure it out, make it work. She'd see it. Take him back, and they'd be a family again. He had a bead on a construction job in Uvalde. If that panned out, he'd have good money for a few months.

The pump slapped off, the lever snapping open in his hand. Nestor reseated the nozzle and closed the gas tank. Sammy's tacos would fix anything, including this bleak mood he'd found. He left the car by the pump and walked toward the building. The smoky odor of chorizo hung in the air with the smell of gasoline and tires, and Nestor's stomach rumbled. He pulled open the door, waiting to let a pair of men exit before he rounded the entrance.

"It's just for a few days."

Nestor stopped and turned. A man was looking at him, boring into him with piss-yellow eyes. Nestor backed away at the sight of him. Translucent skin, face blotched with wrong colors and hanging off his skull, lips trembling as if he was freezing. Nestor raised his hands, as if the man's appearance would reach out and assault him.

The other man—younger, less ragged—stepped over and pulled the yellow man by the elbow. "Sorry, don't mind him." Nestor took them in. The old man, a brace on his arm, clothes loose and stained with sweat. The younger man, shirt smeared with filth, eyes straining in their sockets. Christ help them, what had they been through?

Nestor watched as they left through the door. The old man hesitated, but the younger man insisted. Nestor shook his head as he turned toward Sammy's counter. He had his own problems today. He didn't need distractions.

As Nestor walked through the aisle, he called out, *"¡Oye, Sammy!"* The cook poked out of his window and saluted him, his face breaking out a crooked smile. Nestor held up four fingers, and Sammy nodded, getting to work on the tacos.

Nestor walked over to the coffee counter, putting together a large coffee for himself. He carried the coffee to the refrigerator. Scanning the rows of beverages, he found the chocolate milk that Armand loved. As he approached the food counter, Sammy had the tacos ready in a brown paper bag for him.

"¿Qué onda?" Sammy asked.

Nestor took the bag, smiled at his friend, and replied, *"Todo bien, todo bien. Hablemos más tarde,* okay?"

Sammy nodded and focused on another customer as Nestor went to pay for his food. He dropped the wad of eight dollars on the counter. Not waiting for the cashier to count it, Nestor headed for the door. The bag warmed his hand. The salty odor of egg and tortillas wet his mouth. His stomach grumbled, knowing food was close. Nestor figured it would be okay to eat on the way to Armand. His son wouldn't mind.

He backed out of the door, pushing it open with his ass and turning to face the day. Sunshine filled the sky; Nestor raised his face to it, thinking about the day ahead with his son. They would play board games, rest, laugh together. Maybe he would even tell Caterina about the job. Then again, maybe he wouldn't.

He walked back to the pump, stopping when he saw the pickup truck where his car should have been. Thinking he was looking at the wrong pump, Nestor walked to the next lane of pumps. It was empty. Nestor stood still, his face falling. He scanned the last row of pumps. His car wasn't there either. Eyes frantic, his chest tingling with anxiety, he scanned the pumps. The lot. The road. His car was gone.

Nestor's food and drink hit the ground.

Chapter 33

CALEB

"**D**ammit, son, slow down a second!" Caleb was frantic, terrified by what Wes had done, yet his voice came out pathetic and whiny. The seat belt yielded in fits and spurts until he landed it in the buckle with a soft clunk. The rush of running from the motel was catching up with him. His body aches became pointed. His breathing couldn't happen fast enough, and Caleb worried that he would pass out. His fanny pack dropped to the floorboard. "You're gonna get us killed, Wes!"

"I'm going to get us out of here," Wes responded, his voice brisk. His eyes bounced from the road to the rearview and back with an intensity Caleb hadn't seen before. Was his son afraid? No, Caleb had seen fear in Wes many times. This was something else. Something far from fear. A smile spread on Wes's face. His son chuckled, and it grew into laughter. Caleb swallowed his discomfort. His son wasn't afraid—this was elation.

As if confirming, Wes released a maniacal yawp and punched his fist into the roof of the car. Caleb withered at the noise, shying to the far side of the passenger seat. He looked to the side-view mirror, glancing back at the truck stop. The man who owned this car wandered the pumps, clutching a paper bag. Caleb's heart dropped when the man raised a hand to his head. Wes jerked the car around a corner. The gas station disappeared behind the highway overpass.

Caleb turned to his beaming son. "We shouldn't have done that! This isn't petty theft, Wes!"

The smile on his son's face didn't falter. "Pop, we'll fix it after Utopia." He dismissed his father with a wave of his fingers. Caleb sighed and turned to the road, putting a hand over his mouth. He could feel his son glance at him. "If you want, give that guy your nice-ass Beamer as a thank-you."

"We left that man stranded back there!"

Wes groaned, "Goddammit, you're ruining this buzz with your moral edge, you know?" The car slowed to a legal speed. Wes threaded the dirty compact through the rolling hill country. "If we hadn't taken this car, we'd be in custody. Waiting for someone else to choose what will happen to us while you fade away."

Caleb's mouth opened as he searched for words. Wes didn't give him the chance.

"Look at yourself, Pop. You're beyond sick now. I may not remember Mom, but I've seen the dying, enough to recognize it." His son looked back at the road for a moment, but returned his steady smile to Caleb. "You don't have the time, Pop. I'm getting you to that boy, come hell or high water."

They sat in silence for a minute. Caleb scanned the spiral backcountry drive as it wound through a mass of small bushy trees.

Wes cleared his throat and said, "Achieving balance requires patience." His tone and cadence mimicked someone else, perhaps the original source of the words. "You've been patient, Pop. You've suffered, and now the universe is correcting itself in this ..." Wes waved his hand at everything around them. "... this glorious moment of redemption."

Caleb licked his dry lips. He shook his head, replying, "I don't buy it."

"What? What's the issue?"

"The logic, it doesn't hold up. Why would the universe need correcting? If this is some ... blessed crusade we're on, why are we hitting any obstacles at all?"

Wes eyed him with curiosity, his smile replaced with a look of interest. "How do you mean?"

Caleb shifted in the seat to find a more comfortable position. "The roadblock, the police finding your car, Irene freezing my accounts? If this is a correction, why would any of those things happen? Why not—hell, I dunno—zap away my cancer while I'm in my bed in New Mexico?"

Wes shrugged, his head lilting to the side. "Regardless, here we are, on the road to Utopia. Because some disembodied voice told us it would help you. And considering we're almost there, I'd say things are going our way."

"No," Caleb retorted, his voice cracking, "no, see, I don't feel the same. This is wrong! We shouldn't have to steal things to make this happen if we're so ..." Caleb struggled with his words. Was he conning himself? Wes was so fixed on the idea that this entire trip was some kind of mission from God. But why hadn't the voice warned him about the troubles they would hit? Let them prepare instead of having to improvise their way across two states?

Wes sighed and pointed toward the road ahead. "Look, we're only forty minutes from Utopia. Do you still have that map in your pack, Dad?"

Caleb reached down, lifting his pack and removing the map of Texas roads from the front pocket.

Wes added, "I penned some marks of our route, once it leaves I-10."

Caleb searched through the folds of the map, looking for their current location, while the rattle of garbage in the backseat filled the silence. He followed I-10 east on the map until he found an ink circle around Junction, Texas. "Looks like Highway 83 south a ways, then a left on State Road 39, and then 187 will take us all the way into town."

Wes repeated the names of the roads, playing with the words out loud. Caleb folded the map, cramming it back into his fanny pack. He held the pack loose in his lap, wondering whom this car belonged to. He opened the glove box. It exploded in a mess of papers on the floor.

"What are you doing?" Wes asked.

"Trying to figure out who this car belongs to." One piece of paper stood out from the pile of receipts and mail. Caleb reached down to pick up the expired Texas vehicle registration. It had a name on it—Caterina Ramos—and an address.

Caleb unzipped his pack again, pulling out the paper napkin and pen. He unfolded the napkin flat on his thigh. Beneath the note describing the waitress, he copied the name and address from the car's registration.

Wes snorted. Caleb glanced up to see his son smirking at him. "You're keeping ... what is that, a crime ledger?" Wes chuckled. "How bean-counteringly unnecessary."

Caleb was in no mood. He finished taking down the address, cramming the loose papers back into the glove box. Something was blocking it from closing. He sifted beneath the raggedy pile of stuff, and his fingers found a solid metal lump. He pulled it out, curious, and held it in his open hand.

It was a toy car. An El Camino. White, with red flame marks on the hood. Like a tiny, clean version of Wes's car they'd abandoned at the motel.

Wes snatched the toy from his dad's palm, holding it up and inspecting it. "Holy shit, it's my ride!" He grinned at the discovery, nodding his head. "See, Pop? Tell me this isn't a sign that we're supposed to be in this car, right now." Wes thrust the car back into his father's hands, closing Caleb's knobby fingers around the toy.

"You keep that, Pop, to remind you. Remind you we have a mission. No one else on earth, Pop. Just you and me. We're doing this thing, and you'd better start believing in yourself. And in your purpose."

Caleb tucked the napkin back into his pack and set it on the floor. He held the car in his fist, thumbing a wheel as he considered his son's logic and the road ahead.

Chapter 34

WES

Dad faded in the passenger seat. Wes couldn't blame him. The adrenaline rush from stealing the car had burned off, and their stomachs were still empty. Driving through the curves and hills required concentration. Wes trusted the road signs and murmured the little travel ditty to himself again. "Highway 83 to State Road 39, then south 187 to the end of the line."

They passed countless outfitters and tubing-excursion businesses. Wes recalled this part of the trip followed a river as it wandered the Texas Hill Country. The road crossed the water now and then, giving him a brief glimpse at a slow and calm waterway. People played in the river, some in tubes, some not. Wes imagined Pop in a tube on the water, healthy, enjoying a beer. The image made him smile.

A signpost showed the turn onto 187 was coming up, and a kick of excitement hit Wes in the chest. He looked over at Dad, who stared out the passenger window at the passing bushy trees that lined the road. "Hey, Pop! This is it, the last road before we get there!" His dad acknowledged him with a weak nod.

After a few minutes, they breezed through Vanderpool. That was the last town on the map before Utopia. Wes's mind started considering their next steps.

"So, once we hit Utopia, should we head straight to that restaurant and wait?" he asked his father.

Pop groaned instead of answering, putting a hand on his gut. His breathing became rapid, shallow.

"Pop? What's wrong?"

He tried to make words, but they wouldn't form on his shallow, staccato breaths.

"Do you need your pain meds?" Wes shouted.

Dad didn't answer and fumbled with his pack. He unzipped the main compartment, spilling the contents on the floor. Bending to collect them, he moaned in pain.

Wes pulled the car onto the shoulder, stopping under the shade of a gigantic oak. He reached into the backseat, pulling a bottle of water from the carton set among the pile of debris. He bolted from the car and ran around to the passenger side. Opening Pop's door, Wes found his medication spilled across the dirty floor mat. Wes knelt, picking up the oblong tablets and placing them back into their bottle.

He placed one tablet into his father's mouth and raised a bottle of water to his lips. Pop swallowed between gasps of pain. Wes wiped spittle from Dad's cracked lips. He was getting dehydrated. "You need to keep drinking this, okay?" Pop nodded, folding his shaking hands around the bottle.

Wes stood and took in the road. Grass fields framed the patched asphalt. The occasional line of trees marked the edge of someone's property. Wes's body retaliated for the morning's fight-or-flight session. He needed to take a piss. He turned around, eyeing the oaks separating the shoulder from a farm.

"Listen, I'm going over there to take a leak, but I'll be right back, okay? Pop? Can you hear me?"

He nodded once, enough to show that he understood. Wes walked across the dirt shoulder toward the trees, the ground hard under his feet. Turning his head back to his father, he said, "You keep drinking that water."

Wes found a gap between the oaks large enough for him to pass. The trees offered privacy from the road. Beyond them, several acres of low ground cover expanded around an open metal barn. The sun beat down through the leaves above, warming Wes's head and shoulders. The light and shadow created a pattern on the ground—eyes staring up at him.

Being watched made it hard to pee. Wes closed his eyes, thinking of the river he'd seen on the way here. Relief came, blissful, bordering on painful. The patter of his stream accented how quiet it was. There was a slight wind stirring the leaves above him. Some grinding bugs somewhere beyond the barn. The natural beauty of the soundscape deteriorated as a puttering motorcycle growled.

Wes finished, zipped up his jeans, and pulled his shirt away from his gut. He turned to make his way back through the trees to their car. The deafening buzz of a siren revved his heart into overdrive.

He peeked around the oak tree. A highway patrolman made a U-turn on his bike, pulling up behind the car.

Wes's gaze traced the car's frame to his father. His dad gaped back at him, a hand pressed against the window, mouth trembling, eyes wide and yellow with fear.

Chapter 35

DEMETRIO

The midday Texas sun pulled the sweat out of Demetrio Cruz. But the breeze created by his Road King wicked the moisture off his skin. He revved the engine, feeling the vibrations through his pelvis and legs as the bike hauled him home. He should wear his helmet. It was the law, and he was a lawman. But the exhilaration of the wind on his face sure beat the hell out of setting a good example.

His shift had been quiet, most of it spent at his desk catching up on paperwork. The night had been boring, but boring nights were the pleasant ones. When things weren't boring for Cruz, people were heading to a hospital or to jail.

After work, Demetrio took his time on the serpentine roads, taking pleasure in each curve. He had two stops this morning. He'd done the first—visiting a small grocery where he packed his saddlebags with fresh fruits and vegetables. Now he was on his way to his second stop—to deliver those foods to Mrs. Park and her family in Utopia. He had made it a point to visit them once a week since her stroke last year. Cruz smiled, thinking about her remarkable recovery. The elderly woman had been nonverbal, confined to a wheelchair on her better days, bedridden on the others. At least, until her daughter brought her to church. The kids doted on Mrs. Park, asking her where she'd been, giving her hugs, and offering prayers. And then, the miracle. She stood. She hadn't gotten on her feet in a year. But then, her frail form straightened from her wheelchair. Her feet popped off the flanges and onto the floor. And she stood. She rose from her chair at the front of the church, wrapping her arms around the boy hugging her. It stole the air from the room. Everyone stared at the living wonder, stunned and silent.

Then came the most incredible moment, at least for Demetrio. She sang. So quiet at first, you could hear it only as an echo, the words to "Amazing Grace" sketched in their ears. But Mrs. Park found her voice. The tentative hums grew into her tenacious alto, which no one had heard in years. Once the congregation started breathing again, their voices joined hers. The space between them disappeared in worship and wonder.

She'd been at church every Sunday since, healthy as ever. More than healthy, even. Her slack face and atrophied muscles came back toned, strong, and supple. She radiated now, engaged with the community in ways she'd never been. Cooking, teaching, leading. It was, Demetrio knew, a genuine miracle of God. Mrs. Park was a living testament to His power and glory.

Demetrio steadied the bike, decelerating as he entered a turn, then opening up again. The center of gravity drifted back under him, keeping him in the tight side of the curve. When he reached the deepest part of the turn, Demetrio twisted the throttle. The bike howled forward, and he relished the sinking sensation in his gut.

The curve passed, and as he merged onto 187, something whacked his forehead. The bike wobbled as he shook off the sting. He reached up, peeling the remnants of the bug carcass from his face. As he flicked the dead bug into the wind, he made a promise to himself to wear his helmet from now on.

Distracted by guts on his face, Demetrio didn't see the car parked on the shoulder until he was upon it. He slammed on the brakes, careful to watch the front of the car for people changing a tire or working under the hood. As he reached the car, he saw the driver's seat was empty, but someone sat in the passenger seat.

Probably out of gas, the driver walking into town to fetch some from Jerry's station. It was a solid three- or four-mile walk, and although Cruz wasn't on duty, he was still obligated to help if he could. Past the car, he worked the bike in a slow arc across the road until he passed it again. He flipped on his lights, accidentally turning on the bike's siren. The still Texas afternoon shook with a dissonant howl.

"Whoops, sorry," Demetrio said to his bike more than anyone else. He pivoted behind the car. A blue Nissan, an older model, Texas plates. He didn't recognize the car. It wasn't common for tourists to take 187, but it happened. The bike came to rest, and he lowered the kickstand with a practiced flick of his heel.

Demetrio dismounted, hoping the shade would keep the veggies in his saddlebags from wilting. He wiggled his belt, setting it on his hips, and took in the scene as he approached the passenger side of the car. Backseat was empty except for some trash—well, mounds of trash. No driver. Passenger was an older male, maybe sixty. Light features, and ... goggling at Demetrio with a look of raw panic on his face.

Something felt wrong. Cruz widened his path around the car, taking in more details. The car's engine ran. It wasn't out of gas. The patrolman turned his practiced gaze to the road, scanning for anyone walking 187. No one. No cars. No people.

"Sir, are you okay?" Cruz asked, his voice carrying authority. He fumbled with the radio on his belt.

The man stared back at him, lips puttering in fear, his eyes wide and trembling in their sunken sockets. Could be drugs. He could be afraid of having the car searched.

"I asked if you're okay. Do you need help?" The radio finally loosed from the holster. As Demetrio brought the radio to his face, he locked eyes with the old man in the car. Cruz flipped the talk button and called his identity into dispatch.

He waited for a response. The old man's gaze left his. It moved past Demetrio and into the space behind him. Cruz followed the old man's wandering attention.

Another man poked his head around the thin line of trees on the shoulder.

If the man in the car was panicked, this other guy was shitting-his-pants terrified.

They stood for an expanding moment. Cruz realized his hand rested on the butt of his revolver. A reflex from his unease. Demetrio took a deep breath, trying to stay relaxed and open to what was happening around him. He asked the petrified pants-shitter hiding in the trees, "Are you two in need of help here?"

The unlatching of the door spun Demetrio back to the man in the car. His voice took on a level of control. "Stay in the car!" He had walked into something that smacked of danger. His training and self-preservation instincts took control.

Demetrio turned to the man in the trees, commanding, "Move to the back of the car! Is there anyone else with you?" He felt the weight of his gun. He knew he'd loaded it with six bullets.

"No, Officer," the younger man said as he inched around the trees, his arms raised, compliant and meek. Cruz chanced a glance at the older man in the car. He braced himself against the open passenger door, clutching at his chest.

The man's eyes gaped in his skull and fixed on Cruz, skin splotched and ruddy. One hand drew his sweat-soaked shirt into a knot. The other clutched the open door in a death grip. The man croaked, a broken, dry whisper. "My chest ... I'm having a heart attack!"

Chapter 36

CALEB

The officer crossed the mirror as he approached the car. Static flared through Caleb's chest, his body tightening into a fist. Why did his pain have to strike now, when they were so close? Why couldn't Wes have just held it a little longer?

No, he couldn't think that way. This officer was on this road with them, coming from or heading to Utopia. There was no avoiding this.

The officer's voice stopped the world, the baritone resonating through the window as if it weren't there. "Are you okay, sir?" His tone was cautious. He knew about the stolen car.

Caleb strained in his seat to see the officer. He was rounding the car in a wide arc now, his posture wary, his movements deliberate.

Caleb turned forward. What the hell should he do? Movement caught his eye. The patrolman was outside his window now. Neither Caleb nor the world around him breathed as the man raised something from his belt. Was it a gun? Too big.

A radio. The patrolman was announcing their location. Caleb sucked in an agonizing breath. They were done for.

Was Wes hiding? Did he know what was happening? The thought pulled Caleb's gaze away from the officer, to the line of trees behind him. Wes skulked by the largest tree, watching them. His face soured with fright. He looked like his father felt.

Caleb pressed a hand to the window. His son's attention turned to the cop. Caleb's eyes followed.

The officer locked on Wes. His hand fell to his gun, his stance widening. Shit. Shit! How could they have gotten this close only to blow it?

The voice. Would it help? "What do I do?" Caleb heaved, his breath locked tight in his chest.

Nothing.

The officer issued a command to Wes. "Move. Move to the car." His tone wasn't pleasant anymore. He knew. He would stop them here.

"What do I do!" Caleb spit, watching his son step over the thick roots, his arms over his head, raising his shirt and exposing his belly.

His deaf ear remained silent.

The officer tracked Wes, turning his body to try to put both men into his field of view. Wes padded out from the trees, glancing at his father. His son mouthed the words, "I'm sorry, Pop."

And that was it. All of Caleb's pain, his good intentions, his forethought to plan a Final Release. It was ruined. The officer would arrest them. Caleb would die today, tomorrow, or the next day, away from home, in a strange place, with no one he loved around him. His heart ached knowing it.

And poor Irene. Instead of a quiet passing, she would need to deal with this mess now. Twenty-four hours of panic they'd caused her. What in hell had he done to his daughter? She would never have accepted what they were trying to do. His chest clenched when he thought of her remembering him this way. The man who ran from death like a damned coward, only to die alone on a dirty Texas road.

His breath stunted, his vision blurred, his son becoming a blob rolling to the back of the car. His son. God, his son. What the hell would happen to him now? These were his last moments of freedom. What would prison do to him? He was soft, a schemer. Not a brute. He'd had a chance, only twenty-four hours ago, a chance at a healthy life. To turn things around for himself. But Caleb took it away from him with this ... this ... this what? This wasn't an adventure anymore. This wasn't a journey of hope. This was a road trip through hell. Pain stabbed through his limbs like an electric current.

Caleb owed his children. There was more he needed to do for them. In his good ear, he could hear the whoosh of his pulse grow louder, feel the pressure of it in his cheeks and face. As if his body was a size too small for his heart.

The waitress, her money. The man they abandoned when they stole this car. He owed them too. The pressure twisted in him, the surge expanding against his skull. Caleb could feel the fear and the static solidify in his chest. It grabbed him, turned from emotion into something physical. This pain was unfamiliar. Each beat of his heart became deliberate, thick, moving sludge through his body.

This couldn't end here. Caleb had so much to fix now.

His hand fell down the window to the car's panel, finding the latch to the door. His heart beat once—thud.

The car door opened before Caleb realized he was doing it. His legs were heavy, his chest exploding. Thud.

His lead feet found the ground. He pulled his screaming body off the seat. Thud. Pressure filled his head. Not the voice. Something else. Something new.

The officer's attention turned to him. Thud. He was shouting now. *Stay in the car.* Thud. The colors of the world pulsed from vivid to gray with each slam of his heart.

He took a step. The edge of the door pushed sharp into the flesh of his hand as he used it to hold himself up. Thud. Caleb's vision narrowed around the officer.

"My chest," Caleb said, staring at the man. "I think I'm having a heart attack."

The officer was on him in a moment.

"Help me," Caleb said.

The officer's voice was clear over his slamming pulse. "Lie down, sir. I'll get you some help." Caleb felt the man's fingers cupping the back of his head, the patrolman's other hand finding the small of Caleb's back. His bottom touched the earth.

Caleb's arms reached up. They wrapped around the officer's torso. "Help ... me!"

"Sir, please, I am trying to help you," the officer said, twisting around to remove Caleb's grip.

Caleb pushed his fear into his arms. He tightened his hold. The officer tensed, eyes flashing with realization.

Caleb glared over the officer, to Wes. The kid was standing there. Mouth open, eyes wide. No idea what to do. "Help me!"

The officer's hands reached for Caleb's arm. The movement was deliberate, strong. Caleb pushed his arms closer, one hand finding his braced wrist, and winced at the sharp pain as he squeezed his arms tighter. The officer cried out, realizing what was happening. Caleb couldn't hold him for long.

Through his clenched teeth, he spit at his son, "I said, help me!"

Chapter 37

WES

Panic clawed at Wes's throat. His breath shortened as he watched the cop ease his father to the ground, as if his dad might shatter.

Pop's hands scrambled around the officer's body. This was it. Dad would die right in front of him. His pain must be immense, skin glowing maroon as he struggled. The officer tried to settle him. He needed to call an ambulance. Why wasn't the officer calling a fucking ambulance!

Dad's arms closed over the cop's waist. Wes's hands lowered—the image made little sense. Dad wasn't flailing. This seemed purposeful.

The officer sensed it too. One hand gripped Pop's arm; the other clambered for the pepper spray on his belt.

The logic of it snapped together. Holy shit! His dad wasn't having a heart attack!

Pop's head appeared over the officer's shoulder. He locked wide and tight eyes with Wes. A look of determination, his teeth gritted behind his lips, peeled back in struggle.

Over the rush of his own heartbeat came Pop's strained voice. "I said, help me! Fucking help me here, Wes!"

A flame raced through Wes, loosening his arms and leaving them flopping about as he searched the ground for ... for what?

The cop found a grip on something from his belt. As he jerked the item loose, he commanded, "Sir, let me go or I'll be forced—"

Wes didn't think as a twitch of panic pulled on his muscles. He looked at the dead branch of the oak tree, somehow in his hands now. He took three strides to the men on the ground, raising the branch over his shoulder. The only sound was the breath of air as he swung, followed by the dull crack of the branch connecting with the crown of the cop's head.

Whatever was in the officer's hand fell to the dirt. He remained frozen, motionless, squatting over Pop, held up by air, for one prolonged moment. Dad stared up at the man, then at Wes, his face wide with horror.

The patrolman slumped forward, landing across Pop's chest, pushing a puff of dirt into the air.

Wes looked back to his hands. The branch had broken, splintered remnants left clutched in his fists. Blood—his own blood—filled the gaps between his fingers, seeped between his palm and the wood. Wes dropped the split branch to the ground. An ache flowed through his arms.

He turned to his dad. The officer's body lay over him. Writhing. Like a caterpillar, rolling forward. Except ... it was

Pop, trying to shove the officer off him. Wes grabbed the cop's shirt with bleeding hands, and heaved him off his father.

Wes looked to Pop. He was breathing heavily, eyes watering, easing himself onto his side. Wes shifted to the patrolman. The officer wasn't moving. His breathing was shallow. The cop's hair matted against his head. Bloody. Dirty. The sound of moving air filled Wes's ears. He realized it was the sound of his own breath, his chest heaving it in and shoving it back out.

His father got to his belly, rose on all fours, coughing as he crawled toward the Nissan. Wes reached for him. Blood covered his hands, and he wiped them across his jeans before helping Dad to his feet. Wes settled him into the car, his frayed nerves starting to tremble in his arms.

Wes picked up the bottle of water from the floorboard. He washed the blood and dirt from his palms. Fetching another bottle from the backseat, he pushed it into Pop's hands and cracked the seal for him. "Drink this, Pop. Try to calm down."

Dad was silent. He shook, but he was safe. Wes turned around and surveyed the scene. The cop was unconscious. Wes couldn't leave him here. They needed to tuck him away. For a day or two, that's all. What else? Wes looked around. The bike. He needed to hide the bike.

His eyes found the road. It was still, no movement except for the haze of heat. He turned back the way they had come. It was empty. A long breath hardened his resolve as he walked over to the officer. Hooking his hands under the officer's armpits, Wes began dragging him toward the trees.

His body was heavy and uncooperative. It took too long to move. Wes's neck twitched from scouring for the eyes he felt on him. He saw nothing except the bark of the trees, the light making patterns like stunned faces.

A grunt popped from Wes's gut as he heaved the bulk of the officer's body around the large oak. A few more feet, and the cop was in the barn.

Wes pulled the cop behind a stack of straw bales. He set the man upright against a rusted steel barrel with a few heavy pops and clanks. Wes cursed under his breath at the noise. The officer was still out. His body pliable, his breathing remained shallow. Blood seeped from the head wound, but not much. That was probably good. Putting fingers to the cop's throat, he found a steady pulse. Wes figured that was a positive thing too.

He looked toward the open wall of the barn. This spot wasn't visible from outside. Perfect. Wes patted the officer's belt, finding the stiff metal of the handcuffs. He opened the cuffs and secured the officer's wrists to the heavy shelving welded to the barn wall. His injured fingers groaned as he fumbled with the officer's belt buckle. After a few pushes and pulls, the belt released and Wes placed it behind him.

His pockets contained a handful of bills and an ancient flip phone. He tore open the cover, pulled out the battery, then tossed them to opposite sides of the barn. In the officer's back pocket, Wes yanked out a folded bandanna.

He fell back on his haunches, considering the cop. He'd take the radio and the gun, and he had disabled the phone. How else could this asshole give himself away? Wes looked around the barn. Organized tools filled the far wall, well out of reach of the cuffed patrolman. Nothing else around him but bales of hay. Or was it straw? Hell, it didn't matter. The only other way this prick could call attention to himself was to yell. Wes stuffed the officer's own bandanna into his mouth as a gag.

He lifted the officer's head by the chin. With his other hand, Wes pried open one of his eyes. The pupil was wide. Was that right? Or wrong? Wes couldn't be sure. Were Pop's pupils wide after he'd collapsed on the street? Or were they narrow? Maybe he should wake the officer. Explain that this was for a day or two, at most. Wes debated, losing count of the unconscious man's shallow breaths. He snatched the officer's belt, stood up, and left the barn.

Back at the car, Wes dropped the belt at Dad's feet. He looked behind the car. The officer's bike stared back at him, headlight wide in appalled judgment. Wes approached the bike, taking the handlebars and wobbling it across the road and into the tall grass. He walked fifteen paces into the field, then let the bike fall to its side. Walking back to the road, he checked his work. The bike wasn't visible, and there was only a slight dent in the meadow where he'd entered.

Was this how Irene felt when she was problem solving? Ticking off the things, making a goal attainable piece by piece?

The thought was random; Wes was unsure where it came from. He paced over to the passenger door, still open while Pop sat slumped in the front seat.

"Can I have ..." Wes looked into the branches above, calculating how much water he wanted before huffing out, "... two of those bottles of water, Pop?"

Dad nodded, reaching into the backseat and producing one bottle at a time. Wes held the bottles in one hand. An unease came over him, a tumbling insecurity.

"Dad, do you ... want to leave a note, or something?"

After a long moment, Pop closed his eyes and shook his head.

Wes returned to the barn. The officer sat hunched where he'd left him, cuffed to the heavy shelving and unconscious. His head painted with blood, it seeped over his face and stained his khaki shirt. Had there been this much blood earlier?

He considered where to leave the water so the man could get to it. A shallow gesture, Wes realized. "You're gagged and bound," he said aloud. "How will you even drink it?"

Wes debated for a moment. He left one bottle on the officer's slumped chest and took the other with him as he walked back out of the barn. He emptied the plastic bottle before making it to the trees, discarding the bottle on the ground

At the car, he fell into the front seat, exhausted. Dad sat silent and still in the passenger's seat. Wes waited a breath, then revved the Nissan and put it into drive. With a heavy yoke, he moved them back onto southbound 187.

Chapter 38

CALEB

The car's bald tires spun on the cracked pavement, filling the space with an unsteady hum. Neither man spoke.

Caleb tried once, turning to his son to check if he was okay. The sight of the glistening streaks stopped him. He hadn't seen Wes cry in years. Caleb realized his own face was wet as well.

Were those tears of sadness on his son's face, over what they had just done to that poor man? Or was he crying at the joy of what they were about to accomplish?

He didn't ask. Wes wouldn't know the answer. Caleb sure as hell didn't know the answer either.

An incessant clanking pulled Caleb's wet gaze to the floor near his feet. As the car moved down the road, the vibrations set the little toy El Camino bouncing against the barrel of the officer's gun. It made a sharp, pinching tap. Metal on metal. Arrhythmic, cacophonic. Caleb reached to his feet, carefully lifting the toy off the pistol. He rose, unsure of where to place the toy. He stuffed it into his fanny pack.

"We're here." Wes's voice was hoarse and dry, yet there was a rise to it. "We made it, Pop."

Caleb lifted his gaze to the road. A sign, whitewashed plywood and hand painted with large red print, greeted him: WELCOME TO UTOPIA. THIS IS GOD'S COUNTRY. PLEASE DON'T DRIVE THROUGH IT LIKE HELL.

UTOPIA

Chapter 39

CALEB

His son had been right: Utopia stuck to the road. A thoroughfare formed the vein of commerce and traffic. Capillaries of ranch roads and residential areas branched into the hills.

Caleb had ridden the length of town in a daze. The shock of what they had done pressed on him. The town's southern edge snapped him out of the fugue. The buildings ended as the road disappeared in a turn, the view obscured by maple trees. They turned around, paying more attention to their surroundings.

The restaurant was easy to find. Wes had recognized the sign from the video. The Silverleaf stood alone, a converted two-story house wrapped in cream clapboard and finished with brick-red trim.

If the roads were veins, and the people were the blood of this small town, then this place must have been its heart. At least forty people had come and gone in the two hours Caleb waited at his table in the corner.

Wes had dropped him here. Caleb was concerned about separating, but Wes was in no shape for public viewing. He said he would clean up, figure out where they could stay, after which he would return. That was two hours ago. Caleb's waiting had turned to worry. Maybe the cops had found Wes. Maybe he had left. Caleb's hand sought the bulge in his fanny pack. He felt a twinge of guilt at doubting his son. Relief that he still had his medication.

"Nothin' else?" the waitress asked, her tone short. It was the fifth time she had asked, and it would be the fourth time Caleb ordered nothing. From her scowl, the waitress seemed irritated at his loitering.

"No, I'm just waiting for someone," he said. He held up his mug and added, "I'd love a reheat, though."

The waitress left, then returned with another cup of hot water and a selection of tea bags. Her smile stopped at her eyes as she left to take care of someone else.

Caleb tore open the single-serving mint tea and landed it in the steaming mug. The sharp and clean aroma did little to calm his nerves or his impatience. Caleb knew he was an awful sight. Sweat and dust stained the cuffs of his shirt. Hemorrhages darkened his hands, but the space between them glowed as the bilirubin built up in his body. He worried about how he was behaving, how people perceived him.

It was more than being a stranger in this town. The incident outside Utopia cracked his core. He hadn't thought about what he was doing until he opened the car door. The voice wasn't offering any help, so he had just acted. And then Wes took action too. The violence shattered Caleb. As he sat alone with his thoughts, he realized why.

Deep down, Caleb had understood what he was doing. How his son would react. Relied on it. Trusted it would happen. He had forced Wes to take action, and he knew what that action would be.

His son swung the branch. It was a terrible choice. But he had manipulated Wes to make it happen. Caleb had made a plan. He put it together in the moments between opening the car door and standing up. It wasn't one choice. It was a logical sequence of events he conceived and put into motion. That he would be so cunning, so thoughtful around harming another person—that's what bothered Caleb more than anything.

Wes had assured him that the officer would be fine for a day or two, until they could get this done. Before they separated, Caleb asked for his phone, and Wes flat out refused. His son didn't trust him not to call the authorities, tell them where to find the incapacitated patrolman. It was a good bet— Caleb had spent the last two hours perseverating on ways to get the officer anonymous help. If he had his phone, he would have caved and called 911.

Caleb repeated the mantra in his head. "Find the boy, fix the cancer, then we can fix the rest." Another day at most. Then he would welcome any punishment given, make any amends possible, if it took him the rest of this new life.

After waiting through the lunch crowd at the Silverleaf, Caleb wasn't so sure. The whole effort was fragile. Illogical. Wes was on his own. Caleb was in a random place, hoping to find a stranger. He didn't know how long he should wait. For the boy. For Wes.

And the damned voice had been silent since this morning. He had reached out to it several times, but heard nothing. Just deafness in his deaf ear.

Caleb sighed, shaking his head. When had he become so prideful? Why would he get to cause so much suffering, only to help himself? He had had enough. He cursed his feeble mind and body for fooling him into nurturing some hope. He would pay for his two-hour tea; then he would walk outside. He'd head to the fire station. Tell them about the injured officer. After that, come what may. He pushed up from his chair.

A warmth moved under his skull, a bliss worming out from wherever the voice lived.

Caleb turned to the room. Near the front entrance, he found his waitress nuzzling a ruddy and dusty boy, talking to him. The kid squeezed her, hands interlocked around her back. As they parted, Caleb recognized the demure child from the video. Heat filled his cheeks. His head spun.

He took a moment, some time to consider his actions. Should he approach them? What would he say? How would they react? Caleb ran his hands over his wrinkled and stained shirt, trying to clear the detritus it had accumulated over the last day. Why the hell hadn't he spent the last two hours thinking about this moment?

The moment was here, now. The opportunity would pass, whether or not he acted. He chose to act. Caleb took a few steps toward the mother and her boy. He looked from his disheveled clothing to find the kid staring at him from across the room.

The look on the boy's face flushed the warmth from Caleb. The boy's mouth was agape. His eyes saucers, hands frantic on his mother's apron as he struggled to move behind her. To protect himself. To hide from Caleb.

The boy was terrified of him.

Chapter 40

EMERSON

Emerson lowered his head into his shoulders. He hoped to disappear into the crowd of kids leaving the elementary wing of Utopia School. His feet shuffled across the wide lawn, his eyes fixed on Main Street ahead. He chanced a look behind him, checking for Henry and his friends. They were somewhere, searching for him. They had promised they would pound Emerson to dust after school.

Emerson had made a mistake during recess. That's why Henry was mad at him, why he and his friends were looking to beat him up. That morning he had seen the kink in Shannon's Lavender halo. Her heart was sick. It would get worse in a few days or weeks. So Emerson stood behind Shannon when she got in line for the swings at recess. He smoothed the refractions through her heart. But his hand ended up stroking her wavy brown hair, just enough for her to notice. She turned around and started calling him names. Creep. Touchy McStalkerson. Shannon was going with Henry. Even though

Emerson didn't understand what that meant, he knew Henry was mad at him now.

Mom would be upset too. She told him to stop helping people on his own. To wait for the right moment. When she was there and could keep him safe. Emerson understood. He'd known for a long time that few people believed he could do what he did. But also, Emerson couldn't help himself. The light was pretty when it was right. When the light was wrong, though, he couldn't look away. Like an itch he could scratch with his eyes. And besides, he was helping people, and helping people was a good thing to do.

Emerson reached Main Street, his heart jumping in his chest. He stopped at the curb and waited for the crossing guard to signal that the street was safe to cross. She was talking with a driver, her halo glimmering with the color of limes as she laughed. Her lovely light did nothing to calm Emerson's nerves. His shoulders hunkered up to his ears, he turned his head back toward school. Peeking through the gaps between the bigger kids, Emerson saw him.

Henry. And two of his friends—Juan and Miguel. They ran down the school yard in his direction, heads circling, eyes searching.

Emerson sucked in a breath. His legs itched to run. They were looking for him. Coming his way. When they reached him, they would tear him apart.

Emerson turned back as the group of kids began moving across the street. He kept his head down. Stayed in the middle of the kaleidoscope of colors shining from the crowd. He reached the opposite side of Main Street. Over the din of kids ready for their afternoon free time, Emerson heard it.

"There he is, man! Across the street!" Juan had seen him.

Emerson hugged his library books to his chest and broke into a run. His backpack slammed against him with each footfall. The binders and books shoved him forward, then pulled him down with each slap of his sneakers. He could leave it. Run faster without it. Deal with the anger Mom would have if he lost his backpack again. Emerson knew it wouldn't matter. Henry and his friends were bigger. And they were faster than he was. They'd catch him either way, and if he dropped his backpack, he would never see it again.

The crossing guard shouted. Emerson turned to see Henry and Juan running across the street. Cutting around the cars stopped in the road, they made a beeline for him. Fear tingled through Emerson's tummy and into his legs. He made those legs pump as hard as they could go.

"Don't you run, freak!" Henry. His voice was deeper than those of the other boys. His body was bigger too, and his light was never still. From what Emerson had seen, Henry was full of rage now. Ugly colors spitting out of him. No pattern. No control.

Emerson had to get to the diner, to his mother. He would be safe there. His feet stung as they beat the dirt. The heavy backpack shoved the air out of him as he ran faster. Faster. Unable to catch his breath. The flops of other feet grew louder behind him. He was three blocks from the Silverleaf. He might make it.

"Here we come, faggot!" Henry hollered. Juan's sick laughter followed the insult.

Emerson bolted into Lee Street without looking. The shrieking brakes of a car startled him, but he didn't stop running. He glanced to see the driver's light twitching with shock. Emerson shut his eyes as he turned back toward Mom. Two blocks away. Maybe she was outside, waiting for him. He opened his eyes.

A blur. Then the ground leapt up at Emerson. His hands took the fall. Emerson's books scattered in the surrounding dirt. Then his bulky pack landed hard on him, sandwiching his body to the ground with a puff of dust. Before he could sense any injury, Emerson felt a yank on his pack. Someone flipped him. Miguel's snarling and pimply face leered over him. Henry and Juan appeared a moment later, Henry panting after the chase.

Henry bent, grabbing Emerson's shirt with two fists and lifting him up, only to slam him back into the ground. The binders in Emerson's backpack ground into his spine and shoulders. Then Henry did it again. The third time, spots filled Emerson's eyes. Not normal spots, like the lights from people. These were all in his head.

Henry dropped a knee on his chest, leaning his weight into Emerson's body. His face eased close, their noses almost touching, the smell of gasoline and bubble gum pouring off

Henry. He waited there, inches from Emerson's face, letting him stew in his fear. Henry was enjoying this now. Emerson saw it in his Silver and Yellow tones. The halo never lied. After a forever moment, Henry spit in Emerson's face and hissed, "You weird piece-of-shit freak."

The large boy rose and balled up a fist. Emerson held his breath as Henry punched him in the gut. The pain was immediate, explosive, brilliant. Emerson coughed, his breath leaving him.

"That's for making me chase you!"

Henry's fist rose. He aimed higher this time.

"And this is for putting your freak hands on my girlfriend."

Emerson gave up. He clamped his wet eyes and went limp, waiting for the pain. Maybe this time Henry would stop after hitting him once. He might split Emerson's lip straightaway, or break his nose on the first try. Then he would leave Emerson alone.

Instead of pain, there was lightness. The other boy's weight disappeared. Emerson opened his eyes. Henry was in the air, held up by his shirt, which wrapped around an immense fist.

It was Mom's new friend, Jaime. His Indigo light shone steady and bold. Henry flailed and kicked, his halo bounding around him like a goldfish out of the bowl.

Henry screamed, "Stop it, man, I was just playin'!"

Emerson looked for the others. Juan and Miguel were gone.

Jaime's eyes lowered to Emerson. "You okay, boy?" His voice was deep, stern, no hint of effort at holding Henry's squirming bulk off the ground.

Emerson swallowed and nodded. Jaime pointed behind him with his chin, toward the Silverleaf. Toward Mom. "Go. It's Wednesday. Get you some kuchen." Jaime turned his face to Henry. "Tell your mom I'll be back in an hour."

Emerson gathered his books, stumbled to his feet, and ran. He didn't look back. Over the slaps of his sneakers on the pavement, he could hear Henry hollering, "Let me go! C'mon, man, just let me go!"

Emerson checked the traffic before crossing Jackson Street. His shoes crunched on the gravel in the road, and he didn't stop moving until he reached the door of the Silverleaf. Mom wasn't outside.

He chanced a glance back toward school as he pulled at the door, but Emerson didn't see Henry or Jaime. He clambered into the restaurant and dropped his bag and books by the door with a puttering thud.

It took him a moment to adjust to all the light, all the people. He recognized Mom by her pattern—the Scarlets and Oranges radiating out and in as she took care of people at the tables.

She saw him and smiled. Emerson waited as she set down her water pitcher and walked over to him. She eyed him up and down, a puzzled look on her face. She would ask him what happened, Emerson realized. How he got so dirty. Why he had been crying. He wrapped his arms around her tightly, squeezing his face into the warmth and safety of her tummy.

She hugged him back. He could feel her kissing the top of his head and listened as she sucked in a long sniff of his hair. She knew. She always knew when he'd tried to fix someone. She said she could smell it on him.

She pulled away from him, and his eyes met hers. He couldn't read them, but Mom's light showed how worried she was. "You did some work today, Em?" Her tone was firm, her voice quiet against the din.

There was no reason to hide it. Emerson nodded, looking back into her belly. She opened the space between them and stooped down, holding his chin so his eyes rose to hers again.

"Oh, Em. We talked about this. It's dangerous to do that when I'm not around." Her face was hard. Her lips thinned. She was disappointed. Her halo didn't say if she was also mad.

Emerson knew better than to look away. "Sorry, Mama. I just wanted to help Shannon." Tears rolled from his eyes again. Not from fear now, but frustration. "She would have gotten sick someday."

Mom smiled at him. "I know, sweetie." She cupped his face in a tender hand and wiped away his tear with her thumb. "And you're a good person for wanting to help her. But not everyone understands, Em."

Emerson nodded again, tears flowing free. He wasn't sobbing, not yet. He swallowed his nerves, waiting to see where Mom went next. Was she only disappointed this time? Or was she angry with him?

"My darling boy," she whispered, the smile spreading across her face and into her eyes. Emerson relaxed into her Pink tones. She pulled a napkin from her apron and cleaned his face. After another kiss on his forehead, she pulled away and motioned to the counter seating. Her voice took on a playful tone as she announced, "It's Wednesday, which means ..."

Emerson lit up around his tears. Wednesday! That meant ... "Kuchen!"

"Kuchen!" Mom confirmed with a bright smile and wave of Red light. Mom moved to the side, wrapping an arm around Emerson's shoulder as she walked him toward the counter.

The lights from the people at the tables mixed with the sounds and smells of the place to weave a tapestry of the moment. The Olives and Sea Greens of comfort, the starbursts and twinkles of laughter, the various Blues as people ate themselves full.

Mom moved Emerson in front of her, and he stopped. Mom asked him a question, but Emerson couldn't hear her. His focus was across the room as he tried to make sense of something he had never seen.

There, on the other side of the Silverleaf, was a man. He was moving. Standing up from his table. It was wrong. There was no reason for this, no sense to it. Emerson's chest tightened, his breathing locked.

The man turned, looking over at him. At Mom. Under his gaze, Emerson felt it again—the rush, the tingle telling him to run. He tried, but Mom held him still.

The man moved, as if he was part of this living tapestry that surrounded Emerson every moment of every day. Except life radiated color. Everyone in the Silverleaf had a shine. A halo. Overlapping hues of Pinks, Blues, Purples, Oranges, and Greens spilled out from the people around Emerson.

Everyone, except for this man. This man had no light at all.

Chapter 41

BLAIR

She stumbled into Emerson. "Dammit, Em," she cursed. "You gotta be careful about getting in people's way!" Blair put a hand against her son's back, egging him forward. He wouldn't budge.

She stooped down to him, her other hand rubbing his chest. A calming gesture she called an Emerson sandwich. "Hey? C'mon, Em, what's up?"

His eyes were fixed. Blair followed his stare, landing on the man that had been bogarting the table for the last few hours. The tea drinker. He was standing now, staring at them. His face made an awkward smile, the kind pleasant men make on first dates.

Blair looked from the customer to her boy, confused. "Emerson, what's wrong, honey?"

Emerson ducked behind her in a flurry of fidgets. She straightened, surprised at her son's behavior. His face buried into her lower back, the bones of his nose and chin jabbing her backbone. His arms held her waist in a death vise. She turned her head, crooked an arm awkwardly around to stroke his hair. She smirked at how shy her boy could be. She hadn't any idea where he got it. Blair wasn't timid. And Emerson's asshole father was about as bashful as a horny dog. And less discreet. Yet somehow together, they had created this sweet boy. She turned, finding the customer approaching them.

"Oh, you can pay your bill at the register, sir," Blair said with her work smile. "I'll be right there."

The man stood there, running a hand through his hair and then over the stubble on his blotched face.

Blair squinted, confused. "I'm sorry, did you need something else?" She pulled Emerson around her, nudging him toward the counter. Her son bolted, reached the farthest stool at the counter. He scurried his small body behind it. His hands whitened as he gripped the pedestal of the stool. Christ, he was upset today.

"Is he your son?" the man asked. There was a lilt in his voice. A tone. It rubbed Blair the wrong way. The words were innocent, but the man's interest in her son was not.

Blair's mothering hackles flared. In a clipped voice, she replied, "I'm sorry?"

His hands fumbled, as if he didn't know what they were for. "My son—" He motioned toward the windows, to the world beyond. "My son and I. Ah, we came all this way."

Blair's brow furrowed. She stepped around the man, placing herself between him and her son. His eyes shot over her shoulder to her boy as the man licked his cracked lips. She slid into his gaze again, hardening her stare. "What is it you want?" she demanded.

"We ... ah ... we saw the video? With the deer?"

The lightness of adrenaline flooded her chest. Christ. That fucking video of Emerson and the deer! She knew it would cause trouble. Her eyes washed the room, looking for Jaime. Where was he?

The man closed the gap between them. Blair backed away, bumping into an empty table.

His eyes went wide, pleading. "Was it real? The video?" he begged. He was already nodding, waiting for the answer he wanted to hear. The loose skin on his cheeks stretched into a hopeful smile. He grabbed her upper arm, his fingers digging into her bicep. "Please, tell me!" he whispered in a quick breath.

The thrush of her blood filled her ears as she panicked, her hands rising up to protect her face.

"I'm sorry," the man gasped. His face fell as he let go and stepped back. Blair leaned farther into the table behind her. "I'm sorry, it's just that ... My name is Caleb. Caleb Allard." He held out a frail and skeletal hand, which Blair met with a tentative handshake. His skin felt brittle, reminding her of onion skin, yet the strength of his grip made her hand ache.

"Blair," she replied, releasing his hand as soon as she could.

"It is a pleasure to meet you, Mrs. ... ?" He trailed off, looking for her last name.

"Miss," she corrected him. She shook her head, folding her arms across her chest. "What do you want from me?"

People were paying attention to their conversation now. They heard the edge in her tone and saw her hardened stance. She could feel the customers' stares on them. That relaxed her a little, gave her a tepid sense of safety. These were her people; they knew her; they loved her. As if to prove it, Hue stood from his table a few feet away. He puffed himself up, his mechanic's coveralls stretching on his lean frame. "You okay, Blair?" he growled. She nodded, keeping her focus on the man in front of her.

The stranger pointed over her shoulder with a crooked finger. "Is it real? Is ... he ... for real?" he whispered.

Blair swallowed. She took a glance at the man's shoes. High-end joggers. Dirty, but new. Expensive. "Yes," she answered, returning to his gaze. "As real as you standing here." She struggled to recall this sickly man's name.

The man exhaled a single whimper, his eyes growing dewy. "I'm ah—" He stopped to wipe his eyes. "I'm sick, and I was hoping ..."

She and Jaime had talked about this. It wasn't safe to discuss Emerson in public. Blair held up a hand and interrupted him. "Not here," she snapped. The man's face wobbled as his voice stuttered. She turned to the clock over the service counter. "My shift ends in about an hour. Meet me in the park across the street from here. There's a wooden gazebo. You can't miss it. We'll talk there."

The man smiled. He wrung his hands and shifted his weight, as if unsure of where he needed to go. "Thank you," he sighed. And again, Caleb looked past her, to Emerson. His face stern, eyes focused. A look of hunger, of longing. He repeated in a breathy whisper, "Thank you so much."

Blair stepped into his line of sight again. "The gazebo, one hour," she said. The man grinned, turned, and hobbled toward the door of the diner.

She watched the man walk. He was frail. His clothes were dirty and stained with sweat. But they were brand-name. Blair called after him, "Oh, mister?"

He turned to her. He wiped tears from his eyes, his lips trembling.

Blair folded her arms and nodded over her right shoulder, toward the register. "You still need to pay your bill."

Chapter 42

CALEB

Caleb stepped out of the Silverleaf into the hazy afternoon. The sun was different here than in New Mexico. Gentler on the skin, it traveled through a deeper sky, and it didn't brutalize the earth like it did back home. In Utopia, the sun felt comforting instead of dangerous. Things had more of a chance to grow here, to fill in the space between buildings and roads. That made the air smell more lush and wet than out west.

Caleb glanced across the street from the shade of the diner's awning. The park was a flat acre of grass with a brown wooden gazebo a few dozen feet from the road. A crew worked on a stone wall at the close edge of the park, their trucks double-parked. He wanted nothing more than to get over there and wait for Blair and Emerson.

The tap of a car horn pulled Caleb's attention to the parking spaces in front of the Silverleaf, where he found Wes parking the Nissan. He walked to the driver's window, spinning a finger so Wes would roll it down. Anticipation had him shaking.

Caleb gasped at the cleanliness of his son's face. He had washed himself off somewhere, his skin shining. Gone was the panicked demeanor of the morning. The car was clean too. Wes had emptied the backseat, save the carton of water bottles. Even the outside of the car was free from the dirt and grime with which it had come.

"Any luck here, Pop?" Wes asked, his voice hopeful.

The rush of excitement splayed a smile across Caleb's face. "Yeah, it went well, son. I found him. I found the boy."

Wes sat up, anticipation widening his eyes. "You did? So fast? Holy shit!" He slapped the steering wheel with elation. He broke out the gummy smile. His honest smile. "I have to admit, Pop, I was afraid it might take a day or two. I wasn't sure the plan would work!"

"Yeah, me too. But it did! I saw the boy, and I met his mother."

Wes's eyes glowed. "So, did you ... ?" He gestured at Caleb's cancer-ridden body.

Caleb shook his head, his grin fading. "Not yet, she said to meet them at the gazebo over there soon." He turned, pointing across the street into the park. "You cleaned up?"

Wes nodded. "Made a few arrangements for us too." He released his seat belt and exited the little car. Caleb considered asking him for details, but decided against it. The day had wrung him out; he couldn't handle any more ups or downs.

They were close now. Minutes away. Across the street and Caleb would be well again. An hour from now, he would be cancer-free. A wave of giddiness tickled his ribs.

Wes handed him a bottle of water, taking one for himself, and they crossed Main Street to the park. The earthy odor of fresh masonry hung in the air. It mixed with the sweet smell from the pile of flowers the work crew pulled up to make room for their wall. Wes's arm snaked through Caleb's elbow. His son helped him move across the lawn and into the musty structure at the center of the park.

Despite his earlier enjoyment of the lazy heat, Caleb was thankful for the shade. Wooden benches lined the octagonal bower. He motioned to the bench farthest from them, the one that faced the diner. Wes eased him down onto the splintering seat.

Time passed, and Caleb kept laser eyes on the diner. Wes paced the edge of the gazebo, turning now and then to track the sound of a car or a voice.

"Is that her?" Wes asked, pointing at a tall brunette walking on the other side of the partially built wall.

"No, Blair's a redhead. Small, but you can't miss her."

A mud wasp buzzed by Caleb. He watched it circle and land on the railing. It crawled into a hollow of a papery nest on a post that supported the gazebo roof. After a moment it reappeared, somehow turning around so its head poked out of the tube first. It paused for a moment, pulsing its thorax before it shot into the air. Thin legs dangled from the insect as it spiraled awkwardly away, as if flying was just within its control.

Caleb's eyes tracked the wasp out of the gazebo. He saw a flash of unnatural red across the street. It was Blair. "There she is," he whispered, unable to contain the tingling excitement brewing inside of him and stealing his breath. He stood from the bench uneasily, his back and stomach complaining about the last hour of waiting.

Blair crossed the street beside a man built like a house. Caleb squinted, looking for Emerson. He couldn't see the boy. The giant stopped just before they reached the narrow paved path from the street to the gazebo. The man turned to Blair, a hand on her shoulder. He was speaking to her; Caleb couldn't hear the words but watched her nod adamantly. They moved toward the park. Caleb felt a chill, a compulsion to avoid the man's glacial stare.

The man entered the gazebo first, with Blair following. She still wore her work outfit, complete with the half-apron around her waist. The two were tentative as they settled against the railing on the other side of the rotunda.

Wes drew next to his father to place a hand on his back. Caleb stepped forward, but stopped. The brute held up a hand, showing they were close enough. Blair crossed her arms, her eyes tight and her mouth a stern line.

Caleb swallowed, missing the lightness of an hour ago. The boy wasn't here. Blair's face was passive. And this enormous man's posture was threatening. Had she changed her mind?

Caleb's throat cracked, and he took a glub of water. "Thank you," he said after wetting his throat. "Thank you so much for coming."

Blair nodded. "Of course. This is my friend Jaime." She nodded her head to the pile of bricks beside her. Before Caleb could acknowledge the man, she continued. "Y'all come far?"

Wes answered. "From New Mexico. It's been a"—he sighed, rubbing a gentle hand on Caleb's lower back—"long trip."

Blair furrowed her brow and pursed her lips for a moment. Her arms opened and her hands found the front pockets of her jeans. Her eyes never left Caleb. He felt her watching. Not just looking at him. Something in the way she was taking him in, like she was measuring him. It made him uncomfortable.

"You're sick," she said. It wasn't a question.

Again Wes responded, "He has cancer. It's terminal. We were hoping the boy—"

Blair interrupted him, "Emerson." Her gaze shifted back to Caleb.

"Of course," Wes continued, his tone placating and friendly. "Emerson. We were hoping Emerson could, you know, do the thing he did with that deer? On my dad?"

Jaime shifted his weight, enough for the wood joists beneath his feet to groan. Blair nodded. Her eyes fell to the floor of the gazebo, to a decking nail stalked several inches out of the floor. She picked at it with her Croc.

"What have y'all tried?" she asked, eyes down.

Caleb cleared his throat. "I mean, everything, I guess? Radiation at first, chemotherapy, stem cell replacement. The whole shebang. Nothing's stopping this disease," he said, putting a hand on his abdomen.

Blair nodded, looking up with a sympathetic smile. Caleb felt a slight unwind of tension as she replied, "I'm sorry to hear that. That sounds expensive and harsh."

"Thank you, Blair. I was preparing to ... for the end, you know? I've just been managing my pain. And then we learned about your son, Emerson. We saw the video—we couldn't believe it was real."

"Then why come all the way here?" she probed, her eyes curious.

Wes replied this time. "We got confirmation from a higher authority." His hand patted Caleb's lower back.

Blair's expression deepened into amusement. Her smile grew, rounding her high cheekbones. "I'll take your word for it," she said. Her face softened, along with her posture as she leaned farther against the railing. "He is the real deal too, ya know? I've seen it myself. Shit, I've lived it." Her face became thoughtful. "I swear, I ain't been sick since he started walkin'." Pride shone on her face, her eyes floating to the roof in a moment of remembering.

The moment passed, and Blair's wistful eyes fell back onto Caleb. She continued, "I've seen that boy heal the sick, Caleb. Seen 'im put broken animals back together. He's a miracle, you know? He's my miracle."

Caleb had no response to that. He believed her.

After a moment of uncomfortable silence, Blair sighed. "Look, I'm sorry to hear about your cancer, Caleb." He swallowed the thick suspense in his throat, waiting for her to go on. Over a sigh, her eyes walked him up and down again. She finally nodded, her face relaxing. "We want to help you, okay?" Her voice was warm now. Caring.

Caleb's breath became light in his chest. He couldn't help his eyes watering. He turned to his son. Wes had a hand to his mouth, as if he was trying to contain a joyous song from spilling out.

"But there are three things you gotta understand," Blair added. Her tone had turned to business. Professional. It pulled Caleb back into the moment, his eyes back onto her. "First, it don't always work, you know?"

Caleb gawked, unsure of what to say. "Sure? Okay? I mean we appreciate you trying. You can't understand—"

Blair interrupted him, "Second, we try it once, but that's it. It takes a hell of a lot out of him." She crossed her arms again.

Caleb nodded, insecurity blooming in his chest. He looked at Wes, who was a mirror of his own confusion. The warbling hum of the wasp returned. It circled behind Wes and then around Caleb's back.

"Of course, of course, I'm sure it'll be fine," Caleb said, turning back to Blair with a forced smile. He felt uneasy about something, but he couldn't find what it was. His voice became tentative, his tone pitchy and unconfident as he asked, "And the third thing?"

Jaime unclasped his hands, making his frame appear more intimidating. Blair's eyes locked onto Caleb's as she licked her lips. She gently cleared her throat before continuing.

"And third," Blair said, letting the moment hang in the air with the wasp, "we're gonna need five thousand dollars. Cash."

Chapter 43

IRENE

The Kimble County Sheriff's Office in Junction was a hell of a lot smaller than the one in Las Cruces. The building was older, but the interior was immaculate. A cloying flowery odor filled the single room, potpourri that was trying too hard. Three small metal desks took up most of the space. A young officer sat at a desk near the door, his work space taken by a CB radio and a laptop. His long face bore an eager smile. He stood, smoothing his pressed brown button-down and adjusting his belt.

"Good afternoon, ma'am. How can I help you?" His voice betrayed his youth. Irene looked at the nameplate pinned to his breast pocket. Leo. She wasn't sure if that was his first or last name.

"My name is Irene Allard," she replied, her voice breathy and impatient. "I'm here because you found my brother's car. It's part of a Silver Alert for my father."

Leo's smile widened. He turned his head, speaking into the room behind him. "Las Cruces was right, Sheriff," he called.

"She came all the way here." Irene leaned her head around Leo's solid build to see whom he was speaking to.

A woman stood from the metal desk set against the back wall and turned around. A loose blouse and dark jeans covered her lean frame. She waved Irene over and pulled a chair away from the empty desk.

"Go on ahead," Leo said, turning back to sit at his desk. "She's been expecting you."

An unease quivered in Irene's belly. The woman's stare was cool, her eyes piercing and sharp. Her face conveyed none of her feelings. She held out a hand as Irene approached. "Sheriff Dietrick," she offered. Irene took her hand. Her grip was solid, but not overbearing. "And you are Irene Allard." The sheriff motioned to the chair and Irene sat. The metal legs rubbed the floor as it took her weight, cutting the air with a sharp scraping sound.

"Las Cruces called us," Dietrick continued. "They told us to expect you. That was less than six hours ago." One corner of the sheriff's mouth ticked up in an amused smirk as she leaned back into her chair. "You must have been hauling serious ass to get here that fast."

Irene's eyes widened with mild surprise. "They called you?" she asked. "Why?"

"To let me know you were comin'," the sheriff replied, her tone showing that it should have been obvious. Dietrick regarded Irene for a quiet moment, crossing her arms. "And why are you here, Miss Allard?"

Dietrick's pale eyes were hard to read. Irene wasn't sure where to start. "I want to find my father. He's very sick, and I think my brother is manipulating him."

"Manipulating him? What do you mean?" Dietrick asked.

"My dad has cancer. He takes a strong opiate to cope with the pain." Irene heard her own words. The details of Dad's terminal illness had somehow become a secondary concern. She shook her head. This had gotten so fucked up.

Dietrick raised her chin. "I'm sorry to hear that—about your dad. How does your brother fit in?"

Irene swallowed her shame. "Wes's a lifelong addict. Not a recovering addict, just an addict. And my dad—Caleb is his name—he's carrying some of the most potent drugs in the history of the universe. He's got enough on him to keep Wes stoned for weeks."

The sheriff's gaze broke from Irene and moved to the floor between them. After a contemplative moment, Dietrick sighed and shifted her weight in her chair. "Miss Allard, is there any chance this is some kind of ... last rodeo?"

Irene knitted her brow, confused. She replied, "I'm not following."

Dietrick met her gaze again. The sheriff's eyes were narrow with concern, her lips pursed in an unasked question. "You said your dad was sick."

"Yes," Irene replied. "Pancreatic cancer."

Dietrick nodded, uncrossing and recrossing her ankles. Her voice softened as she said, "Your father's dying. Maybe your brother is taking him on one last trip? An adventure? Some 'guy time' together to untie old knots before ... ?" She trailed off, leaving the unpleasantness unsaid.

Irene shook her head. "No way. Thinking about someone else would be a first for Wes. Whatever he's doing, it's to benefit himself, I guarantee it. This entire thing is about Wes getting high, or Wes getting money." Her voice had expanded, her body tensed in the metal chair. Irene's fingernails dug into her palm as she clenched a fist in her lap.

"Okay, okay," the sheriff placated. She regarded Irene with a dour frown. Regret spilled through Irene at the look of disappointment on the woman's face. "Does your brother— Wes?—does he have a history of violent behavior?"

Irene fingertips went to her jaw. A reflex. She covered the motion by rubbing her cheek. She could feel the plate in her jaw under her palm. The hard knobs of the screws tightened into her bones.

"No." Conflict roiled through Irene as she said the word. It made her sick—why in hell would she cover for her asshole brother like that? Was she acting like Dad now? Giving Wes a pass by justifying shitty choices and behavior? And yet, labeling Wes as a violent person felt wrong.

"No," she repeated, shaking her head. "Violent" wasn't the right word for Wes, she realized. "Wes's just an idiot, Sheriff. He won't intentionally hurt our father." Irene thought for a moment while Dietrick eyed her. "It's more like Dad would end up abandoned, or find himself in danger because of a choice Wes makes."

Dietrick looked over at her desk. "Got it," she confirmed. A tightening of the woman's lips told Irene she was holding something back.

Irene leaned forward. "Sheriff?"

Dietrick looked up, but past her. Irene followed the woman's gaze, finding Leo taking copious notes. She turned, meeting the sheriff's eyes for a breath. Dietrick stated, "As you know, we found your brother's car at a motel off the interstate. We haven't located your brother or father yet. We finished processing the crime scene an hour ago, and—"

Irene cut in, shocked. "I'm sorry, a crime scene?"

The sheriff leaned back into her chair, nodding. Irene could almost see the dark cloud hanging over the woman's thoughts. "Sheriff!" she pressed.

Dietrick sighed. "While the police were checking out your brother's car, another one was stolen from the station next door. Witnesses describe two men, possibly father and son."

Silence hung while the sheriff ran a hand through her short auburn hair. Irene exhaled in a shudder. What the hell had Wes done?

Dietrick continued, "There's an all-points out. In every adjacent county. Extending as far as San Antonio, Austin, and Fort Stockton." The sheriff leaned forward, closing the gap between them. Her face softened, a kindness rounding her eyes. "Irene, when we find your brother and father, they'll be arrested for grand theft."

Wetness filled Irene's eyes. Sad tears. Angry tears. Because the thing she had feared most since yesterday morning had happened. Wes pulled Dad into some of his bullshit, and now everyone's life—and Dad's death—had become more complicated.

Dietrick's face remained mild and stoic. She opened a metal drawer with a clank, fetching a box of tissues and placing it on her desk. Irene plucked out a tissue and wiped her eyes, offering, "Thank you."

Dietrick nodded as she spoke. "Irene, there's something I don't understand about all this. If your brother just wanted to get high, or sell drugs, he could have holed up nearly anywhere. But he didn't. He's keeping on the move to something. They're going somewhere specific. Whatever's happening here? Wherever it is those two are going?" Dietrick leaned back in her chair, her face knotted in thought. "They seem awful hell-bent on gettin' there, don't they?"

Chapter 44

WES

Wes drove south, heading out of Utopia and into the hill country. Earlier, after leaving Pop at the diner, he spent the afternoon searching out a place to set up camp. Wandering out onto the ranch roads, he eventually found a tiny shack on an apiary. It was away from the major roads, surrounded by clusters of tall cedars and mesquites. The bees were active, but whoever owned the apiary was neglecting it. Most of the hives needed repair, and the weathered hut had been dusty and ignored until Wes cleaned it up. Every sign told Wes they could use the area overnight without being discovered. It was dumb luck or providence. Wes didn't care at this point. Either way, he would take it.

He parked the car beside the shanty. He looked over to where his dad sat puddled in the passenger seat of their car. He was defeated. Resigned. He had been from the moment Blair asked for money.

They'd negotiated. Wes explained their predicament. How they couldn't get the funds before Dad needed to be healed.

All thanks to Irene and her need to be right. Blair didn't care. Wes recognized the situation for what it was. It was a business transaction, like any of the hundreds of exchanges he had taken part in. Cash, if you didn't have it, you could fuck right off.

Wes circled the compact car, opening Pop's door and helping him to his feet. He led them up the two rickety steps to the screen door and inside. Wes had stocked the shack with essentials. He'd replenished their water supply, picked up a few cans of soup and some crackers. And toilet paper for the inevitable.

The ramshackle structure had little to it. A short wooden chair tucked under a small table. A field coat, moldy and ragged, hung from a peg next to the door. One wall was open, covered with a dilapidated screen that wouldn't keep the bugs out. A dusty hammock attached to a support post, intended to stretch to the opposite corner where another hook sat waiting. An empty rifle rack on the back wall completed the space.

Wes expected Pop to balk at the accommodations, but he didn't. Instead, he found the chair, pulled it out from the table, and collapsed into it. Wes shoved the carton of water bottles aside with his foot, giving himself space to sit on the floor.

For a long minute neither spoke. Neither looked at the other. Wes reached around his back, taking a water bottle and cracking the seal before offering it to his father. Pop took the bottle with reluctance. Wes hated to see him like this. To be so close to death and life at the same time. Wes had no frame of reference for what Dad was going through.

"We'll figure this out, Pop. We can still do this," he offered.

Dad drank, swallowing thick gobs of water and then exhaling a wet sigh. "Where the hell are we going to come up with five thousand dollars, Wes?" Dad's voice broke, and he sucked in a breath. It rattled, his chest heaving in spurts to take it in. Wes couldn't tell if it was from emotion or physical pain. "Irene froze my accounts. Even if we could convince her I'm safe and she thaws the money, the police would know. Christ, after what we've done to get here ..." Dad's voice failed him as his eyes brimmed with tears. Wes held his gaze, tried to shine confidence back into his father.

Wes nodded. "I know, Pop, and that's on me. All of it. I'll figure this out, okay?"

Dad sobbed, and his eyes lowered to the floor. Wes put a hand on his knee, but Pop wouldn't look up. Wes's gut dropped. His dad didn't believe he could do it.

Wes closed his eyes, allowing himself to feel crushed for a moment. Like the rehabilitation therapist had instructed him. No running from the negative emotions anymore. Acknowledge the genuine parts. Change the things you can. Start from where you are, with what you have. Wes opened his eyes.

"Okay, so, what cash do we have left?"

Dad sighed as he put the water on the table. He rummaged into his fanny pack, pulling out several bills and counting them. "I've got about seventeen dollars. And whatever you have on you."

Wes emptied his pockets onto the floor of the cabin, taking Pop's money and adding it to the pile. He counted it up, twice. "We have thirty-eight dollars and change."

"Okay, so only four thousand nine hundred sixty-two dollars to go," Dad snorted. There was a grim edge of gallows humor in his voice.

Wes looked at the screen door, to the little blue car. "How much do you think the car is worth?"

Dad shook his head. "Son, it's stolen. How can we—"

"Just guess."

Dad blew out a breath, his head moving side to side with calculation. "Hundreds? Maybe? Not thousands."

Wes nodded, looking for the positives. "Okay, that's something. We can pawn our phones. ..."

Dad lowered his face into his hands. His shoulders slumped forward. "Son, I think it's time we call Irene." He was giving up.

"No!" Wes's voice was loud, surprising even him. A rush of pride filled his lungs. "We can do this ourselves! Look how far we've gotten. We just have this one little wrinkle, okay?" He looked around the cabin again, determined that the answer lay close by. He saw the food, the water, junk from the car. ...

"The gun," Wes thought aloud. "The cop's gun. How much? Maybe five hundred dollars, right?"

"I don't know, son." His tone was dismissive. Wes could see him disengaging, his eyes loose and unfocused. He was slipping into a negative space, and would soon stop making choices altogether.

Pop continued, "Sure, let's use it to force them to heal me at gunpoint. Seems like that would fit our modus operandi."

Wes hated to hear him like this. He knew the headspace Pop was in. The cynical humor. Fatalistic thinking. That mind-set where you no longer see the possibilities. And they were so close now. They got to Utopia. They found the boy. Wes just needed to figure this out for him. Prove to Dad and Irene that he wasn't a total disaster.

He considered the gun. Robbery crossed his mind. He kept the thought silent and in his head. It would tempt fate yet again, but if it came to that, Wes was ready.

Fate! Wes snapped his fingers. Of course! "Ask the voice!" he exclaimed. He slapped his leg, punishment for not thinking of it sooner. "The voice brought us here—it must have a plan! It could see this coming!"

Pop shook his head, waved a dismissive hand.

"Can you try? What could it hurt?"

Dad sighed. His tired eyes wandered up, searching for something he couldn't see. After a long moment, his lips pursed. "Nothing, son. I haven't heard it since this morning at the motel."

Wes's back twitched. He shifted his legs to relieve some stress. As he jostled, his foot knocked into the small pile of money. Panic struck him as a few coins disappeared through the gaps in the floorboards. Wes made a mad grab at the cash, collecting the prize from the floor of the cabin. His heart sank at the knowledge they were further away from making this happen.

Shoving the cash into a wad in his pocket, Wes stared up at his dad. Tears streamed from Pop's eyes. He made no sound, his face eerily neutral.

Dad opened his mouth. His lips quivered. A spark of hope lit in Wes's chest. The voice. Was it here? Would it help them?

"I'm tired, Wes. I need to sleep. When I wake up, I'll call Irene."

The spark extinguished. There was no convincing Pop, not when he was in this mental space. Wes stood from the floor. He let out a slow sigh, mumbling, "All right, Pop. Let me get you settled."

Wes pulled the musty hammock across the shack. He helped his dad up and eased him into the woven cocoon. Dad grunted, squirming until Wes realized the fanny pack was under him. Wes removed the pack, hanging it over the back of the chair.

Pop panted, easing his body still and prone. He motioned a finger toward the chair where Wes hung the pack. "I'm having breakthrough pain, can you, please?"

Wes unzipped the pack, pulling out the prescription. He cracked it open and doled out a pill into his palm. He stared at the pill, his brow furrowing. There was no itch. No draw. It was only a thing now. Wes shrugged off the feeling, put the tablet onto Pop's tongue, and lifted the bottle of water to his lips. Yellows saturated Dad's skin. Wes wondered if the fading light of the setting sun was making it look worse than it was.

"Thanks," Dad said. His eyes fluttered closed. The hammock creaked as his body relaxed into it. "Thanks for trying, son. I'm sorry this got so sideways."

Wes set the bottle on the small table. The air was becoming heavy with damp, warning of a chilly night. Looking for something to cover his father, he took the field coat off the peg and rested it over him. Dad's breathing was deep and regular, a slight rasp marking the change from inhale to exhale. Wes contorted around the hammock, careful not to rock his father, and sat in the small chair.

He took a breath, determination stiffening his jaw. He still wanted to win. To figure this out for Pop. He lined up what he had on the table—two cell phones, the gun, the tiny wad of cash. He emptied his dad's pack. The note Wes wrote at the hotel this morning. Dad's makeshift napkin ledger. The toy El Camino. Wes looked up from the table, through the gaps in the siding to the actual car. He wasn't a math guy, but even he was able to run these numbers. His gaze sank back to the table as he blinked away tears.

A spike of anger thrust through him. He wanted to make this happen. This was to be his atonement. His big win, making up for all the little failures. Instead, it was ending in another defeat. Irene's voice popped into Wes's head. Judging.

Arguing. Wes's responses flashed quick across the screen in his mind. How could he have known this would happen? The voice wasn't helping them when they needed it the most!

Wes's fist slammed into his thigh, releasing a sharp pain. The discomfort faded, leaving a wake of pleasure behind it. He did it again. And again, relishing the endorphins racing through his body to hide the effects of the injury.

Fuck it. Fuck all of it. Wes eyed the script bottle. A thick orange cylinder, about the size of his palm. Inside were enough pills to kill an elephant. Maybe a herd of them. He opened the bottle, shaking out one pill into his hand. His heart skipped a beat. Anticipation of a release. A respite from the shame of his failure.

He wanted it after all.

He looked to his dad and then into the bottle, counting in his head. There were plenty for Pop and for Wes, for what they both wanted to do. Wes shook out another pair of pills. That made three. These were potent as shit. Three should do it. After some thought, he nudged the bottle, bouncing out one more. Four of them would definitely get it done.

Dad breathed steady as Wes closed the bottle with one hand. Wes laid the four pills out on top of the napkin on the table, folding it over to protect them. The last four pills Dad would have. He rose from the chair, pushing everything into his father's pack. He pocketed their phones and secured the pistol in his waistband.

Wes stepped out of the hut, easing the door closed behind him. He walked to the car, throwing the fanny pack into the passenger's seat before looking back at the shack. It glowed in the oncoming blue of night.

Sliding behind the wheel, his jaw clenched from determination. Or was this regret? He started the car. Before driving away, Wes whispered, "I'm sorry too, Pop."

Chapter 45

CALEB

A crisp chill slapped Caleb conscious. It was dark, a musty odor lay on the air, and he could hear a rustle nearby. Trees swaying. Insects creaking. He turned his head, seeing stars through the screen wall. His side hitched, the wobbly hammock making it difficult to move.

Caleb counted in his head, moving through the pain. As careful as he could, he put his feet on the ground. He changed to a sitting position, the hammock stretching at the shifting weight. His pain wasn't local anymore. It radiated through him, from each joint and muscle and bone. Had he missed a dose? He could remember Wes feeding him a pill. Caleb shoved off the worry that this might be the new normal.

A long canvas coat slid off his lap and pooled onto the floor. It gave Caleb something on which to focus. A way to isolate his consciousness from the breakthrough pain. He inhaled, trying to control his mind. "Pain is temporary," the mantra passed through his thoughts. Caleb exhaled, maintaining a steady breath. He spit shaking bursts of air as his muscles spasmed. Minutes passed as he repeated the exercise. Tears formed. Caleb continued to focus on the field coat.

His agony tapered from constant to moments. The sound of his pulse faded in his ears as the pain moved away.

Caleb nudged the coat with his foot. Wes must have covered him with it after he fell asleep.

"Wes." Speaking hurt too, Caleb's mouth dry and cracked despite the cool wet air. He cleared his throat, the flavor of pennies hitting his tongue. He sucked in another batch of air, the chill settling him. He repeated the call to his son, "Wes?"

No answer came over the rapid staccato of chirping crickets and grinding frogs. Caleb moved to his feet, steadying himself with a hand on the cabin wall. His legs took his weight, and he looked about the cabin. Wes wasn't there. He must be asleep in the car.

His eyes eased into the surrounding night. The pale light of a low moon filtered through the trees. Caleb looked to the table, finding a half-full bottle of water. He drank it in small sips, giving his stomach time to wake up.

His pain had ebbed, but he needed to stay ahead of it. Where was his pack? He checked the table again, not finding it. It wasn't hanging off the chair either. Caleb searched the floor with his feet, locating only the hard shell of canned food and cardboard. Maybe Wes took it to the car with him.

He sipped at the water and leaned into the wall. Leaving the bottle on the table, he pushed open the flimsy door. The rusty tension spring squeaked as Caleb found the two steps to the ground. He regretted the clack of the door slapping shut, silencing the insects nearby and potentially waking his son. With the wave of pain receding, Caleb realized he needed to urinate. He wandered around the side of the cabin, finding a suitable target in a young cedar tree.

Relieving himself took longer than he thought it would. Standing still and pushing his abdominal muscles left Caleb dizzy. He took a moment, leaning against the outside of the cabin, while his vision cleared.

The stars in his eyes dissipated, and Caleb looked to the sky. The actual stars in the deep dark watched him from across a wide and clear dome. Trees stood still and tall around him, stretching up as if they were pointing back to the stars.

A jagged thought came to Caleb: this was the last night sky he would see. It wasn't the voice's admonition yesterday. Caleb could feel it now. Death was looking at him. Waiting. These moments were among his last.

As if he needed reminding, a stab hit his gut, and he doubled over to his knees. He breathed through it. He willed it to pass. It subsided after a moment, and he eased off the ground. He stumbled through the gray night to the front of the cabin. He hated to wake up Wes, but Caleb had to have the meds in his fanny pack.

The long rows of beehives captured what little light was available and threw it back out. Caleb heaved himself toward the road, one foot, then the next. The four lines of hives rocked past him.

The scrunch of his sneakers on the loose rock told him he reached the gravel. He looked up the drive. It went straight for a stretch, then bent around some mature cedar trees and disappeared from view.

Caleb's brow knotted in confusion. Wes must have moved the car. He turned around, finding the other side of the cabin. His eyes had adjusted enough to see that the car wasn't there either.

Anxious, his heart quickening, Caleb returned to the cabin. He moved the chair, searching for his pack. Nothing. His meds. Missing. Their phones. The revolver, the officer's belt, all of it, gone. Caleb's anxiety balled up and expanded, his nerves rising in his throat.

He rummaged through his own pockets, and then through the pockets of the field coat. They were all empty. The nausea solidified, sinking in him like a stone.

As he looked around the cabin, Caleb's gaze fell to the table, and to the wadded paper there. He picked it up and opened the crinkled mass. A few small objects fell from the paper and into his palm. Pain meds. Four of them.

He shook open the wad with one hand. It was the note Wes had left him in the motel yesterday morning. "I'll be back. Trust me." Someone's blood stained the corner of the napkin, a memento of yesterday's violence.

Caleb fell to the small chair, clutching the meds and the note in his fists. He couldn't believe it. Wes did it. That petty asshole did it. Wes chose the wrong way again. And like he'd promised he would, his son took his shitty choices and disappeared from Caleb's life.

The sinking stone in him landed. Wes had left him here. To die. Alone.

Chapter 46

IRENE

The duck stared at Irene. Irene squinted back from the bed. The duck had not blinked in the half hour she had locked eyes with it. One wing lifted from its body. Tense, as if the bird were about to snap open in a frenzy of wobbling flight. But the animal didn't move. The floodlight passing through the window blinds left a stipple of light across the black orb of its eye. The waterfowl remained still, on the top shelf of the bookcase, a moment of living captured like a breath in a bottle.

It wasn't the only harrowing object in the room. Taxidermied animals covered every wall. Irene would never have stayed here, but the motel in Junction was a nonstarter. It was the only motel in town, and Sheriff Dietrick had insisted that Irene keep away from it. In exchange, the sheriff promised to call if she received any news.

Irene sure as hell wasn't traveling away from the only lead she had on her dad. So she took a chance on the simple solution. Airbnb listed a single room near Junction. A semiprivate cabin on a large ranch estate just fifteen minutes north of town. Decorated by a man, probably. A man who enjoyed killing things, then making them look alive again. Ducks lined the shelves at the foot of the bed. An owl lit on a tree branch attached to one corner of the room. Perched opposite, a kestrel gazed in endless majesty at the hideous toile wallpaper. The one outlier in the avian flock was the beaver laid out on the wall shelf next to the bed. It stood right outside Irene's periphery, but she could not unsee it. Game birds, birds of prey, and mammals surrounded her in an apneic chorus, and their heavy silence kept her awake.

Out of any animal in the room, this goddamned duck was the only one in the perfect position to watch her sleep.

Irene slapped back the covers. She hoped the air of the room was cooler, that it could temper her growing anger and impatience. Instead it was tepid, her skin sticky. The bed became stifling. She rotated on her side, pushing herself upright with her arms to avoid tweaking her back, and found the floor with her bare feet. She plucked her hair tie from the nightstand and pulled her hair up off her sweating neck. She padded over to the shelf, looking at the three ducks arranged in a parade. Standing on her toes, she reached up to the last follower in the line. Being careful with the delicate animal, she spun the waterfowl a few degrees to her right. In her head, she mapped out the duck's view like a laser coming out of its eyes. Her slight rotation should be enough to shift the bird's empty focus from the bed to the owl in the corner. Those two could spend all night staring into each other's eyes.

The red digits glowing on the clock by the bed read four a.m. Even after trying for six hours, Irene hadn't slept. Instead, her brain did that thing it liked to do—think. Then spin. Then move on to spiraling. Her body and mind had fidgeted for hours. She knew sleep wouldn't come. Not without help. She looked at her backpack on the chair under the fucking owl. She kept a few emergency Xanax in the inside pocket. They might calm her nerves, put her out for a while. She considered the idea for a moment, then shook her head. The last thing she wanted was the mental haze that came with the drowsiness. Fuck it. Her brain said she was awake, so she was awake. That's all there was to it.

Irene moved to the en suite bathroom, fetching a paper cup from the dispenser and filling it with lukewarm tap water. The flood lamp outside created enough light for her to see the puffs under her eyes. She rubbed them with her free hand, trying to wring out the sleepiness from her face. She craved rest. She had gotten no real shut-eye since that nap she took at Dad's place, and she had been running near empty before that.

The buzz of her phone snapped her head back to the bedroom. Irene downed the water in one gulp, leaving the cup in the sink. She scampered across the bed to the nightstand. The clock knocked against the wall as she grabbed the phone.

She checked the caller ID. It was Sheriff Dietrick. Irene answered the call as she sat back on her haunches.

"Sheriff?" Irene spoke in a near shout, unable to hold back her anticipation.

"Ms. Allard, sorry to wake you." The sheriff's voice was even and clipped as ever. "I promised to let you know as soon as something new came in."

"Not a problem, I'm not sleeping." Irene swallowed, girding herself for the worst. "So, what's happened?"

The clacking of a keyboard came through the phone. "Looks like Wes used his cell phone. Once, but we narrowed down where he is."

Irene stood from the bed, the suspense making her body itch. She paced around the bed. "And where is that?" she asked. She started cramming her dirty clothes into her backpack, getting ready for the next phase of this shit show.

Clickety-clack. "San Antonio. The cell tower he hit was on the west side of the city." The sheriff was silent for a breath.

Irene stopped packing, waiting for the news. "And?" she begged.

Dietrick sighed. "Police also found the stolen car abandoned at a gas station in the area where the call was placed."

Irene zipped up her pack. "And my father?" she asked. "I guess you would have led with that if you'd found him?"

"No, I'm sorry, Ms. Allard, no sign of either your father or brother. Your brother's phone was still in the car, though."

Frustration brewed through her cranky body. She sighed a little too hard.

"Irene"—the sheriff's voice rose with curiosity—"does your brother know anyone in law enforcement?"

Irene shifted the phone to her other ear to allow her arm to slip into her blouse. She snorted. "I'm sure Wes is familiar with the whole damned New Mexico law enforcement family, Sheriff. Why do you ask?"

Dietrick sighed, then deflected, "Something they found in the car." Before Irene could ask what the hell that meant, the sheriff continued. "Ms. Allard. Irene." Her tone betrayed an ambivalence to continue.

With her jeans halfway up her legs, Irene had to stop, her body jittering through a flush of panic. She braced herself with a hand on the nightstand. She was as fragile and frozen as the decorations in the room. "What the hell is it, Sheriff?"

"Irene, the police found your father's prescription bottle inside the car. It's empty."

The words spun through Irene's head. She heard them, yet her brain wouldn't put them together. The implications were too dark. She eased her jeans to her waist, fastening them as she sat back on the bed. Around a thick swallow, she asked, "Sheriff, what does that mean?"

Dietrick clicked her tongue on the other end of the call. "I imagine you know already. I'd appreciate you meeting me back at the office as soon as you can."

Chapter 47

CALEB

The sky lightened, but dawn did little to stem the cold and damp. Neither did it calm Caleb's worn nerves.

He slumped on the steps of the shanty, wrapped in the field coat to conserve his body heat. But the chill had reached his bones, and the metallic odor of mold from the duster stabbed his nose.

Three meds left. At the rate he was taking the pills, Caleb calculated these would last ten hours. Twelve if his pain was mild. He had taken one a few hours ago, after finding Wes gone. He kept the pill down through the rubber-banding of his emotions. The wringing anxiety of figuring out what to do. The gut-twisting worries over Wes. The crushing depression as Caleb thought over the impact of the previous two days.

Ten hours. Would he even live that long? Was this place, this lonely pocket of nature, where he would die? Caleb shook off the fear. He had to try. Find someone to help him. He had no car, so he would walk. But where? Tall trees blocked his view of the surrounding hill country. Caleb looked east, to the rising sun. That oriented him at least. Utopia was to the north. But how far was it? The farm roads they'd taken here split and twisted through the hills. Caleb hadn't paid attention when Wes drove them here. Had they passed any houses? He didn't remember.

If he found a phone, he could call Irene. She would figure it out, find him, get him safe, and then do the same for Wes. She would be angry. There was no reasonable explanation to give her around why they'd embarked on this fool's errand. And that's exactly what this was, with Caleb as the fool. It didn't matter. He had no phone. Wes must have taken it when he left.

Caleb had no money. Not that the apiary offered much in the way of services—bees operated on a different economy. He looked over to the hives, hearing the swarm humming awake as the morning warmed their homes.

And then there was the missing voice. Caleb had called out to it. Screamed into the dark for it to answer. Blazed with shame as he begged it for help. He waited for a response. Any response. A word. A sound. Pressure in his head. Nothing came. The universe told Caleb to go fuck himself, and that was harder to accept than Wes's abandonment.

His son skipping out on him had precedent, at least. Wes had a destructive reaction to stress. He got defensive. Closed himself. The ignored problem exacerbated. Wes's reactions deteriorated until his only option was to pass the problem on to everyone else. To Caleb. To Irene. Christ, if Caleb was being honest with himself, he had expected this from Wes. Just as he expected the violence with the highway patrolman.

Wes always met his own needs before thinking of anyone else. He was more of an acquaintance than family. But to Caleb, the voice was a part of himself. It was inside of him. The experience was the same as thinking, or moving his body. Wherever Caleb was, the voice was too. And yet, after a night of tearful pleading, his ear remained silent. When this all started, back in Truth or Consequences, the sound of it was debilitating. But now it was the silence that devastated Caleb. Like he had lost part of himself. A limb. Or maybe his mind.

Caleb sat quiet now on the steps, trying to find calm in the bees tending their hives as the sun rose. The low, murmuring hum of the hives increased in volume with the brightening sky. Caleb tried watching the entire brood, finding it overwhelming. They were uncoordinated, the swarm undulating, dripping, with no discernible purpose. As the day eased closer to the horizon, he tracked the individual bees farther into the air.

Caleb watched a bee fly toward him in an unsteady lilt. The buzzing of its wings grew louder until it passed over his head to his deaf side, leaving a wake of silence behind it. At least the insect knew where it needed to go.

Another hum drew Caleb's attention toward the hives. The sound deepened, filling the air in the apiary. He stiffened, a worry budding in his chest. This wasn't an insect. The sound grew throaty, mechanical. The buzz turned to a rumble, and it moved into Caleb's chest. The pops and thunks of a vehicle on gravel joined the reverberation in the air.

Panic sucked the air from him. Someone was driving up the road to the apiary.

He stood. The engine on the other side of the trees heaved. Caleb's mind scampered. He could hide. Hide in the cabin. That wouldn't work: whoever was coming would look in there. He could move into the trees behind the cabin. They weren't as likely to notice him there. Or he could run. If he started now, they wouldn't see him at all.

Caleb closed his eyes, realizing his arrogance. He was reacting, not thinking. The car was being driven by someone. Someone who would help Caleb contact Irene and the police.

He stepped to the ground in front of the cabin, shaking off the field coat. Looking at himself, he found his clothing stained and dusty. He swiped off what he could, running a hand through his hair, trying to make himself appear less disheveled. A black pickup truck fought its way around the tight bend in the driveway at the end of the apiary.

The truck finished the turn, grumbling toward him. Caleb felt a strange calmness relax his shoulders. Like the bee that buzzed his head, Caleb now knew where he needed to go, too.

Chapter 48

WES

"Who the fuck still drives a stick?" Wes cursed. He was fine when the truck was moving, but the behemoth transformed into a temperamental princess in low gear. The engine throbbed, then revved as Wes tapped on the gas. He released the clutch. The truck bucked forward, the chassis rocking under his feet.

The cluster of cedar trees marked the turn into the apiary. Gravel crunched under the thick tires. The first line of beehives came into view. Small dark spots flitted in and out of the white boxes and through the mist rising from the ground.

The corner was tight, and this truck was a freaking land yacht. Wes eased through the turn, riding the delicate clutch. The truck jerked through the turn as if it wanted to impress its new driver with its raw power. More hives appeared, the turn straightening out to the gravel path.

Pop stood outside the hut. Wes smiled, his shoulders relaxed, relieved that his dad was alive and okay. His smile waned as Pop raised his hands over his head. What the hell was he doing?

Wes let the truck carry him past the hives at an idle. Pop's hands rose higher as the truck got close. He faced the ground in front of him, and his palms splayed open. For a moment, Wes worried a cop had followed him into the apiary.

Twenty feet from the hut, Wes pulled the truck at an angle off the drive. The engine died with a throaty huff. Wes opened his door and climbed from the truck, grabbing the fanny pack from the dashboard.

"Hello?" Pop's voice was trembling. "Please ... I'm sorry," he said. "I need your help."

Wes slammed the door and jogged around the bed of the truck. "What's wrong, Pop? What do you need?"

Dad's face rose. His eyes widened, a smile breaking the stress from his face. Wes smiled back, the warmth of Pop's expression feeding his soul. His dad was glad to see him. Wes stepped forward to give him a hug, but paused when his father's face fell to a scowl as his hands lowered, his mouth falling open.

"Wes." It came out somewhere between an accusation and a question.

"Yeah, I'm here, Pop." His uncertainty carried on his voice. He couldn't read if Dad was glad to see him or not.

Pop's rheumy eyes stayed locked on his. They stood in that moment for a breath. Then, Dad shouted, "Wes!" His voice had an edge now. Wes flushed as his dad's hands closed into fists.

"What? What is it?"

Pop took a step toward him, stabbing the air with his finger. "You abandoned me!"

Wes laughed, "Oh, piss off! I'm right here!"

"No!" Pop screamed. "No! You left me here! No money, no phone, left me here to die!" The words sank into Wes's chest like a searing brand.

Wes stuttered, "No, wait—"

"Where's my phone? Where are my meds?" Dad's lips quivered, his eyes hardened. "I want to call your sister, right now!"

Confused, Wes pointed past his father to the shack. "I left you enough meds to get through today. I wrapped them in the note. Didn't you find them?"

"Yeah, I found them!" Dad was yelling now, his voice at odds with his frail form. "What the hell happened, Wes? Did the damned high wear off? You come back for the rest of 'em? *Huh?*" Pop took another step forward. *"You want those too?"*

A familiar hole opened in Wes's chest. He swallowed the feeling of failure, making the conscious choice to keep it from pouring out of his mouth. "Pop, no ... I ..."

"Shut up, Wes! I'm done with this!" He wasn't listening. He was on a script now, one Wes had heard many times. The heat of shame burned into his throat and cheeks. Wes's ears closed as his dad lashed out with the standard barbs. Hard words carried on his fragile voice. "Selfish," "reckless," "damage," "grow up," "responsibility."

Wes tamped the flames down, willing their embers to die on his ego.

Pop stopped yelling and rubbed his ruddy face with a hand. "Just give me my phone, son." Pop opened his hand flat, as if demanding a cookie Wes had stolen from the jar. "I can't believe I let you get me into this."

Wes crossed his arms to hold back the anger roiling in him. The buckle of the fanny pack clacked against the tailgate of the truck.

"I said give me my phone, son. I'm calling your sister, and she'll figure out how to get us out of this shit pile you created."

There it was: Dad bringing Irene in to fix what Wes broke. Her name was a knife, and it severed Wes's emotional control. "No!" He gripped his dad's shirt collar in his fist, pulling his face close. "No, you listen now!" he hissed between his clenched teeth. Rage spilled into his eyes. "If I abandoned you to get high, I would still be high. And I sure as shit wouldn't be here now!"

Dad's eyes went wide and yellow, his arms rubber at his sides. Wes twisted him toward the cabin, pointing with his free hand. "I left you enough pills to manage your pain for the rest of today. Wanna know why?" Wes whipped him back around to face him. "Because after today, you won't need them, you ungrateful shit!"

Wes released Pop's shirt, and he crumpled to his knees, shock on his face. Wes stepped back, finding the fanny pack on the ground by the tailgate. He swiped it up, unzipping the main compartment. Turning back to his father, he shoved a hand into the pack, finding the tight wad. Wes pulled it out in a fist, letting it fall to pieces in front of his father's gaping stare.

Dad's eyes fell to the pile of money on the ground. His face moved from shock to confusion. Wes could see him counting the large bills, scrunched into disorganized clumps. When he finally spoke, his voice was soft, barely audible over the hum of the waking hives. "You ... sold them?" Pop sounded hurt. Offended. It was an accusation.

Wes snorted. "Yeah, I did," he said, the heat of his anger hardening into righteousness. "I found a goddamned solution. I got the money for you." He flexed his fists a few times, burning off the rage and calming himself before continuing. "Look, I figured I could run them to San Antonio. I'd be back with the money before you woke up." He paused as the night's details flashed through his mind. He debated how much to share with Dad. He wouldn't approve. It didn't matter. Wes didn't need his approval. He needed Dad to get well. "But it took longer than I expected. And I'm sorry."

His father picked up a crumpled bill, opening it flat. His eyes rose to look at Wes. "Who did you sell them to?"

Wes shook his head, his eyes falling to the ground. "Nobody, Dad. You don't worry about that."

Dad stuttered, sitting back on his haunches, shrugging in surrender. He was about to protest.

Wes shut him down with a raised hand. "We had a problem, and I solved it."

Pop's hands lowered. He relaxed, and his eyes turned back to the money.

Wes continued, his voice strong with confidence. "I told you, this is redemption for me. I'm not letting you die if I can help it. So anything I need to do to get you in front of that kid, I'm going to do it. Even if you don't agree with it."

Wes paused, collecting his thoughts. His father's eyes stayed on the bills in front of him. "You have ... this cosmic purpose, Pop. What did the voice say? 'Save everything and everyone'?" Wes waited for Dad to respond, but he only stared at the money. "My conscience is clear on this. Yours should be too. You have the money you need to see the boy. I made that happen for you. Not Irene."

Dad peered at him. His eyes narrowed with concern. Lips moved in self-debate. Wes sighed, the final bits of anger leaving his body. A new peace came to him, and a realization. He could help Dad only so much. At some point, his father needed to make a choice. Take action. Wes couldn't do that for him.

He'd had enough of Pop's ambivalence. His nonacceptance of the gravity of this entire series of miraculous events. Ignoring his own importance. His place in the universe. Pop had been chosen. By God. By Fate. By whatever. It was time he started putting in the effort.

Wes pulled his dad's phone from his front pocket. He tossed it to the ground among the crumpled money. "And now you have a phone to call Irene for help, if that's what you want."

He turned back toward the truck. After a few steps he spit, "Call Irene, and end this. Or come with me and see this through. It's time to shit or get off the pot. I'll be in the truck."

Chapter 49

BLAIR

Blair stood outside the Silverleaf, sucking on a cigarette and enjoying the last of the cool morning air. Her shift had started an hour ago. Once Emerson finished his breakfast, she liked to take a smoke break to watch him walk to school. This had been their routine for months, since Em started kindergarten. Before reaching the drive to the school, Em turned back toward the diner. Blair waved her hand wide over her head, letting the smoke from her cigarette draw an arc in the air. Her heart swelled when the smile broke across Emerson's precious face. He traced his arm in a wide circle—his signal that he saw the arc she made. Then he turned into the school yard, walking out of view, leaving Blair's chest full of warmth. The timing, the moments that defined their morning, none of the details ever changed. The kiss good-bye, Blair lighting the smoke as her boy crossed Jackson. A few minutes of watching Em walk up the road, waiting at the crosswalk, then disappearing into the school.

On schedule, the ember of her smoke reached the filter. Blair stamped the butt into the overflowing ashtray. She pulled her hair back into a ponytail. Walking around the corner of the building to the entrance, Blair smoothed down her apron with practiced moves.

She saw him as soon as she opened the door. The sick man from yesterday. He sat at the counter, in the seat that Emerson liked to sit in after school. He looked down at his hands as they manipulated something on the countertop. Blair tensed, scanning the dining room for the other one—the son. She didn't find him, and her breath released as she walked to the counter.

This sick man—what was his name? Carl? No, Caleb. He was alone, and that was good. On his own, this man was no threat. A stiff breeze would tear him in half. Blair looked him over as she approached. He wore the same clothes as yesterday. His shoes were dirtier. Blair rounded the business side of the counter, and she put on her work face.

"Good morning," she sang. "Good to see you again. Coffee? Tea?"

The man's eyes lit up as they rose to meet hers. She had caught him stuffing a fork handle under the brace on his left hand, probably to scratch an itch. He yanked out the fork and moved his hands to his lap, his frame straightening as if he wanted to impress her. He stumbled with his words, pointing out the window toward the park with a grimy yellowed nail.

Blair shook her head and leaned against the counter, closing the distance between them so she could speak low. She did her best to keep from grimacing. The man reeked of stale sweat and mold. "Caleb, right?" She kept her voice soft.

The brittle man nodded and swallowed. "Yes, that's right. You're Blair." He smiled at her, mouth sticky and teeth yellow.

She returned the smile, hiding her disgust at the man's breath. Jaime had laid out an approach for her to follow. A script. To keep her and Em safe during these exchanges. Jaime wasn't here to take charge of the conversation, but they practiced this enough. The business wouldn't happen here, or at home, but at the church where Jaime worked. Safest place. Controllable. Small. Isolated.

"Were you able to get the money together?"

The man nodded, shifting around in his seat. Blair's brow knotted as she heard a thin snap. Caleb turned back, hauling a large fanny pack onto the counter. Before he pulled open the zipper, Blair placed a hand on his. "No, not here. There's a church right next door." She nodded past the kitchen, toward the church lot beyond. "Round the back is a new annex. A building on its own."

Caleb turned to the kitchen, as if he could see through the wall to Jaime's office. She continued, "You go there after three thirty or so this afternoon. You knock on the door. My friend Jaime, from the gazebo, you remember him?" The man nodded. "Give the donation to Jaime, and he'll let us know. And then we'll meet you there."

A tingle of pride lifted her head. She had practiced the script several times last night. Jaime should have been here to watch her nail it!

"You understand, Caleb?" she asked, giving his hand a brief squeeze.

Caleb's eyes still stared through the back wall of the café. He nodded again, his face loose and eyes dreamy. "I understand. Three thirty, the building behind the church next door."

"Good," Blair stated. "Bring the money. Jaime will take care of you." His face turned back to hers, his eyes hopeful. "For now, how about some tea?" she inquired. He nodded.

She pulled a mug from the rack and filled it with hot water. She set it in front of Caleb with the collection of teas from under the counter. Another patron—Hue from the auto shop down Johnson Street—flagged her over. "Stay here for a minute. I'll be right back, okay?"

The man still stared past the kitchen.

A fresh pot of coffee sat ready. Blair snagged it and walked toward Hue's table. She passed him his check as he dropped $12 into her hand. The movements were shadows of a routine they ran several times a week.

Hue headed for the door. Blair checked on her other customers, refilling their coffee. She returned to the counter, replacing the carafe and ringing up Hue's check. Caleb cleared his throat, and she looked up from the register drawer.

His face was tight with concern. "Is there anything I need to do? To prepare?"

Blair chuckled. "Prepare? Like, don't eat for eight hours before your appointment?" she teased. The image of this twig of a man walking around town in a medical gown made her laugh. His hands fidgeted, wringing with embarrassment. "Mister, there ain't no preparing for it," she consoled. "Don't worry, okay? You just need to show up. Emerson does the rest."

His face relaxed into a weary grin. He was thinking. Wondering what it was like, being healed by her son. She'd experienced the magic so often. The feeling of it was empty. No stun, no bliss, no discomfort, no recognition of change. But it had never gotten familiar. Never became routine. Each time was exactly like the first. Unexpected and new.

He finally put words to his thoughts. "What's it feel like?"

Blair thought for a few seconds, staring at the counter between them. What did it feel like? Thing was, it didn't feel like anything. Em had been healing her for how many years? And she never even knew it was happening. He'd done it while she was asleep, and the experience wasn't enough to even wake her. There was no explosion. No orgasmic release of health. You just changed. One moment, you're injured. The next, you're not. She'd seen Em remove cancer, seen him close bleeding wounds, watched him unclog Jaime's sinuses. There was never a cry, a whimper, or a laugh.

Blair rested her hand on top of the register and met his rheumy eyes with a smile. "Well, it don't hurt none, if that's your worry."

Chapter 50

CALEB

Caleb watched for a bee. Any bee. Coming or going. There had been no activity around the apiary since they returned from town a few hours ago. He noticed after Wes finished inhaling the meal Caleb had picked up for him at the Silverleaf. The quiet after Wes's belch. No hum hanging in the air. The constant thrum of nature was missing.

Wes had stumbled into the cabin. He emptied his pockets onto the rickety table and fell into the hammock, snoring in moments. Once Wes passed out, Caleb moved the little chair outside, in the shade of a cluster of cedars near the closest row of box hives. The hives were active that morning. He didn't know much about bees, but Caleb figured it was odd that the apiary would go silent. Had they swarmed off, en masse? Was that something bees did? Had their presence scared them away?

Caleb reached down, finding the near-empty bottle of water on the ground under the chair. He tilted it up, draining the last few swallows. His thirst was insatiable today, his body a bottomless sponge. At least water was available, since Wes had overstocked their supply setting up camp yesterday. Caleb capped the bottle and dropped it next to the other empties as he counted them. That made two liters he'd consumed since Wes fell asleep, yet his mouth remained dry, his skin tight on his bones.

Continuous intravenous fluids. If he were back home in hospice care, that would be scribbled on his chart. Dr. Pav had warned him, a time would come when he wouldn't be able to drink enough to keep his body working, and machines would force it into him. It was one marker Caleb had identified for his Final Release. When the medical tether became mandatory to keep his body functioning.

Caleb sighed in the warm and still air. The voice hadn't lied—it was happening fast. His flesh was giving up. If he were back home now, the metal box would be in his hands, the button waiting for the slightest pressure. But Caleb wasn't home. He was here. And he just needed a few hours more. His body could give him that. Then it would be reset. He'd have the strength to start over. The time to fix the things he and his son had done in the last few days. The chance to explain everything to Irene.

He trembled up from the seat, one arm bracing his frail body against the cedar as he staggered upright. He was dying, but not dead. His bladder still worked and at the moment, it screamed. Caleb steadied himself before making his way to the pine tree he had been using as a urinal all afternoon. He emptied himself into the ground around the tree. The sound of his stream filled the silence left by the missing bees.

As he finished, he could hear his son's thick feet slap the wooden slats of the cabin floor. He was awake, groaning a low rumble. It was a sound Caleb recognized—bending stiff joints and stretching tight muscles. Caleb moved to the screened door, finding Wes sitting up in the hammock.

"Sounds like your warranty expired overnight," he said to his son. "Hate to tell you, but each morning feels better than the next one, kid."

Wes chuckled. Caleb watched him through the screen as he rubbed the sleep from his face. He stood up and stretched. Shoving open the door, he stepped into the afternoon. "You're peeing a lot, Dad. That's the fifth leak you've taken since we got back."

Caleb nodded and sighed, "Yeah, I can't hold it. I think it's the sun."

Wes shielded his eyes as he looked to the sky. "Yeah, I guess we're closer to the sun here in Texas than we were in New Mexico."

The joke made Caleb snort, and he relaxed at the levity returning to their relationship. Whatever had happened overnight, Wes had come back with an edge to him. Caleb had asked once—what happened in San Antonio? Wes had refused to talk about it. Caleb didn't have the strength to press him, but he kept revisiting the questions in his head. God knew what the hell Wes had done to get that money together. What damage had he inflicted? How many lives had he derailed? Regardless, it honed his son's temper and purpose. There was resolve in him now, the likes of which Caleb had experienced only from his sister.

Wes looked at his watch. "We'll leave in a few minutes, Pop. You got the money in your pack, right?"

Caleb answered by patting the bulging pack at his waist.

Wes nodded. "Good. I'm gonna take a few minutes, go over to those trees, and make like a bear."

Caleb missed the reference, furrowing his brow. Wes held up a roll of toilet paper, grinning at his own joke. As his son walked stiff as a scarecrow into the small grove of trees beyond the truck, Caleb scoffed, "Show-off. I haven't been able to take a crap since before the hospital in New Mexico."

Wes's voice carried from behind the trees. "Well, make sure the kid fixes that too."

Caleb laughed, but not at his son's wit. The thought of being well again titillated him, filled him with energy. After the pointless cancer treatments, the fuss and worry, the trouble he'd created getting to Utopia, Caleb's new purpose was an hour away. He needed to get to the other side of his sickness. There was so much to undo now. The shame of his actions forced a grimace on his face. He longed for his chance to make things right again.

He closed his eyes and raised his face` to the sun. The air was still, warm enough that he felt it on his skin. Without the sunlight on his face, Caleb wouldn't know where he stopped and everything else began.

A sound came soft to him, a perturbation through the air like a growing sigh. Caleb opened his eyes. In the sky, beneath the sun, distant dark wisps reached up over the tops of the trees. They flowed like currents of water, cresting and breaking, then fell apart and re-formed in billows of heavy smoke.

Caleb felt a hand on his back. Wes. His son asked, "Ready to go, then? First day of the rest of your life, and all?"

"I am, son!" He raised a hand, pointing above the trees. "You see that? I think those are the bees. I guess they're swarming?"

Wes took his hand back, shielding his eyes from the sun, squinting. He shook his head. "Nah, I don't see 'em, Pop." He turned and moved toward the truck. "C'mon, let's finish this thing."

Caleb followed his son, veering off to the passenger side of the truck. He looked back over the trees at the ebb and flow of shadows in the sky. The trees around the apiary were close, hiding the distance to the blob. The swarm would be near the horizon. Caleb blinked at his confusion, trying to process how a swarm so large could form, how it could appear so fluid.

He heard the truck door open. He turned to his son. "You don't see that?"

Wes stopped, turning back. Caleb gestured up above the treetops behind him. Wes followed his hand into the sky, frowning.

"Look there, way in the distance. They're swarming or something."

Wes scanned the sky for a moment and shrugged. "Guess you're seeing shit now too, Pop," he laughed. He turned toward the cab and hauled himself into the driver's seat.

Caleb took one last gander. The movements were soothing and steady. Natural. Beautiful. His contentment spread to the smile on his face. He placed a hand on the door latch as his right ear crackled. His grin faded as vibrations bloomed in his skull. Caleb braced both hands against the truck before the voice arrived.

Caleb.

His grip tightened on the door handle as the voice shook him.

This is it, you're almost done.

Caleb breathed through a deep rattle as the voice boomed through him. The pressure in his head was tolerable, the compulsion that came with it manageable. Around the voice, Caleb found something surprising. Rage. Anger at the abandonment. The inattention that had led him and his son to such awful action. All of it was unnecessary.

"Where the fuck have you been? We've been struggling here!" Caleb spit. He kept his voice to a harsh whisper.

And yet, here you are, right where you need to be. You're doing fine. Everything is coming into place. You're here, the boy is here. It's working itself out.

"Working itself out? Are you fucking kidding me!" His voice rose. He opened his eyes, finding his son's worried face through the window. Caleb turned away, his voice rasping, "Do you have any idea what the hell we've had to do in the last twenty-four hours?"

Uh ... no, not really. But you seem okay.

"Where have you been? Do you have better shit to do? Is that it!"

Caleb, what is this? Where is this anger coming from?

Caleb turned his head skyward, screaming, "You want to know why I'm angry?"

Yeah, I do. Did Wes do something?

"Wes did what he had to! I'm pissed because you can't be bothered to help us!"

Oh, I see. You're upset that this wasn't all easy-peasy.

"No! I'm confused that we keep finding so much trouble! You should be able to help us with this stuff! The roadblock? The police at the motel? And that poor guy locked up in the barn! We could have avoided it all. Instead, we keep hurting people. You said I have a bigger purpose!"

That's right, Caleb. You have a significant role to play in this universe. In how it plays out for everyone.

Frustration cramped in his leg, and Caleb stomped at the dirt, sending up a cloud of dust. "Then why is this so damned difficult! Why did I have to steal to get here? Why is that injured man cuffed in the barn outside of town?"

Caleb, all I can say is that things are moving as they should. I'm sorry I can't explain it better for you or make you more comfortable with it all.

Caleb sucked in a rattling breath. Through clenched teeth, he asked, "But why did you disappear on us? On me?"

Nothing filled his dead ear. Caleb used the space to calm himself before continuing. "Look, I'm not asking you to make things easy, okay? But it would help me if I knew you're here, that you haven't abandoned me in ..." His voice trailed off as he gestured broadly to the Texas scrub country.

The sound of the truck door opening pulled Caleb's attention around. His son stood on the other side of the truck bed, eyes wide, concerned. "What is it?" he pleaded. "The voice?"

That's fair. I apologize, Caleb.

Caleb processed the words, nodding. "When this ... all of this ... when it's all over, are you going to leave me alone?"

Is that what you want?

Caleb closed his eyes. Was that what he wanted? Return to the banality of merely existing in the moment? Losing this experience and connection to everything around him? He'd cut off an arm as soon as abandon this extraordinary perception.

"Yes." The sound of his own voice surprised him. And then it didn't. This sense wasn't one he governed. The limb wasn't his, and he would never control it. "Yes, if I can fulfill this purpose without you in my head, that's what I want." Caleb stepped toward the truck, reaching for the door handle. The throb of the voice froze him.

Then yes, when this is over, I'll leave you.

"Good. I want to fix everything you made us do to get here."

I didn't make you do anything. You made your own choices.

Caleb closed his eyes, his other hand finding the truck to steady himself. He waited for a long moment, not speaking, hearing just the throb of his own heartbeat in his head. Did the voice expect a response? What could he say to that?

Caleb?

He opened his eyes, sighing through his frustration. "What?"

Are you ready to fulfill your purpose?

He scoffed. "Of course I am. I've come this far. I'm seeing this through to the end." Caleb opened the door to the truck.

Good. Don't forget the gun.

Chapter 51

WES

Wes looked across the cab. Dad was standing outside, waiting for something. Maybe he was having trouble with the door of the truck?

"Oh sorry, hang on, Pop." Wes pulled on the latch, hearing it click. Then Pop leaned against the door, pushing it closed again. "Dad, back off, let me open the ..."

A chill froze Wes. Pop's face spasmed, his right eye slamming shut and his mouth twitching into a nasty sneer. Wes recognized it—the tics that came when Pop heard the voice. The terror melted into elation.

Dad spun away from the window. His hands chopped through the air as he started shouting. Screaming, incoherent. Something was wrong.

Wes bolted from the seat, throwing open his door and moving around the truck bed. Pop stood a dozen feet from the truck, his face up, hollering gibberish into the sky.

"Jesus! Are you okay?"

Dad turned to look at him. His eyes were stark and narrow. His face wrenched in a scowl, skin darkening in a flush of anger. He hissed at Wes. Not words. Not even syllables. Just feral sounds.

"Dad!" Wes insisted. "Is it the voice? What's the matter?"

His dad grunted something further, his face turning to the sky. He stomped back to the truck, slamming his hands against the passenger-side window.

Wes ran around the truck to him. He heard his father's phlegmy lungs heaving air in and out of his broken body. Pop leaned his head against the truck window, seeming to catch his breath for a moment. Wes reached out, wanting to take his hand. Before he could, Pop opened his door.

"Christ, Dad! Are you all right?"

Dad stopped, holding the door open a few inches. "What?" he rasped. Dad's voice was thin, hesitant.

"I asked if you're okay."

Pop didn't respond. He stood still as stone.

"Hey, Pop?" Wes grabbed his father's shoulder, giving him a shake. Dad's grip on the truck door supported his frail form. Wes pried him away from the truck and then regretted it. Pop's hands fell limp. He spun into his son, eyes dilated and unfocused. His mouth hung open, a thin line of spittle hanging from the thickest part of his lip. His legs crumpled beneath him, bringing him hard toward the ground. Wes caught him at the waist, easing him the last few inches to the earth.

Wes hovered. He waited for Pop to move, twitch. Fucking breathe. Instead, his father's eyes stared past him into the sky. His body relaxed against the ground, one leg twisted beneath him. His arms splayed to the side as if he were performing some macabre dance. Wes listened, watched. No part of him moved. He was still far too long.

Was he dead? Wes's eyes flitted across the apiary, retracing his dad's steps as though he'd dropped a clue somewhere to explain everything. Dad had stood by the truck, alive, a moment ago. And now he lay prone in the dirt at Wes's feet. Could it have happened? Just now? So close to the win?

He knelt over his father. Memories of the accident at the greasy spoon came rushing back. Dad had moved then. He'd spoken. Cried. Wes moved his hands over Pop's face and chest, unsure of what to do. "No, no," Wes howled, "not like this, come on!" He took his father's shirt in his hands and gave him a throttle, hoping to thrust the life back into him. Dad's limp form flopped inside of the loose shirt.

"No, no, no!" Wes screamed. They were just leaving! They were about to see the boy! They only needed another hour! He released the crimped shirt and stood, his hands finding the sides of his head and clenching mounds of his hair. Wes turned away, exploding his frustration in a violent bellow that scorched his throat and rattled his vision.

How could they have come so far, guided by God, only to fall now? Was this a cosmic joke? A fucking game with his family as the pawns?

The sting of tears came to his eyes. The world blurred around him. Wes had no control over it. No control over what was happening to his father. No way to help. To fix it. To back up, move sooner, skip the nap, stay in town. The possibilities flipped through his mind. They agonized and tantalized him with what-ifs and should-haves. He hated being this helpless. He hated himself. Who did he think he was? A millennial apostle? Wes's knees hit the ground, followed by his palms. He sucked in a dusty breath, his chest exploding and collapsing toward hyperventilation.

The questions came like a battering ram. When had he fucked it up? Had he pushed Pop too hard? Should they have waited at the diner? Should they have kept driving in Junction? What if they had spoken with Irene before they left, what would have happened? The possibilities grew. The regrets multiplied. Wes's breath heaved faster, but no air filled his lungs. Shimmers appeared at the edge of his vision. A tingle reached from his chest into his legs, where his muscles began to shake.

A percussive snap derailed the freight train running through his head. Wes turned to the sound, his torso following until he fell onto his backside. He stared to the ground where his dad's body had been. It was empty. Dad was gone.

Chapter 52

CALEB

His anger tempered to confusion. "What?" Caleb snapped. "Why would I need the gun?" The sun grew blistering suddenly. Sweat worked its way down his face, and he swiped it away with the heel of his unbraced hand.

To complete your purpose.

Caleb scanned the hillside, as if an explanation were hiding in the scrub. "I ... I don't understand. We're heading to Emerson now. Let me get healed, and then I can do what you need me to do. Hold your horse for another hour or two."

His head rattled. The voice moved in him. Impatient. Unable to rest.

You don't have another two hours, Caleb. You need to make this a priority, or it won't happen.

How could something omnipotent be so obtuse? Caleb pleaded, exasperated. "We're leaving now, Emerson will cure me, and then we can prevent that ... that ..."

The end of everyone and everything?

"Yeah, that!" Caleb snubbed. "Give us a damned minute to do the first thing first. I can't help you if I die from cancer, can I?"

That's what I'm saying. You will die, Caleb. You will die today. In less than two hours. If you want to come through for me, the time is now. There is no later. Not for you.

Caleb stopped moving. The truck door lilted closed. It clicked in front of him as his mind made sense of the voice's words. "But the boy ... Emerson," Caleb mumbled. The annoyance dissolved into his gut, the heat of his impatience tempering to a chill. "We came all this way so Emerson could heal me."

His son's face appeared in the window. Wes said something he couldn't process. Caleb turned away. His voice assertive, Caleb sputtered, "No! We did awful things to get to the boy! To cure my cancer!"

What? No, Caleb. No, I'm sorry. That isn't why you're here.

A hole formed in his chest. A familiar void. Caleb recognized the shape of it. The tender edges. The scarring left behind as the tangled roots of hope ripped out of him.

You're not here for salvation. You're here to act. To close that cosmic gap before your cancer kills you.

The void in him opened. Became a chasm. Separating Caleb from his petulant dreams of a longer life. Of knowing a sober and responsible Wes. Of living vicariously through Irene's success. Of making right all the things he'd set wrong. He felt it slip away, a treasured gift morphing into a malicious prank.

His lungs shook as Caleb inhaled, his body revolting against the voice's words. The world blurred beyond his tears. His jaw panged from the pressure of clenching teeth. "That's not right," Caleb spit. He shoved away from the truck. The apiary spun around him as his eyes scoured for something on which to focus. "That can't be right!"

I'm afraid it is, Caleb. I am sorry if you thought you would live through this, but it's not possible. It never was.

"But why!" Caleb yelled. His face turned to the sky, to the empty pale blue, and he filled it with his scream. "Why would you let me think I was going to live!"

Caleb, I never said that. I offered you a purpose. That's what you wanted, and it's all I'm able to give you.

Wes came at him, frantic. "Jesus, Dad! Are you okay?" Caleb looked back to the truck. Wes was out of the cab, his mouth and eyes agape with worry.

"Not now, son," Caleb scolded. He turned his attention back to the endless Texas sky. Searching. Wanting the face of the voice. To grab its throat and throw it to the ground. Rage replaced his blood, thrashing through his good ear, building pressure through his body, a vise closing around him. Fists clenched. They pounded on the truck window. His voice exploded into the air, "Explain yourself, you manipulative shit!"

I can do that.

The apiary shimmered. The grid of hives unfolded into a cube. Caleb leaned into the truck, trying to keep his balance as the world split open around him. The chassis of the truck bent toward him, away from him. Caleb kept his eyes locked on the center of the window. A glint of light, an indirect reflection of the sun at the center of the kaleidoscope forming around him. The sky's reflection in the window expanded in directions Caleb couldn't name. He focused. On the pinpoint of light in the reflection. On his breathing. He fought to stay inside his body.

Let go.

"What?" he asked. It came out in a tight whisper as Caleb tried to breathe through the experience.

I need you to let go, Caleb. Let me pull you out of this moment.

Caleb resisted. His mind pushed against the voice. Tried to force it out of his ear. But the compulsion hit his head like bullets: act; choose; let go. The gleam in the window expanded, along with the sky, the ground. The scratches in the truck's body panel grew to canyons. The wide sky shrank to a speck. His consciousness exploded against the moment.

Caleb didn't want to see this. He didn't want to explore possibilities, to be aware of every atomic detail around him. He wanted a simple answer. Why? Why wouldn't he live?

I don't know, Caleb. I can't help you with that. I just know it won't happen.

Anger should have flooded him, but Caleb felt nothing. The dimensions twisted around him, and his feelings did the same. He was neither peaceful nor belligerent here. He merely existed, but he wanted so much more. To rage. Scream. Destroy this moment and all others in a seething tantrum.

Why was he here? What was the point?

I realize we haven't communicated effectively. This thing we're doing now—being able to talk like this—it's new to me. That's not an excuse. The stakes are too high for the imprecision of language. It's time I show you. Explicitly.

The moment collapsed. The universe passed through him as Caleb stared into the brilliance of countless burning stars. He recognized this space. The familiarity should have shocked him, but Caleb felt nothing. The boundless light of this realm where every possibility floated alongside the others. This was where he experienced the strange vertigo of the empty tear. The void where choices no longer existed. The end of everyone, and everything.

Caleb, here's how you will stop the cataclysm.

Chapter 53

WES

Wes fell to the ground, gutted. They had it all but done, but his redemption slipped from his fingers. A drop of failure in an ocean of defeat. His face lifted to the sky. To wail. To scream after his father's soul as it sailed into the endless pale blue of the Texas heavens. But a second sound—a rustling knock—took his gaze to the cabin.

His heart leapt. The screen door was open, his father using it to brace himself as he hobbled down the steps. The field coat lay across his free arm, a bottle of water in his hand. He walked toward Wes, his face powdered with dirt, his shirt still wrinkled with the peaks created by Wes's fists.

"I'm ready," Pop rasped, motioning to the truck with his chin.

Wes swallowed, hope filling the pit in his stomach. He shook off the stun of finding his father alive. "I thought you were dead, Pop."

"I wasn't. I'm not." Dad's voice was gloomy, quiet. He sounded tired. No, something more than that. Sadness hung on his face. It pushed against the wave of Wes's positive feelings.

"You sure you're okay?" Wes asked, concerned. "What the hell happened?"

Pop's eyes wandered away from him. For a moment he feared they would dilate again, that Dad would fall back to the ground. Instead, Pop stepped around Wes and proceeded to the truck. Over his shoulder, he replied, "It was the voice. It was showing me things again."

Wes sat fixated in the dirt.

His father opened the passenger door and laid the field coat and water bottle onto the seat. He turned, his face stern. "We should get going."

Wes nodded. He stood, dusted himself off, and took a step, patting his pockets for the keys. A mild panic swelled in him until he remembered they were in the ignition. He walked around the truck, lifting himself back into the driver's seat and closing the door. He stole a look toward his father. Pop sat with the field coat in his lap, his braced hand rubbing his temple.

"You sure you're okay?" Wes checked.

Dad sighed, dropping his hand. "There's no time like the present."

Wes turned the key, and the truck roared as the engine came alive. He released the brake and negotiated the powerful machine through the apiary.

The truck bucked as he downshifted for the turn onto the road that would take them back to 187. From there, it was straight north to town. "The Silverleaf?" Wes asked, realizing he had no specific destination.

Pop stared through the windshield, his face drawn into a stoic mask as he answered, "That works."

They rode in silence for several minutes. The road switched and twisted through the low-rolling hills and brush. Wes pampered the clutch to prevent the truck from stalling on the turns. A metallic odor tainted the cab—the vapors of the mold-crusted jacket on his father's lap. The smell pinched the inside of Wes's nose. It reminded him of the stink of the ashtray on his front stoop during the monsoon season back home.

As he drove, the pinch turned to a tickle, which progressed into a steady stab. Wes snorted, his sinuses swelling at the acrid vapors. "Dad, can we ditch that thing? The odor's getting to me."

Dad placed his hands on the coat, but didn't respond.

"We can toss it in the truck bed," Wes continued, reaching behind him to slide open the rear window. "Do you mind?" he asked, nodding back toward the bed while keeping his eyes on the road. Wes was having trouble hiding his aggravation. Between the temperamental transmission and that disgusting odor pecking at his brain, he was losing patience.

The road straightened out, and State Road 187 loomed in the heat-hazed distance. Wes glanced over, seeing the coat in Pop's lap.

"Look, that thing stinks, and it's pissing me off." Wes reached over, finding the canvas coat with his fingers. He heaved it over the seat in an awkward motion toward the window. Wes tried to keep his torso straight, to hold both feet on the pedals. One hand gripped the steering wheel, while the other tried to underarm the long jacket through the window. The coat snagged something, refusing to move. Wes brought the truck to a stop on the empty road, so he could focus on getting rid of the damned thing.

Glancing down, he found what was keeping the coat where it was. His father's hands clawed into it like it was prey.

"Pop, what the hell?" he asked. "That thing is gross—you don't want it." He yanked the coat, slipping the musty canvas through Dad's fingers.

His father's hands clambered for the jacket as he cried, "No, wait!"

Something thudded to the floorboard. Wes's eyes found what made the sound: the revolver sat at Pop's feet.

Wes's eyes bounced up, expecting Dad's face to mirror his shock. Instead, his father's eyes were tensed, brow crested, mouth agape. He swallowed, his gaze shifting between his son and the pistol. Pop was afraid.

"Jesus," Wes said. "You gotta be careful with that! At least let me know you had it on you! It might have gone off!"

Wes moved the coat through the back window, hearing it land in the metal bed of the truck with a slap. He turned, reaching for the gun on the floor.

It wasn't there. Wes scanned the cab. He found the revolver in Pop's lap, his hand cupping the grip.

"Pop, we're not gonna need that," he said. "You should put it away." Wes leaned over, opening the glove box.

His dad didn't move.

"Please, it's not safe having that out. Put it away."

"No, thank you," he replied, his voice cracked and dry. "It's okay."

Wes sat up straight, adjusting his foot to keep pressure on the sensitive clutch. "No, thank you?" he parroted. "Seriously, we don't need it."

Dad turned to face the passenger window. The rumble of the idling engine marked the silence. Wes looked down, brow furrowing in confusion as Dad's hand tightened on the grip of the gun.

Wes swallowed. "I know this is scary, Pop, believe me. This has been the road trip from hell." He reached over, putting a gentle hand on the gun. "But we're nearly there, okay? We have the money. We found the boy. We don't need this now." Wes felt Pop's fingers move beneath his hand, his hold solidifying on the weapon.

"Don't," Dad hissed, his voice now a coarse whisper. "I need it!"

Wes shook his head. "No, Pop, I don't think you will. We're just gonna give them the money and—"

Dad's face turned from the window, his expression derailing Wes's thought. Dad's mouth contorted into a deep frown. Eyes wide. In fear. Sadness.

No, not sadness. Wes knew this face. It was the face he'd had when Wes broke Irene's jaw. This was anger. Resignation. Betrayal.

"I need it!" The words spit from his father's lips. "I need it to kill Emerson!"

Chapter 54

CALEB

Wes's grin twitched. "That's not funny, Pop. Let go."

Caleb swallowed. It burned. His throat was drying up again. He shook his head. "I can't do that, Wes."

The smile melted off his son, his eyes blinking away the confusion. "No, Pop, that's not the thing we're doing." The words sputtered out, his son's way of cobbling thoughts together from broken pieces.

Wes shook his head, and the pieces seemed to snap together. He licked his lips, his mouth clicking as he whispered, "What the fuck?"

Caleb's chest heaved. "Please, let's get moving. I'm running out of time. We need to go to town."

The truck lurched as his son twisted in his seat, shifting his foot on the clutch as he turned toward Caleb. Wes found his eyes and held them with his own. His stare bored into Caleb, searching for a sign that his father meant to say something else. Wes's eyes widened, not finding what they were looking for.

"We're not going anywhere," he rasped. "Not until I understand what the fuck is going on."

Caleb broke the gaze, peering out the windshield. The highway was a hundred yards away, rising heat making the pale asphalt shimmer like a mirage. He heaved in a breath, holding it, unsure of where to start. "The voice ... it came to me before we left. It showed me ... It told me ..." The experience ran through his head again, the flashes of things that could be, the endless branching of possibilities. How the hell would he explain this to his son?

"The voice told you what, exactly?" Wes's voice steadied.

Caleb swallowed again. The burn down his throat cleared the rubble from his thoughts. "My purpose. The reason for all of this. The voice showed me. My purpose is to kill Emerson."

A silence weighed on the air in the cab. Wes broke it with a harsh whisper, "That's not right. That can't be right, Pop." His voice crescendoed as he spoke, building toward clarity and anger. "Tell me what it said!"

A throb bounced against the inside of Caleb's skull. An echo from speaking with the voice. The insistence, the betrayal, the emotionless manner in which it was conveyed. Caleb continued to stare out the front of the truck. "It came, the voice. It came, and it said, 'You're almost done now.' Then it told me to get the gun." His voice cracked then, his eyes thick with the threat of tears. He pushed the shame away, but it kept his voice a thin warble. "It said I'm not here to be healed." His eyes watered, despite his dehydration. "The voice said I'm here to stop the boy. That's all."

Wes shifted in his seat again, his hand tightening around the revolver's frame. "Stop the boy? Stop him from what? What in hell does that even mean?"

Caleb stuttered, "I don't ..." Heat fanned his face, sweat licking his temple. The cab was stifling.

"Tell me," his son demanded.

Caleb took a breath to calm himself. He thought back through it all. The branches of things to come. He turned to face his son's hard stare. "The voice ... it showed me ..." It showed him what? "I can't find the words here, son, I'm sorry."

"No! You need to explain this to me! What did it show you? What!" Wes was livid, his voice raw and loud. His anger trembled into his hand as it tightened around Caleb's fingers. Around the gun.

"The future? Or maybe, what the future could be?" Christ, what the hell did that even mean?

Wes shook his head. He grunted through his clenched teeth. Caleb saw a shadow on his face, one he recognized, a portent of violence. Caleb's breath caught.

"Son, it was too much to take in. It was ... everything. It was all the things that will happen. That could happen. A ... map. An endless one. Of anything that may come to pass." Caleb heard the words flow out of him, his thoughts melting just prior to pouring out of his mouth.

"Pop." Wes's tone came soft. Caleb hadn't expected that. His son closed his eyes and took a breath. "Let's focus on one thing. Focus on the thing that made it real for you."

Caleb recognized the language—"What makes it real for you?" The tone of voice—calm, placating, benign from judgment. It was from their family therapy sessions, to ensure that they could communicate well enough to keep Wes from relapsing. The therapist would ask, "You say your father's disappointment in you is a trigger. What makes his disappointment real to you?"

His son's eyes crept open. The anger was missing. Not at bay, not held back. His son had shut it down.

The therapist had asked, and Wes responded. Those responses focused on emotions. Caleb's behavior triggered a feeling in his son. An inadequacy, helplessness that despite doing his best, it was not good enough. The shame of not being as smart and organized as his sister. Guilt at not holding his shit together. Fear of developing new coping skills, when self-destruction worked so well for him.

Caleb closed his eyes now, and he sought back for that feeling. He replied, "It was ... like a tree. Or ... a road. It started ... here, and now. And then it moved forward. But the way forward twists. It breaks into branches. ..." He shook his head. He was moving through it too fast.

Wes encouraged him, "It's okay, go on."

Caleb considered it. Space bending around him. Possibilities laid out to infinity. Eternity pierced by an infinite number of sparks. Each comprehensible on its own, but the whole of them were blinding. Then, the vertigo of being in that empty abyss. The insignificance of an individual, standing on the rim of oblivion. The abandonment. Boundless fear. Resignation. Surrender.

"It was overwhelming. The voice, it tried to show me, but I couldn't see the whole thing. The thread—the branch or whatever—the voice showed me the one we're on. The one that leads me to the boy. It splits and twists from there. It branches whether I kill the boy or let him live."

Caleb opened his eyes, looking for some sign this was making any sense to Wes. His son was listening. A soft smile found Wes's lips as his son's eyes encouraged him to say more.

Caleb started nodding too. He held the image in his head. The threads countless, always unraveling. "The thread, the one where the boy lives. It goes on for a ways, splitting and twisting. But that all ... everything just ... ends."

Wes's brow perked up. "It ends? What do you mean?"

Caleb shrugged with his eyebrows, stammering a bit, "I mean, there's nothing. Nobody. All the branching ends in nothing."

"Like, how?" Wes asked. "End-of-times kind of stuff?"

"I don't know, I think so?" Caleb replied. The explanation came easier. "Those branches where the boy lives on, those disappear into a void, where nothing comes out. But the ones leading off from his death, those go on. They continue for as far as I could see."

Wes huffed and considered him for a moment. "And you said that the dead end happens if you don't kill the boy?"

Caleb nodded.

"And the path if you kill him? Where does that go?"

Caleb tried to remember. Every possible outcome, none of them determined. Endless sparks in the dark. "I don't know. It was too much to know. All I can tell you is that it just ... keeps going."

They held the moment, the rumble of the antsy engine a metronome to their tension. Wes sighed hard. "Look, Pop. You must not have understood. The voice leaves a lot to be desired in the communication department."

Caleb shook his head. "No. I know the voice isn't giving us a script here, but this part was spelled out. Everything ends if Emerson lives. He dies, things carry on."

An incredulous breath blew through Wes's lips. "But why, Dad? And how?" The heat was returning to his voice.

"I don't know, son. I couldn't understand. I tried, but—"

Wes's grip on the gun tightened again. He turned his face away, and Caleb watched the spit fly from his son's lips as he spoke. "Fuck this. Kill a kid? God would never ask you to do that."

Caleb was unsure what to say. Wes stared through the windshield, his jaw knuckle throbbing with energy. The truck smelled like anxiety, a mixture of sweat and uncertainty.

Wes sighed. The sound was even, calm. His face pivoted back to Caleb, his mouth turned down in a hard and broken expression. His other hand moved from the steering wheel and wrapped around the gun.

"Give me the gun, Pop." The resolution in his tone shocked Caleb. Wes wasn't asking. He was threatening.

"I can't." Caleb was crying again as the brief respite of calm in him evaporated.

"Let go," Wes demanded. "This is over." His hands closed around the cylinder. Caleb's fingers were pressed between his son's swampy palms. "We'll call Irene. She'll figure out what to do." A tremble had moved to Wes's voice too.

Caleb swallowed the dryness in his throat. "No, son. This has to happen."

"You're sick, okay? Give me the gun, let's call Irene, and we can go home."

"I can't do that, Wes." The tears were steady now. His son's face was a blur. "You keep saying I need to accept my role in this." Wes's hands clenched. Caleb tightened his grip around the gun. "You're the one who keeps pointing out how things have moved us here. Saying we need to trust our purpose here."

"Let go, Pop." Wetness fell from Wes's eyes and down his cheeks. Caleb could hear the break in his voice. The staccato of emotion in his throat cracking the hardness of his resolve.

Caleb shook his head no.

Wes's hands closed tight. "Please," he begged, as he twisted the gun in Caleb's hand. "Just let go of the gun."

Caleb's fingers tightened, a futile gesture against the strength of his son.

Wes rotated farther in his seat, and Caleb lost the leverage he had around the grip. His good wrist bent backward, the gun slipping, the textured handle scraping across his palm.

Pressure exploded in his wrist as Wes shifted his weight. The clutch groaned as it slipped from beneath Wes's sneaker.

The gears engaged. The engine shuddered with power. The truck bucked. Caleb's back pressed into his seat. The barrel twisted toward him. Its blackness was bottomless.

A cough from the engine. The truck stalled as Caleb fell forward into the sudden silence. The gun rattled in his hands as the dashboard slammed into his face.

The punch of a gunshot filled the cab.

Chapter 55

IRENE

Irene disconnected from the video call. The sheriff's office came back into focus. The smell of work—a familiar mix of body odor, sweat, printer toner, and shitty coffee. She stole a glance at the clock on the wall. That was the sixth meeting she'd joined in the last hour. That call had included the Travis County Sheriff's Office. The one before that, Webb County. Then Bexar County. Kerrville police. Hondo police. Uvalde, too.

She had to give a nod to Sheriff Dietrick. The woman got shit moving. It had taken Irene twenty minutes to drive back to the sheriff's office. In that time, Dietrick stirred the pot across southern Texas. At five in the morning, she followed up with the San Antonio police about the stolen car. She inserted herself into their workflow, and data started pouring in.

First came photos of the stolen car. Close-ups of her father's empty prescription bottle. Wes's cell phone. Irene recognized those items. There was other trash in the car too: bottles of water, piles of fast-food wrappers, a small bag of hand tools, and a utility belt. None of it was familiar to Irene, and she had to admit that she wasn't sure what, if any of it, belonged to her brother.

Then the deluge of data began. Photos came in via email and fax, and to Dietrick's cell. Stills, dash-cam footage, even grainy CCTV. "Irene, come look, this person fits the description of Wes or your father," became too much for the sheriff to say each time. So it soon shortened to, "This one?" Over the first hour of the morning, they pared it down to a bare-bones grunt. The rising one-syllable noise from Dietrick told Irene that her eyes were needed. Irene would look, shake her head no, and return her attention to her laptop.

Deputy Leo had been vigilant too. He'd been on the phone since Irene arrived at the sheriff's office. He followed up with law enforcement, culling emails, or weeding out leads using the little detail Irene provided on Wes's appearance.

For the first time since Dad disappeared, Irene was grateful for those around her. The sheriff and the deputy fell into the same set of people as Dr. Pav. They were helpers. They took action. They did the small things required to get to the big thing. A steady workflow operated now. Leo collected and culled the data. Irene offered analysis. Dietrick governed the flow in and out. This felt familiar to Irene. Productive. A process she respected.

And Irene had respected it. For almost nine fucking hours. And there was zero progress finding her father or brother. But this was how things worked. She trusted Leo and Dietrick; she trusted the process, and she knew her place in it.

"The McLennan office is sending in photos," Leo announced to the room as he cradled his landline. "They're coming in via email to you, Sherriff."

Irene tabbed over to her geoplot of Texas on her laptop. She was unfamiliar with the layout of Texas counties, the locations of cities, how far things were from one another. So she had built up a plot of the state, overlaying counties, cities, and roads. She added McLennan to the list of things she wanted highlighted in the map. A rotated rectangle, just east of the center of the state, started filling in with a red hatch pattern. McLennan was a county. Most populated city in it was Waco. The map updated with new annotations. A note next to Interstate 35 identified the three-hour driving time between Waco and the last place Wes had been—San Antonio.

Earlier in the day, that might have been useful information to have. At this point, Wes could have driven out of the state. Or out of the country. Irene sighed. Massive areas of her Texas map remained unshaded. The number of unknowns was staggering. The only way to resolve them—to make them known—was to work the process. Get the data. Clean it. Build a picture, atom by atom, until the pattern showed itself. Respect the process. The process worked.

Out of the corner of her eye, Irene saw the sheriff rotating her laptop toward her. They'd done this so many times today, her response approached a reflex. Irene leaned her chair back toward the officer's desk before Dietrick made her come-look-at-this grunt. The view in the photo was from high up, the face of the man obscured by the angle. It was a crappy black-and-white still from a video camera. A young man paying for something at a gas station register. Irene could make out the light hair, like Wes's. The bowl cut didn't match. Add the T-shirt and jeans hung from a beanpole of a frame. The person was not her brother.

"Nope," Irene huffed. "Too skinny. Wes's shorter as well."

The sheriff shrugged, turning her computer away. "Leo?" she called.

"On it," he replied, lifting the phone to his ear and dialing.

The sheriff had asked for recent photos of her father and brother. Irene delivered on her father—she had pictures from just days ago. But she had no photos of her asshole brother. She should have grabbed one from Dad's house. Hindsight was a crystal-clear bitch. Instead, the sheriff requested mug shots from Las Cruces. There was a single profile and face to work from, and they were three years old. Not ideal.

Now it was up to the pattern-matching engine between her ears to verify the photos. If she had more pictures of Wes, she would automate the process using her laptop. Facial recognition was a commodity now. You got it for free if you knew where to look. But you needed example data. The more, the better. With only one old photo to work from, Irene relied on her eyes and her memories of her asshole brother. A pattern cannot be gleaned from a single data point.

She scooted the metal chair closer to the desk. The legs vibrated against the concrete floor, squeaking out a brassy toot with each movement. At first, the noise amused her. The lowbrow sensibility required to appreciate a solid fart joke had been a sledgehammer to her anxiety, shattering it into manageable pieces. Now the sound was glue. Each little squeak marked a dead end, refitting another sharpened sliver of her anxiety back in place.

A harsh metallic rattle pummeled the room as Irene's cell phone rang. It vibrated against the metal desktop, creating a percussive onslaught of taps and bumps. The sound had occurred several times throughout the day. Each time everyone jumped like they had the hiccups. Deputy Leo shot her an annoyed glance, covering his open ear with a hand as he murmured into his phone.

Most of the official channels communicated through Leo. Except fucking Las Cruces. No matter how many times Irene corrected them, they kept calling Irene for updates. She lifted the cell, taking a mental note to disable the vibration after this call.

She turned it over, and her eyes stuck on caller ID glowing against the black glass.

First, Irene registered something unexpected. It wasn't the Las Cruces Sheriff's Office. Then she read the name on her screen.

Caleb Allard.

"It's Dad?" The words fell out of her mouth, a hoarse whisper at the end of an exhausted breath. She gripped the phone harder, shouting "It's Dad!" as she stood, her knees knocking the metal desk. Leo's eyes fixed on her as he eased his phone back into its cradle.

"Please answer that, Irene," Dietrick insisted.

Irene thumbed the connect icon and lifted the phone to her ear. She turned toward the sheriff. Dietrick was standing now, holding a pen against a pad, her jaw set and eyes homed on Irene.

The line connected with a quiet snap. Irene could hear noise from her dad's phone. Breathing.

"Dad?" she gasped. *"Dad?"* she shouted into the phone, her emotions teetering between anxiety and relief. "Are you okay!" The pressure of the last few days reached her eyes. Tears came, feral ones that poured out of her by their own will. Anxious ones. Angry ones. Hopeful ones. Terrified ones. "Are you safe?"

She held her breath, listening to the noise coming through the line. Heavy. Ragged. Wet. "Dad?" she repeated.

Endless seconds passed.

Then, a gasp. A shuddering heave of a breath. "Irene."

Her heart sank. Her body collapsed into the desk chair. The motion pushed the chair back, filling the pregnant room with a flatulent squeal.

She recognized the voice. From one data point, she knew who this was. But she couldn't help herself. She had to ask.

Verify her assumption. Because one data point cannot make a pattern.

It was possible she was wrong.

Dear God, please let her be wrong.

"Wes?"

Chapter 56

WES

"Irene," Wes stammered into the phone.

There was a pause. Three excruciating heartbeats of silence. Then, his sister's voice. "Wes?"

"Irene, I fucked everything up," he said. His voice was shaking. Tight. He had to remember to keep exhaling.

"It's okay. Is Dad there? Is he with you?"

Wes's eyes snapped across the gore-filled cab of the truck. Shiny, thick rivulets of blood ran down the windshield. Over the console. Down the front of the glove box. The sun came in through the open passenger-side door, putting a sheen on the rusty streaks.

"Wes, is Dad with you?" Irene's voice was insistent, but far away now.

No, Pop left.

"*Wes?*" she hollered.

"No, Pop left," he said into the phone. Wait, where's the phone? It had fallen from his ear. Wes felt around himself with trembling fingers. The hard case was on his belly. He picked it up. It was slick now too. "Dad's gone," he said. "He's heading back to town." He panted through a few pulses of pain. "Irene, listen, okay? I've been shot. And it really fucking hurts."

Irene had been speaking. Wes didn't realize until she stopped.

Her voice quickened. "You're hurt?" she asked.

He looked down at his leg. The red bloom on the thigh of his jeans was growing. Slower now, though. One hand braced a gnarled branch of mesquite, holding pressure on a makeshift tourniquet his father had made of Wes's belt. If he held it tight enough, it kept the artery closed.

"Wes! Did you say you've been shot!"

There was still a lot of blood, though. His vision was fuzzy. Fading. The hand on the branch was bleeding as well. He lost a finger when the gun fired. The index one.

"Yeah. Dad ... he fucking shot me. Where's my goddamned finger, Irene?" Where was his goddamned finger? It throbbed, as if the digit still belonged to his hand. But it wasn't there.

"Wes," Irene's voice came clipped, commanding. She was the authority now. "Wes, I need you to count to five, collect yourself. Can you do that? Will you count with me?"

"Well, yeah, I can count to five. Just not on my hand. Not anymore." His finger was missing.

Irene talked him through it, making him breathe before each number. It helped. Wes found the moment he was in.

"Okay," he said. "Yeah, I'm shot." He focused on keeping his breathing steady. "In the leg. Lots of bleeding." He glanced at his wound again. His pants had turned a sickening purple color, as if a bruise bloomed in the denim. He didn't need a medical degree to know he was in dire trouble. "I need an ambulance. I'm holding a tourniquet on the leg, but there's a lot of blood."

Irene's voice fell to a murmur. She spoke, but not to him. Wes took one steady breath through the burn. His mind wobbled, threatening to topple before she returned to the phone. "Where are you, Wes?"

He had to think. They took a trip. "We took a trip," he parroted. The pain in his leg oscillated with his heartbeat. Jesus Christ, it hurt.

"To Texas?" Irene asked. She had always been able to get him talking. Help him figure things out. Yes, Texas.

"Yes, Texas. Utopia." She was a good big sister to him.

Irene's voice returned to a murmur. Who was she talking to? Was it him? Because he couldn't hear her very well. "I can't hear you very well. I'm bleeding, Irene."

"Did you say you're in Utopia?" she asked.

Yes, that's right. He and Pop took a trip to Utopia, Texas. To heal their father. See, there's this boy ...

"Wes?"

"Yes, that's right," he remembered to speak this time. His hand ached. From holding the tourniquet tight. From the hole where his finger used to be. His eyes fell to find the source of the slow, thick dibbling sound. Blood saturated his jeans. His blood. It dripped to the vinyl floor mat. It smelled too.

Metallic and sulfurous. He tasted pennies in the air. "Dad," Wes said to himself. He tightened the pressure on his leg.

Hot pain burned off the mental fog.

Dad!

"Dad has a gun, Irene. He wants to kill a kid."

A bumping sound passed through the phone. "Wait, say that again?"

The strobing pain turned into a metronome, ticking away the events taking place right now. Right here. Dad. The gun. The boy. "Oh God, Irene," Wes cried. "Dad's got it in his head that he needs to kill this boy in Utopia. He's heading there now. There's a restaurant. The Silverleaf. He's heading there."

Irene's voice was incredulous. "Dad's gonna kill somebody? *What the fuck?*"

A brief shuffling sound carried through the phone, and an unfamiliar voice came over the call. "Mr. Allard, this is Sheriff Dietrick of the Kimble County Sheriff's Office. Please repeat what you just said to your sister."

Wes stammered, the words falling out between flares of agony. "My dad ... has a gun. It went off and ..." He stopped speaking to breathe through the fire in his thigh. "My dad shot me in the leg. It was an accident, but I'm bleeding bad. Dad's going on to Utopia. He's planning to shoot this kid to ..." He breathed again, clamping his eyes as the pain crested. "He thinks he needs to kill this kid in Utopia to save the world or some shit."

"Where is your father now, Wes?" The woman's voice was sharp, tense.

Wes's eyes opened. Through the blood smears on the windshield, he could see the dusty asphalt ending in another road. The one that cut a beeline north to Utopia. The ground moved in the air. A wiggle. It must be hot outside still. He didn't know where Pop was.

"I ... I'm not sure. He made a tourniquet on my leg. Then he left." The throbbing continued to ebb, accompanied by a chilling tingle in his toes. "I think I need an ambulance."

"Okay, I can work on that, but I need to know where you are. What road are you on?"

Wes peered through the splatter on the windshield, to the shoulder of the road. There were no signs here. Everything faded, the edges of his consciousness blunting from the hammering pain. Didn't he make up a song about the road trip?

"I made up a song about it," he slurred. Damn, he was losing it. "Highway 83 to something-with-a-nine, then 187 to the end of the line." His singing voice sucked right now. That's okay, this shit hurt something fierce.

"You're on road 187?" she asked. "Near Utopia?"

His mind wandered. Vision blurred. "I can see there from here," Wes mumbled. "I'm the guy in the truck with the blood all over it." The throb in his leg wasn't helping him stay focused anymore. The moment faded further from him with each thrush of his pulse. "You can't miss me."

He looked at his leg. Blood gushed. When did he let go of the branch? Shit, he couldn't do that. Wes twisted the branch around, tightening it again. It hurt. More than before. It was hard to hold. Slippery. His finger was missing. That fucking hurt too. Where did it go?

"You know what? I think I'm dying." The words dribbled from his lips. He could hear them dripping on the floor.

The sheriff talked, but Wes couldn't hear very well. He had dropped the damned phone again. Where was it? He looked around the cab.

On the dashboard, pointing back at him from a pool of thickened blood, Wes found his severed finger instead.

Chapter 57

CALEB

His sneakers crunched on the road. The sound was a pendulum, and Caleb used its momentum to keep moving. The sun was falling, the collected heat of the day rising from the asphalt. It was sweltering under the field coat, but he didn't dare take it off. The moldy duster made Caleb look like a hobo. But it was a hell of a better choice than walking around in his blood-covered shirt and pants.

Jesus. Wes had been wresting the gun from him. Caleb hadn't even been holding it tight. The truth, if Caleb was honest with himself, was that he had been about to let go of it. Succumb to Wes's bigger will and younger strength. He had seen it in his head, one fluid motion. Caleb letting go, Wes moving the pistol out of reach. Calling Irene to set the world back on the right path before his body gave out on him.

That hadn't happened, though. The sound, the impact of that moment, had been immense, like the voice itself. It filled his head, pushed on his body, froze his thoughts. The first change was a chemical bitterness in his mouth. The next change was incomprehensible.

It arrived as a heavy whine in his good ear. Neither Caleb nor his son moved. Still as stone, they gaped at each other. Wes's eyes were wide, searching over Caleb for an injury, while Caleb scoured his son.

The tentative thought had formed in Caleb's head: we're both okay. It was irrational. A false hope that despite the blood on everything, the warm wetness on his own face, they could put it back where it came from.

That's when Wes started screaming. A spray of blood—his son's blood—was hitting the windshield. Caleb followed the spray to the spreading stain on Wes's thigh. It saturated the denim and worked its way into the bench seat beneath him.

Caleb had to stop the bleeding, or his son would die in front of him. He pulled the belt from his son's pants, snaked it under the injured leg a few inches above the wound. He tightened it as hard as his failing body allowed. His strength wasn't enough—the spray slowed, but it was still steady. He needed leverage, something to compound the pressure. He jumped out of the cab, found a solid length of dry hardwood, and worked it between the belt and his son's leg. He rotated the stick like a winch, got three revolutions in before his arms threatened to shake off. He put Wes's hand on the branch, telling him to hold it firm. That's when he saw the stub on his son's hand. The flash from the revolver had severed his finger.

The recollection quickened his step. His son's blood, a timer counting down Wes's life one drop at a time. He walked through the growing stitch in his belly. Caleb needed to find someone to help his son, get medical attention to him before Wes bled out. They had holed up in a remote area on purpose. There was nothing between the apiary and Utopia except a few miles of road, scrub, and sky.

Caleb needed a phone. Call an ambulance.

You don't need to do that.

"You shut the hell up!" Caleb spit, taking another heaving step north, toward town.

No, it'll be all right.

"I said be quiet!" he screamed. The sound disappeared into the wide space around him. Caleb could see Utopia from here. It was miles down the road, yet there it was. Across the flat, unremarkable landscape, he made out the individual boards in the siding on the buildings in town. The structure and the road swayed in the haze of heat and breeze. The mirage of movement stoked Caleb's hope that someone was on the way to him. Coming to help.

Stop worrying about Wes. He's called Irene. She's working on it. Keep moving toward the boy.

Caleb stopped, raising an arm to help release the catch in his ribs. "What? When?"

Um ... just a few minutes ago, I guess?

"How the hell did he call his sister?"

Your phone. He had it in his pocket.

Caleb shut his eyes. A wave of rage and shame washed over the breakthrough pain as he tightened his fists. Through his gritted teeth, he spit, "Why the fuck didn't you tell me he had my phone on him!" He turned in place, searching for a target for his ire. "We could have called for help back at the truck!"

Well, sure, I guess I could have done that. But then you would have waited there, right? And we don't have time for that. Look, it doesn't matter. Wes phoned his sister. She's close. On her way here. She'll get someone out to help Wes.

The stitch in his belly reasserted itself. Caleb breathed through the pain. "And you know this for sure?"

Yep.

"So ... Wes's gonna be okay?"

There was an emptiness in his deaf ear. It lasted only a moment, but long enough for a kernel of doubt to form before the voice answered.

The Utopia Volunteer Fire Department is aware of Wes's location and situation. They're on it.

"But you know, right? You can see the ... branches or whatever. The possibilities. So you know for sure, he'll be okay?"

Silence. This wasn't right. A sickening hole opened under his pain. "Listen, I'm not taking one more step until you tell me ... no, you fucking show me that Wes lives through this."

A sigh filled Caleb's deaf ear. A balloon of emotion, expanding and releasing against the inside of his skull.

It's not that simple, Caleb.

"No. No more until you assure me Wes will be safe." Caleb looked for a place on the road to sit and rest. A fence. A stump. A rock. There was nothing but dirt and brush.

I can try to explain it to you. Or rather, show you, but ... okay, hang on a second.

Caleb scoffed. "Now I'm supposed to wait? For what, exactly?"

Okay, take one step forward.

Caleb swallowed. His feet and back ached; each step released a wave of agony in his gut. The tumor in his liver pulled on his diaphragm with each drop of his heel. He didn't want to continue on anymore. He could die right here, in this spot. And that would be okay.

Please, Caleb! I know you're tired, but this is a time-sensitive step I'm asking of you.

Caleb sighed, the impulse to move turning to a compulsion. An undeniable desire to act. He lifted his right foot, feeling the lumps on his liver shift. He brought the foot forward, setting it on the road. As he shifted his weight, something cracked beneath his shoe. There was a buzz, a crunch, and then silence again. Lifting his shoe, Caleb saw the remains of a thick beetle on the road, torn apart between the asphalt and his sole.

There! Your choice to take that step has saved a countless number of lives.

The voice spoke with an air of pride, but Caleb couldn't appreciate it. He looked around at the still air. Nothing had changed. He looked at the broken bug. Shaking his head, he said, "I don't understand."

A rumble filled his head. Caleb stumbled, then left his body. He watched himself slam into the road, wincing at the sight of his face hitting the pavement. He noted the rough facets on each pebble, discerned the individual pores and hairs on his skin as the road abraded it. He felt nothing from the fall. No discomfort from his sickness. No air or sun on his skin.

The translucent threads appeared. An endless and dense tapestry wove through the moment. Thick swatches speared out toward the town, and thinner strips wandered off into the hill country around him.

Now, I will show you what would have happened if you didn't step on that beetle. I've never done this before, so bear with me. Let me know if it hurts.

The perspective changed around him. Colors disappeared, turning the scenery to clay. He stood on the road now. The beetle was on the asphalt in front of him. Caleb noted one of its legs was in the air, that the insect's mandibles were half-opened as it cleaned them off. This was the moment he'd stepped on the bug.

Look here.

Caleb knew where to look. A single translucent fiber stood out from the rest, a thread that spiraled through the beetle.

Follow it.

Caleb knew how to follow it. The next moment came, in full color, the scene living and real. The beetle moved into the field on the side of the road.

Faster.

Caleb knew how to move faster. Moments came and passed in rapid flashes. Details accumulated until he found the beetle rummaging under some rough growth. He couldn't feel it, but Caleb knew the air carried a chill now. The season had changed. Murmurs filled the space. Not people, geese. They waddled through, bickering and picking at the rough ground vegetation. One goose clamped its bill around the beetle, crushing the bug before swallowing it. The beetle's thread spun down the bird's gullet, then intertwined with a new thread. The thread of the goose.

Follow it.

Another series of flashes, and the goose was in the sky, Caleb's view following the goose as if he were flying himself. The effect should have been nauseating, but Caleb felt nothing. The flock spanned forward and left. The ground passed far beneath them at a plodding pace. With a snap, another moment arrived. The formation broke as a bird of prey landed on the goose leading the flock. Caleb saw the thick talons of the eagle. Each scratch and gouge in the sharp nails was apparent as they passed through thousands of delicate barbs in the goose's feathers. They sank into the flesh as the remaining geese scattered in a show of flapping wings and terrified honks. Caleb's goose plummeted, following a few of its flock as they broke to the right.

Another sound joined the fray—the purr of an engine. A small, single-engine plane. Caleb experienced it for only a moment before the goose disappeared in a spray of blood and feathers. The thread of the goose knotted around other threads, ones that passed through the Cessna. Five of them. Five living things in that plane as it fell out of the sky. A path of smoke highlighted their fibers as they ended, knotted into the burning ground.

None of this happened, thanks to you.

Caleb's perspective shifted again. He pulled away from the crash to see other branches reaching out, past this moment. Above it. Below it. The frustum shifted. A plane landed. A bundle of threads stretched away from the event. Faces came to him. Tens, then hundreds, then millions of faces raced past Caleb as he dragged forward.

These people will exist because you took that step. Without that choice, none of them would.

Caleb registered none of it now; the faces became a blur of white noise. Years. Millennia. Epochs. They passed around him like wind. The tapestry from that one event branched into a forest of possibilities. People. Futures. A saga of humanity.

A snap in his head, and everything was dark. He felt something. Warmth, under his fingers. He blinked. He was in his body, facedown on the road. He eased to his knees, checking for fresh injuries. He rubbed the road grime from his face, specks of stone, dirt, and sweat falling off his cheeks. His head throbbed from the experience, but it hadn't been painful. It had been exhilarating. Too much so for his broken body to absorb.

You've saved an infinite number of lives by making a single choice.

Caleb stood, his breath catching again. The tumor in his liver asserted itself with a sharp pang.

Every moment—every choice—is like this. There are endless outcomes, each leading to an endless number of other choices.

Caleb was upright. His breath heaved, his body shuddering with each throb of his heart.

The forward outcomes are impossible to predict. No one can tally them all. Not even me.

"Why show me this?" Caleb huffed between labored sighs.

Because there isn't a ledger to the universe, Caleb. I'm only trying to keep things moving forward. Keep things from ending.

He shook his head, clearing the haze left by his out-of-body experience. "What does that have to do with Wes?" He looked around him, as if he would see the voice standing next to him. "You said you'd explain how Wes would be safe?" Caleb's heart leapt. "No, you could show me! Show the threads to follow where Wes lives, and I can figure out how to get to them!"

Caleb, look ...

"No, dammit!"

Caleb ...

"Not until you show me!"

No! Caleb, I can't!

"You can't? We just finished a literal fucking goose chase! Don't tell me you can't!" Caleb was screaming now. He twisted his body around, searching for something, anything, on which to focus. "Or you *won't?* You want me to kill that boy, you need to show me how it keeps Wes alive!"

I can't show you that, Caleb.

"Show me, or I'll sit down right here and die!"

The sigh filled his head again, but there was no shift in his perspective. He stayed in his body, left with a lingering shadow of sadness as the voice filled his deaf ear.

I can't show you a path where Wes survives.

Caleb's eyes blurred.

Because I can't find any. The choices that would have changed that have been made.

Stinging tears fell down Caleb's road-rashed cheeks. His shoulders fell, and he struggled to stay standing. He knew the truth in the words. The things he'd done to get here—the lying, the stealing, the lives ruined—it guaranteed this outcome. Whatever choices they'd made—the choices Caleb had made—solidified this current moment. Guaranteed it would occur.

A bubble of spit shook on Caleb's trembling lip. Despite himself, he whispered, "You lie."

I've never lied to you. Your situation, this moment—this isn't bad or evil. It's not good either. It's just ... the way things have gone. Wes won't survive the day. Neither will you. But you can both still make choices. You can choose how to live it out.

"You lie!" Caleb spit, his voice rising. "You let me think I would live! That this boy would heal me!"

No, Caleb. I never said that. I said you had a purpose. I said the boy was the key to your purpose. That you needed to get to the boy. And all of that is true.

"That's still a lie! A lie of omission!" he yelled. "You knew what you were implying, what you dangled in front of me to get me here!"

I did what I needed to do. But I never promised you anything beyond a purpose, Caleb. Any "lie of omission" is what you read into it.

Caleb wiped his eyes on the sleeve of the duster. He turned away from Utopia. Toward his son. He could get back to him. Wes didn't have to die alone.

The landscape had changed. Drab with shadow. Smoking. Was there a fire? Caleb looked closer. Fragments dissolved from the distant hills and lifted into the air. Waves and tendrils of color eased into the sky, where they joined other currents moving there. They flowed together, wisps wrapped around larger fingers, leaving a stale and lifeless putty color in their wake.

He recognized this. The fluid motions. The serpentine flow. This was the swarm he'd seen at the apiary. It spanned the entire Texas horizon now. Swaths of color dissociated from their matter, flowing away as far as Caleb could see. Hills, brush, and even the road smeared into the sky, leaving behind bland clay forms of themselves.

"What the fuck is this?" Caleb hissed.

Your choices are collapsing.

"That ... that wave? The color disappearing?" he asked. "It's like that space you take me to. When there's no color."

Yes. Moments are becoming fixed for you now.

"That's ... death," Caleb said. His voice was distant, his breath stolen by the apocalyptic scene in front of him.

That's a way of understanding it. Your death.

Caleb swallowed. There was nowhere to go. It was consuming everything he saw. "Can I still get to Wes?"

No. He's behind the wake. You'll die before reaching him.

"Can I save him?"

No. I told you. His path is set. He won't survive the day.

The front of the wave crested another hill between Caleb and the Texas horizon. A spiral of sienna and sage broke away from the earth and lifted into the sky.

Turn around, Caleb. That's where your choices are now.

Chapter 58

IRENE

Once Wes stopped responding, Sheriff Dietrick had turned to Leo. "Utopia. The Silverleaf. It's an hour away. Unless you drive—then it's more like forty minutes."

She wasn't joking. Irene sank into the backseat of the deputy's custom Dodge Challenger as he sped out of a curve. He handled the overpowered car on the delicate edge between control and chaos. The tires squealed in protest as the engine insisted they race forward.

Leo was a statue of concentration, his focus on the snaking road ahead. Sheriff Dietrick worked her phone and portable radio. She was trying to organize medical help for Wes and a police presence at the restaurant. Her tight shoulders and clipped tone told Irene it wasn't going well.

"What's the problem?" Irene asked. "Did the ambulance reach Wes yet?"

The sheriff turned in the front seat, giving Irene her profile. "I'm having trouble getting a coherent picture from Utopia

dispatch. I got ahold of a friend over at the fire department."
She shook her head, dismayed. "Says help will be on its way to
your brother soon, but everyone is working a scene north of
town." She looked back before adding, "What are the damned
odds of that?"

Irene nodded. Her stomach reached into her throat. She
wondered if it was because of her own worry, or if it was from
Leo floating into another wide turn. Her fingers dug into the
leather seat as the car sped up again. The sheriff didn't seem at
all perturbed by the offensive driving tactics, and she turned to
face the deputy.

Dietrick's voice lowered, still yelling over the guttural
engine noise as she spoke to Leo. "Something's up in town.
Everyone's cagey, I can't get any direct answers."

"That's probably it right there," Leo offered, one of his
fingers shooting toward the windshield. Irene's eyes followed
it. The road straightened out, and ahead of them highway
patrol cruisers blocked their way. Their strobing red and blue
lights made the scene painful to view straight on. An
ambulance was parked on the shoulder. Paramedics and
officers scuttled over the area near the road.

Physics released Irene from the seat as Deputy Leo
decelerated. He reached to the car's console, flipping a switch.
Emergency lights flashed from under the dashboard.

Dietrick nodded to the scene ahead. "Yep, here's why we
can't reach anyone. Wonder what all the fuss is." As the car
eased to a stop in front of the blockade, she opened the door.

As she closed it behind her, the sheriff turned to Irene, saying, "Stay here, Ms. Allard. We'll only be a minute."

Irene was alone before she put her protest into words. The windshield provided an unobstructed view of Dietrick approaching an officer, Leo stepping into his boss's flank. Irene watched the conversation, trying to pick up any detail she could. Heads shook; faces were drawn. She wasn't able to make out words from watching their lips.

"Come on," she groaned. She looked at the road ahead. She saw no town. Just fields. Trees. Dad was down there, somewhere, coming her way. Wes was farther away, bleeding to death. And Irene was stuck here, waiting in the backseat of a tiny-penis-mobile.

She punched the headrest, releasing a modicum of her frustration. She turned back toward Dietrick. The sheriff had her hand over her mouth. Leo and the patrolman stared past her. Irene followed their eyes to a long, thin cluster of trees. Two paramedics heaved a large black sack, working it over the gnarled roots that wove the trees together.

Her heart slammed against her chest. Her fingers dug into the headrest. Not a sack. A body bag.

She pushed on the seat in front of her, fumbling until she found the release on the side. She was out of the car, feet on the ground, moving into the scene. A hand gripped her shoulder. It was Deputy Leo.

"Ms. Allard, you need to stay in the car." His voice was firm, but his eyes were round with care.

She looked to the black bag framed by the paramedics as they hauled it toward the ambulance. Her hand rose to her mouth. "Oh God," Irene cried, "is that ... my father?"

Leo shook his head. "I assure you, ma'am, it ain't your father."

"Let me see," she screamed. "Show me!"

The sheriff closed the distance to Irene, stepping between her eyes and the ambulance. Irene tried to look over her tight features, searching for an explanation. Dietrick leaned in close, her breath hot on Irene's cheek as she whispered, "Irene, it isn't your father. It's a highway patrol officer."

Irene shook, her hands wandering to her cheeks, then her belly.

Deputy Leo's arm went around her shoulders. He prodded Irene back toward his Challenger. "You need to be calm and wait in the car." His head turned toward the officer on scene. His tone became guarded as he whispered, "Things just got a hell of a lot more complicated for everyone."

Irene stood, one foot in the car, the other on the ground. She watched the paramedics hoist the bag into the back of the ambulance, the boxy chassis rocking from the weight. The doors closed, the body hidden. The ambulance pulled into the road, its siren wailing. Irene watched it shrink away, the pitch and volume of the siren falling.

Voices stole Irene from her reverie. Yelling. Her eyes found the sheriff. Another officer screamed at her, the sheriff's hands raised in placation. What the hell?

The patrolman's head swiveled, and his eyes locked on Irene. His stare was bitter. It was more than professional stoicism. He scowled at her. The man's skin went ruddy; his lips sneered with vitriol.

Sheriff Dietrick turned her head to Irene. Her face pleaded, her eyes motioning to the car. The deputy placed a hand on Irene's head, pressuring her into the backseat.

He closed the door, and held a hand to the window, a universal sign of "wait here." He returned to the sheriff's side. She engaged the patrolman in a verbal confrontation. Irene couldn't hear them from inside the car. Dietrick's hands opened, her movements intentional and slow. The other officer puffed his chest, his hands fisting closed and open.

Then the patrolman pointed past the sheriff and the deputy. Toward the car. His eyes rose to Irene. He pointed right at her. He glared, spit frothing as his mouth slapped open and shut. The sheriff moved to block his view as the deputy rounded the front of the vehicle. In a moment, they were back in the car.

"Come on," Dietrick said, "let's haul ass to the Silverleaf before this gets any worse."

The car started with a controlled growl, and Deputy Leo eased it around the blockade. The screaming engine aggravated the tension between them as the car opened up on the road.

"What the hell was that about?" Irene asked.

The question hung in the air, unanswered. Leo stole a pleading look to his boss. Dietrick puffed out a sigh and turned in her seat to face Irene.

"The body they pulled from the barn was a highway patrolman. Someone murdered him."

"Jesus Christ," Irene said. "Murdered?"

The sheriff nodded.

Irene shook her head. "That's terrible! But ... why was that officer angry at me?"

The sheriff chewed her lip, eyes fixed on Irene. She debated something; Irene sensed ambivalence radiating from her.

"What is it?" Irene demanded, steeling her gut for more dreadful details.

Dietrick released her lip. "Your brother was shot."

Irene nodded.

"By your father," the sheriff continued.

"That's what he said," Irene confirmed.

"And your father doesn't own a gun?" Dietrick worried. Her brow wrinkled, eyes wide. The sheriff hoped for a specific answer.

Irene shook her head. "He doesn't, no. Why?"

The sheriff's face fell a bit. "And Wes?"

"I ... I don't know," Irene admitted. "I can't imagine he would be able to get one legally, with his record."

The sheriff didn't blink. Her eyes hardened, her lips thinned as she swallowed. "That patrolman they pulled out of the barn? His gun is missing, Irene."

Chapter 59

CALEB

"But why does it need to be me?" Caleb asked. "Why don't you just ... I dunno, drop a rock on the kid? Cause a car accident?"

Oh, believe me, I tried.

The shock of the flippant response stopped Caleb in his tracks.

Yeah, I mean, that video of the deer getting crushed? I was aiming for the boy. I did what I could, but it didn't work out.

Caleb's mouth fell open. "But how could it not? Aren't you ..."

I can't make anyone do things. It's a "free will" thing, you know? People have to act on their own. Make choices. Each choice results in a moment. More choices.

"So you ... what?" Caleb asked. "Talked the driver into murdering the boy?"

Oh, no. That whole thing, it was more of a Hail Mary. He loved animals, was on that road at the right time, with a paranoid squirrel in exactly the right place. Most of the time that's the way it is. You've seen it—there are just too many possibilities to track.

"But why is this happening? Why me?" Pride and terror battled in his chest as the voice remained silent. What made him special? Was he created to do this one thing?

He stopped walking as a shudder of resignation ran through his body. He recognized the emotion, the gesture. It didn't belong to him.

Caleb raised his open palms, annoyed. "Are you ... shrugging?"

Yes, sorry. You can't see that, can you?

Caleb sighed, turning around. The rising smears of color had expanded. The sky was full, walls of color ebbing and flowing like the surface of rising water.

Keep moving. The church is two streets right, three streets up.

"I know," Caleb snubbed. He walked the last dozen steps before the town's first intersection. He turned off the road to a side street that ran by the church. The town was still, save a thin wail rising in the air. Across a small yard was a boxy, prefabricated building. The annex. That's where he needed to go.

The wailing blossomed into a piercing siren. It rose and fell in pitch as an ambulance raced through the intersection beyond the church.

It was heading south. Straight for the wall of dissolving colors. Straight toward Wes.

Focus, Caleb. You're so close now.

A shudder racked his chest. Not physical pain. This was bitter regret, shaking the breath from Caleb's lungs. "Is he gone yet?" he worried.

Who?

Caleb's unbraced hand ran over his face, wiping past his frustration. "Wes, who the hell do you think?"

Oh, right. Let me see. ...

Caleb stepped into the churchyard. The annex was featureless and unremarkable. It squatted on cinder blocks, the bulk of it taking up what was once a basketball court. The plank siding of the Silverleaf walled the far side of the yard. He wondered if the boy was there now. Beyond the diner and across the street, Caleb saw the wood gazebo in the park. His hand reached for the fanny pack under his coat, finding it bloated with cash. Then it moved to the revolver in his pocket.

Looks like he's hanging on. Shouldn't be long, though.

Caleb looked to the annex. Wood stairs led to the only door in the structure. Three steps, each a choice he needed to make. A tremble came to his lips. He didn't want to move. He didn't want to hurt anyone else. A story played out in Caleb's head. He could take out the gun. Put it under his chin. End himself before he caused any more damage to the world. One choice. One last moment. A squeeze, then nothing. No ten seconds of awareness like he'd have with the Final Release. It would all end in a flash.

Don't you puss out on me, Caleb! We've come too far for that! You need to see this through!

The voice stabbed through his mind. Fresh pain, a crushing fist, gripped him. His chest tightened. The tumors in his belly ground against his rib cage. His posture bent at the angry force shoving his body forward. "Stop," he croaked. "Please, stop! I'll do it!"

The pressure abated, and Caleb stumbled to catch himself. Hands on his knees, he caught his breath. "Please, don't. I'll do it," he grunted.

Get on with it, Caleb. The universe has time. You don't.

Caleb nodded. "I will. I'll do it. But ... I want to see Wes one last time. Before he's gone."

What did I say? We don't have time for this, Caleb!

"No," he replied. His breath calmed as his body relaxed. "No, we do have time, don't we? You can take me into that ... that space. With the threads? Time doesn't pass when we're in there. Does it?"

His deaf ear was silent.

Caleb stood up straight, a sharp pang pinching under his ribs. "Well? Am I right?"

The snap in his head was his answer. Caleb expanded beyond his body. The moment shifted around him, his mind racing back the way he had come. Blazing over tepid-colored scrub and hills. South. Toward his son.

The clay ambulance was turning off State Road 187. On the farm road was the truck. Wes. Caleb was with him now, his putty statue slumped in the pickup, the details sickening. Blood dripped from his leg and pooled on the floorboard. It was the same neutral color as Wes's form, making it appear as though his son were melting in the afternoon sun.

See? There is your son. Right where you left him.

The voice was flat, colorless as the environment that surrounded them. Caleb ignored the cynicism and focused on his son. He looked past the excruciating details for what he knew was underneath. And he found it. Wes's thread.

Caleb, what are you doing?

He traced the thread backward, through their afternoon in the apiary. Further, back to Junction and I-10.

This won't change anything.

Caleb ignored the voice, moved along the thread. Faster. To Truth or Consequences. Further. Wes arriving at the hospice office. Caleb lurched along the glassy fibers, heaving past Wes's recent time in rehab. Past his previous stint several years ago. Caleb groped past years, stumbling through moments of his son's young adulthood. Wes sitting in a small classroom, dozing. Wes running through the street with other children as a monsoon opened above them. Caleb searched. Scoured.

Caleb, are you trying to delay your responsibilities?

Caleb wanted to know. When was it? What was the deciding moment?

Oh, I see.

What choice had he made?

You want to understand how you fucked up your son?

He would have chosen other words. But yes, that was what Caleb wanted to know. What did he do, as Wes's father? What was the tipping point that nudged Wes onto his path? The laziness. The drugs. Violence. Bleeding out in a truck, alone.

I can help you with that.

Caleb settled into a specific moment. The stale palette made forms difficult to distinguish. As he eased into the scene, his mind wormed into the exquisite details. The boat, on Elephant Butte Lake. Waters calm, except for the dozen ripples from the pontoons as they rocked against the weight they carried. The sun fixed high in a clear sky. The air still. Irene seated under the boat's metal canopy, unwrapping a clay Popsicle. Caleb standing on the deck. Holding his boy. Playing the game they both loved. Counting. Teasing. Building the anticipation before tossing Wes over the railing and into the water. In the static moment, Caleb held Wes's thick-boned body prone, about to release him out over the water.

What was this? Why this moment? How could this have set his son on such a destructive path? Wes loved their time on the boat. They all did. It was one of the few times the kids enjoyed each other. This was a moment filled with love, one he wanted his children to cherish. How was this where things went so wrong?

It's tricky, though, Caleb. This moment is ... was ... the last time you took them out on the pontoon boat. Do you remember what you were thinking?

He remembered. Wes was getting too big for the game. Too heavy to throw. They wouldn't be able to play it much longer, unless Caleb wanted a back injury.

Yes, but do you remember the choice you made here?

Caleb could not remember. What choice?

As an answer to the question, two fibers became obvious to Caleb. They knotted together in the chest of his putty statue, passing into Wes. They split there, one curving over the left side of the boat, the other over the right. Caleb didn't comprehend.

You always flung Wes over the left side of the boat. That's the side that has the ladder in the water. This time, though, this one time, you went the other direction.

The scene played out, Caleb's form splitting as one released Wes to the left, the other to the right. Both Weses silently broke the water, sending ripples through the clay-colored surface. What was Caleb supposed to see?

Look deeper, Caleb. Look at what's happening in your son's brain.

Caleb moved into the microscopic details. Brain cells. Neurons. Chemicals spewing across endless chasms of space. Both Weses had the same rush. Neurotransmitters shoving the impulse from cell to cell. Feelings emerged as the event arced through his son's brain. Anticipation. Excitement. Joy.

The patterns diverged. Caleb slipped back to the boat. Left-Wes reached the ladder, his brain falling back to something stable, something calm. Right-Wes slapped through the water to reach the pontoon. He pawed hand over hand toward the front of the boat, his brain flooding with new chemicals. Unfamiliar feelings. Different thoughts. Fear. He couldn't get out of the water. Terror. He was drowning. Betrayal. Dad knew he was a shitty swimmer.

Experiencing Wes's thoughts should have unsettled Caleb. The lack of privacy should have embarrassed him. As before, in this strange place, Caleb felt nothing. It was one minor detail on an infinite pile of emotionless data points.

That right there? That set it all in motion.

But how?

Subtle changes in neural pathways, solidified by the body's reaction. It changed your son. How he responded to things. What he expected from people.

Caleb couldn't look away. His mind captured every painful, writhing detail as his son thrashed in the lake. Eyes saucered, Wes splashed around the front of the boat.

Not all at once. Like, he wasn't swimming here thinking, "Damn, now I'm an unmotivated drug addict." But this was the first chink in his armor.

The moment moved forward. Wes—both Weses—were on the boat. Left-Wes reaching up to Caleb for another toss into the drink. Right-Wes shuddering under a towel next to his sister.

A slight change already, see? Changes have a way of accumulating.

Caleb rushed off the boat. Two fresh moments splayed around him. Wes was years older. Maybe eleven. He was walking into his two-story school building with other students. Left-Wes stood midstride, in a group of his peers. Smiling. Eyes homed on a boy standing next to him. Engaged. Happy.

Right-Wes stood a few yards back. Alone. Eyes on his shoes. Ignoring the world and the people in it. Shoulders stooped as if he was trying to disappear altogether.

More moments, more choices, more disparity.

The scene flashed ahead. Wes was older. Midteens now. In a hardware store. He wore a utility smock, a name badge pinned to a polo shirt. He worked here. And he didn't. The other Wes skulked in a corner, pocketing something from a display.

Moments came faster. One Wes buying groceries, the other buying weed. One finishing high school, the other skipping class. One in technical school, the other in rehab.

How was Caleb supposed to know? How could he have known that one insignificant decision would lead to this? More moments raced around him. Wes starting an HVAC servicing business. Wes relapsing into treatment. Wes grieving over his father's death. Wes dying under the Texas sun.

Caleb wanted to stop, longed to leave this space. There was one Wes now. Getting married. Knowing love. Having children. His own boat. Caleb's adult son, standing on the bow of a new pontoon boat, holding his daughter—Caleb's would-be granddaughter—by the armpits. Faces bright. Eyes twinkling with anticipation. Like Caleb used to do with his son.

He longed to feel something. Anger. Sadness. Guilt. Something to acknowledge the lifetime of misery he'd caused his son. To grieve the moments that could have been. That should have been.

You can't dwell on that, Caleb. You made a choice, yes. Wes made his own choices too. It's impossible for anyone to see it all. The infinite outcomes and interactions. Hell, I can't even do it. All you can do is move ahead. Make the next choice.

The moments folded on themselves. Caleb found himself back in front of the church annex. Color throbbed into the scene as his emotions reasserted themselves. Rage at the loss of his son, preventable by a single choice so long ago. Frustration at not seeing it in time. Despair that he would never have known any better. Broken over the moments that would never be.

Caleb pulled in a creaking breath, the pain of his disease blossoming once again. Its grip had tightened, an anchor dragging from his belly. Tears seeped from his eyes, blurring the annex door to a smudge. He wiped them away.

Would you like to see Irene too?

Of course he wanted to see his daughter. Yet, Caleb shook his head. He knew he wouldn't be able to resist unraveling the threads. He would learn why Irene was the way she was, while her brother's life came to an ugly end. It would break him in two.

Season of Waiting

If it's any consolation—

"It isn't," Caleb interrupted. As he placed his foot on the first step to the annex door, a new siren blared from the road. He looked up, followed the sound of squealing brakes as a muscle car tore down the road. Several police cruisers followed, and the vehicles stopped at the intersection past the diner, blocking the road through Utopia.

Behind the cars, in the park across Main Street, a thin streak of rust and brown pulled away from the gazebo. It tangled with the stale greens and grays effervescing from the grass, mesquite trees, and stone wall as the colors of the park broke apart and rose into the sky.

Then you need to hurry. This can still go sideways. You have a few choices, Caleb. Make them count.

Caleb rapped on the door.

Chapter 60

WES

One. Two. Three. Four. Five.

Wes opened his eyes. He looked down at his leg. His forearm still wedged the tourniquet tight. The makeshift clamp held. His lids drifted back closed.

One. Two. What were those numbers Pop had said? When he lay in the road? What did Irene call them? Oily numbers, or something. What were they? Two, something, right? Wes struggled to remember. Who remembered such a stupid thing, anyway?

Shit. Shit! He opened his eyes again. Was the tourniquet still holding? He grappled against the weight of his eyelids. His head leaned forward onto the steering wheel. He was so tired. His leg numbed as his body shivered from the chill. Maybe he would take a short nap.

The crowbar of a siren forced open his eyes. Just as fast, the sound stopped. Had he died? Was that moment his last one? The spattered windshield throbbed with the red emergency lights, making the spots and rivulets pulse. No, he wasn't dead.

His door opened. His body moved. Not by his choice. Wes wanted to help. But the pain held him in his seat. The slurp of breaking suction. The scream from his thigh. He pushed against his own mind, willing it to stay conscious.

He must have failed. He was prone. Fresh agony, on his leg. Tearing. They were cutting off his jeans, ripping the coagulated blood from his wound. Ragged pain. He bled again. It wasn't warm. He should be able to feel it on his skin, right?

Wes heard his name. He looked up, at a stranger. Round face. Weak beard. Wes nodded. More words from the round face. A single word stood out.

Morphine.

No, no morphine. I'm an addict. Had Wes said it or thought it?

The round face turned away.

Are you listening to me? I can't have morphine.

The round face turned back. Wes felt a pressure on his arm. Don't ...

The needle pricked his skin.

I said no ...

The pressure on his arm released. Then, the pressure on his body released.

That familiar warm bloom lifted Wes above his misery. His suffering was there, but distant. His wounds were still a part of him, still identifiable, the pain stitched into his sensory fabric.

Wes acknowledged them, but they did not concern him anymore.

Wes recognized the space around him. He had spent so much time in this deceptively safe and gentle place.

He found the eyes of the EMT. "You shouldn't have done that."

Round Face bounced as he spoke. "Please, lay still."

"Yeah, but you shouldn't have done that." This was important. Round Face needed to listen. Air passed over his exposed legs. His jeans were off now. A nugget of modesty joined the pain of his wounds.

"Stop moving. You've lost some blood, but you'll be okay," said the jiggling face. Liar, liar, pants something something.

"On fire." Wes found the words. They were there the whole time, in his salty and sticky mouth.

"How's that?" Round Face asked. "You should feel pretty great about now."

Wes pointed at Round Face with his missing finger. "You shouldn't have done that, though." Gross. His hand was a mess. It needed a bandage or something.

Round Face frowned as he reached around the small space. Wes knew they were moving. His body shifted on the gurney. Round Face wobbled over him.

"How's that?" Round Face asked again. He poked at parts of Wes's body.

"I'm an addict," Wes said. I won't test clean. They won't let me back. I'll have to start again. From the beginning. Had he said that last part?

"Buddy, let's focus on getting you through right now, 'kay?"

Yeah, okay.

Fresh pain joined the old, a whisper on a wail. Wes peered over his bloodied body. A clean bandage wrapped around his thigh. His dick lay out in the open for everyone to see. Well, for Round Face, at least.

Wes was what? Fourteen maybe? He made up that song about it. How did it go? "Hung like a baby, hard like wood, gonna rub it raw cuz it feels real good!"

Wes chuckled. That song was dumb. They couldn't all be winners, though.

Chapter 61

JAIME

Strobing lights penetrated the thin curtains, tinting the inside of the temporary building with purple tones. Jaime pulled back the curtain again. Something was happening at the Silverleaf. Police poured into the street from their vehicles. Whatever it was, the restaurant sat between Jaime's window and the action.

He felt his stoic mask crack as his face grimaced. Those cops could be coming for him. Had someone already found that dumb-ass kid from Emerson's school? Jaime shook off the thought, like dust off his confidence. Jaime had stuffed the kid's body in the abandoned well because it was so remote. Away from town, miles from anyone. And it hadn't even been twenty-four hours yet. Besides, no one gave a shit about Henry. No way the town would pull together this level of response for that brat. Hell, his parents were too stoned to realize their kid was even missing. But what about the school? Henry would have been absent today. Jaime snorted. Henry's teacher was most likely grateful that the little fucker didn't show. She wouldn't have looked any further into it.

Jaime dropped the curtain and checked his watch. The afternoon was getting away from him. He had expected the sick man—Carl?—almost an hour ago. Maybe he bit the dust already. If so, that was disappointing. This would have been an easy five grand. And even though he never let it show, Jaime enjoyed watching Emerson work. The faces of people as Em shrugged off the yoke holding them down. It was magic.

He sighed through his growing disappointment. While he debated how much longer to wait, two hollow raps sounded from the door. Surprise crawled into his ass, an image of the police surrounding his office running through his head. He swallowed the worry. Cops didn't knock, he figured. And if they did, it sure wouldn't sound so meek. Jaime peeked through the door's peephole.

Warm satisfaction filled him. There he was! That shrinking sick man. Carl, or whatever. Jaime smiled. He pulled his phone from his pocket and texted Blair, "He's here. Better late than never. Get M ready."

When Jaime first caught wind of the angle Blair was working, she had been operating out of the goddamned Silverleaf. Where she worked. Where anyone could have witnessed the miracle firsthand. Once he realized what they could do together, he offered to manage the business and build a smarter workflow. One that was safer for Blair and Em. Blair had jumped on his offer. She confided that their clients were sometimes less than satisfied with the value they received from the transaction, reactions ranging from nonpayment to violence. Once, a man put his hands on the miracle boy. And that was fucking unacceptable.

Jaime mapped out a better exchange. The precautions were of his own design, although he borrowed from what he'd learned selling dope in Del Rio. It was a staged process now, isolating the money and the product from each other. Money came first, before anyone lifted a finger. Jaime met the client in a controlled location. He accepted the cash and notified Blair when everything was ready. She brought Em over, he did his hands-on stuff, and then they left. Regardless of the outcome, Jaime made sure the client stayed put until Blair texted that the boy was safe. They'd practiced it a ton. And this dying man would be their first live customer experience.

Jaime hardened his face and opened the door. Carl stood on the bottom step, swallowed in a duster that consumed him to his bones. The sick man stammered, and rather than wait for him to find words, Jaime waved him into the office. As the man passed through the doorway, Jaime pointed him toward the molded plastic chair set against the narrow wall of the room.

"Sit down," he commanded.

Carl eased into the chair with an unsteady wobble. A vapor had followed him into the annex. A cloying mixture of sweet body sweat, metallic mold, and earthy dust unseated the smell of the recent construction. Jaime felt the odor crawl into his sinuses. He swallowed through his gag reflex. This man needed a shower more than a healing.

Jaime stared at him for a moment. The man was a mess. The stale coat covered the man's mud-splattered clothing. His short hair was dusty and matted in cowlicks. Bruises and dirt splotched his scraped-up cheeks. His eyes had yellowed like piss, and they stayed fixed on the floor in a picture of shame. In the silent space, Carl pulled the coat close around his rattling bones.

"You look like hell," Jaime offered. "You really do need a miracle, don't ya?"

Carl swallowed. He nodded as he asked, "The boy?"

Jaime sighed and shook his head. "The money," he retorted, adding a condescending drawl to his voice.

The waif of a man eased up in the chair. It seemed to take a massive effort for him to reach under the coat. He shifted his body, and there was a clacking sound. From under the coat, Carl produced a black leather fanny pack. He held it up to Jaime like a child holding a fish they just pulled out of the water—enamored with the thing but disgusted by it at the same time. Jaime took the bulk of the pack in his fist, setting it on the desk as he sat in his chair.

Jaime opened the main pouch and reached in. He found wads of bills, packed tight into the pouch, as if Carl had found all this money stuffed in his damned couch. Jaime shot a glance at him, an eyebrow raised in irritation. Carl continued to stare at the floor.

It took several minutes for Jaime to flatten each crumple back into a recognizable bill. Twenties and hundreds. A few odd denominations crumpled together into a heavy ball. As Jamie teased them apart, he hid his confusion at finding a toy car at their core. Carl was full of fucking surprises. He rolled it over in his palm. The miniature metal vehicle was something that Emerson might play with. Hell, the kid was probably playing with his Hot Wheels right now.

"I'd like to keep that." Carl stared at the toy. Jaime nodded and handed over the little metal car with a shrug.

With the bills organized, Jaime pulled his ledger from its drawer and opened it to the bookmarked page. His eyes followed his finger down the first column until they landed on the last entry: Caleb Allard. Caleb, not Carl. Shit! Had he used the wrong name out loud? Whatever, the man was morose. He wouldn't have noticed.

His finger moved across the columns until Jaime found accounts receivable: $5,000.00. He tallied up the money. As he double-checked his math, Jaime worked to keep a smile off his face. Taking the pen from his shirt pocket, he jotted the total into the next column of the ledger: $6,330.00. The chump had overpaid.

Without a word, Jaime closed the ledger and locked it back into its drawer. He collected the bills into an envelope. As he stood from his desk, he crammed the thick bundle deep into his pocket.

Payment received. The rest was gravy and intimidation. Jaime enjoyed this part too. He moved his bulk around the desk to face Caleb. Caleb, not Carl. Staring down at him, Jaime waited for the man's eyes to rise from the floor. They didn't.

"Hey, Caleb," Jaime said, snapping his fingers. The sick man's gaze broke away from his shoes. His eyelids fluttered as his rheumy stare locked on Jaime. Caleb's face hung, despondent despite the wonder he was about to experience. Jaime fidgeted his fingers. He wasn't expecting that. Customers should champ at the bit for what Em offered.

"Before we start, let's go over what'll happen," Jaime said. He queued up the prepared script in his head as he pointed an index finger into the other man's caving chest. "You will sit right there. You will not move. Your hands will stay at your sides, at all times."

Caleb's mouth opened, and Jaime raised his other index finger to his own lips. "You won't talk. The boy and his mother will come here shortly, and you will not speak to either of them. You will not touch either of them."

The sick man nodded and swallowed. The sadness drawn on Caleb's face deepened. For a moment, Jaime lost his place in his script. He covered by lowering his hand to his side at a deliberate pace.

"You are not to touch either of them. They won't touch you, but the boy will come close. Stay still. If you move toward the boy, if you touch him or Blair ..."

Jaime's lips tightened. He used her name. He needed to practice the script more. Run scenarios. Blair could help with that. He blinked away the stress of the minor mistake and continued. "If you touch the boy, or his mother, this ends, and I'll escort you far, far away from here. Do you understand?"

Caleb nodded once, his eyes falling back to the floor.

Jaime folded his arms across his barrel chest, making his girth as intimidating as possible. "Once it's done, the boy and his mother will leave. You'll continue to sit there until I tell you otherwise. Do you understand?"

Caleb wiped his eyes against the dirty sleeve of the coat. Jaime turned and opened the door. "Wait here, Caleb. Just a minute." He stepped out of the door and down the steps to the churchyard.

Jaime walked to the corner of the annex building and pulled his phone from his pocket. He texted Blair, "Ready when you are. Meet me outside."

Jaime pocketed the phone. He poked his head around the corner of the annex, wanting a look at the activity near the Silverleaf. Red and blue emergency lights bounced against the flat walls of the diner and the metal-walled garage across Jackson Street. Voices and tension carried from the intersection. Jaime furrowed his lips as he sucked in a deep breath.

What the hell was going on over there?

Chapter 62

EMERSON

The van slammed into the Batmobile with a breathy explosion. Flames licked the sides of the boxy vehicle. It rocked on its wheels, easing past the tipping point until it landed on its side with a crunch. Imaginary sparks flew from the metal frame as it slid toward the edge of the kitchen table.

"Make sure you finish eating while you play, Em," Mom called. Emerson paused the demolition derby and looked up. Mom was still scrubbing the mac and cheese burns from the bottom of their cooking pot. She made dinner super-early today. He didn't enjoy having dinner for snack time, but sometimes that's what they did. Mostly when Mom wasn't that hungry, and she ate whatever Emerson wouldn't finish.

He picked a carrot from the plate and nibbled. It was bitter, like dirt. But he ate it. The bowl of mac and cheese was almost empty. After making sure Mom was still staring out the window over the sink, he scooped the last of the yellow tubes into his fingers and dropped them on the floor. Barfly leaned out from beneath the table, and her scouring tongue lapped up the cheesy treat.

Emerson turned back to the battle royale on the tabletop. The van was destroyed, the Batmobile unscathed, but another threat loomed. A sleek, futuristic police car bounded onto the arena, looking to put an end to Emerson's derby. It was one of the coolest cars he had. It had laser guns! The Batmobile didn't have lasers, so it ran.

As the police cruiser charged up its side blaster, a series of quick buzzes filled the trailer. Emerson looked up as Mom dropped the pot and brush into the small sink with a tinny clatter. The noise was loud enough to spook Barfly out from beneath the table. The dog skulked back to the bedroom. Mom wiped her hands on her jeans and grabbed her phone from the charger cubby by the door. As the Batmobile screeched into a drift to avoid colliding with the burning van, Mom approached the table.

"Time to put your toys away, Em," she sang. She pocketed her phone and smiled at him, the bold Scarlet halo matching her hair. She was excited about something. Emerson hoped she was going to tell him what it was.

He picked up the police car and slid it into its slot in the storage container beside him. Each car Emerson found on the playground at school had its own specific place in the container. The van lived on the bottom level, with the rest of the regular things. The top level was where Emerson kept the special cars, like the Batmobile and the laser-blasting police car.

He plucked up the Batmobile with a fist as Mom continued, "Before you start homework, there's a chore we need to take care of, okay?"

Emerson flicked at a wheel of the car in his hand, nodding. "Are we helping someone?" He wasn't ready to end the pretend, but he enjoyed helping people more.

Mom tossed his hair. "Yep. Like we do, Em."

Emerson smiled, patting his mussed-up hair. "Okay!" he chirped. He tucked the car caddy back into its home on the shelf, keeping the Batmobile stuffed in his fist.

Mom opened the door, and she nodded sideways toward the sunshine as she held out an open hand. Emerson grabbed it and asked, "Where are we going?"

"Just down the street, to church," Mom replied. Outside was warm and sticky and it reached through the open door.

"Can Barfly come?" he asked. At the sound of her name, the dog reappeared, shoving past them and out of the door. Mom let Emerson lead, and he heard the door smack shut as they walked into their yard. Barfly pranced along Oak Street, bouncing between shadows created by the stretching trees along the road.

Straight ahead, Emerson could see Jaime standing outside his office. He turned and waved to them, and Emerson waved back with his Batmobile-filled fist. Jaime's colors were off. They shifted, like in a kaleidoscope. As if he couldn't decide what color to be, so he was trying them all. Seeing Jaime, Barfly broke into a goofy run. She veered past him at the last second, like the Batmobile did with the van.

Mom squeezed his hand as they crossed Jackson Street. Emerson looked up to find her staring off. His eyes followed hers to real police cars. Their lights were on and everything, and they had stopped in the road around the Silverleaf. Emerson smiled. That must be where they were going!

They reached the yard. The brick church peeked over Jaime's new office trailer. Mom tapped Emerson's hand with her fingers as she let go of him. "Wait here, sweetness," she said.

Mom walked up to Jaime. He couldn't hear what they were saying. They pointed toward the police cars and lights and shrugged with their shoulders and halos. Maybe they were discussing how to help. Jaime thumbed back toward his office. Then he started moving toward the Silverleaf. Emerson wondered if it was a car accident on Main Street.

Mom returned, the dog following her. Her halo was shy, folding in on her the way the sunset drains into the horizon. She took his hand again, and they walked toward the office, stopping a few paces from the steps.

Emerson glanced at his mother's face. She stared past the building, in the direction Jaime had gone. "Mommy?" he asked.

"We're just waiting for Jaime," she answered.

"Wait for him to do what?"

"He's checking out what happened over at the diner. You saw the police lights?" she replied.

"Yes. Is that where we're going?"

Her light flickered Yellow and Purple. "No, Em. The person we need to help is in here." She nodded her head toward the office. Her face smiled; her halo showed Emerson her fear.

Barfly found a spot of sun in the grassy yard a few feet away. She collapsed into a ball to lick herself. Mom let go of his hand and pulled her cigarettes out of her shirt pocket. She put one between her lips and lit it, the orange tip glowing in a pulse with her relaxing halo. Emerson hated the odor. They smelled dirty and stale. And it dimmed her light. He made a small groan, a sound his mother recognized.

"I know, Em. I'm just nervous," she said. Her eyes stayed fixed, waiting for something to appear around the corner of the building. "We'll go help the man once I'm done, once Jaime is back, okay?"

Emerson flicked the wheel of the Batmobile in his hand. Mom left the stinking cigarette between her lips. The smoke lifted around her eyes as they watched Jackson Street. Her halo shook, fading to the color of a deep bruise with small rays of Orange. Mom was panicking.

Emerson leaned closer and placed his free hand near her lower back. His fingers knotted around the source of the light, twisting her color back to the natural contented Ruby. Back to Emerson's favorite color. It was a trick he'd learned a few months ago. It calmed her enough to stop her from smoking. It made Mom happy again.

The cigarette fell from her lips to the ground. Mom tamped it into the grass with the toe of her sneaker. She smiled as she looked at the diner, her light back to the color of cherry Ring Pops. Emerson smiled too. Mom's light shone calm now. Whatever was upsetting her, it wasn't anymore. The trick worked. It worked every time.

"Can we go help now?" Emerson asked.

Mom's gaze broke from the Silverleaf and fell to his face. Her smile beamed through the Scarlets and Reds bursting from her in steady waves. "I don't see why not, sweetness." She shrugged. She took his hand again, and they walked up the steps to the annex. Mom opened the door and led him inside.

The smile faded from Emerson's face as a well of fear overflowed in him.

That man. The one from the diner. The empty, lightless man. He sat in a chair in Jaime's office. Emerson turned away, to the open door. He pulled toward the yard, but couldn't move. Mom had a hand on his shirt. She held him in place. In the shrinking space around the closing door, Emerson saw Barfly panting in the sun.

Chapter 63

IRENE

"Is that it?" Irene asked. "Is that the place?"

Neither Dietrick nor Leo answered her. The Challenger ground to a stop across the open parking spaces in front of the restaurant. The sheriff was moving out of the car before the engine was off, her deputy following. Irene spilled out of the backseat to the dusty road. Her eyes scoured the outside of the restaurant. The rusted metal sign read SILVERLEAF, and it hung from the covered porch of a clapboard building. A few chomping faces stared from the windows—diners concerned at the commotion. None of them were Dad.

Irene turned south. The road pierced the town, then disappeared into a curve a few miles away. Mature maple trees obstructed the longer view. A few figures milled about, none of them Dad either. Over her throbbing pulse, Irene heard the fading siren of the ambulance they'd followed here as it raced away to save her brother before he bled out.

Had her father made it here already? She turned back to find the stern face of Sheriff Dietrick between her and the diner.

"Irene, you need to wait here." Her hand landed on Irene's shoulder as she tried to push past the officer. "Let us take stock of the situation first. For your own safety."

"Well, you can fuck that idea, because I'm going with you." She tried to slide around Dietrick.

"Irene, please!" the sheriff pleaded. Deputy Leo moved ahead of them, opening the door as he reached a hand around his boss to block Irene.

Irene gripped the deputy's wrist, ready to remove his arm to get inside that building. Her dad might be in there. After the last two days, nothing would keep her from finding him.

"Ah, shit." The words eased from Leo's mouth, his eyes looking at the street behind her. She turned around. Three highway patrol cruisers screeched to a stop on the road. They blocked the entire intersection. Irene hadn't noticed them on the way here. She hadn't realized the sound of their sirens was getting louder. They must have been following Leo here from the accident.

The deputy reversed his force against her, yanking Irene into the diner. He slammed the door closed behind them. Irene combed the patrons for her father. She found only blank stares from concerned strangers. Leo kept her moving across the floor, where Sheriff Dietrick was holding court.

"Everyone, I need your help." Her voice filled the tense space. Despite her compact form, the sheriff captured the room in her gravity. Leo released Irene's wrist with a reassuring squeeze and went to stand behind his boss.

"We're looking for a man named Caleb Allard. Caucasian, fifty-nine years old, he's very sick." She turned to Irene. "Pull up a photo, please."

Irene pulled out her phone, struggling to find the photo-gallery app she used every day.

"Leo," the sheriff grumbled, lowering her voice, "get the staff from the kitchen in here too." The deputy nodded and moved behind the service counter.

"Irene?" Dietrick held out a hand for the phone. Irene found the last photo she had taken of her dad. His thin frame sat at his dining room table. They had been working through a stack of Final Release paperwork. His eyes were tired, but calm. Or resigned. Things were in their places then. As Dietrick's callused fingers took the phone from her, Irene noted the date in the photograph's corner. Less than a week ago now. A few days with Wes had turned the serenity in that photo on its ass.

The sheriff scurried to the closest table, holding out the photo to the patrons and repeating Dad's full name. They shook their heads, the man balancing a forkful of pasta in front of his face, the woman clutching her purse tight to her chest. Impatience gnawed at Irene's bones. She jumped at the sound of the kitchen door banging open. Leo corralled two tense cooks and a waitress into the dining area.

Dietrick moved to the next table. The lone man chomped on his sandwich and played with his fries, giving the photo a cursory shake of his head. "This is Caleb Allard. Are you sure you haven't seen him?" the sheriff asked.

Movement caught Irene's eye. Behind the service bar, a small view of the kitchen was visible. A house of a man padded past the stove tops. Based on his sharp clothing, he could have been the manager. Or the owner.

Dietrick turned to the cooks and waitress, holding up the phone. "We are looking for this man, have you seen him?" she asked. "His name is Caleb Allard."

Irene flushed. The gigantic man in the kitchen froze. His eyes saucered. His brow clenched. His neutral face opened in surprise.

He had recognized her father's name.

Chapter 64

EMERSON

The man's empty eyes bored into Emerson. His face carried no smile. No frown. His skin yellowed and thin. How could skin have a color without light? And the man smelled. The way Barfly stunk after Uncle Terry's. Like the deer on the road. Metallic, sour. The smell of broken halos and death.

Emerson turned away and buried his face into his mother's standing lap. His arms clamped around her waist. Mom backed away, but Emerson pushed harder until she stumbled against Jaime's desk. She put her hands on his shoulders, and Emerson dug deeper into her belly.

"Dammit, Em, what's wrong?" she asked.

Emerson shook his head, afraid to let his voice into the room. Mom's hands tightened on him, her movements becoming harsh. She pulled his face away from her warmth. "Emerson Hunt!" she scolded. "What is the matter with you?"

Mom was angry now. Her light became fire. Orange, Yellows whipping out from her chest, bleeding over the Ruby calm he'd created in her earlier. Mom's colors scared Emerson when she was mad. But that terror was nothing next to what he felt standing this close to the lightless man. Mom stooped as tears formed in Emerson's eyes, and he pushed his head back into her.

Her hand slunk between them, her arms prying him out of his safety. His face clenched, his body trying to fold into a ball. Mom held him tight, one hand on his chest and the other on his back. Emerson opened his eyes, and his tears ran for their chance to escape. Her face met his, her eyes bright and fierce. It froze Emerson. He sucked in a lip as she spoke through gritted teeth, her warm spittle spraying his cheeks. "What the hell is wrong with you?" As she finished the question, Mom shoved him once, and the room rattled as Emerson's head bounced back and forth.

She didn't want an answer. Emerson knew he should stay quiet. He spoke anyway. "I want to go," he whispered. It was as loud as he could make his voice. It hurt like a scream, but it barely moved the air between them. "I don't think I can help him."

Mom's face tightened around her eyes. They shot up to the man sitting behind him, softening into an apology. When she turned back to Emerson, her mouth and eyes were firm and cold.

She hissed, low enough so the empty man wouldn't hear. "Well, he helped us, okay? And in return we have to help him back." Mom whipped Emerson around on his feet, so he faced the lightless thing in the chair. Her warm cheek brushed his, her voice turning bright. "All you gotta do is try, sweetness."

The man's face blanked, blurred from Emerson's tears. Mom stood up behind Emerson, and the lap he had run to for safety now shoved him into danger.

"I'm sorry, he's never been like this before." Ochre flares of her annoyance betrayed the calm tone of her voice. Emerson planted his feet, but the thin carpet offered no traction as Mom pushed him closer.

The man stared at him. After a boundless moment, the man's gaze lifted to Mom, and then fell to the floor at Emerson's feet.

The man smiled. Why? Was he happy? Excited because he thought Emerson could fix him? Was he thinking about a joke? Or was that a frowny-face that looked like a smile? Was the man angry? At Emerson for not being able to fix him?

Without the light to guide him, Emerson was blind.

Chapter 65

CALEB

The mother wrestled the boy toward him. "I'm sorry," she said with an apologetic nod. "He's never been like this before."

Caleb's heart pounded against his ribs. The boy was here, terrified. The kid's face was slick with tears. Snot bubbled from his nostrils as he resisted his mother. Caleb leaned into the hard plastic chair. Resignation pushed down on his shoulders. The mother inched the kid forward as the little boy's arms flailed out to brace himself. This was all so wrong.

Motion behind the woman drew Caleb's gaze. In the far corner of the room, the white of the wall fell away in a gentle wave. Wisps of gray from the carpet joined the stream. Like living smoke, the colors wrapped around the ficus tree, pulling out the plastic greens and browns. The color drained in swirls, leaving a taupe blankness that explored the space like a dozen curious fingers.

Caleb's chest tightened, a slice of pain radiating down his arm and through his back. The weight of the thick canvas jacket pressed him into his seat. It wouldn't be long now. Death was here, in the room.

He looked down at the floor. The carpet beneath his feet. The jacket was heavy, holding him in the chair. Caleb wanted to remove it. To stand. He wasn't sure he had it in him.

Something was next to his shoe. A tiny black thing. Was it … was that a toy?

Caleb smiled. It was a toy. Another car. He bent down, the pain in his back thrusting through his belly and ribs. His fingers found the toy as the tumor jabbed into his liver. He crawled back up with small movements, the toy car in his hand.

He waited a breath before opening his eyes. The tendrils of color consumed the far half of the room now. The space behind Blair dissolved into a watery wall of pigment. He looked to the mother and found her scowling frown. She shoved Emerson again with a frustrated grunt. Caleb turned to Emerson. The boy thrashed, as terrified as his mother was angry.

Caleb swallowed. He hoped his voice would work. "Is this yours?"

The boy twisted his face away, pushing back against his mother's torso. She secured him with her hands, nudging him with her legs as she said, "Don't be rude, Em."

"Em," Caleb repeated. "Short for Emerson, right?" The boy's face pivoted, just enough to reveal his chin. A nearly imperceptible nod confirmed Caleb's memory. "I think," he said, raising the car in his trembling hand, "this is yours." The boy's eyes shot from the wall to the car and back. The boy nodded, sucking in the stream of snot dangling from his nose.

"This must be important to you," Caleb offered. He moved the car toward the boy, but Emerson made no move to take it.

Caleb reached out with his braced hand, taking Emerson's forearm and easing it out straight. The kid's eyes clenched closed as he sucked in a breath. Caleb pulled the kid's hand open, resting the Batmobile in his open palm. The boy relaxed into his mother. And she relaxed as well, stroking the boy's hair.

As he closed Emerson's fingers around his toy, the kid let go of the breath he held. In a single staccato huff, Emerson gasped, "I don't know how to fix you." He sucked in another breath, bracing his body as if expecting a blow. The mother mumbled something Caleb couldn't hear.

As the waves scoured the color from the walls and the floor, Caleb released a shuddering sigh. The searching fingers of smoke flowed his way, locking the scene as they went. He moved his hand from the boy's fist, reaching into the pocket of the rotted coat. His fingers landed on the slick and cool metal of the pistol barrel.

Caleb looked into the boy's bulging eyes. The kid must have sensed it. Terror erupted across Emerson's face as he pulled away. His mother cursed and pushed him forward. None of this was okay.

"It's all right, Emerson," Caleb whispered. He tightened his grip around the boy's arm as Emerson yanked it back.

Was it all right? Was anything that happened these last days right? Caleb closed his eyes around his tears. The rough embossing on the gun's wooden handle brushed the tips of his fingers. Life throbbed in his deaf ear.

Caleb?

Words fell from Caleb's lips like a late apology. "There's been a change of plans."

Chapter 66

BLAIR

For fuck's sake, Emerson needed to calm down. Blair had never seen him react this way. He was always tentative, sure. Em was very sensitive, especially around people who were sick or distraught. But he never openly defied her like this. If they were alone, she would whip him with a drop cord.

But they weren't alone. And Emerson needed to earn his keep. He should at least try to help their customer. Blair stroked her son's thick hair, finding it matted with sweat, her hand coming away sticky and wet. Emerson continued to push against her, trying to move away from the man.

What the hell had gotten into him? Caleb looked sick—even a child would see it. And his odor was off-putting, but Christ Almighty, Em had seen and touched a lot worse, all on his own. Her boy stilled, leaning into her as he stopped flailing his arms. Blair adjusted her hips to square the boy up in front of Caleb. Her son's body went rigid, but his panting grew raspy, as if he were out of breath from running from something.

Blair looked up to Caleb, shrugging a smile. But Caleb was looking past her, his face detached. An anxious twitch pulled on her lip. She was losing him. He would want his money back.

Blair dropped her eyes down to her son again. His face turned to the wall, as if Caleb's stink was too much to take straight on. He sniffled and shuddered against her legs. Her mouth trembled again. The kid needed to pull it together, to toughen up.

Caleb grunted, and Blair found him stooped. His wrecked fingers wagged at something just out of his reach on the ground. It was Emerson's toy. Em must have dropped it when he was throwing his tantrum. Straining, Caleb moaned as he grabbed up the toy. As he sat up, his eyes clenched tight and his face grew dour as he breathed in uneven sighs.

His eyes opened, tracing from the ceiling, past Blair, and landing on Emerson. Blair eased her fingers through Em's hair, feeling him flinch when the man held out an open hand, the toy resting on his palm.

"Is this yours?" he asked.

Emerson tightened against her. "Don't be rude, Em," Blair nudged.

Caleb smiled at her boy. The knot in her chest relaxed. As long as he remained hopeful, still held some anticipation at the prospect of leaving this sickness and pain behind him, this could work out. But she needed to get Emerson to work his goddamned magic.

"Em. Emerson, right?" The man's eyes betrayed a longing, but he engaged Em with patience. This was a team effort now, the two of them working Emerson to get the job done. Caleb held the toy closer. "This must be important to you."

Emerson quaked, pushing into her leg. Blair shifted one leg back, her stance too solid for him to move. She ran her fingers through his hair again as Caleb placed the car in her son's hand. Emerson froze for a heavy moment.

The moment ended as Em heaved in a gasp, and words sputtered from his sloppy mouth. "I don't know how to fix you."

Goddammit! Blair groaned, exasperated. Her hand fell from Em's head to her side as she mumbled through her tensed lips, "Dammit, Emerson, you haven't even tried." She pulled in a calming breath and looked around in frustration. She needed to turn this around.

"That's okay, Emerson." Caleb's words surprised her, his tone dark. Her brow curled in confusion. She wanted to tell the man that it was not okay, that Emerson needed to fulfill their part of the arrangement. Before she could, Caleb stammered, "There's been a change of plans."

Puzzled, Blair watched as he leaned to the side. His free hand disappeared into the pocket of the coat while the other held her son's arm. "How do you mean?" Blair asked.

He paused, his hand finding whatever it was looking for. His eyes shifted to the corner of the room, searching for a long moment before they came back to hers. Caleb shook his head, a wry smile stretching across his face. Swallowing, he replied, "I wasn't talking to you."

He pulled his hand from the coat pocket, the shifting weight sliding the jacket across his torso. Blair's eyes widened at the sight of the man's shirt. Spatters of dark and rusty stains dotted his torso. She followed the pattern to his pants, where the spots turned into long organic streaks.

Blair sucked in a breath. "Is that ... blood?" she heard herself ask. As the duster moved off Caleb's legs, the extent of the stains became evident. Blood covered him, from top to bottom. Her arms moved around her son's chest in a protective clutch. She reversed her stance, pulling Emerson toward her. Away from Caleb.

His grip tightened on her son, holding him in place. She reached down and worked to wrench the man's fingers from her son's arm. She looked up, and Caleb's face fell to a frown.

"Let go!" she hissed.

Caleb's lips quivered, as if he was debating how to respond. The quiver expanded, filling the side of his face. As Blair pulled, his face contorted past the grimace, drooping into an unnatural and shaking relaxation. Blair shuddered, heaving on her son as Caleb's right eye rolled back into his head.

Chapter 67

IRENE

A wave of panic crossed the thick man's face at hearing her father's name again.

"Sheriff?" Irene croaked. She turned to find Dietrick. The sheriff and Leo were moving from the cooks back to the patrons. Irene glared back through the service bar. The man had disappeared.

She bolted through the kitchen door. Her heart threatened to beat out of her chest, fueled by adrenaline-spiked panic and hope. She caught a shadow of the man as he rounded the pantry shelving. She jogged to close the distance, her voice cracking as she cried for him to wait.

She turned past the shelf, finding his enormous silhouette in a swath of sunlight as he left the building. He was running.

She followed through the kitchen's exit, into a dusty yard. Her legs pumped to catch up to him. He was moving fast, already across the street, making a beeline toward a trailer standing in the yard.

"Hey!" she called out, her voice working again. "Hey, do you know where Caleb Allard is?"

The man continued running ahead. Irene's swirling hope and panic focused into a rage. It ripped out of her mouth. "Stop right there, goddammit!"

The man stumbled to a stop, his shoulders hunching at the weight of her scream. His hands shook as he raised them over his cowering head. His thick frame pivoted around, his face clenched with fear.

His meek eyes found hers, and then his face wrinkled with mild confusion as he took her in, evaluating her for the briefest moment.

"Do you know where Caleb Allard is?" Irene repeated. She sounded pleading. Desperate. The force of her scream had taken the strength from her voice.

His arms lowered. His head rose and he stretched his neck to one side. An obvious expression of disgust crossed his face as his posture relaxed and his eyes rolled. Irene recognized the look from countless interactions with her peers. Her teachers. Men everywhere. He was ashamed he had felt threatened by her. He turned back to the building, dismissing her with a swipe of his hand.

The fire under her rage flared, igniting her impatience. She pulled in another breath, ready to spew untethered hell upon this behemoth who could take her to her father.

A scream pierced the still air. Not from Irene. From the building ahead. Irene held her breath, unsure of what to do with it. The man startled again. Then he broke into a run.

Chapter 68

CALEB

"There's been a change of plans."

Caleb ...

Caleb's abdomen exploded with ragged, hot pressure. He opened his eyes. Blair looked at him, concerned. Her mouth moved; she shook her head. Caleb could hear only a warble of her voice over the static of his stomach pain.

Behind Blair, the walls and floor faded to the tepid beige of those fixed moments, the color of choices made or lost. The woman's face knotted. She asked him something. She expected a response.

Her words broke through his wall of agony. "What do you mean?" she asked.

Caleb chuckled around the jagged edges of the pain, realizing what she was asking. Her face tightened, confusion turning into fear. He met her eyes and replied, "I wasn't talking to you."

The thrush surged in his deaf ear.

Caleb!

Ripples of color stripped from the walls and floor. Their motions kept time with his own pulse, inching across every surface. Homing on Caleb as if he were a gravity well for death.

Caleb, you need to do this!

"Is that ... blood!" Blair's voice grew loud. Her eyes wide. She pulled on her son. Caleb tightened his grip on the boy. He tightened his grip around the thing in his pocket. The metal parts cool against his fingers and palm.

Do it! Do it now! Kill that little universe-ending shit!

The colorless putty was everywhere. The last of the color surrounded only the mother and child now, as she clutched her arms around her petrified boy. She pulled on him, her strength increasing. Caleb held him fast as he lifted his hand out of his pocket.

This is it! Your choices are running out! One little beetle to crush and your life will have a purpose!

She blubbered. Yanked on the kid. Her noise. The pain. The disappearing colors. It dissolved into an incoherent rabble.

Caleb ...

The boy froze. Eyes bulged. Breath heaved. Tears and snot stuck to his cheeks. Emerson. The boy's name was Emerson.

Caleb?

Caleb raised his fisted hand up to the boy's terrified face. The voice ebbed from his head like a wave flowing back into the sea, giving him space to act. The tide of his own blood flushed in his good ear.

How much longer would he hear it? How many heartbeats did he have left? How would he use them? The wisps of color hung in suspense, curious to know the same.

Caleb! What the hell are you waiting for!

Chapter 69

BLAIR

Why the hell hadn't she waited for Jaime to get back? How did she think doing this without him here was a good idea?

She clawed at the spotted yellow skin of the man's hand. Her fingers worked to pry his fingers off Emerson's arm. She couldn't move him. With all the fury she had, she hammered her fists against the brace on the man's wrist. The skin on her knuckles split open, yet this sickly man's grip remained locked on her son's forearm.

She needed Jaime. Her back and legs heaved, her son failing to move. Where the fuck was Jaime?

Caleb raised his other hand. It was holding something. Blair caught the flash of metal in his hand.

Blair kicked at the desk, searching for any leverage her tiny frame could use against the man holding her son. Caleb pulled harder, and Emerson inched closer to the man as his wadded hand floated to her son's face. Her efforts were pointless—she couldn't release the hold of this dying man.

The thought slapped her mind: She could let go. Leave Emerson here. Run. Let this man take her boy. Save herself. But for what? What would life be without Em? Living in a fucking trailer. On someone else's lot. With her shit job in this shit town. She would die here. Stuck. Waiting. Waiting for death to take her from her shit trailer in a shit town some shit years into her shit life.

No. She deserved better. She deserved Emerson! Resolve coiled in her. Emerson was a gift. A gift for her. For her suffering. The abuse from his father. From men. From the world.

The coil snapped. Her arms tightened. Jaw clenched. Her own scream rattled through her bones, "Jaime!"

Chapter 70

CALEB

Caleb pulled Emerson closer. The boy's mother was fighting him, wresting the boy away. Why?

The voice slammed against the inside of his skull.

Caleb!

Breathing through the boom of the voice, Caleb opened his fist. He held his palm flat, letting it float in front of Emerson, waiting for him to unclench his eyes.

Caleb, no!

Emerson's eyes peeled open. They jumped to Caleb's face.

Caleb smiled, as best as he could through his discomfort. Through the scratching voice in his head. Through the throbbing fingers of color lapping around his shoes.

Emerson's gaze fell to Caleb's open hand. He took a long look at the toy El Camino, and the boy's expression softened. His posture relaxed, shoulders falling as his panting slowed.

Caleb wiggled his hand a little, a suggestion for Emerson to take the car. A smile hinted on the kid's face as he looked between Caleb and the toy. It was the only warmth in this chilled moment. Caleb smiled at the sensation.

The mother stopped yanking on the kid. Caleb looked up at her. She stared down at the toy in his hand. Her hands fisted in the boy's wrinkled shirt. Her face hung in wide terror, but her body stilled, creating a statue of ugly confusion.

Oh fuck! Caleb! What are you doing?

Caleb ignored the voice as best he could. Instead, he turned his focus to the growing pain inside of his belly. "I have a boy too," he said in a whisper. His lungs rattled as he sucked in air. "He drives a car that looks ... just like this one." The sentence came out in spurts, between the throbs of agony radiating from his gut.

Emerson blinked from Caleb's gaze down to the car. He sniffled in a heaving sigh.

A stab shot up from Caleb's abdomen. It lifted with it a wave of nausea and fear. Caleb breathed and counted, pushing it all back down. He needed a few more moments, that's all. He prayed he would have them. He continued, "I mean, his car is bigger of course. We wouldn't fit in this one."

Emerson's smile stretched to his eyes. Caleb moved his open palm holding the toy El Camino toward the boy.

Jesus Christ ...

The kid's eyes bounced from the toy back to him. Caleb relaxed his hand from the boy's arm as Emerson moved to wipe his nose on it. With a croak, the boy asked, "Can I ... can I have it?"

439

Caleb, you're ruining everything! Literally everything in the damned universe!

Caleb smiled and nodded at the toy in his palm. Emerson sucked in his lip and raised a tentative hand. His nimble fingers lifted the car off Caleb's palm.

You can still do it, okay? You can pull out the fucking gun and kill this cataclysmic brat!

Emerson relaxed into his mother, clutching the El Camino in his tiny fist. The boy glanced up at Caleb, and the remaining knots of tension between them loosened.

You don't understand what you're doing!

The boy's mother remained vigilant, her hands flattening on Emerson's chest and pulling him away. Her voice was quiet and coarse, "Emerson, we need to leave, okay? Right now."

Caleb? Please! Don't do this!

The door to the office burst open. In the bright Texas afternoon sun stood the hulking frame of Jaime. His sharp eyes took in the scene, moving from Blair to Caleb to Emerson in a tense circle. He snatched up the boy, shoving Blair away. Caleb heard her head connect with the desk, hard enough to make it crack the flimsy annex wall. Jaime turned and bolted through the door, Emerson clutched to his chest.

Oh God, no!

Caleb watched the man run through the open doorway. As they bobbed across the churchyard, color dissipated from his clothing, from his skin, from the boy. He turned back to find Blair. She lay on the floor, a growing pool of blood leaking from her head. The blood dissolved from crimson to a drab beige as the color smoke reached over her prone body.

You asshole. You fucking asshole! You've fucked everything. Do you realize that?

"I made a choice," Caleb replied to the voice. "Emerson will make his own choices too."

Yeah, well, that was a real dick move, Caleb. Way to blow it. Way to ruin the entire universe!

Caleb reached again into the jacket pocket. His fingers found the revolver and eased it to his lap. It had become heavier somehow. Everything felt so big. Everything except Caleb himself.

Do you have any idea how much effort I put into you?

Tiny wisps of putty ate through his sneakers. The colors exploded away with every jolt of pain, grabbing more and more of him. His ankles. One calf. Then the other. The tendrils smoked toward his knees. His feet went cold, and then they weren't there anymore.

What the hell am I supposed to do now?

The effort to lift the gun pulled the eddies of color higher, over his thighs. The gun was so heavy. Caleb feared he would drop it. Lose this last choice. He fit the pistol under his chin using both of his shaking hands.

Chapter 71

IRENE

He disappeared around the front of the building. Irene sprinted after him, her legs burning from the sudden exertion. She threw herself into the same corner, slamming against the building. She felt the heat in her blood as she took in the empty yard, the brick church beyond, the Labradoodle stooping to piss on a spot of glass.

The man must have entered the building. Before she could get her legs moving, a percussive whomp punched the wall behind her. He exploded from the door, carrying a flailing bundle of a kid in his arms.

"Stop!" she demanded.

The dog galloped, shadowing him across the yard like they were playing a game. Irene pushed herself off the building. Running a few steps on shaking legs, she screamed again, "Hey! Asshole!"

As if that was its name, the dog skidded to a stop. It turned around, beady eyes finding her through the curls on its face. It tilted its head and peaked its ears with curiosity. In one motion, the dog's mouth opened, the tongue flopped out, and it leaped toward her in spastic strides.

Irene froze, focused on the man as he ran across the street. The dog raced past her, clipping her leg and sending Irene to the ground. When she got herself upright, the man was gone.

"No!" Irene begged. "I just want to know where my dad is!"

A ruckus turned her around. The dog stood in the building's doorway, lapping at something on the floor. Her muzzle came up dirty. Muddy. Bloody. Irene approached the steps. A woman lay on the floor of the structure, her head leaking blood. Beyond her, around the frame of the door, sat a man in a chair.

"*Dad?* Is that you?" Her voice was thin, its strength gone.

She moved up the steps to see all of him. She stared, willing herself to recognize the man slumped in front of her. His face sunk against his skull. Skin jaundiced and sallow. It had been two days, but Dad had aged years.

Irene had seen it before, in her mom. The disease. It was taking Dad.

His head dipped to one side as he stared down at the woman on the floor. A grimy canvas coat hung on his tender frame, open to show brown stains of dried blood across his chest and legs. Wes's blood. On his lap, cradled between his hands, was a pistol.

Uncertainty cast shadows on her thoughts. "Dad?"

He didn't respond. Didn't look at her. He sucked in a phlegmy breath and raised the gun to his chin.

Chapter 72

CALEB

It consumed him now. It ran into his gut. The color leaked out of him. His body fixed into its final position as the end of his life lapped at him like a rising tide.

Now what the hell am I going to do?

Caleb ignored the voice. It came easy now. It didn't rumble through his bones anymore.

The gun was so heavy. It shook in his hands. He had one moment left, at least one more choice to make, didn't he? He could end this on his terms, like he'd planned. It was just days ago. Or was it longer? Weeks?

This is all shit. Just shit!

His finger found the trigger. The barrel pressed into the soft tissue under his jaw. These were his final thoughts. Wes. Irene. Ivy. The boat. The deep dark waters that terrified and delighted them as kids. They learned to love it, though. They should have spent more time there. Together.

I mean look at this mess. Just look at it!

Caleb closed his eyes as the warmth and color drained from his chest. It was coming fast.

He squeezed. Nothing. He opened his eyes.

Irene. Irene was here? The gun was in her hands now. Where were his hands? He couldn't feel them anymore. Just the rising pressure inside of his chest, his pulse walloping through his head.

Well, hang on ...

The color of her face—her lovely face—dissolved away, leaving behind the clay of the fixed moment. Irene's kind eyes, her tears, her worried lips, solidified for eternity.

Huh.

Her mouth moved. Caleb could not hear her. He was so tired.

Thoughts jumbled. Caleb's chest expanded, heaving in a breath. His last breath. How would he use it? He had to pull one thought, one thread, from the knot in his head. I'm sorry. You look so much like your mother. Don't remember me this way. I'm proud as shit of you. Take care of your brother. Run away from your brother. Your brother is dead. I killed your brother. Whose dog is that? I wish I had done more for you. For Wes. For your mother. For us all.

Okay, how did you do that?

This was it. Caleb had to make this last choice. What could he say to his daughter? After the pain he caused her. The difficulty of growing up with Wes. Without Ivy. And yet Irene persevered. She gave so much back to them. Irene's support. Her intelligence. Her edge. Her humor. Her kindness.

His body racked as he let go of the breath. He wasn't able to push it out. Instead, the words leaked from his mouth like smoke, light on the currents in the air. He didn't hear them, but they were out of him now, floating away with the last of the color he would see.

"Thank you, Starlight."

Irene's face was still.

The world split.

Irene's face was still. Irene kissed his head.

The world split. Irene's face was still. Irene cried. Irene pulled out her phone. Irene kissed his head. The dog sniffed at Caleb's shirt.

I'll be damned.

The world split. Irene stooped over Blair. The dog sniffed at Caleb's shirt. Irene sat against the wall and brought her hands to her mouth. Irene's face was still. Irene kissed his head. Irene cried. Irene pulled out her phone.

The world split. The dog licked its crotch. The dog sniffed at Caleb's shirt. Irene's face. So many of them. Irene?

The world split. It was too much to know. It was too bright to see. Caleb tried to close his eyes, to make it all disappear. To sleep. Where were his eyes?

The world split. Over the rabble of light, the kaleidoscope of moments, Caleb heard it. The pitch falling. Its volume fading. The voice, keeping its promise. Moving away from him. Leaving him behind.

Caleb, I think I can work with this.

Chapter 73

EMERSON

Emerson didn't like the hospital like he'd thought he would. It smelled like old people and the bathrooms at school after they were cleaned. He couldn't remember ever being in one before, even though Mom told him he was born at a hospital. Still, Emerson knew what a hospital was from school and reading stories—it was a building where sick people went to get better.

The hospital he'd built in his mind was far away from the place he stood now. People here were sad, their lights broken or dim. Some were in bed, their halos fading in and out, or shining in pieces instead of whole. People around the beds sputtered ugly colors. Why? Why wasn't this place the most beautiful place ever? If men came here to get better, why was every light so wrong?

Jaime's Indigo and Violet lashed out as he spoke to the doctor. "This is bullshit. The boy needs to see his mother, see that she's all right!"

The doctor's halo held steady, a bold Copper that seemed to brighten even as Jaime got mad. The doctor replied, "I'm sorry, but until she's out of the eye-see-you, she can't have visitors. It's for her own safety." The "eye-see-you" must be where doctors watched sick people. But if the doctors couldn't see halos the way Emerson could, what would they be watching?

Jaime's hands came up. They stayed calm, despite the rage spitting out of his light. "Just for a minute, just let the kid see her for a minute—"

The doctor shook his head, the way Emerson's teacher did when her mind was made up. "I'm sorry," he said with a shrug, "but she's not conscious. She wouldn't even know he's there. You'll have to wait. We can have someone call you as soon as she's awake and able to have visitors."

The doctor turned, but stopped. He looked back up at Jaime. "You're family, correct?"

Jaime paused for a moment, Oranges of confusion tainting his halo. He shook his head.

"Well then, I'm sorry, but this argument is pointless. We cannot allow you to see her. Don't worry. She's receiving the best possible care." The doctor nodded and walked away.

Emerson wanted to tell him he could fix her, but he kept quiet. Because Jaime told him to "just keep quiet" before they entered this awful place. That they would have to figure out how to get into Mom's room. Then Emerson would fix her and they could leave.

His tummy rumbled. Early dinner was hours ago, and he usually went to bed by now. What meal came after dinner? Emerson looked up at the clock again. Almost nine at night. Jaime had been trying to get into Mom's room for hours. But nobody would let them go in there. Not the doctors, not the police.

Emerson tugged on Jaime's pants. The big man looked down at him, his light steadying a bit. "What's up, little man?"

Emerson curled a lip. "I'm hungry."

Jaime looked up at the clock now too. He smiled and said, "Whoa, I'll bet you are!" He slid his thick hand into his pocket and pulled out a few dollar bills. As he handed them to Emerson, Jaime said, "Here. Bring me back a soda, yeah?" He reached to tousle Emerson's hair. Em hated when he did that. He moved away before Jaime could touch him.

They had passed some vending machines near the elevator, and Emerson walked back that way. His eyes stayed low to avoid the light noise spilling out of everyone in this miserable place. He didn't know anything about these people. He shouldn't help them unless he knew they were good people— that's what Mom always told him. She also told him he wasn't old enough to know if people were good or not. And then on the way here, Jaime said in the car, "Em, you're gonna want to heal people in there, but you can't, okay? Promise me you won't." Emerson promised he wouldn't. But there was so much light noise here. He wanted to make it prettier than it was. Make it more right. Or at least, less wrong.

Emerson spied the thick railing that ran along the corridor. He pulled the toy car—the funny car-truck the empty man had given him—from his pocket. Holding the car by the sides, Em rolled the toy along the top of the railing as he walked. The railing ended at a door. The car made a gigantic leap over the doorway, landing on the railing where it picked up again.

It did the same across the next chasm, passing through the rays of Yellows and Greens from the people in the room beyond. Emerson looked up. One last room before the hallway bent around a corner. The car would have to make a hard right to stay on the railing. First, though, it had to make this vault across the last doorway!

The gap approached fast. The car reached the falling edge of the chasm. It launched into the air; moving in slow motion, the jump built up tension with a rising pitch. Would they make it? Or would they fall into the ...

Emerson ran into something. Someone. He felt the car slip from his fingers, heard it skitter on the tiles below his feet. He looked up at the woman standing in the doorway now. Em didn't watch where he walked. Would she be angry with him?

Would Mom?

"Excuse me," she whispered, so quiet Em could barely hear her. Her light flickered, unable to hold a color or shape as she continued down the hall. That's how Mom's light did when she was upset. Not angry-upset like when she yelled about Dad, but sad-upset like when she'd told him they had to sell Barfly. Emerson could fix Mom when she flickered like that.

He could probably fix this woman too. But he'd said he wouldn't.

Emerson turned to the floor, searching for his car. It wasn't at his feet. He peeked around the doorframe, into the room. The weird car-truck had landed upside down near the bed. The bed had someone in it. Emerson couldn't see much of the person in there. The Cinnamon light was dim, pulsing with the man's breath. The person in the bed was asleep.

He padded into the room, heel-toeing to his toy to keep his sneakers from squeaking on the floor and waking up the stranger. He reached for his toy, picked it up, and held it to the light.

"Whatcha got there?" The man's voice startled Em. He spun around. The man in the bed wasn't sleeping. He must be very tired, though. Or hurt. His light struggled out of him where it should have radiated.

Emerson swallowed and took a step back. He watched the man for a moment, then held up the toy car.

The man lifted his head and squinted. He tried to point, but a thick bracelet kept his arm near the railing on the bed. He licked his dry lips. "Is that ... an El Camino?" he asked. His voice sounded like it needed a drink.

Emerson looked down at the car and shrugged. He didn't know. It was the car the empty man gave him. It didn't have a name yet.

The man relaxed into the bed. "I used to drive a car just like that one," he said.

Emerson smiled. Before he realized he was speaking, Em replied, "It was bigger, though, right? Your car? Because you'd never fit into this one?"

The man in the bed laughed. A quiet laugh, but his paling light brightened into a happy flicker. Emerson's smile brightened too, because he could tell the happiness was real. The man stilled in the bed. His chest rose and fell, his light calming to a slow Yellow throb. He slept now, for real.

Em pocketed his toy, feeling it squish into the money in his pocket. The money Jaime gave him for a snack. Jaime would get mad if he knew Em was in here. He'd think Em tried to help the man in the bed. Emerson turned, walking the few steps to the doorway. He looked around it, back down the hall. His eyes followed the thick railing back to Jaime. He argued with two other doctors now, his hands pointing past them to where they had Mom.

The man coughed. Em turned in time to catch it ripple through his halo. It would be so easy to help this man. To straighten his light. Shape it right. Make it whole and strong. He could do it too, right now, with no effort. Mom would be angry if she found out, though. She would know, too. She always knew when he helped someone. She could smell it on him, she said. Plus, he promised Jaime he wouldn't.

But it wouldn't hurt to look, though, right? He didn't have to do anything. Emerson pulled a stool next to the bed, standing on it so he could get a better view of the man and his light. Bandages wrapped his leg and hand. Em could see from the gap in his halo that he was missing his finger. He could fix those things easy enough. There was something else, though— a weird heaviness through his whole body. It made his light crawl instead of run. Emerson knew how to fix that part too.

A voice. From the hall. Emerson turned his head to listen. It wasn't Jaime or Mom, but he could hear what they would say right now. They would tell him to wait until they knew it was safe. That the choice wasn't his to make. Emerson held his breath while he thought about what he would do.

* * *

Around the boy, the universe waited. Between this moment and the next, it waited for Emerson to exhale. To fill that infinitely small void between right and wrong, prediction and error, ana and kata, where all of his choices would be made.

Epilogue

IRENE

Her phone vibrated as she disabled airplane mode. Hiking her backpack to her shoulder, Irene noted the caller identification: Sierra County Social Services. A groan escaped her lips as she walked out of the jetway. She thought she was done with this, that she left it behind in New Mexico a few hours earlier. The current of deplaning passengers poured her into the concourse of the Dallas-Fort Worth airport. She stepped aside and accepted the call with a flick of her thumb.

"Yes?" Her voice projected more than she intended, giving away her impatience.

"Hello? This is Kimberly Rogers with Sierra County DSS. I'm calling for... Irene Allard?"

"Speaking."

"Miss Allard, I'm calling about Caleb Allard. We had a wellness visitation scheduled several days ago, but social workers could not locate him at the address on file. I'm sure you are aware that if we can't verify his safety, we are required to involve law enforcement."

Irene feigned a gasp, "Oh my gosh, really?"

"Yes, Miss Allard. Now, can you tell us where he is?"

"Oh, of course I can. He's right here with me!"

Irene heard the rustling of papers at the other end of the call. "He's there with you, now?"

"Mmm hmmm."

"May I speak with him?"

Irene chuckled, "Oh, I'm afraid not."

"I'm sorry?" The woman's voice rose with the impatience of someone with boxes to check. "Miss Allard, we have called you several times this week trying to verify that Caleb is safe and, according to these notes, you have provided no evidence to that fact."

"Yes, that is correct," Irene stated.

"All I need right now is to speak to your father, ask him a few questions."

"Okay."

"So ... please put him on the phone!" The social worker's tone became sharp, the shrill in her voice making Irene to clench her jaw.

"I told you, no. Not right now. Not ever."

"Miss Allard, I don't think you..."

"I agree, you don't think!" Irene snapped. "Listen, what was your name? Kimmie?"

"Kimberly," the woman corrected, her voice tinny and unconfident. Irene imagined she'd been fighting to outgrow the diminutive nickname for years.

"Ok, Kimmie. My father can't talk right now. Because he has no mouth. Or body. He's just ashes in a fucking urn." As she spoke, the corner of the box carrying her father's cremains rubbed against a rib, prompting her to hike the container a little higher. Its compact size was deceptive, as if something heavy and dense filled the void around Dad's ashes.

"Excuse me?"

Irene swallowed down a spark of irritation at having to repeat herself. "My father. He's dead."

"Oh well..." More papers rustled. "Then I'm going to need a death certificate to close this case, Miss Allard."

"I know you do. Want to know how I know you need a death certificate?"

"I don't see..."

"Because this is the third fucking call I've received from your office this week, and the previous agents told me the same goddamned thing!" Irene's voice exploded, drawing the eyes of other travelers as they shuffled by. Yet the heat of her embarrassment was a flicker in the inferno of her anger. "Apparently no one in your office can keep track of their own ass with both hands and a map!"

"Okay, look, I'm sorry about your father, but..."

"No! I don't need you to be sorry, I need you to dig a little deeper into that file you have open in front of you before calling me again, you bureaucratic twit!" Papers moved, a shaking breath coming through the line. Irene shifted her weight, releasing a modicum of the tension the flight from Las Cruces set in her body.

"Um, okay, yes," the complacency in Kimberly's tone collapsed to humility. "I see now, there's a note here..."

Irene huffed. "And the note says what, Kimmie?"

The wet clicks of Kimmie's tongue licking her lips filled the pregnant gap. "It says that the death certificate is being sent over by Vital Records this week. I'm so sorry Miss Allard."

"I don't need your apology. I need you and your office to take care of your own shit."

"Yes, I understand. This must be a hard time for your family."

Irene chortled. Her family? What family? Dad was gone. And as much as she prepared for his Final Release, she wasn't ready to watch him blow off his own head. That moment had burrowed deep in her mind: Dad's head raised, mouth slack, face relaxed and content, his fingers squeezing the gun in his hands. The image of it was a parasite that wormed out of her to feed on good feelings. It haunted her daydreams and nightmares. Irene clenched her eyes, letting the tears sing for a moment before blinking them away. In two days, her family had dissolved into memories and shadows."Um, Miss Allard?" Kimberly's tentative voice pulled Irene back to the present.

"Have an awful day, Kimmie." Irene disconnected the call and slid her phone into the front pocket of her jeans.

Season of Waiting

She needed a drink. A quick check of the flight monitor revealed her connecting gate was only a short walk away, so she had the time to spare. She scanned the concourse and made a beeline for the first bar she saw.

The space was tight, just a few open stools around a wandering bar top shaped to maximize seating capacity. Irene dropped her pack to the floor in front of the high seat, then debated what to do with Dad's cremains. Setting him on the floor seemed wrong. Not that she believed it would offend his ghost, or anything like that. It just felt impolite to drop him on the floor. So she set the box in the open seat next to her, gingerly balancing the weight of it on the small chrome stool.

As the young bartender approached, Irene fished her wallet out of her backpack and showed him her Massachusetts driver's license. He nodded, asking what she wanted to drink, and her eyes drifted to the glass castle of liquor displayed behind the bar. She debated the relative effects of each variety against her shitty mood, and decided something simple and safe was the best choice. She ordered a gin and tonic.

While the bartender fixed the drink, Irene pulled her day log and pen from the front pocket of her pack. As spent as she felt, she still wanted to be productive. To do something—anything—that was normal. Thankfully, colleagues back at the university were open to discussing the drug proliferation model Irene developed while scouring for Wes. They encouraged her to pull on those mental threads and see where the ideas could take her. Data sources discovered working with

Sheriff Dietrick would allow her model to track arrests and seizures in real-time. And the information from less urban areas provided decent power to predict the flow of drugs along major highways. She opened the notebook to the attached bookmark and scanned her notes. It took her a moment to decrypt her own sloppy shorthand, then another to set her mind into the context of the last problem she was thinking through. The clunk of the thick glass tumbler on the wooden bar top distracted her.

"Here you go," the bartender said with a thin smile.

Irene lifted the drink to her lips, the pungent aroma of juniper and lime carried on the vapors of alcohol tickling her nose. She pulled a slow sip, the cool burn blunting the edge on her nerves. The liquid landed in her empty stomach, and she relished the moment of warm satiation.

"Hell of a thing, eh?" the bartender asked.

Irene looked up from the beverage, finding his name tag. Kevin. "The drink? Yes, it's delicious, thank you."

Kevin shook his head. "No, I mean that." He thumbed over his shoulder, turning his face to the television mounted above their heads. Irene followed his gaze. A news anchor's lips flapped silently on the screen, above a chyron reading UVALDE HOSPITAL EXODUS: ANOTHER PATIENT FOUND SAFE. "You following this story?" Kevin asked, not taking his eyes off the screen. "It's crazy." The meaning of his words were disjoined from the airy wonder and awe on which they were conveyed.

Season of Waiting

Irene gulped another thick swallow of the cocktail. She hadn't been following the story as much as the story was following her. Hell, she lived the story. She had been there, at Uvalde County Hospital, trying to help police cobble together the events of the previous two days from her brother's morphine-greased ramblings. All she could get out of him were disparate pieces of the picture. The voice Dad claimed to hear, pushing him east. First to find a child. Then to kill the child.

Her composure dissolved when Wes broke down, blubbering that he didn't know Dad was evil, that what was happening to him was evil. It was classic Wes—deflection of fault, abdication of responsibility. But for him to lay blame at the feet of their dead father, after stealing her last precious moments with him? Taking what should have been his gentle passing and churning it into this public riot? It was too much effort to contain her anger. The impulse to beat her brother bloomed in her. The desire to choke him as he lay in that hospital bed carried through her blood the way a scent arrives on the air: overwhelming at first, then suddenly normal, her mind adapting to the notion that this is the way things needed to be. She had to get away from him. So she did. She carried her rage out of the room. Across the hall. Down the stairwell. And outside, where she collapsed on a bench in the hospital's small courtyard.

Somehow, after days of crying—from fear over what was happening to Dad, the anxiety of being separated from him, the relief of finding him, and finally the grief of losing him all over again—Wes had wrung more tears out of her. Rage tears. They came ugly and noisy, without impediment, Irene having lost any concern over her appearance or social grace. The colors of the tended landscaping melted in her vision, bright yellows and purples from the flowerbeds blending with the sage hedges, the liquid edges of which spilled into the pale blue afternoon sky. A blur moved through her watery vision, someone pacing through the surrounding space, their essence reduced to an amoebic blob of shifting hues.

Irene had worried about being alone. When Dad was sick, her thoughts had focused on life without him. The Caleb-shaped holes he would leave behind in her life. Those dumb jokes of his, that you still had to be smart to understand. Soft encouragement when he could afford attention away from Wes. A conduit to the memories of her mother. Now, the foundation of her grief lay exposed to her. Irene wasn't alone—she was worse than alone. Of all the spaces Dad filled in her life, it was the one between her and her brother where she most wanted him back. Where he would keep the focus of Wes's thrashing and clutching off of her, shield her from her brother's shitty choices. Dad was gone, but Irene grieved for the thing she gained. The shame of knowing that she was already letting Wes consume the space she wanted for her memories of her father brought her anger back on herself.

It was then Irene had noticed the watery blur growing in the courtyard. Approaching her. Then standing in front of her. Waiting. She cleared her eyes, bringing the smeared colors back into a definitive shape. A person. A woman. Elderly. Thin limbs swallowed in a billowing patient gown. Irene's vision cleared enough to see the woman's gaunt face—mouth slack, eyes disoriented, hair matted to her scalp as though she hadn't bathed in a year. Irene's self-pity became concern as the woman's effluvium musk reached her nose.

"Do you ... know who I am?" the woman rasped through a dusty throat.

That's when the screaming started. Not from the woman, but from inside the hospital. Then alarms blared, sharp and constant, adding to the cacophony. Through the windows, Irene saw people crowding into the hallways. Patients. Walking out of their rooms. Tubing and wiring flowing from under their loose gowns, ripped from the medical machines they were intended to serve. Some moved with purpose and determination, searching for something or someone. Others wandered lost, like this woman in the courtyard, as if baffled to find themselves here.

In the commotion, it had taken twenty minutes to find help for the lost woman in the courtyard. Medical staff scrambled to prevent patients from hurting themselves, to corral them back into the safety of their rooms and beds. Irene worked her way through the crowd. Shoving past the families hugged in tight bundles of joy and relief. Avoiding the viscous rivers of suspect fluids left by medical tubing dragged behind wandering patients. Ignoring the hollers of doctors begging patients not to rip out their breathing tubes. Back up the stairs to her brother's room.

Only to find it empty. During that inexplicable chaos, Wes had skipped out, somehow hobbling through his near-fatal injuries to save his own ass from being arrested for murder.

The wall of ice hitting her lip pulled Irene back to the present, to the bar in the airport. In her reverie, she had downed the gin and tonic in a few swallows. The cascade of alcohol soothed her from the inside, the sharp edge of the tonic's quinine drying on her tongue. She looked to the television again, to the smiling faces of a family reunited, folks who had beaten the odds.

Wes hadn't been the only person to disappear that day. Hundreds of patients had wandered out of the hospital. A few had loved ones with them. A few others found their way home. Some tried to leave, but bled out before reaching the edge of the parking lot. Many, including her brother, left the hospital and wandered into the expansive Texas hill country and remained missing.

"Wow, you're a good drinker!" Irene's eyes fell to Kevin, who nodded with appreciation. "Another?"

Irene set the glass down, pushing it towards the bartender. She wasn't a good drinker, not at all. And she hadn't eaten since this morning. But a haze was building in her head, one that promised to blur the details of her questions around what the hell had happened to her father and brother. To blunt the edge of her anger towards her dad. Towards herself for missing him for the wrong reasons.

"Yes, please. And the tab." As Kevin went to work putting her drink together, Irene slipped her phone out of her pocket and checked the time. She knew she had plenty to spare before her plane opened for boarding, but why trust when you can verify? As she looked, a text notification appeared on the black glass. It was from Sheriff Dietrick: *Still nothing on Wes. Sorry. Have a safe flight.* Irene sighed. The sheriff promised to update Irene at least twice a day. But since he disappeared from the hospital, there had been no trace of her shithead brother.

For the next fifteen minutes, Irene nursed the drink as her intoxication bloomed. The news moved from the "miracle at Uvalde" to more mundane stories. Politicians lying. Businesses stealing. People hurting and killing each other. The stories arrived and passed in moments, each one taking a small piece of her and leaving her more exhausted.

The cackle of the airport PA system pierced the noise of the bar. "This is a call for general boarding of flight 2718 with service to..." Irene recognized her flight number before the announcement dissipated into the din of conversations around her. She downed the rest of her cocktail, leaving money under the glass before collecting her notebook and pen back into her pack. Hoisting her father to her chest, and her backpack over her shoulder, she stumbled from under the weight of the negative news and out of the bar.

Her gate was a short walk away, just out of sight along the curving hub-and-spoke concourse. Irene moved at an unsteady pace, her legs slogging through her viscous inebriation. The stream of people ebbed and flowed around her, as content to ignore her as she was to be ignored.

"Come on, they just called our flight! We're gonna miss it! Let's get to the freakin' plane already!"

The man was not speaking to her, but near her. His voice and accent tugged at a thread in her mind, one attached to fond memories and feelings. The vowels launching wide off his tongue, his inflection animated with a gruff impatience, the undercurrent of Bostonian attitude impossible to mistake. That accent sounded like home now. To hear it warmed her heart, reminding her of the friends and life waiting for her back east. She smiled, following the stranger-from-Boston as he and his companion cut a wake through the disorganized flow of travelers.

Her smile waned as they slowed. The man stood on his toes, searching over the heads of the throng in front of him. "For the love of Pete," he declared, "are these people in line? Or are they just in the way?" They had reached their gate.

Glancing at the marquee in front of the jetway, Irene verified the flight's destination: Boston, Massachusetts. Her face fell. The time had come to say goodbye. Not to these strangers. To Boston. To school. Those friends and that life she had planned for herself there. Moving around the crowd, Irene hugged her father a little tighter to her chest as she continued to the next gate. Her gate. A hopper flight to San Antonio, Texas.

The choice hadn't been easy. She wanted almost nothing more than to return to the safety of what she knew. Classes, teaching, research. Lose herself in data and hypotheses. Relish the lust of systematically unraveling the intimate secrets of the universe. To seek truth through the scientific method. A process she could trust and follow.

Yet there remained the rock under her mind. The unanswered question that irritated her consciousness at every moment. *Why?* Why had Wes taken Dad all the way to Texas? What was Dad thinking? What happened in those two days that turned everything into a shit show? She wanted to find Wes. Needed to find him. When she did, she'd wring information out of him until she understood. Until the jigsawed pieces she carried now fit together into a sensible picture. When this need was met, she could return to the life she wanted.

School would be there. After discussing her situation with her advising professor, the university had offered to extend her leave of absence for two years. After a lot of introspection and some therapy, Irene took the opportunity. That gift of time, combined with the resources left to her by Dad, meant she didn't have to worry about anything except locating her asshole brother. Irene merged into the group of boarding passengers and trudged her way towards the plane. The line of people swayed in front of her. She was solidly drunk. Maybe she should have eaten something with the booze, but the opportunity had passed. She stumbled her way down the aircraft's center aisle, relieved to find her seat open and waiting for her near the window of row twenty eight.

She side-stepped into the row, then carefully tucked Dad-in-the-box beneath the seat in front of her. Before stowing her bag there, Irene pulled out her day log and pen. Her mind was too clouded to get anything done, but an open notebook aggressively displaying data model designs and equations lessened the chances of someone making small talk. She had no use for it on a normal day, and while alcohol tended to loosen most tongues, for Irene it did the opposite. She wanted to be alone with her thoughts, let them swim in the gin and tonic until they could swim no more, and then see where they ended up drowning. The notebook open on her lap, pen in her hand, Irene watched through her window as the ground crew buttoned up the plane.

A flight attendant announced that they were ready for departure, and Irene offered silent thanks for the empty seats beside her. The flight would be quiet, give her an hour to reset. Think about next steps. Maybe she could hire a skip-tracer to find Wes. Were they really a thing? Or was that just in movies and television?

The runway sped past the window, dropping away to reveal the urban sprawl of the Dallas-Fort Worth ... what did they call it? A metroplex? As the plane rose into the sky, concrete spread like a disease below, fingering into the wide and flat expanses of nature that made up most of the state. Her eyes followed the land to the horizon, where the embered sun hung from a line of clouds as it reached precariously for the edge of the world. Color exploded out from there, their luscious flavors and depth perhaps amplified by the alcohol in her brain. Golden rays and long shadows caressed the land, while the thick layer of clouds burst with spirals of orange and purple, creating a phosphorescent eye staring across the sky. Across the wide, flat expanse. To this plane, this window. Holding Irene's wonder with color and light. She held her breath, wanting to keep her grip on that moment and its beauty as long as she could.

She knew better, though. Every moment had to pass, as this one would.

The eye blinked. The plane jolted. Irene gasped as she tried to make sense of things. Through the window, the runway sped past again. The sun was well below the horizon somehow, leaving the sky cold and dark behind the line of trees that throttled past the moving plane. She shook off the haze, surprised that the flight had passed so quickly. Was she so drunk that she had passed out?

The plane roared and rattled as it slowed, and Irene began collecting herself and her belongings. She felt Dad with her feet, smiling with relief that he hadn't gotten up and run away during her inadvertent snooze. Her notebook had slipped off her lap at some point, and she found it by her feet. Irene closed her pen and stowed it in her pack, then pulled the day log off the floor of the plane.

The attached bookmark dangled free, failing to do the one thing it was meant to do. As the plane moved to the gate, Irene thumbed through the pages, looking for the last set of notes she made in the log so she could set the bookmark in the right place. Her eyes watched the inked pages flip, catching when the spreads became blank again. Irene turned to the last page of notes, smirking at her own chicken scratch. It was near indecipherable, even to her.

As she moved the bookmark into place, her face fell. Below her scrawled and wandering notes sat a single line of print. Neatly oriented to the lines on the page. Letters crisp and clean. The familiar endearment broke her heart and then her mind.

HELLO STARLIGHT.

Author's Note

Thank you for reading *Season of Waiting*. I sincerely hope you enjoyed it. Creating this book was an emotional journey, as elements of my life formed the foundation for many of the characters and themes. It is my terrifying privilege to share it with you.

This is my first published novel, and I hope to write many more. Leaving a review will help make this book more discoverable by readers like you (the smart, good-looking ones). Having more of those readers motivates and promotes my writing career. So please, take a moment to pop back to Amazon or Goodreads and share your opinion.

If you'd like to keep abreast of when my next book will be available, please visit my website: https://jim-christopher.com. There, you'll be able to subscribe to my mailing list. In exchange, you'll get access to resources available nowhere else—such as discussion guides for you book club and chapters that never made it into the final draft. On the site, you'll find links to my online profiles as well, including twitter, Amazon, Goodreads, and Facebook.

Acknowledgements

Writing a novel is hard. As I learned by creating this book, it's also the easiest part of the process.

I have no shortage of people to gush upon for their support, hard work, and encouragement. Kid[0] for prompting me to finish the process this time with some well-chosen gifts. Kid[1] for helping with decisions on cover visuals; how did you get such an artist's eye? Julie Smith for the continuous love and support, the reminders of why I'm putting so much energy into this, and for showing me the emotional impact of the story. Liz Dunbar for the writing upgrade and book club resource ideas. Ray Christopher for story and character debugging. Audrey Hammonds for the early-early reader feedback and stoking the fire under this project. Don Jones for technical, process, and motivational support. Geoffrey Hummelke for proofreading and excitement. Michele Alpern for cleaning up my copy. Nichole Lecht for capturing an unwieldy story in a single image. Angela Greenwell for giving me the emotional structure and coaching to accomplish this along with so many other goals. And Gunner for the reminders to leave it alone every once in a while, go for a walk, and enjoy the moment.

Then there is everyone who has supported me indirectly, through their content and resources. There are far too many to list, but I am compelled to call out a few. Randy Ingermanson and his book *How to Write a Novel Using the Snowflake Method* allowed my software brain to break the authoring process into small, iterative steps. His approach is the only reason I finished writing a novel this time around. Joanna Penn and her insightful, positive books on managing your own self-publishing career have been vital in navigating the "Now what?" void that opens after the first draft exists. Her books, blog, and podcast were the cat-herders for my own publication and launch efforts. You can find these resources on Amazon or other ebook retailers.

About the Author

J im Christopher lives near Charlotte, North Carolina, and makes a living as a technologist and learning sciences adviser. His work history is a crooked path, meandering from stagehand, audio engineer, carpenter, cognitive psychologist, behavioral researcher, musician, software developer, to whatever he might be doing today.

To relax, Jim writes, cooks, crochets, builds tiny houses, and walks his dog.

Made in the USA
Columbia, SC
17 November 2020